RANDOM HOUSE
LARGE PRINT

I Still Dream About You

I Still Dream About You

a novel

FANNIE FLAGG

R A N D O M H O U S E
LARGE PRINT

Copyright © 2010 by William Lane Productions, Inc.

All rights reserved.
Published in the United States of America by
Random House Large Print in association
with Random House, New York.
Distributed by Random House, Inc., New York.

Cover illustration: Wendell Minor

The Library of Congress has established
a Cataloging-in-Publication record for this title.

ISBN 978-0-7393-2735-7

www.randomhouse.com/largeprint

FIRST LARGE PRINT EDITION

Printed in the United States of America

10 9 8 7 6 5 4 3 2 1

This Large Print edition published in accord
with the standards of the N.A.V.H.

For Jonni Hartman-Rogers,
my friend and press agent for over
thirty years, with love and gratitude

Prologue
September 1955

It's funny what a person will remember so many years later; what sticks in your mind and what doesn't. Whenever he thought back to the year he had worked at the Western Union office, he remembered that little girl.

At the time, the entire city of Birmingham was surrounded by a number of smaller suburban neighborhoods, each with its own name and shopping area. Most had two or three churches, a drugstore, a grammar school and high school, a bank, a Masonic hall, a J. C. Penney's, and a movie theater.

In East Lake, where he worked, the Dreamland Theatre sat directly across the street from the Western Union office, between the barbershop and the grocery store. He had been sitting at his desk, looking out the window, when he had noticed the pretty brown-haired girl in a green plaid dress. She was the tallest of the three or four little girls walking home from school together that afternoon. It wasn't an unusual sight to see groups of kids going by that time of day. He was used to that, but just as they passed the barbershop, the tall girl stopped in front of the theater, waved goodbye to her friends, then turned and walked inside the two big glass doors and disappeared into the lobby.

Dreamland didn't open until seven P.M. on weeknights, and he wondered what she was doing going into an empty movie theater all by herself. He even thought about walking across the street to check on her, but a few minutes later, a light came on in a second-floor window, next to the big neon sign, and he could see the silhouettes of a woman and the girl walking back and forth, so he assumed she must belong there.

But still, every afternoon after that, when he wasn't busy, he would look over to make sure she'd made it home safely, and eventually, right before she went inside, she would turn and shyly wave at him, and he would wave back.

About three months later, he was shipped off to serve in the army, and by the time he got back to the Western Union office, the theater had closed down for good, and he never saw her again.

He had six granddaughters of his own now, but to this day, he still wondered what ever happened to the pretty little girl who had lived upstairs in Dreamland.

Once to every man and nation comes
the moment to decide . . .
And the choice goes by forever 'twixt
that darkness and light

—JAMES RUSSELL LOWELL

I Still Dream About You

The Big Decision
Monday, October 27, 2008

Today was the day Maggie had been thinking about, obsessing about really, for the past five years.

But now that it was actually here, she was surprised at how calm she felt: not at all as she had imagined; certainly not as it would have been portrayed in a novel or in a movie. No heightened emotions. No swelling of background music. No beating of breasts. No nothing. Just the normal end of a perfectly normal workday, if anyone ever could consider the real estate business normal.

That morning, she had gone to the office, worked on newspaper ads for Sunday's open houses, negotiated a washer and dryer and an ugly monkey chandelier to be included in the sale price in one of her listings (although **why** her buyers wanted it was a mystery), and made a few phone calls, but nothing out of the ordinary. She had known for some time it was coming, but she wondered why it happened on this particular day, instead of one last month or even next week? Yet not more than two minutes ago, as she drove past the pink neon Park Lane Florists sign, she suddenly knew this was **the** day. No bells, no whistles, just the sudden realization of a simple fact. She sat and waited for the red light to change and then turned off Highland Avenue and pulled up to the black wrought iron gates, pushed her gate code, and drove into the large cobblestone courtyard. At first glance, seeing the tall, flickering gas lamps lining the sidewalks and the ivy growing up the sides of the walls, a stranger might have guessed they were in a quaint little mews somewhere in London, instead of in Mountain Brook, just five minutes from downtown Birmingham. Mountain Brook had always looked more English than southern, something that had always surprised her out-of-town buyers, but most of the iron, coal, and steel barons who had settled it had been from either England or Scotland. Crestview, her very favorite house, that stood atop Red Mountain and overlooked the city, had been built by a Scotsman and was an exact replica of a house in Edinburgh.

A few seconds later, she eased the new light blue Mercedes into her parking space, took her purse and keys, and headed up the stairs leading to her townhome. When she got inside and closed the door behind her, thankfully, the loud, jangling five-thirty traffic noises quieted down to a soft muffle.

Her building was just one of the many stately old red brick apartment buildings built in the twenties and turned into condominiums in the eighties, when this side of town had gone condo-crazy. Her unit was a well-appointed two-story townhouse in the elegant, high-end enclave known as Avon Terrace and was kept immaculate at all times. The dark brown parquet floors were polished and shined, rugs vacuumed, kitchen and bathrooms gleaming and spotless. They had to be. She was the listing agent for the entire complex, and her unit was the model other realtors showed to potential buyers. Today, she didn't stop to check the mail in the silver dish on the small table in the foyer, as she usually did, but walked straight through to the small den off the living room and sat down at her desk.

She knew it must be written by hand. Something like this typed up on the computer would be far too impersonal and certainly not in good taste. She opened the right-hand top drawer and pulled out a small box of monogrammed stationery containing ten sheets of thin blue paper with matching blue envelopes. She took out a few pages and one envelope, then reached across the desk and fingered through a bunch of pens she kept in a brown leather penholder with gold embossing, searching for something to write with. As she continued to test one cheap plastic pen after another, she wished she had kept at least one good fountain pen and that bottle of maroon Montblanc ink she had saved for years. Every one of her old black felt pens had dried up, and now she would have to use the only thing she had left that still worked. She stared at it and sighed. Life was so odd. Never in a million years could she have imagined that she would wind up writing something as vitally important as this on ten-year-old stationery with a fat, bright red ballpoint pen with silver sparkles that had **Ed's Crab Shack: Featuring the Best Crab Cakes in Town** written on the side.

Good Lord. She had never been to Ed's Crab Shack in her life. Oh, well. Nothing to be done now. She carefully dated the upper right-hand side of the page with tomorrow's date, then took a moment to think about exactly what she wanted to say and how best to say it. She wanted to strike just the perfect tone: not too formal, yet not too casual. Businesslike, but personal. After reviewing the specific points she wanted to make, she began:

To Whom It May Concern,

Good morning, or afternoon, whatever the case may be. When you read this, I will be gone for good. The reasons for my action are varied and many. In the past, I have always strived to be someone my state could be proud of, but I feel that my leaving at this particular time will not cause as much attention as it once might have.

On a personal level, as I do not wish to upset my friends or co-workers or cause any-one undue stress, this letter is to inform you that I have already made all the necessary final arrangements, so please do not worry about finding me, and I apologize in advance for any inconvenience this may cause. But please be assured that although I . . .

The phone inside her purse on the floor suddenly started ringing to the tune of "I'm Looking Over a Four-Leaf Clover." Still concentrating on her letter, she reached down with one hand, rummaged through the purse, and finally dug the phone out and answered it. It was Brenda from work, all excited.

"Have you seen the paper yet?"

"No, not yet. Why?"

"Guess what? The Whirling Dervishes are com-ing to Birmingham!"

"The who?" asked Maggie, not wanting to be rude, but also not wanting to lose her train of thought.

"The Whirling Dervishes from Turkey! The men with the tall cone hats and long skirts that twirl around in a circle. There's a picture of them in today's Entertainment section."

"Really? The real ones?"

"Yes, the real ones! And they're coming to the Al-abama Theatre for a one-night-only performance. The Chanting Monks from China or Tibet or somewhere had to cancel, and they got the Dervishes to fill in at the last minute."

"Well, that was lucky."

"And guess what else? I can get us two free tickets from Cecil. Aren't you just dying to see them?"

"When are they coming?" Maggie asked, still trying to concentrate on her letter.

"November the second. Look at your calendar."

"Now?"

"Yes, I'll hold on. You know everybody in town will be scrambling for tickets."

Oh, dear. Maggie could tell Brenda was going to pin her to the wall on this, so as a courtesy, she reached across her desk and picked up the Red Mountain Realty calendar with the photo of the entire staff on it and flipped the page over to November; then she said, "Oh, honey, that's a Sunday, and I don't think I can make it. Darn, and I really would have liked to see them. Why don't you take Robbie?"

"Robbie?"

"Yes, she might enjoy it."

"You know I can't get my sister to go anywhere at night, much less go and see any Whirling Dervishes. Oh, come on, Maggie, you have to go! When in your lifetime will you ever get another chance to see real Whirling Dervishes? You know, you're not going to Turkey anytime soon."

"Well . . . that's true . . . but . . ."

Brenda did not let her finish. "I don't care what you say, we're going. I'm calling Cecil first thing in the morning. Goodbye!" Brenda hung up before Maggie had a chance to say no. Oh, Lord.

Maggie started to dial her right back and tell her she really couldn't go, but then hesitated. What excuse could she give? She hated to lie. She supposed she could say she would be out of town. In truth, she really **would** be out of town, but knowing Brenda, she would insist on knowing where she was going, who she was going with, and why. Oh, Lord. **Why** had she answered the phone? Now that she had finally made the decision, she wanted to go ahead and do it, and sooner rather than later. It had taken her long enough to get to this point.

Naturally, doing something like this would never have been her first choice, but after having made out list after list of all the pros and cons of her life and thoroughly exploring every other possible solution, it had become painfully clear that she had no other option. Oh sure, it would have been easier if she could have somehow unzipped her scalp, taken her brain out, and held it over the kitchen sink, and just rinsed away all the old regrets, hurts, and humiliations right down the drain, and started over, but that was impossible. All she could do was get out now while she still had the mental and physical faculties to do it. Thankfully, all the major preparation and planning of **how** she was going to do it, method, logistics, etc., had already been completed. Just one last quick stop at Walmart in the morning for some equipment, and she was good to go.

But she was torn about what to do about Brenda. Should she call her back? Or should she simply drop it? Brenda wasn't just any casual acquaintance. She was her real estate partner, and they had been through so much together. Especially after Hazel died. Had it been under any other circumstances, she would have been more than happy to go with her, especially considering all the nice things Brenda had done for her. Just last month, when she had been so sick with that terrible flu, Brenda had insisted on coming over and cooking all her meals. She had taken such good care of her. Oh God, the very last thing in the world she wanted to do was to have to let Brenda down. But now, thanks to her stupidly picking up the phone, it **would** be the last thing.

She sighed and looked at the calendar again. It would be so much more convenient for her to do it tomorrow or the next day at the latest, but Brenda had sounded so excited, and the poor thing had been having such a hard time lately. November 2 was only six days from now, and considering everything was almost in place and ready to go, she guessed there really was no great rush. So, maybe waiting until the morning of the third wouldn't make all that much difference. It was the decision **to** do it that mattered most and sticking to it, not when. There was certainly no danger of her changing her mind. It would just mean a slight delay and it might be nice to have a little extra time to get things in order and do a rehearsal to make sure there were no last-minute glitches. After all, this was something you had to get right the first time. And Brenda had made a point; it really would be a shame to miss the Dervishes.

When she was eleven, she had seen a photograph of the Whirling Dervishes in one of her father's **National Geographic** magazines, and they had looked like something right out of the **Arabian Nights,** so exotic in their tall cone hats and long swirling skirts. And seeing them the night before she left for good would be a nice send-off for her and certainly make more of an occasion out of it. Besides, it was so important to support the arts, but most of all, she wanted to do something nice for Brenda, as a sort of farewell gift. It was the least she could do for a good friend. She picked up the phone and dialed.

"Listen, Brenda, when you speak to Cecil, ask him if it's possible to get us seats in the middle, and if he could, to try to get us as far up front as he can. We want to get a close look at their outfits."

Brenda said, "Don't worry. If Cecil knows you're coming, they'll be good seats. But I'm bringing my binoculars so we can get a really good look at them, okay?"

"Okay."

"Oh, I'm so excited! Hey, Maggie—what do you suppose they wear when they are not in their twirling outfits?"

"Oh gosh, honey, I don't have a clue."

"Me neither. I just can't wait until November the second. Can you? I'm so glad we're going. Yeah!"

Maggie smiled. "Well . . . I'm glad you're glad."

"See you tomorrow."

"Yes, you certainly will," said Maggie.

Something to Look Forward To

❧

*B*renda was so happy about seeing the Whirling Dervishes, she almost did a little dance in her kitchen. Now they had something fun and interesting to look forward to, and God knows they deserved it. She was under a lot of stress. Real estate was going to hell in a handbasket, and they were predicting that prices hadn't hit bottom yet. It seemed all they did every weekend was hold open houses on every midlist tired old dog on the market and watch the really good high-end "over the mountain" listings, properties that even had a chance of selling, get snatched up by their main competitor, Babs Bingington. (Not her real name, as Brenda was quick to point out to anyone who didn't know.) Babs had only made it up because it sounded good in her slogan, "For the best in Birmingham, call Babs Bingington Realty"—a slogan that, along with her photograph, Babs had plastered on every shopping cart, billboard, and bus stop bench in town. But in local real estate circles, Babs was known as the Beast of Birmingham.

By now, everyone knew just how ruthless she was. She would stop at nothing to steal a client. It was said she had married and divorced two of them just to get their listings. Ethel Clipp, their office manager, often said that Hazel Whisenknott, the beloved founder of their company, would just be turning over in her grave if she knew the lack of real estate ethics going on in town today. Hazel had built Red Mountain Realty's reputation on a code of honesty and ethics; Hazel had even been one of the founders of the Better Business Bureau of Birmingham, for God's sake! But ethics weren't helping them much in today's market. In the past six months, they hadn't had enough sales to cover their advertising, much less make a profit or pay the office rent. How Maggie managed to remain so cool, calm, and collected was a wonder to Brenda, but most things about Maggie were. With all the mean backbiting and cutthroat tactics going on all around her, Maggie never got ruffled or said an unkind word about anybody. Brenda guessed it just must be easier for someone like Maggie not to let anything bother her. But then again, why should she? Maggie was tall, thin, and beautiful, with those perfect teeth and that thick straight hair she could just whip up in a ponytail and still look like a million dollars. And Maggie didn't have a single living relative pulling on her night and day. Brenda had so many brothers, sisters, and nieces and nephews always wanting money for this and that nonsense that she could hardly save a dime, much less buy that fifty-inch high-definition television set out at Costco she had her eye on. Sometimes, she had to laugh when she thought about Maggie, always so perfectly groomed, never a hair out of place, always so pleasant, just floating along through life on a pink cloud. She didn't know how lucky she was, and you couldn't explain it to her if you tried; she had the world by the tail. Brenda just wished she could be more like her.

After Maggie hung up with Brenda, she opened the desk drawer and found a small bottle of Wite-Out and changed the date on her letter to November 3 and continued writing the letter where she had left off.

> . . . have been depressed for quite some time,
> I was always so proud of being from Alabama
> and extremely grateful to have been given the
> honor and the privilege of representing my
> state in the Miss America Pageant.
>
> Sincerely,
> Margaret Anne Fortenberry

She usually added a little smiley face to her signature, but she didn't think it would be appropriate here, so she just left it plain. She then looked it over for any spelling mistakes, because you couldn't be sure where it might eventually end up. After rereading it a few more times, she felt she had made her points; she had offered some information, but not too much. It wasn't her intention to be mysterious, but in her case, some things were best left unsaid. She was sorry the letter had to be so generic and impersonal, but she couldn't address it to either Brenda or Ethel and tell them not to open it until a certain date without having them become suspicious. And she certainly couldn't trust Brenda not to open it. Her sister Robbie said that last year, Brenda had opened all her Christmas presents even before Robbie had a chance to wrap them. Also, Maggie knew that if, for any reason, they found out what she was planning, they would try to talk her out of it. It was sweet of them, of course, but often, well-meaning friends try to stop people from doing things that in the long run are really best for everyone.

Although she wasn't particularly pleased with all the wording, she did feel the overall message was clear. "I'm leaving. I have my reasons. Don't look for me." But she wasn't a fool. She knew, no matter how hard she tried to make it easy on everybody, some people were still going to be shocked. They would wonder, "Why? When she seemed so happy?" Which was true. She had always tried to appear happy. Some might ask, "Why? When she could have had any man she wanted?" Not quite true. And besides, after Richard, she didn't want anyone else. Or "Why? When she was so pretty?" And no question about it, being pretty is grand while it lasts, but good looks alone don't bring you happiness; an awful lot of perks, yes, but not a good enough reason to go on. And some would be disappointed that she hadn't gone into greater detail about her reasons, but she had them. Just last week, she had jotted down sixteen perfectly good reasons, and she was sure there were many more she hadn't thought of yet.

Still, she hated leaving people up in the air. But what could she possibly have said? She couldn't tell them the truth. So, it was best to just bow out gracefully and be grateful she had at least accomplished a few of her goals. She had never smoked, cursed, raised her voice in public, or received a traffic citation or a parking ticket—no mean feat, considering she still couldn't parallel park after years of trying. But now, at age sixty, too young to retire and not smart enough to learn a new profession, what was the point? It was obvious that the best of her life was behind her. So, why continue to struggle? Toward **what**?

Without Hazel, life had become as hard as trying to balance a stick on her nose and juggle six rings in the air while standing on one leg on a big rubber ball. There were times she just wanted to go stark raving mad and run down the street naked, screaming at the top of her lungs, but of course, she couldn't do that.

Not in this day and age, when everybody and his brother had a camera on his phone. There was no privacy left in the world anymore. Somebody was sure to get a photograph of her and put it on YouTube, and something like that could wind up on the Internet for years.

Brenda was lucky. She still had a lot of goals left. Just last week, she announced she wanted to run for mayor of Birmingham and fire the entire city council. Brenda had ambition and a family who cared about her. Even Ethel Clipp, who they said was at least eighty (nobody knew for sure), had her hand-bell choir and her two white Persian cats, Eva and Zsa Zsa, that she adored. Brenda and Ethel wanted to keep going and, evidently, so did the world, but she didn't. So really, it was best that she just step aside and let them go on their merry way.

She was simply, quietly and discreetly, and with as little fanfare as possible, leaving life a little earlier than expected, that's all. An extreme avoidance tactic (perhaps), an inability to face reality (of course), a preemptive blow against old age (most certainly). But on the positive side, by leaving now, she would be saving the government an awful lot of Social Security money down the line; making much less of a carbon footprint; using less oxygen, gas, water, food, plastics, and paper goods; and there would be fewer used coffee grounds in the garbage. Al Gore should certainly appreciate it.

She put the letter in the envelope and placed it in the drawer, underneath the stack of old telephone bills, and was reminded that she had to make sure the rest of her bills and credit cards were paid off before she left. She never wanted to give anyone the chance to say that a former Miss Alabama was a deadbeat. She sat up and glanced around the room. Although none of the furniture was hers, she still had a few little personal items to get rid of, but that was about it.

Dear God, from where she had started out, after all she had aspired to be, where she had actually ended up had come to Maggie as a complete surprise. It was clear now that she had seen far too many movies as a child . . . and had just naturally expected a happy ending.

The Ice Cream Incident

A few minutes later, Brenda was across town with a spoon, eating out of the pint of her sister Robbie's mint chocolate chip ice cream, ice cream she was not supposed to be eating, having been diagnosed as prediabetic, but she needed to celebrate. Besides, Robbie, an emergency room nurse, was working at the hospital and wouldn't be home until nine. She was only going to eat a little around the edges of the carton, then mash it around, and Robbie would never know the difference anyway. Brenda was deep in thought. Surely, when the Whirling Dervishes were not whirling, they had to wear regular clothes, at least when they traveled. They couldn't fit on a plane in those tall cone hats, particularly not on the small jets where the ceilings were so low, but maybe they traveled in buses like the country-western stars did. Buses had tall ceilings. But then, she realized, they couldn't take a bus all the way from

Turkey, and so they had to fly sometimes or maybe they took a boat. She glanced over at the photograph in the newspaper again, and those tall hats looked very heavy to her. She began to wonder how much they weighed or if the Dervishes ever got headaches from wearing them, and before she knew it, Brenda looked down and saw that she had gone through half the pint of Robbie's ice cream.

Oh, damn it! There was no way she could hide that now. She was going to have to run out to the convenience store and buy a new pint to replace it. The last time she had done this, she'd filled the carton with water, but when Robbie had opened it and seen that it was mostly ice, she had suspected something. Brenda turned the carton over and looked to see if Robbie had put a mark on the bottom. Robbie was on to all her ice cream tricks and sometimes put an X on the bottom to try to catch her, but there was no mark on this one. Good. She couldn't afford to get caught cheating on her diet again.

She had been caught red-handed just three months ago, and with Robbie being a nurse and worried about Brenda's health, it had not been a pretty scene. Even though Robbie was her younger sister by seven years, she was very bossy. She was also much taller than Brenda was and as skinny as a rail. Unfortunately, Brenda had taken after their mother's side of the family and was only five foot five, and at the moment, she was at her medium weight of around 166 pounds. Her good weight was 150 pounds, and 178 pounds was her top. Consequently, Brenda had three different sets of clothes hanging in her closet, labeled GOOD, MEDIUM, and FAT AS A HOG. She had not been in her GOOD range since Hazel Whisenknott had died, over five years ago. "I eat out of stress," she told Robbie, and now, between work and nephews driving her crazy, she was just on the verge of having to switch from her MEDIUM to her FAT AS A HOG wardrobe again, which meant she was going to have to switch shoe sizes as well. Robbie said she was the only person in America who gained weight in her feet.

Brenda went ahead and finished the last of the ice cream and wrapped the empty carton in tin foil and hid it at the bottom of the garbage can under the sink. She rinsed off the spoon, dried it, and put it back in the silverware drawer, then picked up the stalk of bananas in the bowl on the counter. She took a carton of milk out of the refrigerator and grabbed the new box of Cheerios from under the counter and put them in a paper bag, put her new Tina Turner wig back on, grabbed her purse, and headed out the door. She didn't want to go out, but if she got caught eating ice cream again, there would be all hell to pay, especially after what had happened just three months ago.

When she and Maggie had found out that the house they had in escrow and had worked long and hard to sell had major structural problems and the buyer had backed out, Brenda had been very upset. Not only had they lost the sale, but she was hoping to buy that new fifty-inch television set with her part of the commission. Brenda knew darn well she shouldn't have done it, but that afternoon, she had driven over to a part of town where no one knew her (and Robbie was unlikely to see her) and stopped at an ice cream place. She went in and ordered a large hot fudge sundae with whipped cream, three cherries, and nuts on top. She was heading back to her car with it when, suddenly, a boy ran up and tried to snatch her purse right off her arm. The good news was that he didn't get her purse, but the bad news was that the next morning, the entire incident wound up being reported in the **Birmingham News.**

HOT FUDGE SUNDAE
FENDS OFF ROBBER

Miss Brenda Peoples of 1416 Second Court South said she was in no mood to give up her purse to a "would-be purse snatcher" and fought him off with a large white plastic dish containing a hot fudge sundae she was holding at the time. A bystander who witnessed the incident said that she "whaled the living tar out of him." When the police arrived at the Foster's Freeze parking lot

where the altercation occurred, they reported that although not seriously in-
jured, the 18-year-old perpetrator was
"a real mess."

Everyone who read the article thought it was the
funniest thing that had happened since a man tried
to hold up the Alabama First National Bank with a
live lobster, but Brenda had been furious that they
had printed her name in the paper. Not only had
Robbie found out that she was cheating, but also,
she had been attending Weight Watchers at the
time, and thanks to that nosy reporter, everyone in
her group found out, so she never went back. She
told Maggie that if she had known they were going
to put her name in the papers, she would have just
given the fool her purse and finished her hot fudge
sundae in peace.

The only consolation she had was that after the
attempted purse snatching, the ice cream people
made her a new sundae, free of charge, to replace
the one she had used as a weapon. Of course, this
was something she did not mention to Robbie.

Upon Further Reflection

⁓

The more Maggie thought about it, the more she guessed she shouldn't have been so surprised how her life had turned out, considering all the really bad decisions she had made. Oh Lord, why hadn't she married Charles Hodges III when he'd asked her? His parents had adored her, and she had liked them. They had been wonderful to her. On her birthday, they had taken her to the Birmingham Club, atop Red Mountain, and she had been enthralled with its rotating glass dance floor of colored lights, where beautifully dressed people sat at ringside tables and drank exotic cocktails, and Miss Margo played piano every evening in the Gold Room, overlooking the city. Charles was a tall blond boy with blue eyes and skin as pretty as a girl's.

The night Charles had asked her to marry him, he had taken her there for dinner and had planned such a lovely evening. She had just been crowned

Miss Alabama, and when she walked in, the band played "Stars Fell on Alabama" in her honor. She was on cloud nine. They danced all night and after the last dance, when they returned to their table, upon his instructions, a black velvet box with a large diamond engagement ring had been placed on her dessert plate.

It had been a magical year. She and Charles had been the golden couple and had gone to so many parties and dances that summer. Charles was a wonderful dancer and looked so handsome in his tux and black patent leather shoes with the bows. She had loved how he felt when they danced. He had held her so tight that she could feel the warm dampness of his body through his jacket. He held her so close, it was hard to tell where he ended and she began. When she came home at night, the smell of his cologne would still linger all over her and her clothes for hours afterward. She had been too young to know that the magic of that summer wouldn't last forever. She thought there was plenty of time for everything.

And if she hadn't married Charles, she should have at least kept up her harp lessons. But she had only learned to play two songs before she stopped. Two had been enough to win Miss Alabama, but she couldn't make a decent living playing "Tenderly" and "Ebb Tide" over and over again. And why had she chosen the harp in the first place? It was almost impossible to travel with. Why not the piccolo, the flute, or the violin? She'd never been very good on the harp, but she had learned to do a lot of large swirling movements that made her look and sound much better than she was. Even her harp teacher had remarked, "What you lack in natural musical talent, dear, you make up for in flair and style." It was the story of her life and probably how she had survived this long: with a little talent and a lot of flair. Few people realized she owned only six or seven really fine suits and dresses, but they all had style. Thanks to the designer discount malls and the fact that she could tie a scarf in over forty different and interesting ways, she had always managed to look good on the surface; what was inside, however, was a different story. She didn't know why, but she had always been a little unsure of herself and for years had been second-guessing every decision with "I should have done that" or "I should have done this," so afraid of doing something wrong, always looking for some sign from the universe to help her decide what to do, that she usually wound up doing nothing. But today at five-thirty, thank God, she had finally made a decision that felt exactly like the right one. What a relief.

Maggie walked down the hall and picked up the mail in the silver dish in the foyer. Nothing but junk and a flyer advertising Willow Lakes, a retirement community for active seniors; she threw it in the trash can. When she went into the kitchen and turned on the light, she saw a business card on the counter from Dottie Figge from Century 21 Realty, who must have shown her unit again today. Dottie was a hard worker and had brought the same couple from Texas through at least three times in the past three weeks. At present, there was only one two-bedroom unit for sale in the complex, but Maggie suddenly realized that her unit would be available after November 3. She should probably call Dottie tomorrow and give her a heads-up. She wouldn't tell her which unit, only that one would be available soon. She liked Dottie. They had been in the Miss Alabama contest together. Dottie had played the trombone and tap-danced, but now she was just another struggling agent like herself, hanging on by a fingernail. Two years ago, Dottie had announced that she was no longer a Southern Baptist and had decided to "embrace the Eastern." She said that if it had not been for OM Yoga and her daily devotionals to Goddess Guan Yin, she would not have been able to keep going. It had been a little strange at first, seeing hundreds of little Buddhist prayer flags flying at Dottie's open houses and crystals everywhere, but she was so sweet. The last time Dottie had sold a unit in Maggie's building, she had given Maggie a ying-yang bowl as a thank-you gift. She didn't know exactly what you were supposed to do with a ying-yang bowl, but she didn't want to hurt Dottie's feelings by asking.

After Maggie poured herself a big glass of wine, she went into the living room and sat down, kicked off her shoes, and put her feet up on the coffee table. As she sipped her wine, she thought about what else needed to be done to make sure everything went smoothly from here on. She wanted to leave not only debt-free, but worry-free as well. She was too tired tonight; first thing in the morning, though, she would make out a "Things to Do Before I Go" list. She couldn't trust herself to remember every detail unless she wrote it down. She didn't know if it was because she was so tired, but lately, she had started forgetting things, like people's names or the name of a certain movie star she used to love. Last week, she'd forgotten Tab Hunter's name. He had always been one of her favorites; how could she ever forget him?

She took another sip of her wine and thought about the Whirling Dervishes again. Oh, Lord. She hoped the Arts and Lecture people wouldn't put them at one of those big ugly convention hotels downtown. Hazel had always said, "People always come to Birmingham expecting the very worst, so it's doubly important that they leave having seen the very best." She looked at her watch. Too late to call Cathy at her office now. She would call in the morning, and if Cathy hadn't booked a hotel yet, she might be able to casually suggest something with a little more local charm, like the Dinkler-Tutwiler or even one of the lovely guest cottages at the Mountain Brook Country Club. But they did have a strict dress code there, and other than the annual Scottish Society Dance, men in skirts might be frowned upon.

She took another sip of her wine. At least, one thing she didn't have to worry about: she knew the Dervishes would be entertained royally while they were in Birmingham. Last year, when the opera singer Marilyn Horne came, she had received over sixty-five "Welcome to Birmingham" fruit baskets. People in Birmingham were famous for their friendliness and southern hospitality. If anything, some people said they were overly friendly, too eager to please, so much so that when visitors left town, they were usually so exhausted, they couldn't wait to get back home and rest.

But besides just being friendly by nature, Maggie thought the other reason they fell all over themselves wanting so much for people to like them was that they were still trying to live down all the bad press Birmingham had received during the civil rights movement. It had been devastating. Even now, whenever there were racial problems anywhere in the world, it seemed they still drug out the same old newsreels of Birmingham and the dogs and the fire hoses and ran them over and over again. It broke her heart. Not because terrible things hadn't happened. They had. But the press had made it seem like every single person in Birmingham was a foaming-at-the-mouth racist, and it just wasn't true.

In her letter, she had used the word "depressed" because it was a word people easily understood.

But the best word to describe how she really felt would be "sad." Maggie had never told anyone what had happened to her in Atlantic City the year she was Miss Alabama, and she never would. People in Alabama, and Birmingham in particular, had heard enough bad things about themselves to last a lifetime.

The Lady with the Frozen Arm

Brenda was standing in the Five Points convenience store with her arm stuck deep inside the large freezer. In the past ten minutes, she had moved around what seemed to her to be a hundred cartons of ice cream, looking for a pint of mint chocolate chip. They had tons of rum raisin, coffee, butter pecan, vanilla, and strawberry. But not one pint of mint chocolate chip. Great. Not only was her entire right arm frozen until she couldn't feel her fingers, but now she was going to have to drive all the way over to Bruno's Supermarket out on the Green Springs Highway and try to find it there.

As she went across town, having to steer with her left arm because the right one was still numb, she became more and more irritated at Robbie. Why couldn't she buy just plain chocolate or just plain vanilla ice cream? She liked vanilla. Why didn't she buy vanilla? But no, she had to buy mint chocolate chip, a summer ice cream that Robbie knew darn well was hard to find in the fall. And when she knew Brenda would be tempted, why did she keep ice cream in the freezer in the first place? But then, there was something wrong with Robbie anyway. How could any normal person "forget" to eat lunch? It nearly drove Brenda crazy. Robbie never finished everything on her plate, and at her own birthday party, Robbie had eaten only half a piece of cake. Brenda had never eaten half a piece of anything in her life, and she didn't understand those who could.

Thirty minutes later, when Brenda finally came out of Bruno's Supermarket with a pint of mint chocolate chip ice cream, she struggled not to look to the right, because she knew the frozen yogurt place next door would still be open. But she was upset and stressed, and she needed something to calm her down, so after the shortest struggle known to man, she headed over. She figured since she had already eaten an entire pint of ice cream and blown her diet for the month anyway, she might as well get herself a small cone of nonfat sugar-free frozen yogurt. It couldn't hurt now.

She walked in, took a ticket from the machine, and stood waiting in a long line, still mad at herself for eating Robbie's ice cream. But then, it wasn't all her fault—it was a family disease. For years, she had done nothing but fuss at her older sister, Tonya, for being an alcoholic and had even put together an intervention and paid to send her off to rehab—

twice. But she was really no better; Tonya couldn't have just one drink without going off on a bender, and evidently, she couldn't have just one bit of ice cream. Oh, well. Tomorrow she would stop eating all sugar for one month.

As the line slowly moved up, she observed all the other fat people waiting with her and decided she would not have any bread or potato chips either. She had to lose that weight before next summer. Last summer had been pure hell; there was not enough talcum powder in the entire world to keep her from chafing in the hot, humid Alabama heat, and lately, her knees and her hips had started to ache from carrying all that weight. She had not mentioned any of this to Robbie, because she would just say, "I told you so." It was pure hell living with a medical professional.

She looked up at the clock. It was already a quarter after eight. She had to get that ice cream back in the freezer by nine, and if that boy working behind the counter didn't hurry up, she would have to leave before she got her cone. She just hoped Robbie wouldn't come home early and decide to have some ice cream tonight of all nights. Chances were she wouldn't, but with the way Brenda's luck was running lately, you never knew. The minute the boy started ringing the bell on the counter, Brenda knew, she should have turned around and left right then and there. He was calling someone from the back to come out and help him, because the woman in front of her had just ordered ice cream for the entire sixth-grade girls soccer team, who had won their game and were outside waiting in a van. Wouldn't you know it? Just when she was in a hurry. By the time Brenda finally did get up to the counter, the machine was malfunctioning, and she had to wait another ten minutes.

Later, as Brenda drove into the garage, she saw Robbie's car. Thank heavens she had hedged her bet and had the sack with the milk, cereal, and bananas with her so she could tell Robbie that's why she had gone to the store. She put the pint of ice cream in her purse. She would stick that in the freezer later, after Robbie went to bed. When Brenda walked into the kitchen carrying the sack, Robbie, who was still in her scrubs, looked surprised.

"Hey, where did you go?"

"Oh, we needed a few things from the store, so I just ran out and picked them up."

"Oh, what did we need?"

"Bananas, milk, and Cheerios," she said as she put the things back where they had been earlier this evening.

Robbie looked puzzled. "That's weird. I thought we had a bunch of bananas this morning. Didn't we?"

Brenda didn't want to be caught in a lie, and she remembered something Hazel had once said: "If you don't want to answer a question, change the subject with great enthusiasm." So, she immediately turned to Robbie and said with great enthusiasm, "Guess what? The Whirling Dervishes are coming to Birmingham!"

"The who?" asked Robbie.

Brenda quickly grabbed the paper and showed her the article, and to her relief, Robbie forgot about the bananas. God bless Hazel, gone five years and still saving the day.

Meanwhile, Back at Avon Terrace

~

Although Maggie was certain she had made the right decision, she still wondered, Why today? Something must have triggered it. She thought back on a conversation she had had with Ethel earlier that afternoon.

When Maggie had come back from lunch, Ethel had said, "God, I miss Hazel. After all this time, I still can't believe she's gone."

Maggie agreed. "Me neither . . . every Sunday, I still expect her to call me up and say, 'Hey, Mags, let's go roaming.' She loved to drive that big old car of hers all over town, doing things, and enjoying every minute of it."

"Oh yes, no matter what she drug us through, she always had a good time."

Maggie said, "Ethel, you knew her better than

anybody. Do you think she ever got tired of being so cheerful and always on the go?"

Ethel shook her head. "Not for one minute . . . **we** got tired, but she didn't, and it was exhausting. Remember all the things she got us into? The softball team, all the parties, the Easter egg hunts, the crazy trips. That woman kept me so busy, I had to get my divorce over the phone."

"How did she keep it up, I wonder?"

"I don't know, but she wore me out trying to keep up with her. We got older, but she didn't. Do you remember when she made us all take hula lessons and march in the Do Dah Parade? My hips were sore for two months."

Maggie had to be careful how she worded her next question. Ethel was very sensitive about her age. "Ethel . . . what's the worst part of . . . uh . . . getting older . . . for you?"

"The worst part?"

"Yes."

Ethel thought for a moment. "Oh, I guess the older you get, the less you have to look forward to. When you're young, you look forward to growing up and getting married and having children, and then you look forward to having them move out."

Maggie suddenly realized that was it. Ethel had hit the nail right on the head. She had absolutely **nothing** to look forward to. Other than missing spring (the flowers and the dogwoods in Mountain Brook were so beautiful) and fall, when the leaves turned such pretty colors, she didn't have a single reason to hang around.

Maggie looked down at her watch. It was already nine-fifteen. She figured she'd better eat something or else she would get a headache. She still had to work tomorrow, so she got up and went into the kitchen and pulled out a Stouffer's frozen dinner, baked chicken breast, mashed potatoes, and vegetables, and stuck it in the oven. She never fixed anything at home except frozen dinners or pop-up waffles because (A) she didn't want to have to clean up the kitchen and (B) although she could set a beautiful table and fold a napkin in over forty-eight different and interesting ways, she had never been very good at cooking. Not that she hadn't tried. The first year she went to work for Hazel, she had attempted a small dinner party for the girls in the office, but the yeast rolls she served had not been fully cooked, and after the girls went home, the yeast in the rolls continued to rise, and later that night, all of them wound up at the University Hospital emergency room, except for Brenda, who felt fine. After that, Maggie just stopped cooking all together. But like everything, you paid a price. All the sodium in the frozen dinners made her hands swell.

As she sat and waited for her dinner to heat up, she picked up the New Age magazine Dottie had left for her with a Post-it note that said, "Great

Stuff!!" She leafed through, but all she saw were pages of advertisements for yoga mats, meditation candles, and numerous self-help books: **The Wisdom of Menopause, The Orgasmic Diet, How to Nurture Your Body and Your Libido at the Same Time,** and one entitled **100 Secret Sexual Positions from Ancient Cultures Around the World.** Good Lord. She didn't want to hurt Dottie's feelings, but this was not anything she was interested in, certainly not now, so she threw it in the trash can and picked up today's newspaper.

Just as Brenda had said, on the front page of the Entertainment section was a large photograph of the Whirling Dervishes twirling in circles, and they looked exactly like something right out of a movie . . . but then, to Maggie, almost everybody **did.** Richard had looked exactly like Eddie Fisher.

When she first met Ethel Clipp, their office manager, with her thin purple hair that stood straight up on her head and her large purple-tinted glasses that made her eyes look twice as large, she had looked to Maggie exactly like an alien bug right out of a bad science fiction movie. In 1976, Ethel had had her colors done by a colorist out at the mall and had been told her best colors were purple and lavender, and she had worn nothing else since. Hazel had nicknamed Ethel "the Purple Flash." She called Brenda "Thunderfoot," because she said she could always hear her coming, and Maggie was "Magic City Girl."

After Maggie finished dinner, she cleaned up after herself, put the glass and silverware in the dishwasher, and turned it on. She then went to the bedroom, undressed, took a hot bath, brushed her teeth, got into bed, and clicked on the television set to watch the news. As usual, it was all about the upcoming presidential election. Lately, people just said the ugliest things about one another. Then something dawned on her. She wouldn't be here on November 4 to find out who won. So why watch? The news just upset her. It was always bad. And she had never cared much for politics. She wasn't like Brenda, who was very involved in politics, or Ethel who was addicted to twenty-four-hour news. Ethel wanted all the news all the time. Not Maggie. She only watched so she could carry on a halfway intelligent conversation with her clients. But now, the idea of not having to watch seemed wonderful. So, she turned it off. And if anybody did ask her something in the next few days, she would just say, "I'm sorry, I don't know."

In truth, there were a lot of things Maggie wished she hadn't known. Maggie was stunned at what people you just met would tell you about their personal lives. She had never discussed Richard with a living soul, much less a stranger. Maybe she was a prude, but to her, there had always been something so lovely, so civilized about **not** knowing the graphic details. She really preferred people to be a little more vague, but now, especially in real estate, you couldn't afford to be vague or the least bit sensitive about anything. Today, in order to even stay in the game, you had to be tough, and in Babs's case, ruthless. Maggie had tried her best to be tough, but she simply couldn't do it.

Just another reason she should have married Charles when he'd asked her, but she had been determined to go to New York and become rich and famous and make her state proud. The only problem: she hadn't thought about **how** she would become rich and famous. She couldn't sing, act, or dance, and with her obvious lack of musical talent, all she could really do was look good in clothes. But as she found out, in New York, at only five foot seven and a half, she was not tall enough to be a professional runway model. And after a year, the only modeling job she had been able to get was in the mezzanine tearoom at Neiman Marcus's department store in Dallas. The other career she might have pursued was that of an airline stewardess, but back then, ex–Miss Alabamas did not become stewardesses; they married well and had 2.5 children.

Maggie could have married well. Most of the kids she had gone to high school with were from the old iron, coal, and steel families, and even though her parents were quite poor, there had been quite a few wealthy "over the mountain" boys who had tried to date her, but the only one she had liked was Charles.

When she had turned him down, he had been a complete gentleman and had not acted very upset, but she heard later that he had been to the point of almost drinking himself to death after she left for New York City. Why hadn't he fought for her? Why hadn't he insisted that she stay home? Why hadn't he come after her? There was that moment in time, before she left New York City for Dallas, when, if he had come, she would have gladly headed for home. If he had, she would never have met Richard. Lord . . . why had Charles been so noble? Why had he been such a gentleman? Both their lives could have turned out so differently. But she guessed he couldn't help being what he was any more than she could help being who she was: so incredibly stupid.

After she'd moved home from Dallas, she'd lived in fear and dread of running into Charles again, but thankfully, she hadn't. Most people had been kind and not mentioned him at all. Only once had a girl she hardly knew, who had married a mutual friend of theirs, asked, "Do you ever hear from Charles Hodges?"

"No, I'm afraid I don't."

"Oh, we don't either. All we know is that he married some Swiss banker's daughter and moved there for good, I hear."

She hoped Charles was happy. He deserved to be happy, just like she deserved to be as unhappy as she was. She had, after all, brought it all on herself.

So Rare

1965

〜

*T*here were a lot of pretty girls in Birmingham, but Maggie Fortenberry was one of those rare pretty girls who grew more beautiful the longer you looked at her, and Charles Hodges III, who could stare at her for hours, tried to figure out what set her apart from the others. He finally came to the conclusion that it was her eyes. There was an expression deep down in her brown eyes, something so sweet, so shy and vulnerable; it made him want to protect her from the whole world.

He had come from quite a social background and was able to converse with everyone, young and old, but around Maggie, he often found himself at a loss for words and, to his embarrassment, kept repeating, "God . . . you're pretty." But she was. Charles was an amateur photographer, and he had taken photograph after photograph of Maggie and found that no matter what angle he shot, it was impossible to get a bad picture of her. She didn't have a bad side as far as he could see. But he was in love.

He must have been. That summer, he had driven Maggie and her harp from one event to the other, had gone to all the Miss Alabama affairs, and had stood in the back as people fluttered all around her. He didn't mind; he wanted to spend the rest of his life with her. And after a private talk with her father to get his blessing, he had spent hours selecting just the right ring for her. An entire evening was planned: dinner, dancing, and, later, the proposal.

Maggie didn't know it, but his parents had already made a down payment on a house for them. After she said yes, he was planning to drive her up the mountain the next day and surprise her. His parents would be waiting inside with champagne to celebrate. But she had said no.

She had decided to go to New York first. He had been so torn about what to do. He didn't want to stand in her way, but he also knew that if she went, she was sure to become famous, and he would never see her again.

The day she left for New York, he stood with her parents and smiled and waved, but as the train pulled out of the station, he knew he was losing her. He couldn't blame her; she couldn't help being who she was. But he didn't think he would ever get over her. No wonder he stayed drunk for the next five years.

The Purple Flash

Monday, October 27, 2008, Midnight

Long after Maggie had turned off her light, Ethel Clipp was still sitting up in bed in her purple flannel nightgown with the cats on it, rolling up her thin purple hair in bobby pins, busy clicking from local news to CNN and Fox TV and back. At this point, Ethel didn't care who won the presidential election. She didn't like either candidate. Still, she wanted to know what was going on, so she could have something to complain about in the morning. Of course, Brenda was all hoo-ha for Barack Obama, and Maggie never discussed politics, so she didn't know who Maggie was voting for. She herself hadn't liked anybody since Harry Truman. In fact, she hadn't liked much of anything since 1948 and was quick to tell you about it. Ethel could be a little blunt at times. She was quite a bit older than she cared to admit (eighty-eight last May), was deaf in one ear, and had terrible arthritis in both knees, but regardless of her age, she never missed a day of work at Red Mountain Realty. She liked work. It kept her heart going. She supposed some people looked forward to retiring and traveling, but not her. There was a time when people traveled for pleasure, but as far as Ethel was concerned, there was nothing pleasurable about it anymore.

She used to like to take the train, but since the government took that over, what was once gracious dining with white linen tablecloths and fine silver was now just a snack bar full of people in flip-flops eating bad microwaved sandwiches, drinking beer and Diet Snapple. And forget flying. Standing in those long lines, being prodded and poked to a fare-thee-well, treated like a criminal. Hell, she didn't want to take her shoes off in front of strangers and stick them in some dirty plastic tub. Years ago, when you took a plane, you were served a fully cooked hot meal: roast beef and gravy or lobster with a nice wine and a dessert. Now it was just water and a bag of peanuts. And even if your plane was on time, there were no more redcaps to help you with your luggage anymore. At the end of her last flight, when she'd tried to grab her bag, she had been dragged halfway around the carousel, and if that man hadn't caught her, there was no telling where she would have ended up. And then it hadn't even been **her** suitcase. They had lost hers. How a bag clearly marked Birmingham, Alabama, could wind up in Butte, Montana, on an entirely different airline was beyond her.

And God knows you couldn't drive anywhere with all of the big eighteen-wheeler trucks running up your behind, blowing their horns, and scaring you half to death. And even if you did make it to where you were going without having been squashed along the side of the road, it wasn't the same. Years ago, when you checked into your hotel, they used to be happy to see you and say, "Welcome!" Now it was just some kid behind a desk who didn't even look at you. No hello, just "Do you have a reservation?" So, she was staying home.

Besides, she couldn't go anywhere anyway. As long as Maggie and Brenda were willing to hang in and keep Red Mountain Realty going, she would hang in there with them. And with Babs (the Beast of Birmingham) Bingington circling around their office like a big shark, Ethel needed to be on guard twenty-four hours a day. She already suspected a few things, and she'd be damned if she'd let Babs pull the same dirty rotten tricks on Maggie as she had on Hazel.

Ethel was a Christian and all that, but she still couldn't forgive Babs for what she had done to Hazel. She was working on it, but so far, no luck.

The Beast

B abs (the Beast of Birmingham) had blown into town years ago from New Jersey and by her second year there, was already a member of the Diamond Club and had been the city's top producer of sales for six years in a row. A dynamo in business, yes, but it would be more than generous to say that Babs wasn't a nice person. She didn't even have the courtesy to fake being nice—unless, of course, she was with a client. Babs not only had two faces, she had two voices as well. When dealing with her employees or with other agents, she snapped orders in a loud, nasal tone that could crack ice, but with clients, she always used some fake oozy, syrupy voice, her attempt at a southern drawl that Brenda said was enough to gag a maggot. They say that eventually, everyone gets the face they deserve, and in her case, it was true. Someone (Ethel) once said that Babs looked exactly like a well-dressed wharf rat, a terribly cruel thing to say, but accurate. With her tight little beady eyes, tight little face, and long sharp nose, there was definitely a rodent vibe going on somewhere. Once, at a Women in Real Estate cocktail party, when Babs had been across the room nibbling on a piece of cheese, Ethel had poked Brenda and said, "See, I told you she was a rat." But Brenda said she thought Babs looked more like a whippet wearing a pair of bad earrings.

And it wasn't just her looks that Ethel objected to: it was the harsh way she conducted business and her loud and crass advertising style. Babs's company used ads written in big bold headlines that screamed at you:

HURRY! HURRY! HURRY!

WON'T LAST LONG!

RUN, DON'T WALK!

BRING YOUR TOOTHBRUSH!

Whereas Maggie's ads used more subtle terms like "Prepare to fall in love," "Elegance of the past," "A house to build a dream on," or "Your lovely new home awaits you." When Maggie wrote ads for less expensive homes, she said, "A rare opportunity for the discriminating buyer," "Adorable and affordable," or "Perfect for the first-time buyer and those wishing to scale down." Babs's ads for the same homes screamed at you:

CHEAP! CHEAP! CHEAP!

A REAL STEAL!

GRAB IT WHILE YOU CAN!

A LOT OF BANG FOR YOUR BUCK!

Maggie's ads for the high-end, upper-market, "over the mountain" homes and estates were especially discreet and simply stated, "Price upon request." Babs's idea of selling an expensive home was:

IF YOU HAVE TO ASK,
YOU CAN'T AFFORD IT!

If Maggie's ad said, "A large spacious home, perfect for the collector and gracious entertaining," Babs's said:

GOT ART? WALLS GALORE!

PLENTY OF ROOM TO PARTY!

Ethel said Babs was about as subtle and discreet as a Mack truck, but as the years went by and Babs Bingington's office started outselling Red Mountain Realty's office three to one, it was obvious that much of the public was responding, and it made Ethel so mad she could spit bullets.

By now, everybody in the business knew that Babs was taking kickbacks from some of the new real estate developers in town. When they saw a house on a lot they liked, usually one of the beautiful older homes, Babs would approach the owners and talk them into selling to the nice young couple she hired to pretend to be the buyers. And then, after it was sold and escrow closed, the next day, the developers would move in and bulldoze the existing house down to the ground and, almost overnight, throw up a cheaply built, brand-new six- or seven-thousand-square-foot, bright orange, fake Mediterranean-style mega-mansion that looked to Maggie like a giant Taco Bell. And, as Ethel often said, "What the hell does Mediterranean style have to do with Birmingham anyway?"

Sleepless in Mountain Brook

⌐

Maggie tried to sleep, but she kept thinking about all the things she had to do to get ready to leave on the third. She had already decided she would donate all her clothes and jewelry to the little community theater around the corner. Her neighbor Boots volunteered in the costume department and said they were always in need of clothes. Everything else—sheets, blankets, towels, dishes, pots and pans—would go to the Salvation Army, but she was still unsure about what to do with her Miss Alabama trophy and her sash and crown. And what about all her family photographs and newspaper clippings? She didn't know anyone who would want them, but she didn't want them to wind up at some garage sale either. She supposed she should probably take them down to the office and put them in the big paper shredder in the back room, if she could figure out how to work the thing. The last time she had tried, it had shredded one of her good scarves into a hundred pieces.

After Maggie tossed and turned for another half hour, she finally gave up and went into the kitchen and made herself a cup of tea and started her "Things to Do Before I Go" list:

1. Cancel subscriptions to **Southern Living, Veranda,** and **Southern Lady** magazines
2. Drop a hint to Dottie about unit becoming available
3. Clean out desks at home and work, all drawers and closets
4. Decide what to do with crown and trophy
5. Buy cardboard boxes
6. Pack up clothes for theater
7. Go to Walmart
8. Close out checking account
9. Pay off all credit cards, except MasterCard
10. Finish going through papers
11. Send whatever money left to Visiting Nurses and the Humane Society

She hoped there would be some money left over. The visiting nurses had been so helpful with her parents, and although she had never been able to keep a pet where she lived, she had always loved animals.

She then walked down the hall and started pulling down some of the boxes from the top of the closet. She hadn't gone through them for years, and she wasn't sure how much she had, but she saw that she had three entire hatboxes full of Miss Alabama stuff alone, so she thought she might as well get a head start on trying to figure out what to throw out and what to shred.

Later, she sat in the kitchen looking at all the old pictures of herself taken the night she had been crowned Miss Alabama. It was hard for her to believe she had ever been that young. But there she was, in photo after photo, with her bouquet of roses, just smiling away, so happy, so naïve, with absolutely no idea what was to come next.

Maggie wished she could just crawl back through the years and somehow stop time. If she could, she would have stopped it that very night. But time only moves forward and drags you along with it, whether you want to go or not.

As she continued going through the photos and old newspaper clippings, she began to think about the series of events that had led up to today's decision. She guessed it had all started with the incident in Atlantic City, losing Charles, then Richard, and, later, both her parents in one year. But for her, the final blow, really, had been Hazel.

One day, Hazel was in the office laughing and then the next day, she was gone. When she had died so suddenly, it was such a shock. For weeks afterward, everybody at the office half expected her to come bursting in the door with her daily joke, to make them laugh, cheer them up, flatter them, to make them all feel so smart. Everybody tried to continue on as usual, but as time went by, they all came to the slow, painful realization that she would not be coming back, and life at the office was suddenly dull, the work hard, the days long. There wasn't a day that passed that someone didn't start a sentence with "Remember when Hazel said this or when Hazel did that?" or ask how Hazel would have handled a problem. She had been the motor that had kept them all running happily for so many years. Without her, their incentive to work hard and the pride of being a part of Team Hazel was gone. They all missed her terribly. But for Maggie, losing Hazel had kicked the very foundation right out from under her. The year Maggie lost her parents, Hazel had quietly stepped in, and without her even realizing it, Hazel had become her rock, her mentor, her own personal cheerleader. And in a world increasingly lacking in role models, she had been the one person Maggie had admired and looked up to. But then, everyone who had ever known Hazel had looked up to her. Ironic, considering that Hazel Whisenknott had only been three feet, four inches tall.

Hazel Whisenknott Begins

September 21, 1929

"*T*his is the tiniest baby I've ever seen in my life!" is a phrase most people have heard a few times, but in Hazel Whisenknott's case, it was true. When she was born, her father had been able to hold her in the palm of his hand, but even so, both parents had been shocked when the doctor informed them that their little girl was never going to grow much bigger than three feet. It wasn't until the second grade that Hazel herself began to notice something odd. She was not getting any taller while everyone else in her class was. When she asked her parents about it, they were ready with answers, and if she ever resented it or felt sorry for herself, they didn't know it. Somehow, her mother had said the exact perfect word at the exact right time. Hazel was told that she was to be different than most, but "special," and Hazel had liked that word. She would settle for that and make the best of it. What her parents didn't know was that inside that small body beat the heart of a natural born businesswoman, and she could hardly wait to get started.

Just five short years later, Mrs. Mae Flower was at the sink rinsing out her deviled egg plate when she heard a knock on the front door. She wiped her hands on a tea towel and wondered who could be visiting her this time of day, but when she opened her door to find out, no one was there. She was about to close it again when she heard a voice from below saying, "Good afternoon, ma'am." She looked down to where the voice was coming from, and there stood the smallest person she had ever seen in her entire life, wearing a pair of tiny little overalls and a pink barrette in her hair.

"Good afternoon, ma'am," the small person repeated. "I hope you are having a pleasant afternoon."

Mrs. Flower was so completely surprised to see the tiny talking person that she clapped her hands in delight.

"Oh, if you are not just the cutest little thing . . . I could just pick you up and squeeze you to death, and just look at those little teeny feet and hands. Why, you are just a walking, talking little doll."

The little doll flashed a beautiful smile. "Thank you, ma'am."

Mrs. Flower threw the door open and said, "Well, come on in, precious, and let me get you some pie or something. Oh, I wish my husband were at home to see you. He's never going to believe me. Are you here with the circus?"

"Oh no, ma'am," said the little person. "I live here in Woodlawn, over on Thirteenth Street South, about five blocks from here." She pointed to the car parked at the curb. "My mother drove me over."

Mrs. Flower looked out and saw a full-sized lady sitting in a green Chevy smile and wave at her.

Mrs. Flower waved back and led the little person into the living room and indicated for her to sit. "What can I do for you, darling? Are you collecting money for anything?"

"Oh no, ma'am, I was just wondering if you had any weeds you wanted pulled today."

"Weeds?"

"Yes, ma'am, when we drove by, I noticed you have quite a few weeds that need pulling." The little person walked over to the living room windowsill, which came up to her nose, stood up on her toes, and sized up the lawn. "I'll tell you what; I'll pull the front yard and your side yard for a dollar."

"You mean . . . pull up the weeds?"

"Yes, ma'am."

"Are you sure you want to do that? That's mighty dirty work for a pretty little thing like you."

"Oh, I don't mind the work. I like it."

Mrs. Flower crossed her hands over heart and said, "Oh, honey, I don't want you to have to do that. Why don't I just give you a dollar? It was worth it just to get to see you at my door. You've just cheered me up so."

The little person frowned. "Oh no, ma'am, I couldn't take any money if I didn't earn it."

Mrs. Flower could tell the girl meant it, and she hated to have her leave empty-handed, so she sighed. "Well, honey, if you want to pull some weeds, go ahead, I guess."

A few minutes later, when Mrs. Flower was busy cutting a piece of pie and preparing a tall glass of iced tea for her tiny unexpected visitor, her next-door neighbor, Pearl Jeff, the judge's wife, came to the side screen door, still dressed and wearing her strand of good pearls from attending an earlier bridge club luncheon.

She said sharply, "Mae, do you know there's a midget sitting in your yard?"

"Yes, I do. Come on in," she said, wiping her hands on her apron.

The judge's wife stomped in, looking very concerned. "Why is there a midget sitting on your front lawn?"

"Well, Pearl, she just showed up, knocked on my door, and said she was looking for work pulling weeds. I told her I would just give her the money, she didn't need to pull my weeds, but she said no, that she wanted to pull my weeds, so what could I do? So, I said, 'Well, if you want to, go ahead.' So, she's going ahead, I guess. I don't know what to think, but she's as cute as a button."

The judge's wife pulled back the curtains and observed the small person. "Well, my word, have you ever? How old is she?"

"I couldn't say, she could be anywhere from six to sixty. I don't know, how can you tell how old a midget is? I wouldn't even know what to look for."

Still peering out the window, the judge's wife said again, "Well, my word, you just don't know what to expect from day to day, do you?"

"No, you don't. If you had told me at eight o'clock this morning that a real live midget would be knocking on my door today, I wouldn't have believed you."

The judge's wife, still looking out the window, said, "Well, who would? It's like having a pink elephant show up and sit down at your table for dinner. You don't suppose she's a gypsy, do you?"

"Oh no, she just lives a few blocks from here. Her mother's out in the car waiting for her. I think she looks like a little teeny tiny Shirley Temple myself . . ."

Two days later, the judge's wife called her neighbor on the phone.

"I'll tell you one thing, Mae, your yard never looked better. I told the judge about the little midget girl who pulled your weeds, and he said when you saw her again, have her come over to our house. We're just about eaten up with dandelions.

Our poor yardman is so old and blind anymore, he never gets them all. All he does now is trim the hedges, mow, and leave."

What the judge's wife said was accurate. Mrs. Flower's lawn had never looked better. It was as if someone had laid a fresh new green carpet in her yard with not a weed to be seen. As it turned out, little Hazel, being so close to the ground, could see the weeds much better than someone looking down from above. And she was fast: scooting on her little bottom across the yard, she could cover more ground in an afternoon than a grown man could in an entire day. As word spread, pretty soon, little Hazel Whisenknott was pulling weeds for everyone for blocks around and for most of the ladies in the judge's wife's bridge club. And they all agreed that once little Hazel Whisenknott had worked in your yard, the weeds didn't seem to come back. It was like some mystical thing, they said, and they wondered if maybe she had some secret midget knowledge. Mrs. Jack Mann, over at Sixteenth Street, said she thought that Hazel might really be a leprechaun.

But in the meantime, although she was only eleven, little Hazel was saving every dime she made to one day send herself through business school, and by age thirteen, she had been interviewed by the Home & Garden section of the **Birmingham News.** Asked what constituted a good weed puller, she gave an answer that appeared under her photo-graph, captioned:

> Little Hazel Whisenknott, The Weed Puller of Woodlawn, says, "Not only does a gardener have to love beautiful lawns, they also have to hate weeds."

Her father had puffed up with pride and had bragged to his co-workers out at the Birmingham Ornamental Iron Company, "Only thirteen years old and already quoted in the paper!"

Hazel had been a success from the very begin-ning. In high school, she was voted president of her class and head cheerleader. At football games, when she ran out on the field dressed in a smaller version of the blue-and-gold Woodlawn High School cheerleader outfits, doing a series of back flips, the crowd would roar with delight, even those there to cheer for the other side.

After Hazel graduated from high school, her fa-ther took her to see a mechanic he knew, who rigged up a car for her with special hand pedals and brakes. She then started driving all over town and selling magazines from door to door, and with the money she made, she sent herself to business school at night and became a CPA and got her real estate license. Al-ways ahead of the curve, she knew that after the war, housing would be in big demand. And so, in 1953, she set up a little one-room office and, six months later, hired Ethel Clipp, her first employee. Up until then, real estate had been mostly a man's profession, but Hazel quickly changed that and hired only women. She gave them great benefits, and they loved her for it and worked doubly hard, and by 1955, Red Mountain Realty had opened eight new branch offices and was on the way to becoming the largest real estate company in the state.

Hazel also believed in promoting herself and had been an occasional guest on the popular **Good Morning Alabama** television show. On the afternoon of July 31, 1968, she walked into the WBRC television station manager's office, looked him in the eye, and said, "Mr. Slinkard, I am by far the most unique individual you will ever meet. I even fascinate myself! So, I got to thinking that maybe I should have my own show."

Several months later, after **House Hunting with Hazel** went on the air, he had to agree. The ratings shot through the roof. Hazel introduced people to new neighborhoods and new subdivisions they'd never known existed. She interviewed experts on obtaining a mortgage, buying, selling, renting, decorating, and landscaping. Suddenly, women all over Birmingham wanted to get into real estate, and people who didn't even know they wanted to move started selling their houses and buying new ones. Hazel soon became a local TV celebrity and loved every minute of it. Sometimes, on her lunch hour or when she had nothing scheduled, she would make Ethel go downtown with her and stand on the corner of Twentieth Street, in front of Loveman's department store, shaking hands and handing out business cards. After about an hour, when Ethel's feet were killing her, Hazel just seemed to get more energized and would ask, "Don't you just love people?"

Ethel, who had always much preferred cats to people, would reply, "Only in small doses." Hazel, surprised, would say, "Well, I don't know why—I just can't get enough of them." And it was true.

In 1971, Hazel informed Ethel she didn't like being alone at night and was going husband hunting. And that year, when she went to the Little People of America convention, she found one and came home with a little husband. Little Harry, an Italian dwarf from Milwaukee, just like the rest of the world had fallen under Hazel's spell. It was a very good marriage—she adored him, and he adored her.

But years later, after Hazel died, Little Harry was devastated. He turned the business over to a management firm and moved back to Milwaukee to be with what family he had left; like everybody else, he was lost without her.

They all missed her. That smile lit up the room, and her heart was as big as the moon. Of course, Team Hazel couldn't help but think of her every time the phone rang. Hazel had her favorite song programmed into all the cell phones. It was annoying to have to listen to "I'm Looking Over a Four-

Leaf Clover" all day long, but nobody had the heart to change it.

So many things reminded them of Hazel. Even the color of their cars. Hazel had worked out a great leasing deal with the Mercedes dealership, for all her agents to get a brand-new blue Mercedes every year. Hazel liked blue; she said it reminded her of her other favorite song, "Blue Skies." Hazel always did love a happy song, and a happy client.

One of Hazel's biggest assets in business was her ability to compromise. Negotiating the sale price of a house, when she was within range of the exact price she wanted, she would bang the table with her little fist and exclaim, "Close enough!"

"Always leave everybody thinking they got a little something," she said. Hazel's motto for selling a house: "Put its best face forward. Move it fast. Don't let it linger."

Good Timing
Tuesday, October 28, 2008

At four A.M., just as Maggie had finally drifted off, the loud beeping of a garbage truck backing up in the alley woke her. As she lay there in the dark, looking up at the moon outside her window, for some reason, she began to think about the Whirling Dervishes again. Where was Turkey anyway? And why did the word "Ottoman" come to mind? Was she thinking about the country or the footstool? Oh Lord, just another regret. She should have gone to college instead of charm school. She had learned how to gracefully enter and exit a car and how to hold a teacup correctly, but not much about world geography. Charm used to be so important that they taught it, but now Maggie, who had made all A's in the subject, found that even she was beginning to run out of charm. Real estate, as it was today, could kick the charm out of anybody.

She had personally been bitten by several mean

cats, numerous dogs, a hamster, two parrots, and a ferret. She had opened attic doors and had bats fly up her dress and get caught in her hair, fallen down slippery basement stairs, and dropped Open House signs on her foot. And she had almost been terrified to death when a seller had failed to mention the eighteen-foot pet boa constrictor left in the upstairs bathroom tub. That, plus having to deal with lookie-loos, real estate hustlers, and hysterical clients all day, could go a long way toward helping you forget your manners.

Lately, she had found herself speaking to the television set and saying, "Oh, shut up!" to whoever was talking at the moment. At present, she only said "Shut up" in the privacy of her own home, but who knows when she might slip and tell someone in real life to shut up? She would hate to think all her years of being polite and pleasant would be wasted, but she felt she was in real danger of behaving badly in public. Something was bubbling up under the surface. There had been other little signs along the way. A few months ago, she had deliberately recommended the worst restaurant in Birmingham to that rude couple from Virginia, and only last week, something even more alarming had happened. She had been sitting in her car, waiting for the light to change, when Babs Bingington, the Beast of Birmingham herself, had walked across the street, right in front of her. Of course, she knew Babs didn't like her, but she didn't know why. She had never done a thing to her. But still, she didn't hate Babs like Brenda and Ethel did. She just avoided her as best she could. However, that day, as she sat there, she suddenly remembered what Babs had done to Hazel, and for a split second, she actually entertained the idea of stepping on the gas and running her over. She not only had a motive, but opportunity as well.

Luckily, in the split second she was thinking about it, a jogger ran across the intersection, and the moment passed. It was probably the first time in her life when indecision had actually worked in her favor, but she knew if she didn't do something soon, she just might suddenly go berserk and wind up on the television show **Snapped,** which featured stories about women who had suddenly flipped out. She could see the CNN headlines running under a newsreel of her now, dressed in an orange jumpsuit and handcuffed, being walked into the jail: "EX–MISS ALABAMA RUNS OVER RIVAL REAL ESTATE AGENT." Of course, she might have gotten away with it. Brenda always said that if Babs was ever murdered, every realtor in Birmingham had a motive and had threatened to kill her at one time or another. But the fact that she, who had a hard time even killing a spider, had actually thought of running someone over in broad daylight made her realize it might be time to remove herself from society, sooner rather than later. Red Mountain Realty had enough problems right now, and they didn't need one of their listing agents going to the chair. Or worse yet, going completely insane and winding up in some asylum like poor Olivia de Havilland in the movie **The Snake Pit.** She was already talking to the television set. It was clear to Maggie that she was getting out, not only at the right time, but just in time. She was obviously not coping.

Growing Up in Dreamland

The truth was, Maggie really **had** seen too many movies as a child. Not surprising, considering where she had grown up. Her father had been the manager of the Dreamland, a small neighborhood movie theater, and they had lived upstairs in a one-bedroom apartment, right next door to the projection booth, until she was eight. Looking back now, she supposed it had been somewhat unusual to enter and exit your childhood home through a movie theater lobby, but at the time, it had seemed normal to her and, in fact, quite wonderful.

To reach the apartment, she had to walk through a narrow, dark, carpeted stairway that was always cluttered with a few old broken spotlights and signs that read COMING SOON or HELD OVER ANOTHER WEEK and cardboard boxes full of black plastic let-ters for the marquee. Inside, the bare concrete-block walls were painted a pale mint green, with dark brown speckled linoleum tile on the floor. The bathroom had a claw-foot tub and one hanging light bulb. The kitchen was only a counter with a hot plate and a small refrigerator under the sink. It was not much to look at in the daytime, but at night, everything changed. As soon as it got dark, everything in the entire apartment, including herself and her parents, would suddenly start to glow a beautiful pink color from the reflection of the big neon Dreamland Theatre sign outside the window. Everything looked so pretty and cheerful. It had been like living inside a cartoon. And in the small alcove where she slept, there was a porthole in the wall she could open to look down and see the big movie screen downstairs. Every night, Maggie would lie in bed, watching the movie, and eventually be lulled to sleep by the whir of the movie projector next door, the voices coming from the screen, and the sounds of soft laughter coming from the audience below. And on hot summer nights, when her parents left the apartment door open to get a little breeze, she would hear the big red popcorn machine popping downstairs and the cash register bell ringing at the candy counter, and if she was still awake after the last show, when they had closed the doors, the sound of wooden seats being slammed up row by row. Then later, the roar of the big vacuum cleaner sucking up leftover popcorn and an occasional candy wrapper. All her life, the smell of popcorn and candy could transport her right back to that little apartment like it was yesterday.

She had loved growing up in the theater, but Maggie now suspected it was the main reason she had always had such a hard time facing reality. She'd read somewhere that the ages of one to four were formative years, so it must have affected her.

She had been raised in the era of Glorious Technicolor, the time of all the great movie musicals filled with cheerful songs and pretty people, where in the end, the boy always got the girl. And even though she was the only child of older parents, she had never been lonely. Her friends and playmates had been the movie stars, and she had been perfectly happy. But then television became all the rage, and like so many other little theaters, the Dreamland closed down for good, and they had to move into a regular apartment. What a shock that had been.

Out in the real world, there was no background music playing, no popcorn and candy downstairs or pink glow at night. Or even a plot she could follow. Her father had managed to get another job, selling shoes, but money was always tight, and afterward, they had been forced to move from one gloomy, airless apartment to another, and Maggie began to feel lost and anxious. The world around her seemed so strange and unfamiliar. She didn't say anything to her parents, but she had an uneasy feeling that somehow a mistake had been made, and she was not where she was supposed to be. She didn't know where that place was until one hot muggy afternoon in August when she was ten. Her mother had just started working as a seamstress's assistant to make a little extra money and had taken Maggie along to a dress fitting for a lady who lived in Mountain Brook. Maggie had never been to that part of town before, and when they drove up Red Mountain and she saw Crestview, the big, stately red brick Tudor mansion perched at the very top, the sight of it had taken her breath away. To Maggie, it looked like a castle in the sky, exactly like something right out of a movie. And as they descended down the other side of Red Mountain, into the cool, lush green world of Mountain Brook, with its leafy streets and ivy-covered brick and stone homes with long, rolling, graceful lawns, Maggie felt just like a kidnapped child who had been brought back home again. This was where she belonged, and she felt she could breathe again.

Of course, at the time, she was living across town in a dingy basement apartment with pipes on the ceiling, but even so, seeing Crestview had given her something to dream about. At night, she would lie on the lumpy pullout sofa and fantasize about the big house on the hill. She would imagine herself sitting on the side terrace, sipping tea, looking down on the city below. It had been a foolish childish dream, but it had soothed her during all those years of never being settled, of living in cramped, dark places. Over the years, Crestview became more than just a place to her; it became her ideal, something to strive for.

Many of the seamstress's clients her mother worked for were women who lived "over the mountain," and Maggie grew to love going along and seeing the beautifully appointed homes, the furniture, the art, the Oriental rugs, the long staircases leading up to large open and airy bedrooms with balconies overlooking the city. No one had minded her coming; she was always well behaved and quiet. All the ladies had been kind to her, but Maggie had fallen in love especially with Mrs. Roberts, at first sight. To Maggie, she was all elegance and grace. Mrs. Roberts had no daughters of her own, and she had taken a special interest in Maggie and, from time to time, would ask her mother, "May I take Maggie to tea?" or "May I take Maggie to Easter brunch at the club?"

Maggie had loved going to the Birmingham Country Club, with its big floral chintz chairs and sofas, and she had liked the people "over the mountain" right away: their manners, their clothes, the way they took such good care of everything. She had been fascinated seeing all the exotic foods they ate: Camembert cheese, artichokes, caviar, black olives, smoked salmon. So different from the Franco-American spaghetti from a can she was used to. When she was twelve, Mrs. Roberts had arranged a scholarship for her at Brook Hill, a private girls' school. If it had not been for Mrs. Roberts taking her under her wing, Maggie could very well have wound up never knowing there was such beauty and grace in the world. Mrs. Roberts had taught her how to appreciate the finer things in life.

And even though she was one of the wealthiest ladies in Birmingham, there was nothing pretentious about her. When she donated money to support numerous causes around town, she did so anonymously. Never class- or race-conscious, she opened her home to all, and all were treated well.

Mrs. Roberts was everything that Maggie had aspired to be. She had spent the rest of her childhood looking in on the seemingly graceful lives of those who lived "over the mountain," just waiting to grow up and move there. It never occurred to her that it wouldn't happen. She had always just assumed that she would wind up there someday, living in a beautiful house, married to a wonderful man; but as with so many other things (Richard for one), she had been dead wrong.

Maggie wished she could have ended up like Mrs. Roberts and all the other "over the mountain" ladies. They had such a neat, orderly way of living she so admired. After their husbands died, they sold the big house and moved into a little garden home in English Village. Then, after a certain age, they went on out to St. Martin's in the Pines, the lovely Episcopal retirement home they all favored, to spend the rest of their days with old friends, most of whom they had gone to grammar school with, playing bridge and being taken on the St. Martin's bus to theater, museum, and flower show outings.

St. Martin's was a three-part facility that made all the unpleasant things about the end of life so much easier. First the little cottage on the grounds, then as a resident's health started to fail, they were moved to the assisted living section, and thereafter, on out to the family plot. A lovely, practical, and predictable ending, but unfortunately, Maggie didn't have the money or the desire to wait that long. True, she wasn't getting the Technicolor ending she had expected, but she couldn't have asked for a more wonderful beginning.

Another New Day

After Maggie had finally gone back to sleep, she dreamed it was a warm summer night and she was young again, dressed in a white evening gown and dancing under a thousand stars on a terrace overlooking the city. Was it Charles she was dancing with? She couldn't quite tell, but it was such a vivid and beautiful dream that when she first woke up, she still felt so warm and happy—until a few seconds later, when that same old familiar wave of cold gray dread washed over her, and the warm glow faded into the harsh reality of the present. It was seven A.M., and once again, she had to summon the strength to get up and face yet another day. She wished she wouldn't have those dreams; it just made it harder. She felt the hot tears running down her face and reached over and grabbed a Kleenex. Oh Lord, now she would have swollen eyes, and she was showing a house later on this morning. That's all her client needed was some weepy real estate agent moping around.

After a moment, she got up and went into the bathroom and looked at herself in the mirror and, just as she'd suspected, her eyes did look swollen and puffy. Now she was going to have to put tea bags on them. She would have loved to just go back to bed, but she couldn't. She had a lot to do today, and she wanted to get an early start. She was meeting Brenda at noon, and it was her turn to buy the wine and cheese for the realtors' open house, and also, she wanted to call Cathy Gilmore at the Arts and Lecture office and find out about the Whirling Dervishes' hotel situation.

As she sat there with the tea bags on her eyes, she realized that at this point, it was completely idiotic that she should even care where a group of perfect strangers she certainly would never see again stayed, but she did care. At exactly one minute after eight, Maggie dialed Cathy at her office. She hoped to reach her before she got on the phone with someone else. They didn't call her Chatty Cathy for nothing. Fortunately, Cathy picked up right away.

Twenty minutes later, when she was able to gracefully slip in the question about where they were putting the Dervishes, Cathy told her that they were arriving the afternoon of the performance and leaving for Atlanta right after the show that night. They weren't even going to spend the night in Birmingham.

As usual, Maggie had been concerned over nothing, but at least now she knew and she wouldn't have to think about it anymore. It was so irritating. All her life, she had wasted so many hours, days, years even, worrying about this and that. It was a serious character flaw. Why couldn't she have been more like Hazel? Hazel never worried. Even when they lost the big new insurance account to Babs Bingington: everybody at the office had been devastated, but when Hazel came in, she just brushed it off and then turned to an agent and said, "Hey, Maxine, ask me why the woman shot her husband with a bow and arrow." As upset as she was, Maxine tried to smile and asked and Hazel said, "Because she didn't want to wake up the children." That afternoon, Hazel had sent them a dozen roses with a card: "Remember, girls, it's always the darkest right before the glorious dawn." Hazel had always been so optimistic about the future; unfortunately, Maggie wasn't Hazel. But then, who was?

Brenda's first meeting with Hazel, like most people's, had been memorable. Brenda had just moved back home from Chicago to be closer to her family and had seen an ad in the paper that interested her. Red Mountain Realty was looking for people to train as real estate agents, and Brenda had called and spoken directly with the owner and set up a meeting.

When she walked into Hazel's office, a tiny little woman, no bigger than a child, jumped down from her chair, walked over, reached up and shook her hand, and said, "Hi, I'm Hazel! Do you know any good jokes?" And the next thing Brenda knew, she was hired. A few minutes later, when Brenda came out, she was still in a little bit of shock and walked over to Ethel, who was typing up her papers, and said, "Excuse me . . . is that lady in there really the owner?" "She sure is," said Ethel, pushing her purple glasses up on her nose. "Oh . . . well . . . does she know she's a midget?" "Why, no," said Ethel, never looking up. "But I'm sure if you want to go back in and tell her, she'll be delighted to know why she's so short." "Oh no . . . I didn't mean it that way . . . What I meant was that she acts just like a real person . . . Oh . . . I'm not saying she's not a real person. It's just . . . well . . . she didn't sound like a midget on the phone."

"Oh, really."

"I thought they all had funny little voices like the Munchkins in **The Wizard of Oz** or something. Well, anyhow, I'll see you Monday morning . . . I guess," Brenda said as she tripped all over herself trying to get out the door before she made more of a fool of herself. Ethel, unfazed, went back to her typing. She was used to people's first reactions. She had been with Hazel from the very beginning and seen it over and over, but after the initial shock, people quickly forgot Hazel's height, mostly because Hazel didn't make a big deal out of it herself. She had certain limitations, but she either overlooked them or worked around them. Hazel always carried a small stepladder in her car to help her if necessary and a magician's extending wand in her purse, in case she was in an elevator alone and needed to punch the button for a higher floor, but other than that, she managed very well.

Of course, she sometimes needed assistance reaching things when she was grocery shopping, and getting on and off buses, but it had never been a problem. As she once said to Ethel, "I've had to depend on people my whole life, and they haven't let me down yet."

In 1982, Hazel was listed in the **Guinness Book of World Records** as "The Biggest Little Real Estate Woman in the World." And it had tickled her to death.

The Perfect Plan

Maggie knew she had a few more days to get ready, but before she did anything else this morning, she thought she would just go ahead and run out to Walmart and pick up the last of her supplies and get it over with, so she wouldn't have to think about it the rest of the week.

Twenty minutes later, Maggie walked into Walmart at the big mall and headed back to Aisle 10. Luckily, she knew exactly what color and what size she wanted, and she paid in cash. It was part of her plan to leave absolutely no clues as to her whereabouts, and having a record of the purchase of a rubber raft show up on her credit card bill so close to her departure might tip someone off. After all the planning, she certainly didn't want to make a mistake at the very end. She had assumed that making the decision to do it would be the hard part, but coming up with a viable and working plan for just

how she would do it had not been as easy as one might think.

Pills were never a sure thing. A gun would be much too violent (and oh, didn't the press just love to portray all southerners as gun-happy?), and her being a former Miss Alabama? They would just have a field day with that. So no, a gun was definitely out. Sticking her head in an oven had never been an option; all the kitchen appliances at Avon Terrace were electric, and it certainly wasn't anything you would ever do in someone else's kitchen, or at least she wouldn't. Her car was a company leased car, so driving off a cliff was out as well. No matter what method she had come up with, she'd found there was just no surefire way to do it and remain attractive, and no matter how shallow it may seem to some, she felt she had a responsibility to always try to look her best, no matter what.

It had taken quite a while to figure out something that would meet all her specific requirements, but six months before, she had been at the gym working out with wraparound ankle weights in her Stretch, Flex, and Strengthen class, when she had come up with the perfect plan. On the designated day, now November 3, she would go down to the Warrior River, get in the rubber raft, row all the way out to the middle where it was very deep and very calm, wrap two ten-pound weights around her ankles plus two ten-pound weights around her wrists, then jump in.

She had some concerns that the Velcro that held the weights together might come undone underwater, but the man at Big B Sports had assured her that the Velcro they used was completely waterproof. However, just to be on the safe side, she had gone to the As Seen on TV store and bought a tube of fast-drying 100 percent waterproof glue, guaranteed to last a lifetime. So, on the third, when she got to the middle of the river, she would apply the glue, wait the necessary twenty minutes for it to dry, then jump. It was a perfect plan. It was so perfect that it really was a shame she couldn't tell anybody about it.

When she got back home, she still had a few hours before she had to meet Brenda at the open house, and that was good. She could use the time to start culling through a few more boxes. Maggie had just reached for another cup of coffee when something suddenly occurred to her. Oh, my God! Today was Tuesday, and she had a nine-thirty hair appointment with Glen, but with so much on her mind, she had completely forgotten about it. How could she have been so stupid? Oh no, with all she had to do, she didn't want to waste two hours getting her hair done. Oh Lord. Why hadn't she thought about it yesterday? She could call and say she was sick, but then she would have to stay home and not be seen for a day at least, and she couldn't do that.

The shop had a twenty-four-hour cancellation policy and if she didn't show up, she would be charged anyway, and she couldn't just drive over and pay him without letting him fix her hair. Of course, she could always mail him a check. But knowing Glen, if he received something from her in the mail after she was gone, he would just freak out, and the last thing in the world she wanted was to upset anyone, especially Glen. His partner of twelve years had just run off with an ice skater, and he was already on the edge. She looked up at the clock, wondering what to do. After thinking it over, she supposed the best thing was to just go and finish with the boxes tonight.

At 9:42, Maggie was sitting in Glen's chair, and he was busy wrapping streaks of her hair with tin foil and telling her all the latest about his ex. Other than the fact that she felt rushed, it was really very pleasant at the shop this morning. As usual, a lot of the ladies from St. Martin's in the Pines were there having their hair done, happily chattering away.

Maggie sat there thinking about how upset poor Glen would be if he knew that all of his hard work was for nothing when she heard Fairly Jenkins say to Virginia Schmitt, "Gin, I heard a rumor that Dee Dee Dalton might be thinking about selling her house."

A couple of months ago, just hearing that someone might be thinking of selling, Maggie would have jumped up with her hair still wet and run out the door and tried to get the listing. Considering that she was leaving the real estate business in a few days, however, the fact that someone might be selling shouldn't have meant a thing to her; but hearing **what** house might be for sale threw her for a complete loop.

Glen continued telling her all about his ex, but Maggie didn't hear a word. Her mind was going a mile a minute. Everyone had always assumed that Mrs. Dalton would never sell Crestview in a million years. How could she even think about it? It had never been on the market before; why was she selling it now? Crestview wasn't just any house. It was a landmark, and her favorite house in all of Birmingham. The thought that it might be going on the market was very upsetting. The longer she sat there, the more agitated she became.

Oh, no. She knew the minute Glen finished blow-drying her hair and she paid her bill, she would have to fight off the urge to drive up the mountain and take a last look at it. But what would be the point? Why make herself miserable today, of all days? She was on a tight schedule as it was. She shouldn't be concerned about anything else today, except making sure that everything was taken care of before Monday. She had a plan, so she should stick to it and just concentrate on that.

She paid her bill, went out, got in the car, and headed straight up the mountain. It was stupid and childish, she knew, but she couldn't have stopped herself if she'd tried. She parked in front of Crestview and began to get more upset by the minute. There it stood, like it always had, so stately and proud, overlooking the city. To Maggie, it was the perfect house, perfectly proportioned, elegant, and understated. Of course, she had never been inside, but Mrs. Roberts, who had been a friend of Mrs. Dalton's, had said that it had lovely wood-paneled walls in every room and the most beautiful set of white marble stairs she had ever seen. When Maggie was growing up, she had dreamed about those white marble stairs.

In the past, she had watched helplessly as Babs Bingington had sold off so many of the beautiful old homes over the mountain and, one by one, they had been torn down. Seeing those lovely old homes go and all the ugly new ones overbuilt on the lots had been a bitter pill to swallow. But if Babs got this listing, it would be a disaster. Babs Bingington had single-handedly been responsible for tearing down blocks and blocks of charming little thirties bungalow homes on the south side and developing new cheap four-story fake Swiss château swinging-singles apartments with a bad pool in the middle. The more she thought about it, the more agitated she became. Babs really had no business selling Crestview. She would run in, slap it on the market, and treat it just like any other property. She had no sense of the history and what it had meant to the people in Birmingham. She would view it with her cold fish eye and be willing to sell it to the highest bidder.

The thought of Babs Bingington marching through Crestview, like Sherman through Atlanta, gave Maggie a sick feeling. Babs had no loyalties to the town or the neighborhood. In the past, there had always been an unwritten law among real estate agents about selling homes on the mountain; even if it meant taking a cut out of your own commission, you did not sell those houses to people you knew would not take care of them or appreciate them. But not Babs. She was only interested in the sale. And who knows what could happen? Some young dotcom millionaire could buy it and put a basketball court in the living room. Or worse yet, it might be sold to a developer. If someone tore Crestview down, the entire skyline of Birmingham would change; it would be like looking at a beautiful woman with her front tooth missing. Or even worse, if one of Babs's developer cronies got a hold of it, a beautiful woman with a big bright orange tooth. Thanks to Babs, there were some streets Maggie couldn't even drive down anymore.

Oh no, here came that strange rage again. She could feel her cheeks starting to burn and her face turning beet red and her heart pounding a mile a minute. What was going on? She had never lost her temper in her life. This was twice in one month. It was either late menopause or some weird form of road rage—or, in this case, real estate rage. Whatever it was, she realized she'd better calm down. She didn't want to have a stroke before she had a chance to finish up all the loose ends she still had to deal with.

As she drove across town, she tried to calm herself. First of all, it really could just be a rumor that Crestview was coming up for sale. With the ladies from St. Martin's, you could never be sure; being of a certain age, many of them were a little deaf and often got things mixed up. Maggie hoped and prayed that this was the case today. And it really made no sense. Why would Mrs. Dalton be selling? The Dalton family had owned Crestview for as long as she could remember, and they certainly didn't need the money, so surely, Fairly Jenkins must be mistaken. Still, Maggie hated to have to spend the next six days wondering about it. But how could she find out? She couldn't just call Mrs. Dalton and ask her outright; it would be far too rude and pushy. Oh Lord, why, of all the houses in the world, did it have to be Crestview? She should have canceled her hair appointment when she'd had the chance. Then she never would have even known about it. With all she had to do in the next few days, the last thing she needed was one more thing to have to worry about. And even if by the slightest chance it was true, and Mrs. Dalton **was** selling Crestview, there was not a thing in the world she could do about it now. Besides, she didn't have time to think about anything but the task at hand. She would just have to try to put it entirely out of her mind and get on with her day. Dear God, what next? That was the point: she didn't want to know what next. She didn't need any more surprises. Life had surprised her enough.

Magic City

⌒

*I*f Maggie had lived most of her life under the spell of her childhood, she wasn't alone. A lot of people still had a few stars left in their eyes, and no wonder, growing up in a place called the Magic City, with all of its lofty aspirations and illusions of grandeur. You could see it everywhere you looked, from the towering smokestacks of the iron, coal, and steel mills to the grand mansions atop Red Mountain to the sparkle in the cement in the downtown sidewalks. The city was bustling and alive, with block after block of elegant stores, where mannequins stood in haughty poses, dressed in the latest fashions and furs from New York and Paris; blocks of showrooms filled with fine rugs, lamps, and furniture, displayed so beautifully you wanted to walk in and live there forever (or at least Maggie had). There had always been an excitement in the air. A feeling that Birmingham, the Fastest-Growing City in the South, was right on the verge of exploding into the biggest city in the world. Even the streets had been laid out extra wide and stood waiting, as if expecting a tremendous rush of traffic at any moment. From the beginning, Birmingham had been bursting with ambition and hated being second to Pittsburgh in steel production and having the second-largest city transit system in the country. Even the towering iron statue of Vulcan, the Greek god of fire and iron, that stood on the top of Red Mountain was only the second-largest iron statue in the country, and during the war, when headlines announced that Birmingham, Alabama, had been named the number two target city in America to be bombed by Germany and Japan, everybody was terribly disappointed; they would have loved to have been first! Their only consolation: they did have the largest electrical sign in the world, which greeted all visitors as they came out of the train station. It blazed with ten thousand golden light bulbs that spelled out WELCOME TO MAGIC CITY. Birmingham was a city with a pulse that you could hear beating, working, and sweating, striving to become number one. The giant iron and steel mills clanked and banged and spewed out pink steam and billowed thick smoke all hours of the day and night. Coal miners worked in shifts around the clock. Streetcars and buses ran twenty-four hours a day, packed full of people either going to or coming home from work.

In the afternoon, parents used to drive their children up the mountain to Vulcan Park to watch the sun set over the city, when the sky would come alive with layers of iridescent green, purple, aqua, red, and orange that streaked across the horizon as far as you could see. Everyone thought it was a special show the city put on just for them. It never occurred to them that the beautiful colors were caused by all the toxins and pollutants spewing out from all of the mills surrounding the city. They also never dreamed that one day, most of old downtown Birmingham, its magnificent movie palaces, restaurants, and department stores with the beautiful shiny brass doors and silver escalators, would all be shut down for good. But they were.

The Open House

Maggie crawled along through heavy traffic, and a good half hour later, she stopped at the Contri Brothers Gourmet Deli for cold cuts and then at Savage's Bakery to pick up five dozen assorted cookies. Everyone said that Red Mountain put on the best realtors' open houses in town. Even in the 1980s, she'd heard, when the market was hot and it had been hard getting agents to show up at all the newly listed houses, Hazel had never failed to draw a huge crowd and had always managed to come up with some attraction. She would send out announcements to "Come and meet Matilda, the World's Oldest Chicken" or "Henry, the Cat with Fourteen Toes." But all they could offer today was a free lunch. Maggie was still feeling thrown by what she had heard at the beauty shop, but she forced herself to just keep her mind focused on what she wanted to get done today. She thought that she probably should start dropping a few subtle hints to Brenda about her plans, but it would be tricky. She didn't want to alarm her, but she did want to try to prepare her as best she could without tipping her hand. She loved Ethel, but of all the people in the world, she guessed she would miss Brenda the most.

Hazel had put Maggie and Brenda together from the very start. Maggie had the looks, the contacts, and certainly the charm to sell real estate, but she couldn't do the paperwork if her life depended on it. The only reason she had gotten her real estate license in the first place was that Hazel sat on the real estate board. Maggie's grades had not been quite high enough to pass, but Hazel had glanced over it, declared, "Close enough," and pushed it through. Brenda, on the other hand, was a master at reading contracts, crunching numbers, obtaining mortgages, and closing a deal. Any information you needed she could bring up on her BlackBerry in seconds. She was a real treasure in every way: Brenda had been one of the first girls in the Birmingham school system to take Shop, instead of Home Economics, and could fix anything. She always had a large hammer, nails, a wrench, several screwdrivers, measuring tapes, light bulbs, extension cords, and a big flashlight in her purse; anything you could ever need, Brenda had it, including snacks of all kinds. Maggie told her that the boy in the frozen yogurt parking lot who had tried to snatch her purse probably couldn't have lifted it anyway.

As far as Maggie was concerned the two of them were a perfect pair. Maggie always felt so safe with Brenda around. Just last month, when a creepy-looking man had shown up at an open house because he had liked Maggie's photo in an ad, Brenda had picked him up and thrown him out the front door. Other than Hazel, Brenda was the most capable woman Maggie had ever known. She just hoped Brenda wouldn't be too upset at her leaving her in the lurch at work, but it was really only a matter of time. Theirs was the last of the Red Mountain Realty offices that had not been shut down, and it was sure to be bought up by one of the larger companies any day now. Maggie wouldn't be surprised if it was Babs Bingington's company, and she was just as glad not to be around when that happened. The way Babs hated her, she was sure to be fired on the spot.

Of course, she should have quit real estate after Hazel died, but at the time, everybody on Team Hazel vowed to carry on out of loyalty; as the business got worse, however, people started to leave. Now there were only three of the original team left: Ethel, Brenda, and herself. Maggie figured that Brenda would be leaving real estate soon to run for mayor, but thank heavens, she hadn't left yet. Brenda was the only person who could still make her laugh.

Last St. Patrick's Day, Brenda had come into the office dressed entirely in green—green dress, green shoes, green wig—and had held out her arm to Maggie and asked, "What color would you say I was?"

Maggie looked at Brenda's arm. "Oh, I don't know, sort of brown?"

"I **know** that! What sort of brown?"

Maggie looked again. "Well, maybe reddish brown?"

Brenda was delighted with the answer. "That's what I think! Reddish brown! Mother was more caramel, and Daddy was dark brown, but I'm more of a reddish color, aren't I?"

"I would say so. Yes."

"I want one of those DNA tests. I've got some freckles; who knows? There could be an Irishman in the woodpile somewhere."

Brenda had such a good sense of humor about herself—a trait you more or less had to have if you worked for Hazel. Brenda and Hazel had a lot in common on that score. In Brenda's lifetime, she had gone from being Colored to Negro to Black, and now African American, and it was a running joke between them. Hazel would come in the door and ask Brenda how she was feeling today, and Brenda would say, "Well, I felt very black yesterday, but today I'm feeling a little colored. How about you?" Hazel would think and say, "I think I'm feeling a little more short-statured than height-challenged today."

Brenda always said to the new people, when they were surprised at some of Hazel's humor, "She may not be politically correct, but she's hired more minorities than any other company in town."

Maggie had hoped to drop a hint while they were preparing the food platters, but when Brenda arrived at the open house, she was in such a state that she couldn't. Evidently, something had happened to her favorite purse, the one with twenty-seven secret compartments she had ordered from the TravelSmith catalog, and as they were putting out the wine and cheese, Brenda was going on and on about it. "I could just cry. The whole inside was ruined, and I had to throw it out in the garbage." Maggie was still somewhat confused about the details and asked her why there was a pint of ice cream in her purse in the first place. Brenda made a face. "Oh, you don't want to know."

"Yes, I do . . ."

"No, you don't."

"All right, I don't."

Brenda sighed. "Oh, well," she said, throwing a bunch of grapes on a plate. "It was all Robbie's fault!"

"Robbie? Why?"

"Because she buys summer flavors just so she can catch me, that's why! Anyhow, I had to run out and get another pint to put back in the freezer, but when I got back, Robbie was already home, so I put it in my purse and I forgot about it until this morning. When Robbie got up, there was this green gooey stuff leaking out all over the floor."

Maggie had heard something like this before; only the last time, it had been an entire coconut cake Brenda had hidden in the top of the linen closet, and Brenda had blamed the ants for her getting caught.

"Oh dear. What did Robbie say?"

"Oh . . . you know Robbie. She said, 'I guess that pint of ice cream just jumped out of the freezer into your purse when you weren't looking, didn't it?' "

"What did you say?"

"What could I say? Anyhow, I didn't forget to call Cecil. We have two tickets for the Dervishes. I'm sorry I'm late, but I had to take everything out and wash it all off. My checkbook is just ruined, but enough about me . . . what did you do last night?"

Maggie started to say something, but a gal from Ingram Realty walked in, and the open house started.

Thankfully, a lot of agents had shown up, including Babs Bingington, who had marched through and, as she left, made her usual snide remark: "Well . . . it's not Mountain Brook." Unfortunately, she was right. Since the market was down, Brenda and Maggie had been happy to get a call from the owners of a midpriced home in a part of town they didn't used to handle. But the minute they walked inside, they knew it would be a problem trying to show it. The wife, "Just call me Velma," collected what she lovingly referred to as "pinecone art." Everywhere you looked, there were hundreds of pinecones with little plastic eyes, dressed as Santa's elves or as Scarlett O'Hara in evening dresses, and pinecone babies in diapers or in tiny pinecone cribs, and she informed them with a happy smile, "I've got lots more up in the bedroom and out in the garage."

Oh, dear. How do you tell a nice woman like that that potential buyers wouldn't find the pinecones just darling, "like part of the family," as she did? How could they explain, in a nice way, that the pinecones and all the geegaws had to go? Collectors were always a problem. Trying to separate people from their eight hundred spoons from around the world or their collection of ceramic chickens, pigs, cocker spaniels, cats, elephants, cows, birds, deviled egg plates, teapots, or whatever they collected was always difficult. They'd once had a client with forty-two toy Chihuahuas, all named Tinker-Bell. Trying to show that house had been a nightmare. But thankfully, Maggie had managed to talk Velma into letting her put away some of the pinecones for today's showing.

After the open house, Brenda said she was late for one of her many political meetings. Maggie told her to go on; she would see her later at the office. Maggie didn't mind closing up. It was nice to see Brenda so excited. Brenda loved politics. The only really strong opinion Maggie ever had about politics, she had learned in the movies. After seeing **Doctor Zhivago,** she knew she could never be a Communist. The scene when poor Dr. Zhivago (Omar Sharif) came back to Moscow after the war and found that his beautiful family home had been taken over by a horde of strangers had really bothered her.

Before she left, Maggie had to put all the pinecone art she had hidden back where it had been. She then went into the kitchen and gathered up all the realtors' business cards they had left on the counter and noticed that Babs had left two cards with BIRMINGHAM'S NUMBER ONE TOP-SELLING REALTOR stamped across the top in bright red ink—just to rub it in.

As usual, when she had come through the house today, Babs had completely ignored Maggie and been rude to everyone else. Maggie had always been so uncomfortable around Babs; it was hard to be around someone who just hated you, particularly when you didn't know why. As Maggie was locking up, something occurred to her. The next realtors' open house wasn't until Wednesday. Today was the last time she would ever have to see Babs Bingington again, and if that wasn't something to look forward to, she didn't know what was. In fact, as of Monday, she would be saying goodbye to the never-ending saga of real estate forever, and not a minute too soon.

Besides being physically dangerous, real estate was also an emotional roller coaster. Dealing with people selling their homes was always tricky. Some would not leave the house and would follow the potential buyers from room to room. And there were no guidelines to offer help, no official set of rules for real estate etiquette. She was constantly surprised at the cruel things people would say about another person's home.

It was about four o'clock when Maggie pulled into her parking spot behind the office. Red Mountain Realty was located in a charming old stone building right in the middle of the village of Mountain Brook. When Hazel was alive, all twelve desks had been filled with busy agents, the phones ringing, and the place had bustled with activity. But now it was mostly quiet—unless, of course, Ethel was on one of her "in my day" rants.

It was said of Ethel that she was set in her ways, but in fact, Ethel just plain didn't like the way the world was headed and made no bones about it. And this afternoon, she was on her Hollywood rant (again). "In my day, the movie stars were glamorous, but now they all want to look just like everybody else; they go out in public wearing any old rag. Back then, you'd never catch any of them running out to the store in cut-off blue jeans. In my day, the movie stars were carefree and fun. Now they all have causes and take themselves so seriously, running all over the world, palling around with dictators, bad-mouthing America. But they sure don't mind taking all the money they make here. I say they should all just keep their big mouths shut and act."

Brenda laughed. "That would be kind of hard to do."

"You know what I mean, and I just give up on the movies. Every damn one has the same plot: everybody in authority is corrupt, and every lead character is a murderer, a thief, a dope dealer, or worse. Hell, if I wanted to spend time with criminals, which I don't, I could go to the jail and visit for free. Why don't they make movies about nice people? When I go to the movies, I want to be uplifted and feel good after I leave, not worse. Nowadays, if there is a movie about killers, perverts, or child molesters that shows the very worst side of human nature, they just can't wait to give it the Academy Award. I used to watch the Academy Awards, but the year 'It's Hard Out Here for a Pimp' beat out Dolly Parton for best song, I just cut it off and never watched it again. Hell, no wonder Western civilization is on the decline."

Maggie didn't say anything, but she had to agree. If they didn't rerun **The Sound of Music** every Easter at the Alabama Theatre, she would hardly have gone to the movies at all. It was obvious to Maggie that she had lost touch with Hollywood or else Hollywood had lost touch with her; she didn't know which, but she strongly suspected it was her. She was hopelessly out-of-date. After all these years, Doris Day was still her favorite movie star, and she was the only person she knew who actually liked elevator music—it was the only music Maggie knew the words to anymore. And it wasn't just music. In the past ten years, modern technology had suddenly taken several quantum leaps forward and had left Maggie in the dust. Things were changing so fast, she couldn't keep up. By the time she had learned how to work something it was already obsolete. She never had figured out how to program her new oven and couldn't work a BlackBerry if her life depended on it. She hadn't even attempted to learn to Twitter.

Another Unexpected Perk

❧

When Maggie got home from work, she walked in and picked up the mail. It was mostly junk and another reminder of the annual Halloween night Boo at the Zoo gala. When Hazel was alive, they usually went. Hazel loved any excuse to dress up in a costume, but now Maggie hardly went anywhere anymore. She had lost touch with most of her old friends, and it had been her own doing. It was easier not to see them. She knew they were probably as disappointed in her as she was in herself, but they were just too nice to say so. Besides, she wanted to have all her good clothes packed in boxes by Friday, so she wouldn't have anything to wear anyway. She would just send a donation.

She went into the bedroom and was putting on her workout clothes for her Tuesday night aerobics class at the gym when it hit her: What was the point of working out now? Why get in shape now? For what? She hated exercise; and no matter what they said about endorphins, exercise never made her feel better, just glad to get it over with. She now realized she would never have to exercise again. What an un-expected perk that was. No more worry about her upper arms or thighs. If cellulite wanted to form, let it. Have a ball. She then took off her clothes, put on a robe, then gathered the rest of her workout clothes, tennis shoes, sweats, socks, etc., and threw them into a big plastic bag for the Salvation Army and promptly called the gym and canceled her member-ship, and that felt good.

Unfortunately, as hard as she was trying to forget it, the subject of Crestview was still stuck in the back of her mind. But what could she do? She had no way of finding out if it was even true. Of course, she did know one person who would know and might even be able to help, but she really couldn't impose on a friendship like that. Oh Lord, she wished she hadn't gone to the beauty parlor today.

She fixed herself a glass of iced tea and went into the closet and had started pulling out boxes of stuff she had stacked up in the back. She began going through her old papers again when she came across her sixth-grade report card. Her teacher had written across the bottom, "Maggie is a quiet, well-behaved, pleasant child."

Dear God, how perfectly sad. She had not pro-gressed since the sixth grade. Lately, she had begun to suspect that underneath that pleasant exterior was just another pleasant exterior. She had gotten older, but not wiser. She'd always thought she would be so much smarter by now, but she wasn't. If anything, she was losing ground.

Then she opened a new box and came across a few notes and cards from Hazel she had saved. Reading them again made her smile.

Sweetie Pie,
Happy Birthday. Get yourself a
good piece of jewelry!
H.

Baby Cakes,
Keep on keeping on, you are the best!
H.

Miss Maggie Pie,
Let's go roaming on Sunday . . . okay?
H.

Hazel had always been so generous. The first Easter after Maggie's parents died, when Maggie was so in debt, Hazel had given her a big white chocolate Easter dove and later, when she was eating it, she found five one-hundred-dollar bills stuffed inside. When Maggie called and asked her about it, Hazel feigned surprise. "I have no idea how it got there; it must have been an Easter miracle," she said.

Every year after that, Hazel gave her a white dove

with money inside, and every year, Hazel pretended not to know how the money got there. Now, without Hazel, Easter was just another Sunday.

She pulled out another box and found it was full of old photos. She picked up the only photograph she had of Richard and wondered why she had ever thought he looked just like Eddie Fisher. She must have been delusional. He didn't look a thing like Eddie Fisher. Had it just been a case of wishful thinking? Had she been so in love with Eddie Fisher just because Debbie Reynolds had married him? Lord, what had she been thinking? That was the problem; she hadn't been thinking. But after Charles, Richard was the only other man she had been attracted to. To this day, she still wondered how she could have **ever** done such a thing. Even though she'd been as far away as Dallas, she had still lived in constant terror that someone would find out. The very idea of a former Miss Alabama being involved with a married man was shocking, even to her, and she'd been the one who was doing it! If you had asked anyone, they would have said that Maggie Fortenberry was the last person on earth they would ever suspect of doing something like that, and she would have agreed with them. Having the affair was bad enough, but how could she have done something like that to another woman? She would never forgive herself for that.

In her defense, Richard had not been married when she first started going out with him; he had simply failed to mention that he was engaged to another girl, one his parents (or so he said later) had picked out for him. "It was more of a business merger between two wealthy families than a romance," he said. Of course, he hadn't told Maggie about the other girl until Maggie had fallen hopelessly in love with him. And in all fairness, he tried to break the engagement off. He decided to tell his parents he was in love with someone else and wanted to marry her. The night he was to break the news, Maggie sat waiting at her apartment, expecting him to come rushing through the door any minute with his parents' blessing and an engagement ring. Richard's father owned department stores across the South, and Richard said that after they were married, they could live in Birmingham. As she sat and waited, she began envisioning their future life together. First the big wedding, then the beautiful home atop Red Mountain, with an entire wing just for her parents. She would furnish the house with rugs, antiques, paintings, and dishes and silver she would pick up at one of the many shops in Mountain Brook or English Village. She imagined all the Junior League luncheons and Miss Alabama reunion parties she would give, all the small dinner-dance parties under the stars on their lovely terrace overlooking the city. She could just see the large but tastefully decorated Christmas tree she would display in the living room window, oil portraits of her children over the fireplace. It was a perfect scenario for her Miss Alabama bio.

Maggie sat waiting for Richard all night, but he never showed up. The next day, he came over, looking terrible. When he'd told his parents he wanted to marry someone else, his father had threatened to disown him, his mother had fallen to the floor in a heap, shrieking, and his sister had collapsed beside their mother, screaming, "You're killing our parents!"

So, as much as he loved her and wanted to marry her, he just couldn't upset his family. Tearful goodbye, miserable days, sleepless nights.

A year later, just as she was beginning to get over him, a midnight call came from a desperate Richard. "The marriage has been a terrible mistake," he said. "I'm in love with you; I can't go on without you. I have to see you." After months of his begging and pleading, she finally said, "All right. But promise me you won't let me wind up in some clichéd relationship where the man promises to leave his wife but never does."

"Oh, no!" he said. "Never."

Of course, she should have left sooner. Not that she didn't try. Three years into the relationship, when she could see it was never going to change, she told him she was leaving; he panicked and told his wife. She said she could care less about his affair, but as far as she was concerned, they had made a business deal, so no divorce. What could Maggie do? He stayed in a miserable marriage, and she stayed with him. It had been humiliating to have to hide and sneak around all those years, but at least she had never been a "kept woman." She had made it a point to pay her own way. He had tried to buy her things; in the first year, as a birthday gift, he had surprised her with a down payment on a condo, but she had insisted on making the monthly payments and had bought all the furniture. Looking back, she could see now, that entire section of her life had been just like the plot of the movie **Backstreet,** starring Susan Hayward: the wife doesn't really love the husband but won't give him a divorce. When it was going on, her love affair with Richard had seemed like a great tragic romance, but in reality, she had been just another dumb fool involved in just another ordinary, dime-a-dozen extramarital affair. Now, thanks to her wasting all those childbearing years, years she could never get back, her official 2008 Miss Alabama bio now read, "Margaret never married and is presently involved in real estate." Dear God, how perfectly pitiful.

In retrospect, considering her lack of gardening skills, she wondered if she would have made a good parent. She dearly loved flowers, but her garden had never been a success. Every spring, Hazel had sent over Easter lily bulbs, and every spring, she had planted them; she watered them, she waited; but every year, Easter came and went, with no Easter lilies. She didn't understand it. Hazel planted the exact same bulbs, and every year, without fail on Easter morning, she had hundreds of lilies blooming all over her yard. Maggie had wanted to give up, but Hazel had insisted she keep trying. She said, "You just wait, Mags, one of these years, they will bloom when you least expect it." When the cactus she planted died (how can you kill a cactus?), she just gave up and had the entire garden covered over with decorative rocks and stuck a birdbath in the middle. If children didn't turn out right, you couldn't just throw rocks over them and go on; you were stuck for life, so maybe things had worked out for the best. Brenda, who volunteered with Planned Parenthood, said each person who did not breed was doing the planet a big favor in the long run. Brenda said it was not going to be nuclear war that destroyed the world, it would be overpopulation; and she was probably right. Still, Maggie couldn't help but wonder what she had missed. To this day, she couldn't pass by a children's clothing store without mentally shopping for the little girl she might have had.

Political Aspirations

⌒

Maggie was right about Brenda. she did have aspirations to run for mayor. In her opinion, it was about time Birmingham had a woman mayor; the men had been in long enough. And when the last one had been sent to jail for taking bribes, a lot of people had begun to agree.

Brenda Peoples was already a familiar name in local politics. She had served on a lot of different committees in town, and she had personally started the Youth at Risk program. She was the president of the local alumni chapter of her sorority, Alpha Kappa Alpha. She knew that to be successful at anything, it was important to know as many people as possible. This was something she had learned first-hand from Hazel.

In 1979, Hazel had finished her big speech at the Women in Business luncheon with this statement: "And so, girls, in closing, I'll leave you with these three words of advice: Network, network, network." It was a credo Hazel lived by, and Brenda had taken Hazel's advice about networking to heart. Just last month, when she and Maggie had gone to the symphony, Brenda had gone backstage and introduced herself to the entire orchestra and to all the stagehands as well. "Everybody votes," she said to Maggie later. And voting was not something Brenda took lightly.

While Maggie had been busy learning to play her harp and dreaming about becoming Miss Alabama, Brenda had been across town, trying to make some sense out of what was beginning to happen. She knew white people lived in one part of town and her family lived in another. Her parents had informed her in a roundabout way that some white people were nice and some weren't, but it had not affected Brenda much one way or another. Her family had a very full and active social life where they were. Her father was the dean of an all-black college, and her mother was a high school English teacher. They lived in a nice house in a good neighborhood. But when she was about ten, Brenda noticed that the grown people had started talking in troubled whispers about something that was upsetting them.

Then later, when all the upheaval in Birmingham began, her parents, like a lot of their friends and neighbors, had not approved of using children in the protest marches. They were afraid of what might happen. They kept Brenda, Robbie, and their younger brothers home from school the day of the marches. But their oldest sister, Tonya, was thirteen that year, and her best girlfriend told her how much fun the march would be and said to come on and go. She said there would be so many kids downtown, their parents would never find out. Tonya, always up for fun, slipped out of the house and met her friend on the corner of Fourth Avenue North. And it had been fun; the two of them were running around and laughing their heads off, tickled to be out of school, tickled to be downtown without their parents knowing; they were still laughing when they ran around the corner.

To this day, Tonya could still remember how it felt: the sudden shock of the huge round sledgehammer of hard, cold water hitting her in the chest, knocking her down to the ground. She could still remember the sounds of laughter turning into screams of terror; dogs barking, people running, water everywhere. Tonya would always remember the moment when the world stopped being fun.

The next day, when the pictures hit the front pages, the entire city was horrified. How could it have happened? This kind of brutality would never have been condoned if they had known about it in advance. The head of the fire department immediately informed the city commissioner that his men would "never again" use fire hoses on human beings. But it was too late.

If Tonya had been stunned at the sudden turn of events, Maggie was just as stunned. This was not the Birmingham she lived in. She had never heard her parents or anyone she knew say an unkind word against black people. Up until that time, Maggie had had no idea they were so unhappy. She had never gone to school with a black person. She'd been told that they preferred to be with their own. When the black high school bands marched in the parades downtown, they seemed very happy. They were always laughing and looked like they were having a good time. Maggie knew on some level she was better off being white, but she had never given it much serious thought. When she was growing up, teenagers had not been very political, certainly not the ones she knew. They were too busy obsessing about boys and clothes and worrying about pimples to think beyond the next day, much less about social injustices. Sadly, the blacks lived in one world and they lived in another, and they just didn't see it, or at least she hadn't. But unfortunately, history always expects people, young or old, to have known better at the time.

Then later, when four little black girls were killed in a church basement, the city was so shocked, they simply could not believe it. It was such an unspeakable and vile act. A lot of people in Birmingham found it easier to believe it had been radicals from the North who had blown up the church, trying to get more national press, or else it must have been just a horrible accident of some kind. It was too frightening to believe that there was that much cruelty and hatred anywhere, and especially in their own city. But years later, when the white men who had done it were finally arrested and convicted, the city had no choice but to face facts, and it hurt.

What Had Possessed Her?

⌒

*A*fter a frozen dinner, Maggie continued orga-
nizing, and by ten-thirty that night, she had
all her paperwork stacked into the throwaway and
shred piles. Going through all of those old things
and seeing Richard's photograph had brought back
so many memories. What had possessed her to stay
with him so many years?

Richard did have curly black hair and a sweet nature, but she now realized (too late) that he had also
been weak and a little dumb. His father had been
the smart one, though he had been completely
ruthless in business, a trait she did not admire. In
fact, had she met the family first, she might have
had second thoughts about getting involved with
Richard at all. She had been modeling at a charity
luncheon in Dallas when two women demanded in
loud voices that she come to their table so they
could feel the material of the suit she was wearing,

and as they were complaining about how cheap the material was (it wasn't), Maggie happened to glance down at the name cards on the table and realized it was Richard's mother and sister. Oh, dear. Not only were they rude, they were two of the most unattractive women she had ever seen. They looked like frogs with large pop eyes. Through some quirk of genetics gone right, Richard was a prince born into a family of trolls, but you never know when those other family genes might strike again.

Richard never did leave his wife. He dropped dead of a cerebral hemorrhage at age forty-six. If that had not been enough of a shock, three days later, she was handed an eviction notice. Richard's family (armed with a copy of an old canceled check) claimed that he had bought her condo with company money, and not only did they want the condo, they wanted all the furnishings, dishes, silverware, paintings, television sets—things she had paid for. She could have fought them, but in order to avoid a scandal, she left the next day with nothing but the few clothes she was able to pack.

After Maggie left Dallas, she found a job on a cruise ship teaching classes in scarf tying and napkin folding. It sounded good on paper, but the cruise line she worked for was a far cry from the **Queen Elizabeth** or the **Crystal** cruises. She had hoped to teach people who wanted to learn about how to set a lovely dinner table, but her classes were filled mostly with children whose parents just needed a babysitter for an hour. And so when her parents became ill and she had to move back to Birmingham to take care of them, it was a mixed blessing. During the time she had been living in Dallas and she had come home to visit her parents or to attend the yearly ex–Miss Alabama reunions, it had been so much easier to keep up a good front. All anyone at home really knew was that she was modeling for a major department store in Dallas or, later on, working on cruise ships. Both professions had sounded somewhat glamorous from afar (they didn't know the details), but now that she was home for good, it was going to be much harder to maintain even a semi-glamorous image. Her parents' medical bills were piling up, and she had to find a job, and it was not going to be easy. She was getting too old to model, she couldn't type, she had failed algebra (twice), so bookkeeping was out, and a former Miss Alabama couldn't very well wait tables at the Waffle House or Hooters.

After a few weeks of looking, she was on the verge of taking a low-paying, somewhat humiliating job as hospitality director for the downtown Sheraton Hotel. Her duties would mostly consist of greeting people, handing out city maps to conventioneers, making hair appointments for their wives, and arranging shopping tours and visits to the Civil Rights Institute and the statue of Vulcan. But fate stepped in and saved her at the last minute.

The morning of her job interview at the hotel, Maggie was walking through the lobby on her way out the door when she heard a familiar voice.

"Maggie! Maggie Fortenberry . . . Hey, Miss Alabama!"

She looked around, but there was no one there. Then, from below, she heard a woman's voice: "Maggie! It's Hazel . . . Hazel Whisenknott." Maggie looked down and saw Hazel beaming up at her.

"Do you remember me? You used to come to my house for fittings with your mother when you were a little girl."

Maggie knew who she was immediately (how many three-foot-four people do you meet in a lifetime?) and said, "Of course I remember you. How are you?"

"Great, fantastic, couldn't be better. How are you?"

"Just fine, thank you," she lied.

"You look fabulous, as always. I read that you're living in Dallas now?"

"Well, yes, I was, but I'm home for a while; Mother is not in great health."

"Oh, I'm sorry to hear that. She was always such a sweet lady. I still have that Easter bunny costume she measured me for—do you remember that? With the big ears that stand up?"

Maggie laughed. "Oh yes, I spent hours helping

her insert the pipe cleaners so they would stand up, and I helped her sew the cotton balls together for the tail."

"You did a good job; I still wear it."

Hazel cocked her head and looked up at Maggie. "Listen, doll, what are you doing right now? Can I buy you a drink? A cup of coffee? I'd love to catch up with you."

Maggie looked at her watch; she had plenty of time before she had to be home. "Well sure, I'd be happy to."

Hazel talked a mile a minute as they rode the elevator up to the restaurant on the top floor, telling her about all the things that were happening and how Birmingham was on its way to a big comeback and that a lot of the old companies that had left in the sixties were now coming back, and new companies were moving in. When they got upstairs, of course the maître d' knew Hazel and seated them right away.

After they ordered coffee, Hazel said, "I just finished doing a breakfast speech for the Lions Club. What are you doing at the hotel? Are you staying here?"

"Oh, no. I was here for a meeting."

Hazel looked at her quizzically. "Ahhh . . . a meeting."

Even though she was embarrassed, Maggie felt compelled to explain why she'd been in the lobby of the hotel. She didn't want Hazel to think she was a call girl or something. "Well, they're looking for a hospitality director and wanted to talk to me about it, so I met with them."

"I see. So you might be home to stay for good?"

"Well . . . I'm not sure yet, but I thought while I was here, maybe I'd look around for a little something to do . . ."

Hazel's eyes widened in surprise. "You mean a job?"

"Well. Yes. Maybe . . ."

Hazel slapped her tiny little hands together. "OOOOH booooy, when I found that penny this morning, I just knew this was going to be my lucky day." She called out to the waiter, "Hey, Billy, forget the coffee—bring us two martinis," and then she turned to Maggie with a new gleam in her eye.

"Honey," she said, pointing her tiny little finger at Maggie, "I've been searching for someone exactly like you. I need a gal with looks, class, and style to head up my Mountain Brook office, someone who knows the territory, understands the upscale market, and you would be my dream come true. Forget what they offered you here. With me, you can double it. No, triple it. What do you say?"

Maggie had to laugh. "Oh, thank you, Hazel, you're very sweet, but I don't know a thing about real estate."

Hazel looked surprised. "What is there to know?"

"Well, a lot. I wouldn't have a clue about how to draw up a contract, for instance."

"So what? Real estate is more than contracts; it's

instinct, it's emotion, it's presentation, and with your looks and background, you would be a natural."

"Well, thank you, but you don't understand; I'm really not very smart about details and things."

"Now look, baby doll, you let me worry about the details. I have sharp gals working for me who can handle details; all you have to do is look pretty and deal with people. I know you're good at that. What do you say?"

"Well, I'd have to think about it. I've never done anything like that before, and I wouldn't want to disappoint you."

"Disappoint me? How could you? There's no way you can make a mistake. Oh come on, don't break my heart, say yes."

"But what if you're wrong about me?"

Hazel threw her head back and laughed. "Me? Wrong? Oh honey, I'm never wrong. Trust me, you'll love it . . . it's the best business in the world."

The waiter brought the drinks, and Hazel said, "Thanks, Billy."

"Hazel, I'm really very flattered, but I don't know how to sell houses."

"Okay. Let me ask you this: Are you nosy?"

"Nosy?"

"Yes. When you drive by a house, are you just dying to get inside and see what's there?"

Maggie thought about it. "Well yes, I guess I am curious about seeing how people have decorated."

"I knew it! I have instincts. I took one look at

you today and said to myself, 'Now, that's a real estate woman if I ever saw one.' But not just any run-of-the-mill everyday real estate agent. You're a Miss Alabama!"

Maggie hesitated. "Well, I wouldn't want to trade on . . . that."

Hazel's little eyes flew open. "Why not? It's a terrific advantage. Listen, honey, in this life, where we get so few advantages, particularly women, if you have something that can get you in the door, use it. It's what happens after you get in that's important, and using what God gave you to your advantage is nothing to be ashamed of. Look at me: when I was a little girl"—she laughed—"well, littler than I am now, I said to myself, 'Hazel, the doctor says you're never going to grow taller than three foot four, so you have two choices: one, you can feel sorry for yourself or two, you can use it to your advantage.' So, I did." She took a sip of her martini. "I noticed from an early age that people were curious about me. Why? Because I was not your run-of-the-mill person. Once they met me, they never forgot me."

"Well, Hazel," Maggie said, "you are hard to forget."

"That's right! I'm different. And that's our calling card, doll. We both have something of interest about us: Hazel Whisenknott, cute midget. Margaret Fortenberry, beautiful ex–Miss Alabama . . ."

"I hadn't thought about it that way. But still . . ."

Hazel leaned in. "Listen, Maggie, I understand

you have a certain standard to live up to; you can't just take any job. You need it to be a high-level prestige position, and with me, you would be starting at the very top, dealing with only the best clientele. And if you come work for me, I will guarantee you'll never be sorry." Hazel looked at her watch. "What are you doing now?"

"Right now? Well, nothing, I guess."

"Good. I want you to come downstairs with me. I have to do another speech, for the Women in Real Estate luncheon, and then we'll talk some more. I'm not letting you get away from me, young lady, until you say yes."

The enthusiasm in this little teeny woman was amazing, and Maggie found herself getting up and following Hazel right back into the elevator like a large dog trailing after the Pied Piper. She had been forced to make so many decisions lately. It was a relief to just let someone take charge and tell her what to do next. Hazel had already plied her with liquor before noon, and Maggie thought it was a good thing Hazel wasn't a man. With her powers of persuasion, she probably would have been pregnant by now.

Before Maggie knew it, Hazel had her downstairs and in a seat in the back row of the huge ballroom packed to the rafters with hundreds of women. After being introduced, Hazel walked out on the stage to thunderous applause, stepped up on a wooden box, flashed her famous smile, and began her speech the way she always did: "I'm so happy to be here today; I can't tell you how much I look up to all you gals in WIRE"—pause—"but then I look up to everyone."—Wait for big laugh.—"You know, the other day, I was out to lunch with Susie, one of the girls from my office, when a friend of hers she hadn't seen for a while came over to the table and asked her what she was doing, and Susie let out a big sigh and said, 'Oh, I'm just a real estate agent.' After the friend left, I asked her why she had said 'just' a real estate agent. And she said, 'Oh, because she has a really important job.' So, just in case we have any Susies out there who think your job is not important, I'm here to remind you just how important it is. Home ownership is not only the backbone of this country, it is the secret of a successful society. Once a person owns a home, he has something invested not only in himself, but in his country, his state, his city, and in his neighborhood. As a home owner, he has a stake in everything and everybody around him. It's the reason people flocked to America from all over the world, with nothing but a strong desire to work hard and a dream of one day owning a home of their own. Don't forget, private ownership is still a pretty new idea in the time frame of the world, so when you help a family buy a home, you may be fulfilling the dream of generations of that family. And one day, a family member will be able to say, 'This is mine; I own it.' "

She paused and smiled. "Now, I have nothing against renters, you understand. Our rental department does very well. I used to be a renter myself. But with just ten percent down and a forty-year mortgage, I was able to buy a house, and to this day, I will never forget the moment when my real estate agent handed me the key and said, 'Welcome to your new home.' I felt at least ten feet tall, and for me, that's twenty feet."—Another big laugh.—"So, remember, when you help a family buy a home, you're not just typing up papers; you're helping that family make years of memories. If you don't believe it, every Thanksgiving, every Christmas, you ask people what they're doing, and they'll say, 'I'm going home.' I'll bet everyone in this room can close their eyes right now and still remember the house where they grew up. How many times have we heard people say about a house, 'This was where I was the happiest, this is where I raised my children.' A home is a special place that will live in someone's heart forever.

"I know our business is hard work, and sometimes we get caught up with all the little details, but never forget that you are part of one of the most important transactions in a person's entire life, the biggest investment in the future most of us will ever make. Remember, you're not **just** a real estate broker, you are a dream broker. So get out there, girls, and keep on selling those dreams!"

As soon as she finished, the entire room leapt to their feet and cheered, and Maggie, who was not even a real estate agent, jumped up and screamed along with them. She was ready to run out the door and start selling houses that day. But as Maggie was to find out later, in all the years she was with her, she'd never seen Hazel do a speech where she didn't get the same reaction. The truth was, Hazel had never really stopped being a cheerleader. She cheered for life itself.

After going through that terrible ordeal in Dallas with Richard's family, she **had** been depressed. That's probably why the day Hazel Whisenknott had walked back into Maggie's life, she had been like a spring tonic. It had been said about Hazel that she was a person who could change your mind about the entire human race.

Meeting a Friend
1990

$\backsim$

Maggie had been working for Hazel for only a few weeks and was having lunch at Cobb Lane when Mitzi Caldwell Lee, an old school pal from her Brook Hill days, walked in. The minute she saw Maggie, she rushed over to the table.

"Maggie! Oh, I'm so glad to see you; somebody told me you were back from Dallas. Can I sit with you?"

"Of course, Mitzi. It's so nice to see you; please sit down."

Mitzi, still as cute as ever, with short red hair and bangs, sat down and said, "I will, but don't look at me. I know I look a hundred and eight, but you! You still look just like you did in high school."

Maggie laughed. "Well, I doubt that."

"Oh, Maggie, didn't we have fun back then? Don't you miss the good old days when we were growing up?"

"I do, very much."

"What great luck to run into you. I'm only home for a few days. Daddy flopped out on the golf course again, with another heart attack, so I had to come home and help Mother."

"Oh, I'm sorry . . ."

"David says between his parents and mine, we could start our own clinic. Old age, honey, it's a drag."

"I know. How's David?"

"Oh, fine, oh fine, working too hard. I can't wait for the day when we can come home for good. New York is nice, but it's not Birmingham. I said to David, 'When your children start talking like Yankees, it's time to come home.' But what about you? Are you home for a while? Are you still modeling? Tell me everything."

"Yes, I am home for a while, and no, I don't model anymore. Actually, I'm selling real estate now."

Mitzi's eyes widened, and her jaw dropped in surprise. "Oh, my God! I can't believe it! **You** are selling real estate?"

Maggie felt her face flush. "Well, I just felt that while I was here—"

"No! I mean, I can't believe it! It is sheer kismet running into you today. I've been trying to get Momma and Daddy to sell their house, but they won't listen to me. I brought in a real estate agent to talk to them, and still they wouldn't budge. But they always loved you! I hate to impose on our friendship, but would you consider taking the listing? The two of them are just rattling around in that big old house, and I know if you got involved, I could get them to sell and move over to St. Martin's in the Pines, so I wouldn't have to worry about them night and day. Please, won't you talk to them?"

Maggie was lucky. After a meeting with Mitzi's parents, they agreed to sell, and Maggie got her first listing: a large three-story gray limestone house located "over the mountain."

The weekend she and Brenda held the first open house, Mr. and Mrs. Caldwell were out of town for three days, leaving her in charge. A lot of people showed up for the open house, many with young children who ran through the house unsupervised, and considering there were so many expensive objects of art, Maggie felt a little nervous. But after a quick check, everything seemed fine. Brenda left first, and Maggie locked up around five-thirty and went home, happy and exhausted.

Sunday morning, when Maggie arrived to get ready for the next open house, the moment she reached the front door, she heard a strange rushing sound. When she stepped inside, she couldn't believe her eyes. A wall of water was cascading over the second-story balcony, crashing onto the floor in the entrance hall and running down the stairs in currents and into the living room. Maggie immediately ran up the stairs to the second floor, squishing as she stepped on the waterlogged rug. When she got to the second floor, she saw a large rush of water flooding out of one of the bathrooms. She ran in and turned off the faucet. Someone had turned on the water in the bathtub and left it running. Evidently, it had been running all night; the upstairs hall and the entire downstairs were flooded with about an inch of water. All the rugs, the bottom of the curtains, and the handsome hardwood floors were sopping wet. Brenda walked in the door and said, "Good God Almighty . . . what happened?"

An hour later, Hazel walked into her office at Red Mountain, and Maggie was waiting for her in tears. "Hi, sweetie," Hazel said as she threw her purse on the desk and jumped up into her chair.

"Oh, Hazel, I'm **so** sorry. It's my fault; I should have checked everything before I left. The Caldwells are coming back tomorrow, and I've ruined their house."

Hazel dismissed her with a wave of her hand. "Oh, don't be silly. You haven't ruined anything; it's just water. Don't you worry your pretty head about a thing; these things happen. What time are they coming back?"

"Around noon."

Just then, Ethel walked in, still in her purple church outfit, and sat down at her desk with a wave to Hazel. Hazel smiled at Maggie. "You just relax; we'll take care of it," she said as she flipped open her overstuffed Rolodex. Hazel's desk had a row of large black phones, each with five lines that lit up. Maggie had heard that Hazel was a master at working the phones, but she had never really seen her in action before. She watched in amazement as Hazel began dialing and punching from line to line, with the ease and finesse of a concert piano player:

Punch. "John! Hazel. Hey, doll, I'm sorry to bother you at home on a Sunday, but how fast can you get some fans up to Crest Road? We have a little flooding problem. I know it is, but can I count on you, honey? I surely would appreciate it if you could. Ah, thanks, John. You're my hero. Ethel will call you back with all the details."

Punch. "Hey, is Al there? Tell him it's Hazel. I'll hold."

Punch. "Danny? Hazel. Listen, hon. I'm gonna need a cleaning crew A.S.A.P. I know it's short notice, but I really do need you to do me this favor, okay? You know I'll make it up to you . . . Aww . . . Thanks, Danny. Ethel will be calling you back with the details."

Punch. "Pete. Hazel. Hey, doll, I need to have some floors waxed and polished by ten o'clock tomorrow morning. Can you do that for me? Ten? I knew I could count on you . . . Hold for Ethel."

Punch. "June? Hazel. Darling, I need a big favor; I need some curtains dry-cleaned by the morning. You know I'll make it up to you . . . Uh-huh, by around ten? Oh thanks, hon, I'll dance at your wedding for this one . . . And you tell that good-looking husband of yours I said hello. All right. Hold on for Ethel."

Punch. "Hello? Oh yeah, I think six fans ought to do it . . . Okay, doll."

Punch. "Al . . . It's Hazel. We have a little emergency, and I sure could use a big favor. If I get some rugs over to you this afternoon, can we get them cleaned, by in the morning? Hold on, hon . . ."

Punch. "Mrs. Wilmer . . . It's Hazel Whisenknott. Could you have Tom call me A.S.A.P. here at the office? I'm gonna need him to take down some curtains for me and get them over to June and bring some rugs downtown to Al. Right . . . And how's your granddaughter? Good, well, I'm glad she enjoyed it. Hold for Ethel, and she'll give you the details."

Punch. "Al, thanks for holding. Listen, hon, I'm waiting for a call back from Tom, but as soon as I hear, I'll have him call you, and you tell him where he can drop them off. Well, thank **you**, and you're a sweetheart for doing it for me on such short notice."

Hazel looked over and smiled at Maggie. "**See**, honey, everything's going to be fine. This is nothing. I'll speak to the Caldwells and explain what happened, so don't you worry about a thing, sweetie. You just go home, have a drink, and relax, and I'll see you tomorrow." Then she called out, "Ethel . . . get me a Coca-Cola when you have a minute, will you?" **Punch.** "Hey, Tom. Did you get my message? That's right, first to Al, then to June . . . Okay? Hold for Ethel."

By ten o'clock the next morning, every rug and every curtain was back in place, cleaned and dried; every floor waxed and shined; and fresh flowers sat on the entrance hall table, waiting to greet the Caldwells when they returned home at noon. When Maggie walked into the office, she looked at Hazel in awe. "How did you do it?"

"What?"

"Get the house cleaned up."

"Oh, that . . . that was nothing. I told you, you don't ever have to worry about a thing. If it can be done, I'll get it done."

Dear God, was it any wonder they all missed her?

Hazel was right about Maggie. After her initial flooding disaster, Maggie had been very good at selling real estate from the start, and she had been especially skilled at staging a home. Hazel always said, "Good taste doesn't cost a dime, but if you don't have it, you can't buy it for a million dollars," and Maggie certainly had good taste. Brenda and Ethel were still amazed at her ability to deal with even the most difficult clients in such a lovely and graceful way.

How do you suggest (in a nice way) that it would be best for the home owners to remove most of what they own from the house, particularly the family photos? Ethel, who had no patience with people, would have said right off the bat, "The photos of the ugly jug-eared grandchildren have to go," but Maggie always managed to do it without hurting anyone's feelings. As she once said to a couple in West End, "It's not that the gold shag rugs in every room aren't nice, it's just that too much of anything tends to be unattractive."

But as much as Maggie loved and appreciated houses, she had never owned one of her own. However, **where** she lived had still been very important to her. She had never understood people who blew into town and bought the first house they saw. Or those who said that location didn't matter, they could "just live anywhere." Not Maggie. When she had moved back to Birmingham from Dallas, she had spent months looking for just the right location, and the minute she'd walked into Avon Terrace, she'd known it was the perfect spot for her. From her back terrace, she could look up and see Crestview standing on top of Red Mountain.

Why Babs Hated Maggie

They say envy is a coal that comes hot and hissing straight from hell. If so, it had been burning a hole in Babs Bingington from the moment Hazel Whisenknott had introduced Maggie as her new agent. Babs had hated Maggie at first sight. This has-been beauty queen with all her phony manners, just waltzing into the business on her good looks and her "over the mountain" contacts. It made her sick to see how all the male agents in town acted like fools around her, fawning and preening like idiots. It was bad enough that she had to compete with that damn midget; now this.

Three weeks later, when she found out that Maggie had gotten the Caldwell listing, she was livid. The Caldwell house was on a view lot that the people she dealt with at the construction company wanted. Babs had contacted the Caldwells a month before, and they had told her that they were not selling. And now, that beauty-queen bitch had gone behind her back and stolen her listing. And to make matters worse, she had driven by the Caldwell house on Monday afternoon, expecting to see cleanup trucks everywhere, but there had been absolutely no signs that the house had been flooded. The kid she had hired to go upstairs, plug up the tub, and leave the water running had obviously screwed up. The little shit. She had been hoping to get the bimbo fired and take over the listing. And what had made her twice as furious was that before she had enough time to come up with another scheme, the house had sold.

Nothing had ever come easy for Babs. She had never been a natural beauty, and it had cost her a fortune. She had been through two face-lifts, a nose job, a chin implant, and had her hairline moved up before she was forty. People had always been out to get her from the start. A disgruntled employee had done her in in Newark. After she lost her real estate license in New Jersey, Babs had changed her name and moved to Birmingham, where her son was studying medicine at UAB. And that had not been easy, either. She'd had to push and shove every inch of the way to get into the real estate market here. Those southern girls were so clannish; they were nice to her face, but she knew they all thought they were better than she was. Only she would get her revenge on that phony Miss Goody Two-Shoes, Margaret Fortenberry. For now, she was just biding her time.

Making Arrangements
Wednesday, October 29, 2008

The next morning, Maggie woke up and realized: she couldn't have picked a better date if
she'd tried. Leaving on November 3, the day right
before the presidential election, was perfect. Now
that the Miss America Pageant was no longer being
shown on network television, being an ex–Miss Alabama or even second runner-up at the national
level no longer carried the weight it once had. But
you could never be sure. Had she done it earlier, on
a slow news day, some bored reporter could have
picked up the story, and she might have wound up
as a joke on a late-night TV show. Some people
could be so terribly unkind. They didn't understand
the tremendous pressure and the responsibility that
went along with the title or how stressful being a
role model could be, but Maggie did, it had taken
a large toll on her. And now she was bound and
determined not to make her same old mistake:

waiting too long to do something until it was too late to do it!

At least she was leaving while she had some of her looks left; her skin was still nice, thanks to the fact that she had always stayed out of the sun and what little gardening she had done, she had done at night with a flashlight. However, she had noticed that what used to be freckles on the backs of her hands were now starting to look a lot like old-age spots. She had a few gray streaks here and there, but Glen had been able to blend them in with her highlights so they looked natural. Even so, there was simply no two ways about it: she was like a carton of milk whose expiration date was just about up.

Of course, Maggie knew that winding up like this was terribly sad, and she could have spent what little time she had left being miserable and feeling sorry for herself, but there was definitely a bright side to departing this world early. Just this morning, she had made out a brand-new "Pros and Cons" list on the subject, and even she had been surprised at the results.

16 Perfectly Good Reasons to Jump in the River

Pros	Cons
1. No old age (no face-lifts, knee or hip replacements, etc.)	1. Missing spring in Mountain Brook

2. No more hair dyeing
3. No more having to make decisions
4. No more bad TV dinners
5. Dentist or doctor's appointments, etc.
6. No more unpleasant surprises
7. Answering e-mail
8. No more Babs Bingington
9. No more sleepless nights
10. Having to make a living
11. Paying bills and doing taxes
12. Fighting traffic
13. No more regrets
14. Having to watch bad news on TV
15. No more bad news, period
16. No more worries

2. Missing fall in Mountain Brook

When she saw everything written down in black and white, she had to admit that the pros still had it, hands down. Number 16 alone clinched it. Last night, she had lost another two hours of sleep, worrying about Crestview again. Not having to worry about anything ever again was something else she was really looking forward to.

She went down the hall and pulled out the last box of her parents' papers and started putting them in stacks. She guessed she could just throw them all out and not bother to shred them. There was no need to be concerned about identity theft now.

A few minutes later, when she saw their burial policies, something suddenly occurred to her. Since she was not going to be using her cemetery plot, maybe she should give it to some needy person. It was in a very nice spot. But her parents had gone to a lot of expense and had bought the plots on a lay-away plan because they had wanted the family to be together. What would they think if a total stranger suddenly showed up next to them? She didn't know if she believed in an afterlife or not, but she decided that on the off chance they would know, she'd better just leave it empty. Then she suddenly realized something else. Since she was their only living relative, she needed to make long-term arrangements about flowers for her parents' graves, so she pulled out another piece of paper and began another list.

Yearly Floral Arrangements
for Mother and Daddy

1. Christmas
2. Easter
3. Mother's Birthday

4. Daddy's Birthday
5. Mother's Day
6. Father's Day
7. Memorial Day

The only days she could eliminate with a clear conscience would be their birthdays, but even when eliminating the two birthdays, it would still cost around $375 a year. She then made an educated guess at how many more years she might have been around. Considering the fact that she was still pretty healthy, and averaging out the age at which both her parents had died, she thought eighty-five was a fair place to stop the flowers. So, twenty-five times $375 came to . . . good Lord. That was a lot of money, but she couldn't just leave them without any remembrance on the holidays.

She looked in the telephone book for the name of a florist on the other side of town. She couldn't call people she knew, like Bill over at Park Lane or Norton's Flowers; they might suspect something. She looked in the yellow pages and found a florist she had never heard of; a woman answered.

"Bon-Ton Flowers, may I help you?"

Maggie could tell by her accent that the woman was not southern, and she was glad. She probably didn't know who she was, or even if she did, she probably wouldn't care.

"Yes, hello . . . uh, I'm going to be out of town

this Christmas, and I was wondering if I could have flowers delivered to my parents' graves. Do you deliver to cemeteries?"

"Yes, ma'am, we sure do, and I'd be happy to arrange that for you . . . Is that going to be Forrest Lawn or Pine Rest?"

"Forrest Lawn. I have the location numbers. Lot 7, Section 196, and the names are Anna Grace and William Herbert Fortenberry."

"That's Anna Grace and William Herbert?"

"Yes . . ."

"And what price range would you like on that, hon?"

"Oh . . . I was thinking around seventy-five?"

"Seventy-five . . . alrighty then, we can do up something real nice for that, unless you want balloons. If you want balloons, that's fifteen dollars extra."

"No, just the flowers. I think."

"Okay . . . that's fine, and what do you want on the card?"

"The card?" Maggie was suddenly caught off guard; she hadn't thought about the card. "Oh . . . well. Oh dear, uh . . . just say, 'Love, Margaret,' I guess."

"Okay, hon . . . we'll have it out there for them bright and early Christmas morning, and how do you want to pay for this?"

"MasterCard."

"Can I get that credit card number from you?"

"Yes, but I'm also going to need to have you give me the total cost for arrangements for Easter, Mother's Day, Father's Day, and Memorial Day."

The woman sounded surprised. "Oh, I see . . . well . . . just how long do you plan to be out of town?"

There was a pause. Then Maggie said, "About twenty-five years."

The conversation did not go well after that, but after talking to the woman for a while, Maggie convinced her that she was serious, and the woman finally took her credit card number and started the process. Before she left, Maggie would send a check to MasterCard to cover the exact amount plus whatever other expenses she might have.

A few minutes later, Mrs. Thelma Shellnut, the woman at Bon-Ton Flowers, walked into the back and said to her husband, "I swear, Otis, what some people won't do to get out of going to the cemetery."

Otis looked up from his **Reader's Digest** article. "What?"

"You should have heard the tall tale this woman told me: said she was going to be traveling and needed to have arrangements delivered for the next twenty-five years. Traveling, my left foot—she's just too lazy to visit her parents' graves, if you ask me."

The truth was, Maggie was not totally without a living relative. She had one: Hector Smoote, a distant cousin of her father's who lived in western Maine in a double-wide trailer that he and his wife, Mertha, had named Valhalla. Maggie had tried to keep in touch with him after her parents died out of some kind of family obligation, but every time she called, Hector hurt her feelings so badly, that eventually she'd stopped calling altogether. However, under the circumstances, she supposed she should try to end on a good note. Maggie dialed his number.

"Hector. It's Maggie from Birmingham."

As usual, he started in. "Well, hey there, little old honey pie . . . how y'all a-doing way down there in redneck land?"

"Oh, just fine, thank you."

"How's my little old country cousin? Are y'all still watching **Hee Haw?**"

Maggie tried to laugh. "No . . . not lately . . . I think it's been off the air for some time now. Anyhow, I just wanted to call and say hello. I'm sorry we haven't seen each other in so long."

"Yeah, me too. Hey, why don't you move out of that hellhole and come on up here with us? It's not much, but at least we have running water."

"Oh, I'm sure it's lovely there . . . but . . ."

He interrupted her with "Hey, Maggie, they still shooting Yankees down there?"

"Oh, yes . . . uh-huh, the streets are piled up with bodies as we speak. Well, anyway . . . I just called to say hello."

"I'm glad you did and next time, don't be such a stranger; let us hear from you more often. You hear?"

"Okay. Well, my best to Mertha. Bye."

Maggie hung up. It was just no use. She had been thinking about leaving her Miss Alabama crown, sash, and trophy to Hector and Mertha, but it was probably best she didn't.

If Maggie had any passion left at all, it was for Birmingham and Alabama. Like everyone who loved their home, she was probably far too thin-skinned and had lost her sense of humor, but to her, talking to Hector was like pouring salt in a wound over and over again.

Maggie had heard other people say about their state that they "couldn't wait to get out and go somewhere else," but not her; from the first minute she left, she couldn't wait to get back, and if it hadn't been for Richard, she would have come home much sooner. She couldn't imagine being from any other state. What if she had been Miss anywhere else but Alabama? Most of the other girls in the Miss America Pageant had traveled to Atlantic City by plane, an automobile, or by bus, but she had traveled on her own private train car, aboard the beautiful **Silver Comet,** renamed the **Miss Alabama Special** for the trip. She had been given a huge send-off at the station, with bands playing and GOOD LUCK banners flying everywhere; and unlike most of the other girls, she had arrived with an entire entourage of people to see to her every need. She had been so surprised when several of the girls told her that winning the title in their state had been no big deal. That was certainly not the case in Alabama. In Alabama, it was **the** beauty contest, second in size only to the Miss America Pageant, and it offered the largest prize money and scholarship of any pageant in the country.

The reason she had entered the contest was to try and win a scholarship to modeling school. She had done some teen modeling at Loveman's department store downtown, and her mother's friend Audrey, who worked there, had encouraged her to try for it. Maggie had certainly not planned on winning, and that night, nobody was more surprised than Maggie. And for a poor girl like herself, winning Miss Alabama had been a very big deal. She had been awarded ten thousand dollars, which had helped her parents buy their first home. She had been given beautiful, expensive jewelry and a complete wardrobe from Loveman's, designed especially for her, plus a gray mink stole from Carlton's furs, which she still had.

Maggie walked down the hall to the back closet, pulled it out, and examined it. It was still in pretty good shape. She put it on and looked at herself in the mirror. Too bad mink stoles went out of style, but you couldn't wear fur of any kind without offending someone. Just one more thing she would never have to worry about: offending someone. That was one of the reasons she was always so comfortable with Brenda; she was not easily offended, and if you were to ever say something by mistake, she wouldn't hold it against you. Not that she ever had or would purposely say or do anything to hurt someone's feelings. She knew what that felt like firsthand. She knew all too well.

Dropping a Hint

✦

Ethel, the oldest member of the Jingle-ettes, a handbell choir that played out at the mall on holidays, had invited Brenda and Maggie to come during their lunch hour to a first dress rehearsal for their 2008 performance. Brenda said she would drive, and Maggie was glad to have an opportunity to ride with her. It would give her a chance to try to drop a hint again.

Brenda and Maggie sat in the food court and ate their lunch and enjoyed the show. Ethel was a regular virtuoso on the handbells and had a special solo spot during "Rudolph the Red-Nosed Reindeer." All the Jingle-ettes wore blinking red noses, and it was very effective, drawing quite a bit of applause from the crowd that had gathered. Maggie was glad she had a chance to see it, considering she would be missing the holidays this year, and she was surprised to find herself getting a little teary.

On the way back to the office, in keeping with her plan, Maggie said, "You know, Brenda, I don't know if you have noticed or not . . . but I've been a little depressed lately."

Brenda rolled her eyes. "Oh right, Maggie, you have so much to be depressed about. You're **so** ugly. It must be terrible to have to wake up and see yourself in the mirror every morning. If I looked like you, I'd be delirious. I'm the one who's depressed. I swear, I've gotten to the point to where I can't even bear to look at myself anymore."

"Why?"

"Because I look like a big fat Tootsie Roll in a wig, that's why."

"Oh, you do not! Brenda, why do you say those awful things about yourself?"

"Because it's true . . . I'm ugly-looking."

"You are not! You are just as cute as you can be; everybody thinks so. When you're not with me, people always ask, 'How's that cute Brenda?' "

"Who?"

"Everybody . . . everybody thinks you are just as cute as you can be."

"Really?"

"Yes, silly, so stop being so hard on yourself."

Brenda seemed happy for the moment; then she asked, "What's cute about me?"

"A lot of things . . . your personality for one, your smile . . . you have darling teeth."

Brenda looked at her. "Darling teeth?"

"Yes, and you have a great smile."

"Oh, I do not; now I know you're making stuff up. I have buck teeth and a big space between my two front teeth."

"No, you don't, you have a great open face and a wonderful sense of humor . . . everyone says that."

"They do?"

"Yes . . . Hazel always said you had a million-dollar personality."

"She did?"

"Yes, you know she did."

"God, I miss Hazel . . ."

They drove a little while longer and then Brenda said, "People don't say I look too masculine, do they?"

"**What?** Brenda, anybody who wears a size 54 double-D-cup bra couldn't look masculine if they tried. Why would you ask that?"

"Oh, I don't know . . . I just worry. Since I got so fat, I think I look masculine."

"Don't be silly. Does Oprah Winfrey look masculine?"

"She's skinny now . . ."

"Well . . . when she was heavier . . ."

"No . . ."

"Okay, then."

They drove in silence a little while longer, until Maggie asked, "How are you doing with your Over-eaters Anonymous meetings? Are you still going?"

"Yes, I love the meetings . . . it's the not eating

I don't like." Brenda let out a big sigh. "Maggie, if I tell you something, do you swear not to tell Robbie?"

"Of course."

"I'm so mad at myself, I could just scream."

"Why?"

"I had another slip. Doughnuts."

"Oh . . . well, honey, just try to forget it and move on. That's all you can do."

Brenda smiled. "You're right . . . that's all we can do . . ."

Brenda then pulled down the visor and looked at herself in the mirror. "Do you really think I have cute teeth?"

"Yes."

Brenda smiled. "I'll tell you what Maggie, talking to you always cheers me up!"

Oh, dear. This clearly was not the moment. Maggie decided she would try another time.

What Was Bothering Brenda

At Brenda's last Overeaters Anonymous meeting, the leader had said to the group, "The problem is not what you are eating, but what's eating **you**!" And unlike a lot of the other gals in the group, Brenda knew exactly what had been eating at her for years.

When Hazel had hired her, it had still been a pretty rare thing: a black real estate agent in an all-white firm. But for Brenda, growing up when and where she had, she had always been an experiment of some kind. Now, after so many years of having to deal with the "race issue" day in and day out, she was tired. Tired of everybody bobbing and weaving all around the subject, never saying what they really thought, herself included. And tired of always having to be careful about not acting "too white" around her own people or "too black" around white people.

When Brenda had been growing up, the issues had been the big, overt, and glaring oversights of voting rights and segregated neighborhoods, water fountains, schools, and bathrooms. But now it was the small, everyday subtleties that were so wearing. She always felt it when white people were walking on eggshells around her, nervous about saying something that might offend her. She just wished people would act normal. When she had been in college up north, all those obsequious professors fawning over her had made her very uncomfortable.

She would have loved to have had a vacation from race, even for a day. But it was always there. And lately, the way the news media kept pitting one side against the other, she didn't see it going away anytime soon. Everybody seemed to have an agenda where race was concerned. Some to keep people stirred up, others to pretend that it didn't matter.

That's why she liked Maggie. Maggie had no hidden agenda; she was nice to everyone. Sometimes too nice and too trusting for her own good. Maggie once spent six weeks driving an old lady all over town, showing her every property available within a twenty-mile radius, only to find out later that the woman was just lonely and liked to go for rides. Ethel said that if the woman hadn't died, Maggie would still be driving her around town to this day, and it was probably true. Maggie had taken care of her parents for years, and when they'd both had to be put in a nursing home, she had visited them twice a day, seven days a week, and never complained. Brenda admired her, but if she herself couldn't complain about her family, life wouldn't be worth living.

Maggie also did nice things for people and never told you about it, but when Brenda did something nice, she wanted people to know about it. Brenda guessed that was why she had always been so drawn to politics and had decided she was going to run for mayor. A politician **had** to toot his own horn. How else were you going to get votes?

The only college professor Brenda knew for sure had **really** liked her was her senior year English professor. While working on a project together, they had fallen in love and had an affair, and it had ended badly and broken her heart. Anybody who won her heart now would have to be pretty special. She had tried out a few, but no luck so far. And she figured that, as mayor, she'd be much better off not having a husband at all. From what she had seen, the husbands had turned out to be more of a hindrance than a help. She would have been much better off with a wife. They stand by you, no matter what. Even Ethel had said, she would be better off just getting herself a cat. "They clean up after themselves and mind their own business."

Maggie's Rehearsal

⌒

That afternoon, Maggie was going to take a test run down by the river to make sure that on the third, there would be no last-minute surprises; you never knew when or where they might be doing roadwork, and if there were any detours she wanted to know about them now. She took the precaution of wearing dark glasses and a scarf. She didn't want to risk the chance of someone seeing her driving on the river road and remembering it later. She now wished she had maintained a lower profile around town, but after Hazel died, she had appeared quite a few times on **Good Morning Alabama,** offering home-selling tips; now younger people who might not have recognized her as an ex–Miss Alabama sometimes recognized her as the Real Estate Lady. She realized it was just another irony of life; first you want to be famous and in the end, it turns around and bites you.

Fortunately, today she knew exactly where she was going. It was to a certain spot where her father had always gone fishing, and if it still was as she remembered, it was the perfect spot for her purpose. As she drove, she looked over at her latest checklist, on the seat next to her.

River-Run Items
1. Wraparound weights
2. Glue
3. Raft and paddle
4. Raft instructions
5. Reading glasses
6. Cheap watch

She had everything with her today, except for the watch. She wasn't about to jump in the river wearing her good gold watch, but she would need a watch to time the glue. She would go to the drugstore next week and buy a Timex, and on the morning of the third, she would put her good watch in an envelope for Lupe, her housekeeper, along with her money for the week. She wanted to say a proper goodbye to Lupe (hard to do when you don't speak Guatemalan), but she figured a nice gold watch says, "I appreciate you" in any language.

One of the reasons she had addressed the note "To Whom It May Concern," and not to Lupe, was that Lupe could neither read nor speak English. Nevertheless, she was always anxious to please. No matter what you asked her to do, she smiled and said, "Yes," the one word she knew. Unfortunately, she was not a very good housekeeper. She had chipped or broken almost every dish Maggie owned and Maggie wound up having to do most of the cleaning herself, but she was so sweet, Maggie didn't have the heart to fire her.

As Maggie drove along, she gradually realized she had not been out this way for years, and she was surprised to see quite a few of the new Jim Walter manufactured homes scattered here and there; other than that, though, the area was still pretty rural. A few barns still had faded SEE ROCK CITY advertisements painted on their roofs. A good half hour later, about ten minutes past the old Raiford Fishing Camp, she found the little turnoff spot she was looking for and slowly drove her car down the winding red dirt road and parked in the small clearing. It was completely hidden from the highway up above, so she got out and changed her shoes. Thankfully, although it had grown over with weeds, she was able to find the little path that led down to the river. It was a good three-minute walk, longer than she remembered, but the good news was that this part of the river was still pretty deserted, and the few beer cans scattered around the bank were old and rusty. She didn't think anybody drank Schlitz or Pabst Blue Ribbon anymore.

She calculated that two trips from the car and back should do it: one to get the weights and one for the raft. Today, she would just check to make sure that the spot was still here and as perfect as she remembered. It was, and on her next trip down, she would hide everything in the bushes and be ready to go.

Coming up with a method had been difficult, but surprisingly enough, figuring out the logistics had been the most difficult part. She couldn't drive down on the third and leave the car parked up in the clearing; she had a responsibility to Steel City Leasing and would feel terrible if someone were to vandalize it or steal it. She couldn't leave a note saying where it was, because if her car was found anywhere near the river, there was sure to be a search, the very thing she wanted to avoid. She couldn't just ask a friend to drop her off. There were no buses she could take, and she certainly couldn't walk. She finally realized there was only one solution. She hated to do it, but she was going to have to take a cab to the river. It would be tricky, of course; the last time she had called a cab, it had come an hour late. This was one of those times that, just like Hazel, she was going to have to depend on people and hope for the best.

But this decision, like every other, entailed having to make yet another decision. Should she call City Cab, Yellow Cab, or Veterans Cab? Her plan had been to call the cab company from a pay phone so there would be no record of the call on her phone bill. She would order the cab a few days before she was leaving, give the dispatcher a false name, and have the driver meet her at another address, up the street from her complex. Later, she realized that to be on the safe side, it would be best to order a cab from one of the independent cab drivers listed. They drove their own cars, so later people wouldn't be so likely to remember a cab being in the neighborhood on Monday morning. Nothing was simple. You had to think of every little thing.

When she got home from the river, she stopped and checked the mail: nothing but junk and another flyer from Willow Lakes Retirement Community. Before she threw it in the trash can, she happened to glance at it. She was glad she did. Written in big bold letters across the top of the page was this phrase: SOME PEOPLE SLIP INTO RETIREMENT, OTHERS JUMP RIGHT IN. And if that wasn't a sign from the universe that she was doing the right thing, she didn't know what was.

That night, as Maggie was eating another bad TV dinner, she spied something in the kitchen and realized she didn't need to buy a new watch to time the twenty minutes for the glue on the Velcro to dry. She would just take her rooster egg timer and use it. She spent the next few hours packing most of her clothes for the theater and the Salvation Army, and it wasn't until after she finished that she realized that she needed to keep one casual outfit to wear down to the river. She rooted around and pulled out a nice powder blue matching outfit and put it alongside the egg timer.

At two A.M. that night, Maggie sat straight up in bed. Good Lord, what was she thinking? She couldn't wear an expensive workout suit to jump in the river! People in Alabama were serious about their fishing, especially down at the river. They didn't fish in designer clothes, and if for any reason someone were to see her, it might arouse suspicion. She had to be more careful than that. What she needed was a good red herring outfit: something that would throw people completely off the track. After racking her brain, she suddenly came up with an idea for the **perfect** thing. She was glad now that she had watched all those Agatha Christie English mystery shows on PBS.

The next morning before work, she wandered around a few sporting goods stores, looking for some kind of man's sweatshirt or T-shirt in an extra large that she could wear with a pair of jeans. She hit pay dirt out at Sportsman's World. There were all kinds of fishing T-shirts to choose from:

BORN TO FISH, MADE TO WORK

REEL MEN EAT TROUT

CHICKS DIG ME, FISH FEAR ME

KISS MY BASS

She was not sure which to get and kept looking until she found the perfect shirt hanging on the last rack. It was so crude, so crass. Something she would never be caught dead wearing:

FISHERMEN DO IT WITH A BIG POLE

She found one in an XXL, but the problem was paying for it without having someone notice. She managed it by sticking the item in the middle of a pile of WOMEN FISH TOO, GET OVER IT T-shirts and, luckily, the girl at the checkout counter never looked.

Maggie had to admit there were times when it was best that salespeople didn't get personal. She was halfway out the door when something else hit her. What shoes would she wear? Her workout shoes were far too nice. Should she pick up a pair of cheap flip-flops? No, too many rocks; she might trip on the way down. She turned around and headed to the back of the store. She would buy a pair of large men's boots. It would be just another red herring, in case anyone found footprints. For someone who had always felt stupid, she was surprising herself with how clever she had turned out to be. Then again, she had always loved Nancy Drew mystery stories. It was too late now, of course, but she wondered if she should have become a detective. She might have been very good at it, if it didn't require a lot of paperwork.

The Beauty and the Beast

Thursday, October 30, 2008

Maggie was still in a fairly good mood when she got to the office, until Ethel said, "The Beast just called and said she's coming to see you at eleven. Happy Halloween."

"What? To see **me**?"

"Yes, lucky you."

Maggie moaned, "Oh, no." Babs was the very last person in the world she wanted to see, but she knew that Babs had shown her condo at Avon Terrace a few days ago, so she was probably bringing in an offer on the two-bedroom unit that was just like hers. That was the good news; the office could use the commission. The bad news was that Brenda had gone to another political rally, which meant that Maggie was going to have to deal with Babs all by herself. Babs would fight you down to the nub on every point, so she braced herself for a bumpy ride.

At eleven A.M. on the dot, Babs arrived and as always, forgoing the customary friendly "hello"s and "how are you"s, she sat down and pulled out the papers and pushed them across the desk. "It's a good offer, no contingencies, and they qualify." Maggie looked it over, and Babs was right; it was a good offer. But when Maggie read the buyers' names, Tom and Carole Troupe, she realized they were the same couple Dottie had shown the unit to a few times before, most recently on Monday. Babs had a nasty habit of stealing clients by cutting her commission, and she was obviously trying to do it again. Oh Lord, Maggie didn't want to get in a fight with her, but she felt she had to say something. So, she asked as pleasantly as possible, "Is this a co-listing?" Babs looked straight back at her and without blinking an eye said, "No."

"I see, but . . . what about Dottie Figge?"

"What about her?"

"Aren't these her clients?"

"No."

"Ah well, I don't know if they told you or not, but she showed them the same unit at least three or four times."

"So?"

"Well, she did spend a lot of time with them, and I think she was sort of counting on this commission."

"That's not my problem."

"Oh, I know, but in all fairness, Babs, she did show it to them first."

"What's your point?"

"Well, couldn't you see your way to at least giving her two percent?"

Babs glared at Maggie. "Are you trying to tell me how to run my business?"

"No, of course not, I was just thinking that—"

"Look, I'm busy—if you don't want to present the offer, fine. I'll just go directly to the owner and tell them their listing agent is trying to block the sale."

"I'm not blocking the sale, Babs. It's just that I don't feel right about cutting her out all together."

"Why? It's no skin off your nose. You still get your commission."

"I understand that, but it really puts me in a bad position. Dottie is a friend; we were in the Miss Alabama Pageant together and—"

Babs exploded: "Oh, get over yourself. Dottie Figge is an idiot, and nobody cares about all that stupid beauty-pageant crap! Wake up and smell the roses, honey: the world has moved on. Are you going to present the offer or not?"

Maggie was shocked by Babs's sudden outburst; speechless, she just stared at her. After a moment, Babs rudely snapped her fingers at her and said, "Hello, Miss Alabama, anybody home? I'm busy. Yes or no?"

Maggie felt something very hot slowly rising up inside her, and her cheeks began to burn bright red. Then she heard a strange voice she had never heard before in her life saying, "Now, wait a minute, you can say anything you want about me, but you say one more word about the pageant, and I'll knock your block off . . . you . . . you . . . person!"

At that moment, Maggie looked down and realized that she had actually made a fist and was at present shaking it across the desk at Babs. Good Lord, she thought. How had that happened? She had never made a fist in her life. Babs looked at her like she was something that had just dropped out of a tree and said, "You must be nuts," picked up the offer, walked out, and slammed the door behind her.

Maggie just sat there, with her cheeks still burning bright red, stunned that she had actually yelled at someone. Oh dear, had she really said "knock your block off"? How embarrassing. She had never said anything like that in her life. Where had that come from? Some bad movie she must have seen as a child, she guessed. Just then, Ethel stuck her head in. "What was that all about? Her Beastliness just flounced out of the door in a snit; what happened?"

Maggie looked up and said, "I don't know."

She really didn't know what had set her off. Was it because Babs had called Dottie an idiot? Or the condescending way she had called her "honey"? Or had it been how Babs had said "Miss Alabama" in that sneering way? She wasn't sure, but now she was worried. She **had** shaken her fist, and Babs might file a police report saying she had threatened her with bodily harm, which, of course, she had. Oh,

Lord! That's all she needed, to be arrested right now. She was going to have to call Babs and apologize and try to keep herself out of jail. Oh, why had she promised Brenda she would go to see the Whirling Dervishes? If she had jumped in the river when she had wanted to, this never would have happened. God, what next?

A frantic hour later, Babs finally answered her cell phone.

"Yes?"

"Babs? Is that you?"

"Who is this?" Babs snapped in her usual charm-free way.

"It's Maggie."

A long silence, then an even colder, if at all possible, "What?"

"Babs, I am so sorry for speaking to you the way I did. Please accept my apology. All I can say is I guess I've been under too much stress lately with the market and—"

"Spare me the details. Are you going to accept the offer or not?"

"Yes, of course."

After Maggie hung up, she decided she would give Dottie the commission money out of her savings in advance and just say it was from Babs.

That night, when Maggie got into bed, she was relieved that she had been able to smooth it over with

Babs, and thank heavens she hadn't run her over that day when she had crossed the street in front of her. She closed her eyes. Then suddenly, another thought popped up. On the other hand, now that she was leaving for good, if she were to just happen to "accidentally" run over Babs Bingington . . . it really wouldn't be murder. It would be one of those random acts of kindness everyone was always talking about. She would simply be doing the other real estate agents in town a little favor before she left, as a sort of goodbye gift. And like Brenda said, the police would probably never find out who had done it, and even if they did, she would be long gone by then. It was something to think about.

As she lay there, she started to think of all the things you could do if you didn't have to worry about the consequences. It was so freeing, really; knowing you didn't have to worry about the future anymore. It opened up endless possibilities. She suddenly felt sort of reckless, or devil-may-care. She hadn't planned on this. Who knew that jumping in the river could be so liberating.

Ethel Is Aggravated

❦

Unlike Maggie, who always had trouble sleeping, Ethel could sleep; she just chose not to. She was too aggravated to sleep. Tonight she sat up, flipping from channel to channel, sipping on her bourbon. The very gall of that woman to come into the office and upset Maggie. Maggie was too much of a lady to have to put up with that nonsense from anybody, especially from some snake in the grass like Babs Bingington.

But that was the way of the world now. Manners didn't count for a thing anymore. Nobody had any respect for anybody, thanks to all those smarty-assed comedians making fun of everything and everybody. Nothing was sacred.

And there was nothing decent to watch on television anymore. Just a bunch of bad reality shows sandwiched in between erectile dysfunction and bladder-control ads. Body functions used to be private, but not now. Nobody seemed to be embarrassed about anything. There was no shame; so many politicians got caught up in sex scandals and the next day, they were out riding in parades, smiling and waving at everyone, like nothing had ever happened. She paused a moment on a rerun of **Sex and the City** and was appalled and clicked back to Fox News.

What ever happened to the **Pillsbury Bake-Off** show and **Petticoat Junction** or Carol Burnett? That gal was funny. Now it was just one trying to be more filthy-mouthed than the other. Nobody had any class anymore. They wouldn't let you. Now they wanted to drag everybody down in the gutter. Nobody was safe. Even poor Queen Elizabeth was written up in tabloids. Sure, she'd had some trouble with her kids, but who hadn't? Ethel's own granddaughter had come home with a tattoo on her behind.

Maggie was the only person she knew with genuine class. "Damn it to hell!" she yelled to the cats. "What ever happened to people behaving like ladies and gentlemen?" The cats had no clue, and got up and left the room.

As she sat there sipping her drink, Ethel's mind wandered to other irritations. Why didn't they make a car with a place for a woman to put her purse? And why did there have to be so much loud noise everywhere? Cars, buses, motorcycles, planes, leaf blowers, and whose bright idea had it been to have those horrible loud beepers go off every time a truck anywhere in America backed up, night or day, especially garbage trucks? She used to love to shop, but lately, shopping had become sheer torture; every store had loud music blasting out at you at full volume. She remembered when music used to be soothing, a pleasure to listen to. What ever happened to pretty music? Now it was just people screeching off-key at the top of their lungs or rap music booming in your ears, with not a tune to be found nor a lyric to be understood, at least not by her. Now all the kids were riding around town with that stuff blasting away so it almost knocked her off the sidewalk. Brenda had promised Ethel that when she got to be mayor, she was going to make it against the law to play your radio at full volume with your windows down. Brenda had Ethel's vote, on that issue alone.

Still, she hoped Brenda wouldn't leave real estate before Maggie could retire and get all her benefits. She worried about Maggie; she was clearly no match for Babs Bingington, and in this dog-eat-dog world, good guys usually finished last. Look what "the Beast" had done to Hazel.

What Babs Had Done

About six months after Babs Bingington had opened her office, she'd found out that Red Mountain Realty was getting the huge contract from the new insurance company moving to town. Babs knew getting that contract could make or break any office. Relocating a big company's corporate office from Philadelphia meant finding houses for hundreds of people, and Babs wasn't about to let some half-pint, hire-the-handicapped office knock her out of that business. She flew to Philadelphia and called the president of the insurance company and asked for a meeting. She informed his secretary that she was in town representing the Birmingham Board of Realtors and she told him that it was of vital importance to his company that she speak with him in person as soon as possible. When the secretary handed him the message, the president figured it was yet another public relations meeting. By this time, he had almost been glad-handed to death by the entire city of Birmingham, but he wanted to keep everything on a positive note and so he agreed to meet with her.

The next morning, Babs was escorted into the president's office. In her best fake southern accent, she started by saying, "Oh, Mr. Jackson, thank you for seeing me. You just don't know how hard this is for me; I'm a nervous wreck, but we . . . all of us . . . are so thrilled and proud that your company is moving to Birmingham, and it would just kill us if something were to go wrong."

Mr. Jackson was suddenly interested. "Oh?"

"I'm afraid the real estate firm you hired is . . . May I speak confidentially?"

"Of course."

"We feel you need to know that Red Mountain Realty is not a company you should be associated with at this time."

He looked at her. "Really? And why is that?"

Babs affected a pained expression. "Well, you see, Mr. Jackson . . . I have been chosen as a member of the real estate board to warn you that we have privileged information that Hazel Whisenknott is about to be brought up on embezzlement and fraud charges by a federal grand jury, and when it happens . . . well, we feel that you might want to consider the ramifications for your company. I know your reputation means a lot."

Babs reached into her purse and pulled out a lace handkerchief, blinked a few times, and managed to look teary. "Oh, I do wish I hadn't been the one chosen to tell you, but all of us in Birmingham care so very much that you be well represented. We would just die if anything went wrong. In fact, I'd consider it a privilege to handle your account personally and charge only a five percent fee, as a courtesy. That's how highly we think of your company, Mr. Jackson," she said as she slipped her card across his desk. "Of course, it's entirely up to you. You do what you want to do, but at least now you have the information."

After Babs left his office, Mr. Jackson thought about what she had said. He had liked the other little real estate lady, but she was right. Even if the charges were dropped, she was sure to be tied up in civil court. He didn't want to try to do business in the middle of that mess, and he didn't want to start off on the wrong foot in a new city. So why take the chance? He would have someone call and say they had changed their minds.

He picked up Babs's card and looked at it. It must have taken a lot of guts for her to fly all the way here and warn him, and he also liked the 1 percent cut in commission she had offered.

Babs was a master at faking sincerity, and since she was usually dealing with men who could easily be fooled by a woman who could cry on cue, she was successful more often than not.

Hazel, who usually thought the best of everyone, couldn't understand why her office suddenly began losing so many big contracts to Babs's company. But all Hazel ever said was "Well, my hat's off to her; she's a darn good saleslady."

T.G.I.F.

Friday, October 31, 2008

*T*he first thing Friday morning, Maggie had to run downtown to the main branch of Alabama Bank & Loan to close out her account and withdraw what little money she had left. She hoped closing her account so abruptly wouldn't arouse suspicion, but it couldn't be helped. When she drove past the empty lot where the old Melba Theatre used to be, she noticed the big white sign: RAZED IN THE NAME OF PROGRESS.

Driving around the block looking for a parking space she could manage, she had to see it over and over again. She hated that sign. It had stood on so many lots where buildings she had loved had once stood. Of course, the new revitalized downtown, with its tall, sleek, modern buildings was beautiful, but still, Maggie couldn't help but miss the old downtown of her youth. In the late sixties, people had begun leaving the downtown area and moving out to the suburbs. Slowly, one by one, the great department stores had started to close. Gone forever were the gleaming silver escalators leading up to eight and nine floors full of beautiful clothes and the second-floor mezzanine tearooms, where delicate little finger sandwiches of chicken salad, cucumber, and cream cheese were served on soft white bread baked that morning. Gone was the glamour of downtown; no more nighttime window-shopping, no more grand window displays at Christmas. By the seventies, even Santa had moved out to the mall.

For Maggie, it had been like watching a good friend die. Each time she had come home, she could see more places she had known as a child shut down; all the elegant deco buildings with the elaborate facades, deserted and standing empty. Nothing left but empty shells and boarded-up windows; the sparkle in the cement now covered over with dirt and grime. "Urban blight" they called it. "It's happening everywhere," they said. Still, it was hard to see all the places you loved crumble before your very eyes. But when they demolished the beautiful old downtown train station terminal and knocked down the big electrical WELCOME TO BIRMINGHAM sign, it broke her heart. She had loved that train station, with the big glass dome and all the excitement and hustle and bustle of people coming and going. It was there, on Platform 19, where she'd left for New York on her way to try to become famous. And that was the last time she ever saw Charles.

Finally, after Maggie's sixth time around the block, two spaces opened up, and she was able to park and go into the bank. Twenty minutes later, after she was almost finished withdrawing all her money and was ready to leave, the teller must have pushed a button, because the manager came out looking very concerned.

"Miss Fortenberry, is there something about our service you're not happy with? We hate to lose your business. Is there anything we can do?"

"Oh no, I've been extremely happy with everything. It's just that I'm moving . . ."

"I see. Well, we would still be more than happy to handle your account online."

Oh, dear. She had to think fast.

"Oh thank you, but I really don't know how to do that, but I can assure you, it's nothing personal."

She almost ran out of the bank. She hoped she hadn't hurt his feelings. But she hadn't lied. She **was** moving, and she really didn't have a clue how to bank online.

Maggie had cleared her morning and didn't have to be at the office until eleven, so she could try to finish up as much as possible before the weekend. When she got home, she sat down and made out a new, shorter list.

Things to Do

1. Pay gas, electric, water, MasterCard
2. Drop hint to Brenda
3. Call Salvation Army for pickup on the second
4. Call Boots to arrange for pickup on the morning of the third
5. Call and cancel all future doctors' appointments (hooray!)

Her doctor had just informed her that he was insisting that all his patients over fifty-five have a colonoscopy. Something else she was **more** than happy to miss.

After Maggie had made her calls, she was cleaning out the medicine cabinet and thought about Crestview again. Coming home from the bank, she had (of course) gone out of her way and driven by it, just to torture herself one more time, she supposed. She knew it was silly. As she was putting fresh towels in the guest bathroom, she was sure she was worrying about nothing. Fairly Jenkins had to have heard wrong. Mrs. Dalton would never sell Crestview in a million years. She walked down the hall to the linen closet to pack up what was left. She really had nothing to be concerned about. But still . . . just the thought of Babs Bingington even having the slightest chance of getting her hands on Crestview was appalling. She didn't trust Babs as far as she could throw her. In the past, the woman had somehow been able to have zoning classifications changed. Now, in what used to be pretty residential areas, there was a Popeyes Chicken or a Jack in the Box right next door to a lovely home. Who knew what might happen next? Babs could turn Crestview into a suite of dentists' offices. My God, it could wind up just like Dr. Zhivago's home, with strangers running in and out of every room. They would probably tear up the gardens and put in a parking lot. The more she thought about it, the madder she became. GODDAMMIT TO HELL! She should have run Babs over when she had the chance. Oh God, now she was cursing. Something she had vowed she would never do.

Maggie finished packing up the extra blankets and sheets and towels and threw all the bath mats in the washing machine, but as hard as she tried, she just could not get Crestview off her mind. She hated to leave not knowing if its sale was just a rumor. She should at least **try** to find out if it was true, shouldn't she?

As she was putting out the ant traps under the sinks, she began to toy with an idea. Hazel **had** said to use every advantage you had, and in this case, she did have a slight advantage: she knew the lawyer in New York who handled all the Dalton family business. She could go ahead and just call him. Just to ask. She could then find out once and for all, and she could jump into the river in peace. Of course, it felt unethical; not to mention rude and pushy. It was something she normally would never even think of doing. But if by any chance it happened to be true, she could at least try to get the listing for Brenda. Lord knows the office needed the business, and under the circumstances, she owed them that much, didn't she? Maggie looked at her watch. She still had time to make one more phone call.

She sat down at her desk, took a deep breath, then mustered up all the courage she had and called Information. When she dialed the number, the secretary put her through to her old friend Mitzi's husband, David Lee.

"Hello, David? It's Margaret Fortenberry from Birmingham. Do you remember me? I used to be a friend of your sister, Pecky."

The man on the other end said, "Well, hello! Of course I remember you. My God, how are you, Maggie?"

"Just fine, thank you."

"Well, my goodness. Margaret Fortenberry. The last time I saw you was at Pecky's coming-out parties."

"How is Pecky doing?"

"Oh, just fine; she and Buck are still in New Zealand."

"I heard that . . . And how's Mitzi?"

He laughed. "Same as ever; can't wait for me to

retire, so we can get back home. Well, my goodness, it's so nice to hear from you. To what do I owe the pleasure?"

"I hate to bother you. I know you're busy, but I just heard a rumor that Mrs. Dalton might be thinking about selling Crestview, and I was wondering if you knew whether it was true or not?"

"Well, I haven't heard anything; another department handles that. But I can sure find out for you. Are you interested in buying the old place?"

Maggie was tempted to lie and say yes, but she didn't. "Oh, I wish that were the case, David, but no. The truth is, I'm calling on behalf of Red Mountain Realty, and if it is for sale, I'm just curious to find out if they've listed it with anyone yet."

"Oh, I see, okay. Well, can you hold on a minute? Let me see if I can reach anybody downstairs. Hold on."

Maggie felt her face flush with embarrassment at having called someone she hadn't seen in years and for shamelessly using him to try to get inside information. But it was her only hope. A few minutes later, he came back on the line.

"Maggie. You still there?"

"Yes."

"Sorry it took so long. Alex says yes, that it will be going on the market in a few weeks, and it's being listed with somebody named Babs Binging . . . something or another. Do you know who that is?"

Maggie's heart sank. She was too late; "the Beast" had already struck. There was a slight pause; then Maggie said, "Oh yes . . . uh-huh . . . well, thank you anyway, David. It was just lovely to speak with you."

"You too. It was great talking to you."

It was all Maggie could do not to break down and cry. She might have known that she couldn't get out of this world without having Babs Bingington kick her in the teeth one more time. And the worst part was that it was all her fault. She had let all her "over the mountain" contacts slip and had not played bridge at the club in months. If she had been on top of everything like she should have been and not so preoccupied with her own little selfish problems, she might have known about it sooner. Now it was too late. She couldn't have felt worse if she'd tried.

After David hung up with Maggie, he had to smile. Of course he remembered Maggie Fortenberry. She probably didn't remember, but thanks to Pecky roping him in, he had been one of the pageant escorts the night she had been crowned Miss Alabama. Who could ever forget that gorgeous thing, sitting there in the spotlight in her white gown, playing the harp with that gorgeous hair of hers falling down on one side of her face? Mercy! Every healthy red-blooded Alabama male there that night would never forget her. She wasn't trying to be sexy. She just was. So intense, so serious, and playing the bloody hell out of that harp. Good Lord Almighty. Did he remember her? Oh, yes, he remembered her. What was her story? he wondered. Why hadn't she ever married? He knew for a fact that his friend Charles had asked her to marry him, but for some reason, she had turned him down. The minute he and the rest of his friends found out, they all wanted to rush over and ask her out themselves, but Charles was a friend, and you just didn't do that. He knew she had lived in New York and then Dallas, but why had she moved back to Birmingham? She was a mystery. Everybody thought for sure she was going to be famous or, at least, marry someone famous. He wondered what had happened.

He knew Charles had hauled off and married some girl he'd met in Europe and had moved to Switzerland. He had gone to Yale and had married Mitzi Caldwell, his hometown sweetheart, and they had been as happy as clams. But all the guys in his crowd had been just a little in love with Maggie that summer. They had all gone down to the train station to see her off and had been there with roses when she came home from Atlantic City. The thing about Maggie was that she was so nice, not stuck-up or vain. In fact, he'd often wondered if she even knew how really beautiful she was. Damn it. She should have been Miss America that year. The girl that won was not half as pretty as Maggie. Those judges must have been blind.

So Much Hope

⌒

The year Maggie was Miss Alabama, the Miss America Pageant was the most-watched show on television, other than the Academy Awards. Every September, millions of people tuned in to see who would be crowned Miss America, which girl would walk down the runway, clutching her bouquet of roses and crying, while Bert Parks, the master of ceremonies, sang "There She Is, Miss America." Certainly, everybody in Alabama would be watching, pulling for their girl to win. Just like Alabama football, it was a matter of state pride. Before Maggie had left for Atlantic City, hundreds of little girls from all over the state had written her, wishing her luck, and every mayor from every town in Alabama had sent her an official good-luck message.

That year in particular, with all the negative press Alabama had received, more than ever their state needed something they could be proud of.

Maggie was very aware of how much people were depending on her to do well, and she was so scared she might let them down that she could hardly breathe. But she needn't have been. On the first night of preliminary judging in Atlantic City, she wowed the judges with her harp and her looks. By the second day of judging, every wire service, including the AP and UPI, had her placed number one to win. Even Jimmy the Greek, who took bets on these things, had her as the odds-on favorite, and reporters had already started calling her hotel room, clamoring for an interview. Jo Ellen O'Hara, who was covering the Miss America Pageant for the **Birmingham News** sent off nightly press releases that became the next morning's headlines back home.

MISS ALABAMA WINS PRELIMINARY EVENING GOWN COMPETITION!

Last night, Margaret Fortenberry, wearing an elegant white gown from Loveman's department store, swept her way to victory again.

In the days leading up to the big night, the judges privately all agreed that they were very impressed with the girl from Alabama. Although there were many talented and pretty girls from other states, she had that certain poise and loveliness they were looking for, that special something; she was someone every little girl in America could look up to and aspire to become one day.

Back in Alabama, people tried their best not to be too optimistic, but as the good news kept coming in, they started planning parades and homecoming ceremonies across the state. They knew by the third day that unless something terribly unforeseen happened, Miss Alabama was going to be the new Miss America.

Maggie understood that if by some chance she were to win, it would mean being awarded thousands of dollars in prize money and numerous network television appearances, and she would become a national celebrity overnight, and her life would be changed forever. But for Maggie, the most important thing about becoming Miss America that year was that it would give her the opportunity to travel all around the country and tell people all the good things about her state, about all the nice people who lived there.

Only something unforeseen happened, and she never got the chance.

Maggie was still sitting at her desk with a sick feeling in the pit of her stomach over the news about Babs. She realized now (too late) that she should never have called David in the first place. What had she been thinking? Oh, God . . . just another bad decision. She guessed the only good thing was that now she could finally stop obsessing over it and concentrate on the task at hand. Time was running short and there was still a lot she had to do. And if the worst did happen and Crestview was torn down, it was probably best that she not be around to see it.

She looked at the clock. It was time to go into the office. Since she was leaving Monday morning, today would be her last day at work, and she still had a few things to shred, so she went out and got in the car. On the way over, she decided she wouldn't tell Ethel and Brenda about Babs getting the listing for Crestview. Why ruin their weekend? They would find out soon enough.

When she got to the office, Ethel was still at the beauty shop; Friday was her day to have her hair and eyebrows tinted, and Brenda and Maggie were just sitting around in Maggie's office, so Maggie thought this might be a good time to try to drop another hint about her upcoming departure. She took an emery board out of her desk drawer and started filing her nails so she would look casual.

"Hey, Brenda," she said, looking down at her hands, "did you ever think of just giving it all up?"

Brenda looked over at her. "You mean real estate? Every day."

"No . . . I mean just giving up . . . in general, you know?"

Brenda didn't say anything, but kept listening. Maggie continued: "I don't think it means that a person is weak or a coward. Sometimes they might be so tired, they just can't go on. What do you think?"

Brenda didn't answer and, after a moment, stood up and went over and shut the door. She sat back down with a serious expression on her face and looked Maggie straight in the eye.

"Maggie, as a friend, can I ask you something?"

Maggie suddenly felt nervous and thought maybe she had gone too far. But she said, "Okay."

"And will you tell me the truth?"

"If I can, Brenda . . . yes."

Brenda paused, then said, "Do you think I should get my stomach stapled?"

"What?"

"Do you think I should get my stomach stapled?"

Maggie was relieved, but disappointed at the same time. "Oh . . . well, honey, I don't know . . . what does Robbie think?"

"She says I'm not fat enough for the operation; she thinks my losing weight is just a matter of willpower, but it's not. I can lose the weight. It's the keeping it off that I can't do. I'm tempted to sneak over to another hospital and have it done behind her back and not tell her until it's over, but with my luck, I'd die on the table. Then she'd really be mad." She sighed. "But at this point, if I die, I die . . . who cares? I'm tired of eating rabbit food."

"Oh, good Lord, Brenda, don't talk like that; you have so many people who love you and would miss you terribly. You're not like me. I don't have people who would care like you do."

Brenda dismissed her with a wave. "Oh, right, Maggie, nobody cares about you. Every man in this town would have a fit if anything happened to you."

"That's not true, Brenda . . . I don't know why you say that."

"Because it's true! You could have any man you wanted if you just crooked your little finger. Robbie said that Dr. Thorneyhill said he would love to take you out. He's a brain surgeon; do you know how much they make? You'd better grab him now."

"Brenda, don't change the subject. You wouldn't really have an operation without telling Robbie, would you?"

"No, I guess not, but don't think I don't think about it. I tried to explain to her that I don't eat too much; I just have a lower metabolism than she does. But you can't make a point with Robbie; she's a nurse, and they think they know everything." She then looked at Maggie. "On second thought, forget about that Dr. Thorneyhill. Stay away from health professionals; they're just a big pain in the ass. Trust me."

Maggie could see there was no use to keep trying with Brenda. She had done her best, but it was impossible to drop a subtle hint to her about anything. She hated it, but unfortunately, Brenda was just going to have to be surprised along with the rest.

Just then, Ethel came banging into the office in a fit. They went out to see what she was yelling about and understood immediately why she was so upset. Her hair was not the pretty light lavender they were used to. It was more the color of Welch's grape jelly.

"What happened?" asked Brenda.

"What happened? I'll tell you what happened. The new girl Lucille hired can't read what's written on the side of the box, that's what happened. I said, 'Jesus, Lucille, I don't give a hoot if you hire an illegal alien or not, but you ought to make sure they can read English before you let them dye someone's hair.' I just hope to God it grows out by Thanksgiving, I've got a show to do!"

Maggie tried to make her feel better and said, "Ethel . . . it's not really that bad." But it was.

Meanwhile, Back in New York

s the day wore on, the more David thought about his conversation with Maggie, the more he began to frown. He didn't know exactly what it was, but he knew something was not right. Maggie had not said one word against the other real estate woman, but just the tone of her voice had told him volumes about this Babs person. At around three-thirty, he picked up the phone and called the lawyer downstairs again.

"Hey, Alex, have we signed a contract with that real estate woman in Birmingham?"

"Just getting ready to, why?"

"Don't."

"Why? We checked her out; everyone said she's the top agent in town."

"Maybe . . . but not for this property. I want you to go with somebody else on this, okay? I want you to use Margaret Fortenberry at Red Mountain Realty. She knows the house and the neighborhood, and she'll do a good job. Okay?"

"Well . . . okay . . . you're the boss. Whatever you want, but I can tell you, that Bingington gal is not going to be happy. She just sent us a great proposal; she's cutting her commission and giving us a great deal."

David continued, "And listen, when you do speak to Margaret, tell her you checked her out, and you heard that she was the best agent in Birmingham. And tell her we want her to handle the sale personally. Okay?"

Alex sighed. "All right, but she's not going to be happy."

After David's call, Alex pulled out Babs Bingington's real estate contract on the Dalton house in Birmingham and looked it over. He dreaded making the call and toyed with the idea of just e-mailing her. He had not mentioned it to his boss, but the last time they'd spoken, she had more or less promised him a "good time" if he ever came to Birmingham, and he had sort of gone along with it. Under the circumstances, he decided it would be the gentlemanly thing to tell her over the phone, so he reluctantly dialed her number, but her voice mail said she was not available and to leave a message. He didn't want to leave bad news on her machine, especially over the weekend, so he hung up. Alex decided it was no use trying to call her again today; besides, he had to leave early, so he could get home and take the kids trick-or-treating. He would just wait and call both Babs and this Margaret Fortenberry woman on Monday. Waiting a day wouldn't hurt anything.

Babs had had her eye on the Crestview property for some time. One of the construction companies she was getting kickbacks from wanted the lot, and for the last few months, Babs had badgered the owner's lawyer in New York with a combination of sweet talk, promises, and relentless pressure, until she was finally about to get the listing. She already had the fake couple set to put in an offer.

Of course, Babs knew as soon as they knocked it down, the snooty "over the mountain" historic-house snots would probably kick up a fuss like they always did, but she didn't care. They were just a bunch of pain-in-the-ass old dinosaurs trying to hang on to the past. They thought those houses were so special, but to her, they were just some old, outdated, falling-down piles of bricks that needed to come down. So screw them and the buggy they rode in on.

Audrey and the Panty Hose

Saturday, November 1, 2008

*B*y Saturday afternoon, Maggie had packed all the pots and pans in one box and the dishes in another, so she was finished with the kitchen. Now all she had to do was decide what she would wear tomorrow night to see the Dervishes so she could pack the rest of her clothes in the boxes for the theater. As usual, she spent ten minutes flipping back and forth through her closet and finally decided on the black Armani brocade evening suit with the green Hermès scarf, simple pearl earrings, and the black suede Stuart Weitzman pumps. She then rummaged through her top drawer, looking for that last new pair of black hose she knew she had, but when she found the package, she was irritated to see they were not the right size. She must have grabbed a bunch of them without looking. There was no possible way she was going to fit into a size A petite. She hated to buy a brand-new pair of hose to wear just once, but she had no choice. She couldn't wear tan nylons with a black formal evening suit.

Maggie was tempted to run out without putting on her makeup. Just a few short days ago, the very thought of going out in public without it wouldn't have crossed her mind. It was a good thing she was leaving soon. She was turning into someone she hardly knew. Good Lord, she would be spitting on sidewalks next.

She jumped into the car and drove over to the Brookwood Mall. She thought she would just dash in, pick up her hose, and dash out again, but after having driven around the block at least sixteen times, she was running out of patience. After the tenth or eleventh time around, she said, "Oh, the heck with it," and pulled into a handicapped parking space.

She hated to break the law, but the other eight handicapped spaces were empty, and the chances of eight handicapped people arriving to shop in the next five minutes were slim. Just in case anyone was watching, though, she got out of the car and limped into the store.

The minute she walked through the front door, she saw Audrey behind the counter in the jewelry department. Maggie hoped Audrey hadn't spotted her and kept going, but it was too late. Audrey, obviously thrilled to see her, yelled across the store, "Maggie! It's me! I'm working here now." She followed Maggie all the way back to the lingerie department and pushed the regular girl at the cash register out of her way, insisting that she wait on Maggie. She wanted to stand there and reminisce about old times, and if Maggie hadn't been in the handicapped spot, she might have stayed and talked to her longer, but after Audrey had run up her purchase, Maggie grabbed her hose and literally ran out the door, saying she was late for an appointment, which was a bold-faced lie. When Maggie pulled out and drove away and realized what she had just done, how rude she had been to poor Audrey, she parked in front of Books-A-Million around the corner and started to cry. She had not seen Audrey in over twenty years. She **should** have stayed and talked to her.

Audrey had been a good friend of her mother's, and the last time she had seen her was at her mother's funeral. Seeing her today, an old lady with arthritic hands, working behind a counter, was so sad; Audrey had once been a tall, good-looking, stately redhead and had run the entire Ladies Better Wear department in the big Loveman's store downtown. Maggie even remembered the first time she had met her. Audrey was wearing a royal blue wool dress with large square gold buttons and a sapphire pin on her shoulder, and Maggie thought she was as glamorous as a movie star. Over the years, whenever she and her mother came into the store, Audrey would see them and call out to any other salesgirls who approached, "These are my customers!" She had taken care of them like they were part of her family.

After Maggie's mother had developed arthritis and could no longer sew, Audrey would call if something was on sale or if a dress came in that she thought would look good on Maggie. Being a working woman herself, Audrey understood that they had very little money, so whenever Maggie needed a dress for some dance or function or a coming-out party for one of her girlfriends, Audrey always found her something wonderful to wear that had just been reduced. She would wink at Maggie and say, "We can't let our girl go to fancy parties in rags now, can we?" And when Maggie became Miss Alabama, Audrey was as proud as her own parents and announced to anyone who was within a mile, "I've dressed her for years." But now Audrey, who had once been Loveman's main buyer, was relegated to a part-time position in costume jewelry at a small outlet store. Maggie sat there and wondered what she should have said to Audrey. What could you say?

She sat for a minute and then got out of the car and walked the two blocks back to the store and found Audrey again. She walked over and took her hand. "You know, Audrey," she said, "I don't know if I ever told you this, but you have no idea how much you meant to me, how much you helped when I was growing up, always being so sweet and making me feel special, and I just want to thank you."

Audrey looked at her and said, "Oh, darling, you

were always so easy to be sweet to." Then Audrey glanced around the room. "Listen, I know you're in a hurry, but can I grab you for a second?" And for the next thirty minutes, Maggie was pulled around the store, from one department to the other, while Audrey introduced her to everyone who worked there, including a few clueless customers who just happened to be standing around, waiting to pay for something. "This is Margaret Fortenberry," she announced, beaming as if she were introducing the Queen of England to her subjects. "The night she won Miss Alabama, wouldn't you know it, I was home sick in bed with the flu and couldn't go to the pageant, but the very first person she called after it was over was me. I've known her since she was ten years old, and she was the sweetest little thing, always so well behaved." Audrey said this to people Maggie was sure couldn't care less about meeting some old beauty-pageant winner, but they were at least polite. It was embarrassing, but she could see it meant a lot to Audrey, so she was happy to stand there and shake hands.

As Maggie drove back home, she felt a little better about herself; Audrey **had** been the first person she had called that night. Maggie began to wonder why Audrey was still working. Where was her family? Did Audrey have a decent place to live? After a while, she moaned and started talking to herself: "Oh Lord, don't start. You can't help Audrey—you can't even help yourself." And why did those panty hose have to be A petite and not regular? Why had she run into that particular store? She could have just as easily run out to Walmart and picked up a cheap pair, but no, she had to have the more sheer and expensive kind. As she drove home, she decided to leave Audrey her Miss Alabama crown and sash and trophy.

Later, after Maggie had finished packing up all her jewelry and her mink stole and had everything ready to go, she called Boots and told her about the things she wanted to donate to the costume department. Boots was just thrilled and said she would have her guys pick them up first thing Monday morning. When Maggie hung up, she felt good about giving them the clothes. Hazel would have been so pleased. Hazel had always just loved the theater.

The Night-Before
Preparations

⁓

*B*renda was busy rooting around in her fat as a hog section, looking for just the right thing to wear to the theater tomorrow night. She had already picked out her wig. Something simple and stylish, but with a flip. Maggie would look drop-dead gorgeous as usual, but Brenda's intent, since she was planning ahead for her political career, was to start now to affect a bold look. An outfit that screamed confidence. She settled on a smart button-up dark green number she had picked up in the Ladies Plus Size department at a dress shop at the mall.

Across town, Maggie was packing up the last of her jewelry when she found a penny Hazel had given her years ago. She couldn't help but smile when she remembered the day.

Hazel had just received an award as Woman of

the Year from the Birmingham Chamber of Commerce, and as she and Maggie pulled out of the parking lot of the Downtown Club she said, "You know, Mags, I'm smart as a whip and a darn good businesswoman."

Maggie laughed. "Well . . . yes, I agree . . . even if you do say so yourself."

Hazel laughed. "I didn't mean it that way. What I mean is that besides being naturally smart and working hard at it, there's another reason I've been so successful in my life, something I've never told anyone before."

"What's that?"

"Luck."

"Luck, really?"

"Oh, yes. You know, honey, when I was pulling weeds for a living, I found an awful lot of four-leaf clovers. Why, over the years, I must have found thousands. Imagine how much good luck that is!"

"Quite a lot, I would say."

"You bet. Plus finding all my lucky pennies, and you have to admit, aren't I just the luckiest person you know? And what amazes me is that most people don't even bother to look for lucky pennies. I look for them everywhere I go, and I find them, too. It never fails. If I find a lucky one, wham! I get a check in the mail the next day."

"But, Hazel, don't you think you would still get that check even if you didn't find a penny?"

"No, it's the pennies. Don't you look?"

"I thought if you ran across one by accident, it was lucky. I didn't know you were supposed to look for them."

"Sure you are! Listen, babe, you have to search for your luck; it's nice if it just falls in your lap, but I look for my lucky pennies. Last year, I found three brand-new pennies, heads up, out at the mall, and the very next day, we got the Park Towers account. Biggest sales of the year!"

"What do you do with all your pennies?"

"I give them away. It's good to spread your luck around, and it always comes back to you. Here, I want to give you something." She reached inside her purse and handed Maggie a brand-new penny. "This is for you; stick it in your bra, and something good will happen."

"Do you think so?"

Hazel looked at her with a twinkle in her eye and patted her hand. "You keep that penny, and I guarantee you someday, when you least expect it, something good is going to happen; you just wait and see. And when it does . . . think of your lucky penny, and just remember I told you so."

"What's going to happen? Tell me now."

"Oh no," she said, looking up in the air innocently, "that's for me to know and you to find out. Just stick it in your bra, and don't ask questions."

"Hazel, you are a real character."

Hazel broke out in a big grin. "I am, aren't I? Sometimes, I just get the biggest kick out of myself.

I just never know what I'm liable to do next. Little Harry said he thought I was the most interesting person he ever met. And I don't even try. I just am, I guess," she agreed as she slid her huge car into a parking space that Maggie couldn't have parked in if her life depended on it. She had failed Driver's Ed in high school, twice in a row.

The only reason Maggie even had a driver's license in the first place was because of Hazel. Hazel's cousin Jimmy worked at the DMV, and the day she'd taken her driving test, Hazel had come along. When Maggie parked at least three feet from the curb, Hazel opened the back door and looked down and declared, "Close enough." Jimmy must have agreed, because he passed her with flying colors.

Why Ethel Hated Babs

*I*t certainly appeared as if nothing ever bothered Hazel; she said she never got depressed. Still, Maggie always wondered. Hazel's life couldn't have been easy. One day, Maggie had asked Ethel if she thought Hazel was really as happy as she seemed to be. Ethel had sat back in her chair, thought it over, and said, "Frankly, I think Hazel is not only happy being who she is, I think she's just tickled to death over it. In fact, I've never met a person—man, woman, or child—who has such a high opinion of herself. Hazel Whisenknott thinks she hung the moon." Then Ethel had shrugged. "And who knows? Maybe she did. The point is, don't ever feel sorry for Hazel—she doesn't."

And it was true; in all the years she'd worked for her, Ethel had never heard Hazel complain or get upset about anything . . . except once, a few years before she died.

Hazel was busy trying to get an account, and after she'd put in months of hard work, preparing presentation after presentation, flying back and forth to Chicago in the dead of winter and again a few days before the deal was to be finalized, the company called and said they were sorry, but they had decided to go with another firm. A week later, Hazel found out that Babs Bingington had gotten the account.

Within a few days, Hazel was sick in bed (with what would later turn out to be pneumonia) and called Ethel over to her house. She told her to close the door of the bedroom, then asked in a worried whisper, "Ethel, tell me the truth. Am I over the hill? Am I losing my touch?"

"No . . . you haven't lost your touch. It's that Babs Bingington that's causing you to lose those accounts. It's not you."

"Do you think so?"

"Yes. I don't know what she's doing; she could be sleeping with the entire board of directors, but she's doing something underhanded."

"It could be she's just a better businesswoman than me."

"Listen, Hazel, I've been working for you for over forty years, and I wouldn't lie to you. You have not lost your touch."

"Really?"

"Absolutely, I swear it on my purple hair."

Hazel laughed, and after that, she never mentioned it again. But to this day, Ethel blamed Babs Bingington for helping wreck Hazel's health. The doctor said later that the pneumonia had weakened her little heart.

Ethel was right, of course. When Babs had found out that Hazel was just about to close the deal, she had pushed and shoved and manipulated her way into a meeting with the company's three head men and had pulled the same trick she'd played before: telling them she had privileged information and yes, it was so sad, Hazel seemed like such a delightful person, but she was about to be brought up on federal charges of fraud, bribery, and taking kickbacks from developers. When the men had queried Babs about the pending charges against Hazel, Babs had sounded pretty convincing. She should have. She had committed every one of them at one time or another. Before she left, she tearfully advised them, "For your own good and for your company's protection, break off negotiations now, before your company is dragged into it."

After she was gone, the men looked at one another. They didn't know if she knew what she was talking about, but they all agreed that in this litigious climate and with business being as shaky as it was, they couldn't afford to take a chance. Too bad. They had really liked the little lady from Birmingham.

If Hazel's secret of success had been finding lucky pennies, Babs's secret had been fear. She had discovered early on in her career what a powerful tool just the **threat** of being sued could be. She kept two mean little lawyers on staff at all times for just such a purpose. She'd found that people would do just about anything to avoid being dragged into a lawsuit.

Ethel had never been able to find out exactly how Babs had stolen the account, but she still blamed Babs for Hazel getting so sick that winter. Hazel was more than an employer to her. When Ethel had first met Hazel, Ethel's husband, Earl, had just left her with no money and two small children to raise. Thanks to Hazel's hiring her, they had not had to go on welfare, like some. As far as Ethel was concerned, Babs had helped kill the best friend she'd ever had. And then believe it or not, Babs had had the nerve to come to Hazel's funeral and hand out business cards.

The Night of the Whirling Dervishes

Sunday, November 2, 2008

By Sunday, Maggie had managed to get all of her equipment, raft, weights, and rooster egg timer down to the river's edge in two trips and had hidden it all quite effectively. So far, everything was in her favor for an all clear for her departure the next morning; no unexpected detours. The place she had picked was still deserted, and as it turned out, fall was the perfect season for hiding her equipment in the woods. With the leaves and pine needles on the ground, she had been able to cover all her supplies with no problem. Things were looking good.

All of her belongings were mostly packed and ready to go. She had been able to quietly clean out her desk and had shredded all her papers and old photographs without Brenda or Ethel noticing. After all these years, she had finally figured out how to work the shredding machine. It was amazing the things you could do when you really put your mind to it.

She was right on schedule; earlier this morning, she had run over to the pay phone in front of the Western Supermarket and ordered her cab for Monday at ten A.M. Of course, she couldn't use her real name. The man had a foreign accent, so she gave her name as Doris Day. She had the car washed and filled with gas, had air put in the tires, the oil and water checked, so it could go back to the leasing company just as it had been delivered, neat and clean, with all the proper papers in the glove compartment. All she really had left to do now was get ready to go and see the Whirling Dervishes.

That night, Brenda picked her up at seven on the dot. **Why** she always wanted to get somewhere an hour early was beyond Maggie, but she was dressed and ready anyway. No need to make Brenda nervous; she wanted Brenda to have a wonderful time tonight. As usual, Brenda rushed them downtown and parked in the theater parking lot, and they were in the lobby by seven-fifteen, waiting for the doors to open. True to his word, Cecil had left two tickets for them at the box office, and when Brenda opened the envelope, she was even more excited. "Maggie, you are not going to believe this: we have two first-row seats! Isn't that great? I guess we won't need the binoculars I brought."

"No, I guess not."

As they stood there, Maggie looked around the lobby of the Alabama Theatre and felt the same old pride and wonder. Thank heavens, because of concerned citizens at the last minute it had been saved from the wrecking ball and had been completely restored. Hazel and their company had donated five thousand dollars. She still remembered the first time she had ever seen it and being utterly overwhelmed, awed at the spectacle of the four-story lobby with the huge crystal chandeliers heading up the grand staircase, the ushers in uniforms wearing white gloves. The theater had originally been designed as an opera house, with plush red velvet seats and five sweeping balconies rising all the way to the top. Maggie had seen the theater from the stage, as well as from the audience. It was the stage where she had been crowned. As she stood there waiting for Brenda to come back from the ladies room, she remembered that night: the nervous excitement as they lined up, ready to walk out on the runway as their names were called; the smell of hair spray, the rib-crushing longline strapless bras, the four-inch-high heels, the sparkle of the rhinestone earrings, the blinding light of the powerful spotlights from the booth way up in the top of the theater; the thunderous applause as the million-dollar Hammond organ rose up from the floor and hit the first deep chord of "Stars Fell on Alabama," the spotlights hitting them as they circled the runway; the backstage running and scurrying, changing from evening gown to bathing suit to talent-number costume and back to evening gown; the squeals and screams of delight when the winner was announced. She realized it was very fitting that she spend her last night here.

At seven forty-five the doors were opened, and as they marched down the aisle to the first row and found their seats and sat down, Maggie realized that although they were in the front row the seats were not very good. In fact, they were terrible. She had to lean way back and look straight up in the air just to see the edge of the stage. But Brenda didn't notice. She was so excited to be there and had turned around and was waving at friends and strangers alike in the balcony. The good news was that the entire house was packed. Maggie was happy to see that everyone was beautifully dressed. The last time she had been in New York, people had come to Broadway shows in jeans and sweatshirts, but good old Birmingham had not let her down this evening. Later, when the curtain finally started to rise, a hush went through the entire audience, but after it was up, Maggie was shocked to see that except for a row of wooden folding chairs, the stage was empty. She had been expecting exotic backdrops and colorful sets. After an uneasy two minutes, Brenda suddenly poked her in the ribs and whispered, "Look, there they are."

Maggie looked over to stage right and saw seven or eight men in white shirts and shiny black pants waiting in the wings; then, with no fanfare whatsoever, they just unceremoniously walked out onstage and, without a smile or even a nod to the audience, sat down and started playing odd-sounding flutes and some kind of stringed musical instruments. They played one strange number after another, each one sounding exactly like the last one. After at least an hour (or so it seemed), again without a smile, they all stood up and left the stage as unceremoniously as they had entered, and it was intermission.

Maggie already had a stiff neck from looking up, and she had not seen a Dervish whirling yet. After a long twenty-minute intermission, the same men came back out, sat down, and started playing again. Oh, Lord, she thought. The audience was at a loss for what to do, too polite to whistle and stomp their feet and scream, "Where are the Dervishes?" but restless nonetheless. Thankfully, after four or five more musical numbers, Brenda poked Maggie in the ribs again, and again pointed to stage right. Maggie looked over and, this time, saw several men in long black capes and big tall cone hats slowly gathering around. After another endless musical number, one of the men came out and walked across to the other side of the stage and laid down what looked to be two very large bath mats and then left again.

No question about it, this was the strangest show Maggie had ever seen in her life. But at least something was happening. After a while, two older men in tall cone hats and capes came out and knelt down on the bath mats for a while, and then finally, one by one, younger Whirling Dervishes in long black capes and at least two-foot-tall black cone hats entered the stage and, without a smile, went over and knelt down in a row. Everyone was so excited to see them at long last and wanted to applaud, but the men looked so serious, they didn't dare. After another long time of doing whatever it was they were doing, they suddenly stood up and dropped their capes to the ground to reveal their outfits: white shirts with little white vests, flowing white skirts, and little soft brown leather boots on their feet. Then very slowly, one by one, they began turning around in a circle, and soon they were all whirling around and around, faster and faster, all over the stage.

At first, Maggie could tell this must have been a beautiful sight: all these tall, handsome, graceful men twirling all at once with their skirts flaring in and out, like waves in the ocean. Unfortunately, all Brenda and Maggie could see as they twirled by was straight up their skirts: the loose white pants and leather boots; and as they twirled faster, the wind from their skirts blew dirt and dust from the stage all over the people in the first row. But even the little bit that they could see of the twirling was terribly beautiful and exciting. For a while however as the twirling went on and on, after waiting so long see them whirl, Maggie now couldn't wait for them to stop. Her neck was killing her, and her eyes were burning from looking straight up into the lights, and she was getting a headache and a sore throat from all the dust and dirt blowing in her face. Maggie calculated that if they had twirled in a straight line instead of a circle, they could be all the way to Atlanta by now. As she sat hoping that this would be their last twirl, she began to notice a pattern. As they twirled, they always wound up right back at the same spot where they had started. In a way, it reminded her of her own life. All that twirling, and in the end, she hadn't gone anywhere at all.

After another painful forty minutes, the twirling finally ended, and the Dervishes put their capes back on and left as slowly and as quietly as they had come on, followed by the musicians, leaving nothing but a row of empty wooden chairs and a grateful, but confused, audience. They wanted to applaud, but were afraid it would not be fitting. It was clearly a somber religious event, not what most had expected.

Brenda was deeply disappointed. "I thought it was going to be fun," she whispered. Maggie nodded with a stiff neck. "Me, too. Oh well, who knew?" But Brenda was still hopeful. In the lobby, when she saw Cathy Gilmore, she asked, "Is there a cast party?"

"No. They have to leave right after the show."

"Oh shoot, what a bummer. Did you get a chance to meet them before the show?"

"I met the bus when they arrived."

"What were they wearing?" asked Brenda.

"Wearing? Oh, just regular clothes. Why?"

Brenda looked at Maggie. "We just wondered."

As they drove home, Maggie quietly opened Brenda's purse and slipped Hazel's lucky penny inside as a sort of private going-away present. When they pulled up to Maggie's door, Brenda laughed and said, "Yeah, thanks to Cecil we sure didn't need those binoculars tonight, did we?"

"No, we didn't."

"It was different, I'll say that."

"It was . . . Anyhow, I'm so glad we went."

"Me, too; at least now we don't have to go to Turkey."

"No, we don't."

"Well, see you in the morning."

"Well, actually, no. I'm taking tomorrow off, remember?"

"Oh, that's right. I forgot . . . and what is it you're doing tomorrow?"

"Just a few things I need to take care of."

"Ah . . . well, have fun. See you on Tuesday then."

Brenda started to drive away, but Maggie said, "Wait—wait a minute."

Brenda stopped. "What is it?"

Maggie stood there and looked at her for a moment and then said, "Oh nothing, I guess I just wanted to say . . . good night again."

Brenda smiled. "Well, good night, don't let the bedbugs bite," she said as she drove away.

Maggie stood there and watched her until she was out of sight. Sadly, the show had not been quite as exciting as she had hoped for, but still, she was glad she had spent her last evening with Brenda.

Inside, she got undressed and packed her dress and shoes in the box and looked over her last list for tomorrow morning.

Things to Do, Morning of November 3

1. Cancel **Birmingham News**
2. Empty refrigerator and freezer
3. Take out garbage
4. Call Dottie Figge about unit
5. Call phone company and have phone disconnected
6. Leave money and watch for Lupe
7. Make bed and do laundry
8. Check under sink for ants
9. Sweep off back patio and clean out bird feeder
10. Don't forget to leave note on counter
11. Leave spare key under mat when you go

When she got into bed, she wondered why she was suddenly feeling so good. It seemed so wrong. My Lord. To wind up this way, she should be feeling just terrible around about now, but she wasn't. She'd noticed that as the day had gotten closer, she had begun to feel better and better. Was it because she wasn't watching the news anymore? She was certainly sleeping better than she had in years. It was amazing how nice it was to not have to worry about the future. Wouldn't you know it, just as she was getting ready to leave, she felt better than she had in years.

Oh, well.

Đ-Đay

Monday, November 3, 2008

Maggie woke up early and stripped the bed and threw everything in the washing machine and was about to get in the shower, but realized it would be a needless waste of water. She put on her coffee, threw two pop-up waffles in the toaster, and made her first phone call to Dottie and left a message on her voice mail telling her that a two-bedroom unit would be coming up for sale soon. She didn't want Babs to grab that listing before Dottie had a chance to show it to her clients. Afterward, she made a call to the **Birmingham News** and canceled her subscription. Then she called the phone company to have her phone permanently turned off. The lady sounded like it had hurt her feelings, but what could Maggie do? She then washed out her dishes and coffee pot and put them in the dishwasher.

As she waited for her sheets to dry, she put her

goodbye letter on the counter, along with her watch and Lupe's envelope, cleaned out the refrigerator and brought out the garbage, and at nine-thirty on the dot, two boys from Boots's theater rang her bell and took the boxes. So far, everything was on schedule. She ran out and swept off the back patio, pulled the sheets out of the dryer, and made the bed.

She walked around and did a last-minute check. Everything looked in order. Just as she was ready to leave, the phone in the kitchen started to ring. She figured it was the phone company calling back, checking the number, so she just let it ring. She locked the kitchen door, put on a scarf and her sunglasses, grabbed her purse, and walked out the front door. She placed the extra key under the doormat and headed down the block to wait for the cab, hoping that she wouldn't run into anyone she knew. Thankfully, the car was already there waiting for Doris Day, and she quickly jumped into the backseat and slammed the door. What a relief. Nobody had seen her. Safe at the plate! After she informed the driver which way to go, she settled back in the seat and was just starting to relax a little when the cell phone in her purse rang. Oh Lord, she was taking the stupid thing to throw in the river, but had forgotten to turn it off. She didn't want to talk to anyone now, much less Brenda or Ethel, so she just let it ring. But then, she suddenly wondered if it could be Dottie calling with some question about the unit at Avon Terrace. Maybe it had been Dottie calling her earlier at the house. She pulled the phone out and looked at the number calling, but she had just thrown all her reading glasses out in the garbage, and the number was a big blur. She punched Redial, expecting Dottie to pick up, but to her surprise, a man in New York answered.

"Hello" she said.

Five minutes later, Maggie had the driver turn the car around and take her back home. She hated to let go of her river plans for now, especially after all of her hard work coordinating everything so perfectly. But Alex, the lawyer who worked for David's company and handled Mrs. Dalton's properties, had been quite insistent. Maggie had tried to suggest that he work with Brenda, but he had said no, that in order for Red Mountain Realty to get the listing, he had specific instructions that she must handle the sale of Crestview **personally.** So really, what else could she do? If she didn't take it, the listing would certainly go to Babs, and after all, she had called David asking about the listing, so she couldn't very well say no now. Of course, this meant another delay on her river plans, but she couldn't be selfish about it. As really inconvenient as the timing was, she realized that just like Humphrey Bogart said at the end of the movie **Casablanca,** her plans didn't mean a hill of beans in the big scheme of things. This was something bigger than she was. Birmingham had lost so many landmarks in the past, and if she could just find the right buyer, the delay would be well worth it. Despite herself, she couldn't help but feel a little excited. This was Crestview.

Right now, she was just thankful she had left an extra key and could get back into her house. Once inside, the first thing she did was go to the kitchen and take her "To Whom It May Concern" letter back to the desk in the den. She sat down and opened it and reluctantly put Wite-Out over today's date. She decided to leave it blank for now and re-date it after she sold Crestview.

Maggie had been so surprised by the phone call; it wasn't until now that she began to realize that she had a major problem. She had just given away all her nice clothes to the theater, and she couldn't very well ask for them back. Oh Lord, she had even thrown away all of her makeup. Luckily, she could run out and at least retrieve most of her makeup and all her glasses out of the garbage can.

A few minutes later, Maggie was happy she had found her makeup and glasses, but that was the least of her problems now. The lawyer in New York had called and arranged a meeting with Mrs. Dalton for eight tomorrow morning—and she had absolutely nothing to wear! Oh, God! Why had she canceled all her credit cards and closed out her bank account? Now, after sending what money she'd had left over to her two charities, she was flat broke.

Then she remembered that she had put five hundred dollars in cash in the envelope with the gold watch she was leaving for Lupe as a bonus. She went into the kitchen, opened it up, took the money, and put her watch back on. She hated to do it, but when you were selling high-end properties, you had to look your very best.

Maggie was so relieved that she had some cash to go shopping with, but then she suddenly realized that she couldn't very well go shopping in her FISH-ERMEN DO IT WITH A BIG POLE shirt. Most every-one she could think of here at the complex, except Mrs. Sullencroft, was already at work, so she turned her fishing shirt inside out, ran to the end unit, and knocked on her door. When she answered, Maggie said, "I hate to bother you, but I wonder if you have a coat of some kind that I could borrow for just a little while?"

"Oh sure, honey, let me go find something for you."

A few minutes later, Mrs. Sullencroft came back and handed her a large, bright pink, fuzzy wool coat. "Here you go. Keep it as long as you like. I think that color will look good on you, honey," she said.

Maggie thanked her profusely and got in the car and headed out to the mall. When she got there, she put the pink coat on and walked into the Armani outlet store. She was horribly embarrassed to be seen in such an outfit, especially the men's boots, but luckily, right away she was able to find a simple

black suit. Then she went next door to the Saks outlet and picked up earrings, a pair of nice Ferragamo
shoes, and a lovely scarf. And she got everything all
within her somewhat limited budget.

Maggie may not have known how to Twitter, but
she did know how to shop.

At the law firm in New York, Alex had just informed his boss, David Lee, that per his instructions, Maggie Fortenberry had been hired and the
first Birmingham realtor had been informed that
she was not getting the listing. David was very
pleased. But Alex was still a little shaky. Just as he
had suspected, Babs had not been happy. He had
not heard language like that since the men's locker
room at college.

At first, Babs Bingington couldn't understand why
the Dalton lawyer had had such an abrupt change
of mind. "We have decided to go with someone
else" was all he would say. The little prick—and
after all she had promised him.

It took her twenty-four hours to find out just
who the Crestview listing had gone to, but when
she did, she went into a dark green rage. She should
have known it. That damned "over the mountain"
bunch had shut her out again. It never failed. No

matter how hard she worked, when push came to shove, they always stuck together in the end. She wasn't good enough to handle their precious Crestview. But if they thought for one minute that she was going to let them get away with it, they were sadly mistaken.

Meeting Mrs. Dalton

Tuesday, November 4, 2008

At eight o'clock the next morning, Maggie was sitting in the grand library at St. Martin's in the Pines, waiting to meet with Mrs. Dalton and sign papers and pick up the keys to Crestview. There was a saying that no matter how far away Birminghamians moved, they always came back home in the end, and Dee Dee Dalton was no exception. She was from one of the old-guard iron, coal, and steel families and, at eighty-eight, had outlived four husbands and lived all over the world, but when she had returned to Birmingham for good, she'd moved back to her family home and had gone back to using her maiden name. It was easier for her friends. To them, she would always be Dee Dee Dalton, no matter how many husbands she had married along the way.

As she sat waiting, Maggie couldn't help thinking how really odd life was. A few days ago, she had been so upset, and now she was glad she had gone to the beauty shop and had her hair done. Then suddenly, something else dawned on her. Since she had made that phone call to David asking about Crestview, she realized that she had actually **stolen** the listing right out from under Babs Bingington's nose. She had never stolen a listing in her life, and it was a total violation of her code of real estate ethics, but . . . oh well. Too late now. The deed was done. And to her surprise, she didn't feel bad about it at all.

Maggie had dressed in such a hurry, she was busy checking to see if she had left any tags on the clothes when Mrs. Dalton, still a handsome woman with bright blue eyes, walked into the library. Maggie stood to greet her, and Mrs. Dalton couldn't have been nicer. After she signed all the necessary papers, she handed Maggie the keys to Crestview and said, "Here you are, dear. I'm sorry I haven't had a chance to clear everything out of the house, but if there's anything you want—dishes, paintings, furniture—just take it or else give it away. I have no room for anything here."

When Maggie asked if she had an asking price in mind, she said, "Oh my, no, I haven't any idea; I suppose you need to tell me what the market can bear."

"All right, let me check the comparables in the area, and I'll get back to you."

"I hate to sell it, but all my children are dead—can you imagine? Of course, at one time, I had planned to leave it to the city, but now I don't trust them to keep it up like it should be, so I'm hoping you'll find someone who won't knock it down to the ground, at least while I'm alive."

Maggie said, "Mrs. Dalton, I promise you I will do my very best to find the perfect buyer."

"Oh, thank you, dear, I'm sure you will; I have such happy memories of growing up there." Mrs. Dalton's eyes looked wistful as she continued: "We moved there right after word came from England that poor Mr. Crocker had been lost at sea. He had no family, except for one sister who lived in London, but she never came to Birmingham. So after he died, the house was left to my father, who was a partner in one of Mr. Crocker's companies." She smiled. "Of course, Mr. Crocker was especially fond of Mother, and I suspect it was really Mother he had left it to. He and Mother had been grand friends. Mr. Crocker was a confirmed bachelor. Over the years, she had helped him plan entertainments and with the gardens and such, so he trusted that she would continue to take care of it, I guess. And he was right. I think Mother loved Crestview as much as the Crockers had. Of course, I never knew Edward's father, Angus Crocker, who had built Crestview, but Mother said that father and son were as different as night and day." She looked back at Maggie, "Tell me, are you at all familiar with the house?"

Maggie nodded. "Oh yes, ma'am, I am. I've never been inside, but I have admired that house all my life. In fact, I always thought that Crestview was the most beautiful home in Birmingham."

"Oh, really?" said Mrs. Dalton, obviously pleased. "Well, that's just so lovely to know, dear. A lot of people your age don't really appreciate the older homes. And Crestview has quite a history, you know."

Maggie smiled. "Yes, ma'am, I do."

Crestview Begins

Birmingham, Alabama, 1887

*I*n 1862, when it was discovered that the red dust that kicked up around wagon wheels on the mountain was not dust but iron ore ground to a fine powder, word spread, and an entire industry began.

Birmingham had been named after the great iron-producing city of the same name in England. Many of Birmingham's early founders had arrived in Alabama with images of London, Glasgow, and Edinburgh, which they had left behind, still shining in their mind's eye, and they had determined to build something in America to match or even surpass those grand cities.

Angus Crocker was such a man. In 1885, straight from Edinburgh, Scotland, he rode in horse and buggy all the way up to the top of Red Mountain and looked into the valley below and declared to his son, Edward, "Someday, a great city will be built down there." An architect was hired, and six months later, on that very spot, construction on Angus Crocker's house began. He sent home to Europe for the finest stonemasons and workmen he could find, and all the materials: each stone, every brick, every plank of wood had been handpicked and shipped from his beloved Scotland. Although he was known to be tightfisted in business affairs, no expense was spared when it came to the building of his house. Two years later, after construction was completed, his foreman from Perthshire proudly handed Angus the key and declared, "There ye have it, sir, the finest of Scotland, your home on the crest of the mountain with a view to rival no man's." From that day forward, the house was called Crestview, and the name was engraved in stone over the archway of the front door. Carved underneath in smaller letters was the phrase THIRLED NO MORE.

After the house had been furnished and the grounds and gardens completed, Crestview had its formal opening. As it was the first of the grand homes to be built on the mountain, the event was covered by the **New Age-Herald.**

A CASTLE IN THE SKY

June 18, 1887—As Scottish bagpipers piped us up the long driveway, Birmingham industrialist Angus Crocker, with young son Edward at his side, welcomed us to his newly completed castle in the sky atop Red Mountain. After a short ribbon-cutting ceremony by the mayor, an awestruck crowd was given a complete tour of the home and gardens. "Perfection" is an oft overused word; however, all others fail this reporter. In this modern age of slipshod, thrown-together, lean-to affairs jumping up all over town, passing as houses, while style, workmanship, and aesthetics have been left behind to serve the new twin masters of the building trade, cheap and speedy, Crestview now stands above our city: a proud symbol of what is good and noble in the human spirit, a tribute to the might of the individual to create beauty out of stone and mortar, a beacon of light shining high on a hill, beckoning and welcoming all who view her to move up the mountain, giving us all an ideal to strive for.

The reporter, still feeling the effects of the imported scotch whiskey that had been served that afternoon, may have overstated the case, but others who had attended the celebration agreed that Crestview was not only beautiful but also well built. "This house will stand a thousand years," said one man who knew about construction.

After Crestview went up, when all the other successful men began building their homes, they, too, brought in architects with instructions to "do me something English." Residential areas were laid out, shade trees were planted, and streets were given names such as Essex, Carlyle, Sterling, Glenview, and Hanover Circle; imported English lampposts with round yellow globes lined each sidewalk. Soon hundreds of large limestone, red brick, and Tudor-style homes with long winding driveways were built, and charming little shopping villages—Crestline, Mountain Brook, Homewood, and English Village—popped up, with small, elegant shops that offered furniture, silver, linens, and fine china brought from London or the Cotswolds.

Every afternoon, from the day his house was completed, Angus Crocker sat out on his large stone terrace and looked down in the valley below and watched the long, wide avenues of downtown Birmingham being laid out. The city grew not gradually but in leaps and bounds. Every day, buildings climbed higher and higher until what was once a huge dark wooded area had become peppered with new houses and streets that stretched as far as the eye could see. From his terrace, he looked across the valley at the towering smokestacks of the iron and steel mills that surrounded the city, billowing thick orange smoke all the way up to Tennessee and beyond. He had seen a magic city rise up out of nothing to become the great modern industrial center of the South.

Angus had no art in his home. His art was the outline of the buildings of the city against the sky, the red and orange streaks of iron ore in the mountains, and the glowing red-hot rivers of iron and steel that ran through his mills day and night. There was no piano in the living room. The pulse and the pounding of the steam engines, iron banging on iron, steel on steel; the sound of the train whistles in the night as they pulled in and out of the downtown terminal with boxcars loaded with coal and pig iron; this was the only music Angus Crocker liked to hear.

On these nights, Angus wished his father and his grandfathers before him could know that, at last, a Crocker had climbed out of the cold, dirty coal mines and had thrown off the brass collar of serfdom forever; that a Crocker had climbed to the top of the mountain and built a castle in the sky as a monument to all their years of hard work and as a tribute to the country where a man with nothing but a dream could succeed even beyond his wildest dreams.

Perhaps in the eyes of others, **what** he had done to achieve it could be considered a terrible thing. But unlike his ancestors, who had left nothing behind, he had something tangible, something real to leave to Edward, his only child: a great booming city he had helped form, a vast fortune, and a name to be proud of. And no matter the dust and grime below, the air was always clean and fresh atop Red Mountain.

Congratulations All Around

Wednesday, November 5, 2008

O f course, Maggie wished she hadn't given all her clothes away, but as she found out, that wasn't the half of it. After the meeting with Mrs. Dalton, she'd had to run back downtown to reopen her bank account and get a replacement credit card, so she could go shopping and buy food and all new toothpaste, soaps, shampoos, and underwear. And the phone company charged her an arm and a leg to turn her phone back on.

She had wanted to make sure that everything was in order before she told Ethel and Brenda the good news about Crestview. She didn't want to get their hopes up until she was sure she really had the listing, but she had been so preoccupied with buying new clothes that she had completely forgotten that yesterday was November 4, the day of the presidential election. This morning, when she was driving to work and heard the results on the radio, she knew Brenda would be thrilled that her candidate had won.

When she got to the office, Brenda was not at work yet, but Ethel said, "Well, I just hope he can do better than the last one, though I doubt it." Then Ethel went on her usual rant about politicians, which lasted about five minutes longer than the Hollywood rant. Maggie stood there and waited patiently until Ethel was finished and then, as casually as possible, handed her the signed papers.

"What's this?" asked Ethel.

"Oh, just a contract to sell Crestview."

Ethel's mouth flew open. "**What?** When did this happen?"

Maggie hoped it wouldn't sound like bragging, but she couldn't resist. "When I called a friend and stole the listing from Babs Bingington."

"You did?"

"I **did**!"

"I can't believe it! YEE HAW! This calls for a celebration." Ethel then proceeded to take out the bottle of bourbon she kept in her desk and her purple plastic collapsible cup and poured herself a drink. "Hot damn, here's to you, Maggie!" she said as she slugged it down.

A few minutes later, Brenda came straggling in looking exhausted but very happy. Maggie stood up and hugged her. "Oh, Brenda, how wonderful, I'm **so** happy for you. Your man won."

"Thank you. You just can't know what this means,

coming from where we were to this, and in my life-time? Oh, you just can't know."

"No, but I can imagine."

Maggie waited until she couldn't stand it another second and then said, "And Brenda, I have even more good news. We have a new 'over the mountain' listing."

Brenda looked at her in disbelief. **"No."**

"Yes! Not only a listing, but a listing I stole from Babs."

Brenda screamed, "Girl . . . you didn't!"

"I did!"

"She did!" said Ethel and poured herself another drink. Even though she was a Presbyterian, she added, "Up yours, Babs."

After Maggie finished giving Brenda all the details, she said, "And guess what else?"

"What?"

"I have the keys!"

"You don't!"

"I do. Let's go. Ethel, if anyone calls, just tell them that we're at our new listing."

"Sounds good to me," said Ethel.

Brenda couldn't stop talking all the way across town. "I can't believe you got the listing away from the Beast." She repeated this over and over, and she was still saying it as they went up the driveway to Crestview. The truth was, Maggie could hardly believe it herself. After all the years of dreaming about this house, she was about to go inside for the very first time.

So many homes that had looked fantastic on the outside had been such a disappointment once you got inside. She just hoped this wouldn't be one of them. Maggie's heart was pounding as she put the key in the lock, and she held her breath as she opened the big front door and they stepped into the entrance hall. The house had an almost sweet smell of wood smoke and did not have the stale musty odor of most of the older homes she had been in. They switched on the hall light and saw a black-and-white marble floor leading past a grand staircase and all the way down a long hall to the kitchen. And what a staircase! Just as Mrs. Roberts had said so many years ago, the stairs that curved gracefully all the way up to the second floor were made of the most perfect marble Maggie had ever seen. "Wow," said Brenda. To the right of the hall was a large living room with four large French doors that opened into a sunroom. On the left was a formal dining room and a library. Maggie almost burst into tears. The inside of the house looked exactly as she had expected. No, in fact, even more beautiful than she had imagined, were that at all possible.

Angus Crocker had clearly spared no expense in building this home. Every doorknob was made of the finest cut-glass crystal. Even today, every window casement, every hinge, every lock was in perfect working order. As they walked through, Brenda said, "They sure don't make them like they used to, do they?"

As they turned on lights and pulled open drapes, Maggie was so pleased to see that, unlike a lot of the other larger homes, which could be cold and fore-boding, with big, drafty rooms, the rooms here were perfectly proportioned, and the honey-colored wood-paneled walls gave the house a warm, homey feeling. She hadn't expected that.

When they walked through the large leaded glass doors off the back of the house and onto the huge stone terrace overlooking the entire city, Brenda said, "Lord, have mercy, how can you put a price on that view? Can you imagine sitting up here at night?"

"Yes, I can." Maggie had imagined it many times.

Brenda turned and said, "Oh, don't you wish Hazel was here with us?"

"Always," said Maggie.

The kitchen was a large old-fashioned eat-in kitchen with long stainless steel counters and ribbed glass cabinets to the ceiling. Off the kitchen were the servants' quarters, with back stairs leading up to the bedrooms on the second and third floors. As a real es-tate agent, Maggie knew that the older kitchen and white marble bathrooms throughout the house might seem dated to some, but she already felt herself dread-ing the thought of anyone changing a thing. She wouldn't. To her, it was exactly right. To her, being in this house was like going back in time. There was something almost magical about it. She felt like she was walking around in a wonderful old English movie. She didn't have to worry about staging this house. As far as she was concerned, it was perfect.

Since Crestview had never been for sale, and there were no existing statistics on it, she and Brenda were also measuring and counting the rooms as they went, and so far, including the servants' quarters, they had counted five bathrooms, a living room, a library, a dining room, and six bedrooms. Maggie was falling more in love room by room; the rugs, the wallpaper, the simple but sturdy elegant furniture, the understated colors, the floral chintz sofas, everything so lovely and tasteful. Even the books on the shelves were tasteful; they hadn't been bought by the pound by some decorator just for show—these were books that had been read. When they finished with the bedrooms on the third floor, just as they were about to go back downstairs, Brenda noticed something down at the end of the hall and walked over and saw a narrow set of dark wooden stairs. She looked for a light switch on the wall, but there wasn't one.

"What's up here—an attic?"

"I don't know, but there might be bats," Maggie said. "Let's just wait and get the home inspector to go up there tomorrow."

"Don't you want to see the whole house?"

"Of course, but I don't want to get bitten by a bat either."

"You won't; come on, just follow me." Brenda pulled a flashlight out of her purse and started up the narrow stairs.

"Brenda, let's just wait."

But Brenda wanted to see everything. "Oh, come on . . . don't be a chicken."

"All right, but if we're attacked by bats and get rabies, it will be all your fault." At the top of the stairs was a large wooden door. Brenda tried to open it, but to Maggie's relief, it was locked. "Come on, Brenda, let's go back down."

But Brenda handed Maggie the flashlight and said, "Hold this . . ."

"Oh, Lord." Maggie stood there and held the flashlight while Brenda tried all the keys Mrs. Dalton had given her. When none fit, Maggie was glad. But then Brenda pulled a screwdriver out of her purse and started jiggling it up and down in the lock.

"Don't ruin the door, Brenda, let's just wait."

But Brenda, determined to get in, said, "Stand back," and banged the door as hard as she could with her right hip, and they heard something snap with a loud crack.

Maggie said, "What was that?"

Brenda stood perfectly still for a moment, then said, "I don't know . . . I just hope to God it wasn't my hip. I don't want to have to spend my money on a new hip."

"Oh, no. Does it hurt?"

Brenda waited another moment. "No, I'm all right." Then she hauled off and hit the door again, with her other hip. This time, the nails in the rusty lock gave way and the door opened with a loud screech, just wide enough so that Brenda was able to stick her arm inside. She felt around for a light switch but couldn't find one, so she took the flashlight from Maggie and said, "Stay here."

Maggie was not happy about being in the dark and said, "Brenda, I wish you wouldn't go in there," but Brenda had already pushed herself inside. She flashed her light all around the room and saw a large window with floor-to-ceiling curtains. She walked over and pulled the cord, and the curtains, rod and all, fell to the floor in a dusty heap with a loud thud.

"Uh-oh," said Brenda.

Maggie called from the hall, "What was that? Are you all right?"

"Yes, I'm fine. It's just a curtain." After some of the dust settled, Brenda looked around. The room seemed almost empty, except for an easy chair, a small table placed by the window, and two huge steamer trunks standing over in the corner. She flashed her light up at the beams in the ceiling and in all the corners and then called out to Maggie, "No bats. Come on in."

Maggie stepped in and looked around and was pleasantly surprised. "This is a nice-sized room." She walked over to the window and gazed down into the gardens. "Oh wow, you can see the whole yard from here. I'd fix this room up as an office, wouldn't you? Wouldn't you call this a bonus room?"

Brenda didn't answer; she was in the corner, inspecting the steamer trunks. "Look at the **size** of these things. They're as tall as I am. Imagine trying to check these at the airport. Hey, look, they still have an address on them." Brenda took out a tiny feather duster from her purse and dusted the trunks off to see what was written on the large faded yellow tags.

DELIVER TO:

Mr. Edward Crocker
c/o Crestview
1800 Crest Road, atop Red Mountain
Birmingham, Alabama

SENT FROM:

Miss Edwina Crocker
1785 Whitehall
London, England S.W.

PLEASE HOLD FOR ARRIVAL

June 2, 1946

Maggie walked over. "Oh, for gosh sakes, I wonder if there's anything in them?"

"I'm about to find out," Brenda said, pulling out

the screwdriver again. "You said Mrs. Dalton didn't want any of this stuff; if we find anything of value, we could always sell it and give the money to charity, couldn't we?"

"Well . . . yes, I guess so, but I really don't think we should open things until we ask her."

"Oh, don't worry about it; she won't care." Brenda then proceeded to snap open all four locks and pulled the trunks apart. One trunk was packed full of ladies' evening gowns, and the other was full of men's formal clothes.

"Oh heck, it's just a bunch of old clothes," said Brenda.

But Maggie was delighted and pulled a gown out of the lady's trunk. "Oh my goodness, these are just beautiful! I think most of these are originals from Paris!" Brenda held one up. Sadly, they were too small to fit either one of them. Maggie then opened up one of the small drawers on the side and found a pair of black beaded evening slippers with a purse to match. "Oh wow. If Mrs. Dalton doesn't want them, these will be great period costumes for the theater."

"Great," Brenda said, "but before you start giving anything away, let's see if there's anything else in here." While Maggie continued to examine the gowns, Brenda was busy pulling aside each one of the men's suits. Suddenly, she jumped back and said, "Woooooo . . . !"

Maggie looked over. "What? Did you find something?"

Brenda did not answer, but stood there with her eyes wide, pointing. "Woooooo," she said again.

"What is it?" Maggie walked over and looked where Brenda was pointing. At that same moment, a ray of golden sun shot through the window and lit up the inside of the trunk like a spotlight. What Maggie saw then nearly scared her to death. Hanging neatly on a hanger, among the men's evening clothes, was a man's skeleton, completely dressed in a formal Scottish kilt and a plaid sash, with one bony hand still stuck in the pocket of a black velvet jacket.

Maggie grabbed Brenda's arm. "Good God, is it real? That can't be a real skeleton, can it?"

"I don't know, but I'm about to find out. Stand back." Brenda leaned in a little closer and poked it with the screwdriver, and what she hit was definitely hard bone. She dropped her purse and yelled, "Hell, yes, it's real . . . Let's get out of here!"

And the two of them sounded like a herd of buffalo, running back down the narrow stairs. When they finally got to the first floor and caught their breath and could speak again, Maggie said, "I have to sit down."

"I thought I was going to have a heart attack." Brenda, still breathing heavily, held out her hand. "Look at me, I've got the willies—I'm shaking all over. I need a cookie or a piece of cake or something or I might pass out. My emergency chocolate is upstairs in my purse. Will you go get it?"

Maggie looked at her. "**Me?** No, I'm not going back up there! **What** emergency chocolate?"

"Never mind," Brenda said and flopped down on the sofa and started fanning herself with a pillow. Maggie collapsed in the chair across from her and said, "I told you we shouldn't have gone up there. I don't know why you don't listen to me."

"How was I supposed to know there was a dead man up there?"

"We should have just left those trunks alone then—" Maggie stopped in mid-sentence and put her hands over her mouth. "Oh my God."

" 'Oh my God' is right," said Brenda. "That thing was looking right at me."

"No, Brenda. I mean **really,** oh my God."

"What?"

Then Maggie uttered the dreaded word: "**Disclosure!**"

Brenda stopped fanning herself. Suddenly, all their dreams of a big fat commission began to fade away. Both having been in real estate as long as they had, they knew from past experience that people were very reluctant to buy a house where a dead body had been found. And certainly not at anywhere near the asking price.

"Well. There goes my TV," Brenda wailed.

Maggie was shaking her head. "I just can't believe it. Why did it have to be this house?"

"What are we going to do now?" asked Brenda.

"I don't know . . ." she sighed. "I guess the first

thing we have to do is call the police. Oh, I hate for us to get involved in something like this. You know it's going to wind up in the papers," Maggie said, opening her purse. "And who would send a dead body to someone anyway?"

"You're asking me? I don't know."

"And what was it doing in a trunk in the first place?" she asked, looking for her phone.

Brenda said, "Maybe he was a stowaway."

"A stowaway?"

"Yeah. Maybe somebody forgot to open up the trunk on the other end and let him out."

Maggie was still digging around in her purse. "Where's my phone . . . oh, here it is. Brenda, would you call? I'm too nervous to talk. And, Brenda, try not to give the police our names, if at all possible."

"Okay, I'll try." Brenda reluctantly took the phone. "But what should I say?"

"Just say that we're two real estate agents who happened to be rummaging through some old trunks and . . . No, don't say that; they'll think we were trying to steal things . . . Don't tell them you pried them open with a screwdriver. No, wait! You can't do that; they'll see they've been tampered with . . . Oh God, I guess we have to tell the truth. We don't want to be brought up on charges." Maggie put her face in her hands. "Oh no, now we're going to be involved in an investigation. They're probably going to take our fingerprints and everything. But I guess it's too late. It can't be helped now. Go ahead and call. And then I guess we should call Mrs. Dalton and tell her."

Brenda was just about to dial the police, but then she stopped. "Hold on a minute! Before we call anybody, let's just think about this. Nobody knows we found that dead man but you and me, right?"

"Yes. So?"

"So, maybe we don't have to call the police."

"Of course we do. We have to report it."

"Why?"

"Because you have to report a dead body!"

"Why? It's not like it's a recent death or something."

"Because they're dead, that's why."

"Okay, but it's not like Judy Spears's listing, when she found that woman in the freezer. That woman still had a full body; Judy said she was still wearing earrings and a longline girdle. Her husband had murdered her with a pickax."

Maggie winced. "Don't tell me the details . . . what's your point?"

"My point is that hers was a full dead body, and ours is just bones."

"Well, full body or not, ours is still a person. It doesn't matter. We have to call the police. **Lord** . . . I didn't think of that. We don't know how that man died; we might wind up in the middle of a murder investigation."

"That's right. And don't forget, after Judy disclosed that she found that murdered woman in the freezer in the basement, the house never did sell. They wound up tearing it down and putting up a Jiffy Lube shop."

"I know all that, Brenda, but as licensed agents, we have to disclose."

"Why? It's not like we took a Hippocratic oath. You don't want this house to be torn down just because of a few old bones."

"No, of course not, but I don't want to get arrested for tampering with evidence either or wind up being accessories after the fact, and if anyone found out we didn't disclose, it would be considered unethical. We could both lose our licenses."

Brenda said, "Listen, don't you think Babs Bingington has done worse things? You think marrying men to get their listings and stealing clients right and left is not unethical? She still has her license. Besides, a skeleton is not a serious health threat to the buyer, it's not mold or asbestos or a weak foundation, it's just a few old bones, and once removed from the premises, it won't hurt anybody."

"Maybe not, but if somebody were to . . ." Maggie suddenly stopped and looked at Brenda. "What do you mean, 'once removed'?"

"Just what I said."

"Brenda, what's the matter with you? You can't just remove a dead body from the premises. It's not like a set of dishes or a painting. We have a moral and legal obligation to find out who he is, or **was** anyway, not to mention a Christian obligation to notify the family and make sure he has a proper burial."

"We will . . . but it doesn't have to be right this minute, does it? We have to think about the office. We need this sale to keep going, and that man's been waiting to be buried since 1946, so waiting until we close escrow and I get my TV won't bother him. He's dead in a trunk. What does he care?"

Maggie could see that Brenda might have a point.

"Think about it while I'm gone," Brenda said as she stood up to leave.

"Where are you going?"

"To get my purse. Dead body or not, I need my candy."

After Brenda left, Maggie realized that it was something to think about, all right. She had put off her jumping-in-the-river plans in order to try to sell Crestview and save it from Babs and the bulldozers. Maggie was tempted, but as usual, she was still torn about what she should do. She had to think about her reputation; after all, she was an ex–Miss Alabama.

A few minutes later, Brenda came back downstairs with her purse, eating a Hershey bar, and said, "Well . . . have you thought about it?"

Maggie looked at her. "When you said **remove** it, just what exactly did you have in mind?"

"Simple. We remove it from the trunk."

"**We?** I'm not touching it. I'd be scared to touch

it. You don't know what he died of. He could have had the black plague or something."

"Oh, all right. If you're so scared, Robbie has a drawer full of surgical gloves; I'll go get you a pair. Okay?"

"Well . . . if," said Maggie, "and this is just a hypothetical if . . . but if we **were** to remove it, we would have to do it at night."

"Why?"

"Because you can't move something like that in broad daylight."

"Okay. Then let's just move the whole trunk."

"What? You and I can't carry that trunk; it weighs a ton. And we certainly don't want an accomplice."

"You're right; they always squeal in the end," Brenda said. "We'll just take it out of the trunk, wrap it in a blanket, and move it ourselves. We can do it."

"But it just sounds . . . so illegal. I just don't think I can."

Brenda looked at her. "Wrecking ball?"

It was a persuasive argument. Maggie said, "All right . . . let's just say that if we **were** to remove it, where we would move it to?"

Brenda thought for a moment. "How about your place?"

"My place! Where?"

"What about under your bed?"

"Brenda, do you **really** think I'm going to sleep with a skeleton under my bed? Besides, people are coming in and out all the time to show the unit, and Lupe cleans under the bed every week."

"Hey, I know: we can put him in storage. Robbie and I have a storage bin over at Vestavia Mini-Storage, and she never goes in there; it's mostly my stuff."

"Are you sure she never goes in there?"

"Yes, I'm sure."

"Okay, say we do sell the house, what then? How are we going to explain how he . . . it . . . got all the way to Vestavia Mini-Storage . . . that he walked?"

"No. We get someone to bring the trunks over to storage, and then after the house sells, we put him back and say we just opened the trunks and found him."

"Yes, but **why** did we take the trunks to storage in the first place?"

"Simple. We were clearing the house out for showings. Nobody's going to question that."

"No, I guess not," Maggie said, beginning to be persuaded; she had stored things when she had been staging houses before. "But before we decide to do anything, I need to make a call first."

Brenda handed her the phone, and Maggie dialed and closed her eyes while she waited, preparing herself.

"Hello, Mrs. Dalton, it's Maggie Fortenberry. I'm so sorry to bother you, but my partner, Brenda, and I are over at the house, and it appears we don't have all the keys . . . and I was wondering . . . do you happen to have a key to the attic?"

"The attic?" asked Mrs. Dalton.

"Yes, ma'am, on the fourth floor . . . up the little flight of stairs?"

There was a long silence.

"Oh! I know what you're talking about. No, I'm sorry, I don't have a key. We were never allowed up there. Mother said those stairs were off-limits to us, and back then, what Mother said went."

"Ah . . . well, do you know who might have a key?"

"I don't."

"I see. So, you don't know what's up there?"

"No, I'm sorry, dear, I have no idea. As I said, when I was a child, what Mother said went. Not like how it is now; back then, when Mother said, 'Eat your vegetables,' you ate your vegetables."

"Well, no problem, but thank you anyway."

Maggie hung up and felt a little better. The last living resident of the house had no idea there was a dead man up in a trunk in the attic. That was some good news. The bad news was that if they were going to move it, they had to do it tonight. In her excitement over selling Crestview, she had called and made an appointment with the building inspector to come first thing in the morning, and now that Brenda had knocked the door open, he was sure to go in and look around. This was one of those times she was going to have to make a decision and pray it was the right one.

The Big Caper

⌒

Later that night, scared to death, Maggie drove over and honked twice. Brenda came out carrying a blanket, dressed completely in black, and when she got in the car, she handed Maggie a pair of surgical gloves. "Here, put these on." Then she looked at Maggie and made a face. "Where did you get that pink coat?"

"It's new."

Brenda was surprised. Maggie usually had better taste in clothes than that, but she didn't say anything. As they approached Crestview, Maggie turned off the headlights and drove up the driveway in the dark and parked. Inside, Brenda used her small flashlight to help them find their way back upstairs. When they got to the attic, they laid the blanket out on the floor, and Brenda reached inside the trunk and tried to pull the hanger out, but it was stuck. "It won't come out. You're going to have to help me."

Maggie closed her eyes and reached in and pushed aside some clothes to make more room, and it worked. But when Brenda jerked the hanger out of the trunk, they heard something drop.

Maggie asked, "What was that?"

"I don't know, but we got him." Brenda carefully laid the skeleton out on the blanket on the floor, and as she did, it made an eerie clacking noise. Maggie felt as if she might faint. Brenda then wrapped the blanket around the skeleton, picked it up, and threw it over her shoulder, where it rattled with each step. When they got outside, Maggie opened the car door, and Brenda put the bundle in the backseat.

As they drove to Vestavia, Brenda turned around in her seat and checked it out with her flashlight to make sure it was all right. All of a sudden, she frantically started flashing the light all over the backseat and then yelled, "Oh, my God."

"What?" said Maggie, almost driving the car into a lamppost.

"You're not gonna like this—there's a foot missing!"

"What?"

"There's a foot missing. We lost a foot somewhere!"

"A foot?"

"Yes. The thing only has one foot."

"Are you sure it's not on the floor?"

"Yes, I'm sure. Turn around. We have to go back for it."

Maggie did as she was told, and the next thing they heard was a siren, and then they saw the blue lights flashing behind them. Brenda stopped breathing. Maggie pulled to the curb.

"Good evening," said the officer.

"Good evening," said Maggie with a big smile. "Is there something wrong?"

"Ma'am, do you know you made an illegal U-turn back there?"

"I did? Oh, I'm so sorry. But I just remembered something I forgot and had to go back and get it, and I wasn't thinking about what I was doing."

"May I see your license and registration, please?"

"Of course," she said.

"Have you had anything to drink tonight, ma'am?"

"No, sir. I never drink and drive."

As the officer was examining her license, Maggie continued, and said in a matter-of-fact way, "And I'm sure you must be wondering why there's a skeleton wearing a Scottish kilt in the backseat, but there is a perfectly good explanation."

At that instant, Brenda thought about jumping out of the car and making a run for it, but she was now frozen in her seat and couldn't move.

The officer looked at Maggie and said, "Excuse me?"

"I said, I'm sure you're wondering about the skeleton wearing a Scottish kilt we have in the backseat, but there's a perfectly good explanation."

"Oh, yes?"

"Yes. The Scottish Society had its big Halloween bash last weekend, and my friend and I are on the decorating committee, and we were just returning it."

The officer shined his light in the backseat and saw the skeleton's head sticking out of the top of the blanket. "Is that thing real?"

Maggie laughed. "Well . . . it certainly looks real, doesn't it? But no, it's just plastic. One of the members is a chiropractor, and he lets us use it as a decoration every year, and my friend Brenda just noticed that a foot was missing, and I was going back to get it—that's why I made that sudden turn back there. I had that foot on my mind and, again, I am so sorry."

"Well, I'm going to let you off with a warning this time, but you ladies be a little more careful, okay?"

"I will, and thank you so much, Officer. I really appreciate all the good work you do. I know your job is not easy, is it?"

"No, ma'am . . . it's not easy."

"Well, thank you again, and have a good night."

Usually, if he had stopped someone with a skeleton wrapped up in the backseat, he would have been a lot more suspicious, but he figured the story was so crazy, it had to be true. And besides, he hated to give such a pretty lady a ticket if he didn't have to.

As they drove away, Brenda looked at Maggie with brand-new admiration. "You've got more nerve than God. How did you think up that story?"

"I don't know, but never mind that; what about the foot?" Maggie asked.

"Forget the foot; we can find the foot in the morning, but . . . I swear, you deserve an Academy Award for that performance. Honey, Meryl Streep has nothing on you!"

Although she enjoyed the compliment, Maggie figured she had probably offered the officer far more information than she should have. Still, she had seen too many episodes of **Cops** not to know that if you had something in your car you shouldn't have, it was best to tell the police before they found it. Of course, she **had** lied to an officer of the law about it being plastic, but it had kept them out of jail. For the moment, at least.

They managed to get over to the storage bin without another mishap and stashed the skeleton behind a chest of drawers.

After Maggie dropped Brenda off, she couldn't help but wonder about life. She was certainly not a philosopher by any means, but the fact that the very day she was planning to jump in the river was the exact same day she found out that the house she had loved all of her life was for sale was ironic, to say the least. Of course, finding that skeleton had certainly been a shock. She just hoped that she and Brenda were doing the right thing.

Now, the big question was, who **was** that dead man and what was he doing in the trunk? Who or what had killed him? And where in the world was his foot? What had they gotten themselves into? She hardly slept all night, worrying about the missing foot. And just when she had been sleeping so well, too.

Another Big Puzzle
Thursday, November 6, 2008

The next morning, Maggie was back up at Crestview by seven A.M., looking for the foot, and the first place she looked was the bottom of the trunk, where she found a shoe, but no foot. Brenda arrived by a quarter to eight, and together they retraced their steps from the attic to the car and back again. They then looked all over the yard, but no luck. Maggie was worried, but Brenda said, "Look, as long as the foot's not in the house, we're all right. Besides, we don't know for sure if he ever had one. Maybe he was put in there without a foot. And even if it did fall off in the yard, a dog has probably gotten it by now and already buried it. So, we have nothing to worry about."

Maggie didn't like the idea of a dog trotting around the neighborhood with a foot, but what could she do? She was relieved when the building inspector's report was finished. Other than a few minor things, the house was declared to be in great shape. No mold, minimal termite damage, no corrosion in the pipes, no moisture in the walls of the basement.

"They don't build them like they used to," the inspector said.

Later that afternoon, after he left, Maggie had to run back down to the river and pick up all the things she had hidden. There was no telling how long it would be until the house sold, and she couldn't take a chance on anyone finding them. It took her two trips to drag all the things back to the car, and the mud ruined her brand-new Ferragamo shoes in the process. When she got back home, she remembered something else she had to do and called Dottie Figge and told her that the unit in her building she had thought would be for sale would not be available as soon as she had thought.

In keeping with Hazel's method, Maggie wanted to put Crestview's best face forward and get it sparkling clean and ready for next week's showing; the last thing in the world she wanted was for it to linger on the market. Thanks to Mrs. Dalton, the gardens were in great shape; the ivy on the side of the house was green and healthy; the English box hedges that lined the driveway were strong and sturdy. All it really needed was a good cleaning. As she stood on the terrace, Maggie tried to imagine what it must have looked like when it was the only house on the mountain. She knew a Scotsman named Angus Crocker had built it in 1887 for his son, Edward, and that Edward had been lost at sea, but that was about all she knew.

Later, Maggie was standing out on Crestview's front porch, looking at the big door to see if it should be sanded and revarnished. She decided it was fine. All they needed to do was clean the small glass window in the middle and maybe have someone come over and power-wash the stonework in the front. That always freshened up an old house. As she was look-ing up, she noticed three small words carved in the stone archway over the door: THIRLED NO MORE.

Thirled? What did that mean? She had never heard that word before. Had it been misspelled? Was it supposed to be "Thrilled no more"? But that didn't make sense. Was it a family name?

When Maggie got back to the office, she asked Ethel and Brenda, but neither knew what "thirled" meant. Then it occurred to her that since the man who had built the house had come from Scotland, maybe it was a Scottish word. Brenda went to her computer, sat down and Googled "Scotland, Thirled." What popped up surprised both of them, especially Brenda.

Thirled: a term used to describe men who worked in the coal mines of Scotland. A thirled man was bonded for life to a company and wore a metal collar around his neck with the name of his owner stamped upon it. These workers stood deep in the pits and cut coal that their wives and children then carried to the surface in baskets. They were paid two shillings and sixpence (sixty cents) for twelve hours of work, and out of that, they paid for their own keep and were not supplied with food, shelter, or medical care. To survive, many families were forced to work all day and into the night in the freezing and dirty coal mines of Scotland. Thirled men were serfs, and if one removed his brass collar and ran away, he was captured by the sheriff and returned to his owner. His punishment was by the lash. He was punished for having stolen himself and his services from his master. This was the law in Scotland as late as 1799.

Brenda, who had majored in history, had never read anything about this before and said, "No wonder the poor man was happy to be thirled no more."

A Crocker Family History

W hat most people hadn't known was that the Crocker family had descended from a long line of thirled men, and even after the practice had ended in 1799, in the ensuing years, they had not fared much better.

Angus Crocker had been cold, dirty, and hungry much of his life, one of twelve children raised in a filthy hovel that sat outside the coal mine where his father worked, barely scratching out a living. Angus had been a good student, but just like his brothers, when he was ten, he had been sent down into the mines. A boy of his class, with no money, had no hope of ever rising higher than a miner, but when Angus was fifteen, fate stepped in and changed his life. In 1863, during the Civil War in America, there was a shortage of men to work the mines of Pennsylvania, and when a letter was posted that a mining company there was hiring and paying good wages, Angus jumped at the chance. He worked the night shift in the coal mines outside of Pittsburgh and sent himself through school during the day. Within eight years, he had worked himself up to mine boss, then to shop foreman, then to superintendant. Ambitious and smart, he caught the eye of a few men at the top. Impressed by Angus's ability to strike a bargain and control his men, they promoted him to a management position, and he was soon traveling to and from Scotland to negotiate the company's interests there. Kicked up in social status, he was on one of these trips to Edinburgh when he met and married Edwina Sperry, the only child of the industrialist James Edward Sperry. It was a good match. By law, upon her father's death, Angus would have complete control of his wife's inheritance and of all the Sperry mines in Scotland. As a dutiful son-in-law, he gave up his job in America and worked exclusively for his father-in-law. Thirteen years later, after the father died, he and his wife moved into the large family home in Edinburgh, and Angus Crocker took over the running of the mines. With the father's money and Angus's ability, the Crocker-Sperry mines soon became the biggest producers of coal in the country.

At age thirty-nine, Edwina Sperry-Crocker was pregnant for the first time, and Angus was deeply relieved. At last, there would be an heir with both

Sperry and Crocker blood flowing in his veins. For Angus, it meant another large step away from the dirty coal mines of his youth. To be sure that everything went well, he hired a private nurse to attend to his wife's every need in her last important weeks of pregnancy.

When the day finally arrived, the family doctor was called to the home, and Angus paced the floor downstairs, waiting for news. Edwina was frail, but after a long, hard labor, the young nurse, wanting to please her wealthy employer, rushed to the upstairs landing and announced to Angus that his wife had just given birth to twins. He had a son and a daughter! Twins had not been expected, but all Angus cared about was that he had a son, whose name would be Edward. He needed a son to carry on the Crocker-Sperry name and protect the business. Now no one, not even his grimy, greedy brothers and sisters, always looking for a handout, could ever dare steal what was rightfully his. He had an heir! Jubilant, Angus immediately retired to his study, poured a whiskey, and started planning the boy's future. Tomorrow, he would send for his lawyer and change his will; everything he owned would now go to his son. In the unlikely event that he were to die before the boy came of age, arrangements would be made for a generous monthly allowance for his wife and the girl, but the day the boy turned eighteen, everything, the mines, the properties, would be his son's to pass on to his own son after him.

Later, when he left Scotland and built his new home in America, Angus stood and watched with great pride as the stonemason carved THIRLED NO MORE above the entrance.

A Lost Object

Saturday, November 8, 2008

Maggie was anxious to get Crestview on the market as soon as possible, and she had hired Griggs Roofing, the company they always used, to inspect the slate roof. On Saturday morning, when Maggie drove up to the house, she saw that Mr. Griggs was already up on the roof working, and his ten-year-old son, Warren, was out on the front porch. He was a sweet little boy, and Maggie was happy to see him. As she headed up the stairs, she could see that he was busy playing with something. She assumed it was a toy or a ball, until she got a closer look, and then she almost fainted. The object he was scooting all around the stone floor was the missing foot!

Oh, Lord. She had to be very careful how she handled this, so as not to alarm him. She casually walked over and said, "Hi there, Warren."

He held the foot up and shook it at her. "Hey,

look what I just found! It's a foot; it's got toes and everything!" He rattled it at her again.

"Oh, yes, I can see that. Where did you find it, honey?" she asked, trying to remain as calm as possible.

"Down there in the bushes," he said, pointing at the boxwood hedge. "I'm gonna take it to school on Monday. I think it's a real dead person's foot."

Maggie smiled at him. "I know it looks real, but it's not."

Warren shook the foot again. "It looks like a real foot to me."

"No, darling, it's much too small to belong to a real person."

He held it up and looked at it. "Are you sure?"

"Oh yes. You've heard of a lucky rabbit's foot, haven't you?"

"Yes, ma'am."

"Well, what you found is a lucky monkey's foot."

"A monkey foot?"

"That's right. The lady who used to live here lost it when she was moving out, and she'll be so happy you found it. I know she'll want me to give you twenty-five dollars as a reward. Isn't that wonderful? Give it to me, and I'll take it to her right now and bring you back your reward, okay?"

Warren still seemed a little reluctant to hand over the foot, so Maggie added, "Why, she might even give you thirty dollars!" She had been prepared to go as high as fifty, but luckily, Warren settled for thirty.

As she drove back across town with the foot in her purse, Maggie was horrified. What was her life becoming? Just three days ago, she had stolen a dead body and lied to the police, and she had just shamelessly bribed an innocent child. Once you took that first criminal step, it was all downhill from there.

Brenda was waiting for her in front of the storage unit, and when she pulled up, Brenda opened the car door and got in.

"Where is it?" Brenda asked, looking around to see if anyone was watching.

Maggie opened her purse. "It's in here," she said, looking around as well. "Oh Lord, I feel just like we're doing some kind of dope deal."

Brenda took the foot out and put it in a small paper sack from Baskin-Robbins. "Got it." As she climbed out of the car, Brenda added, "I just hope it's the right foot." And she walked away.

Maggie called after her, "What do you mean, 'the **right** foot'?"

But Brenda didn't hear her. Oh great, Maggie thought, now she was going to have to worry about that. Did she mean the right foot as opposed to the left foot? Or did she mean the right foot for that particular skeleton? Oh God, she was being punished for stealing that listing from another agent;

she just knew it. Finally, Brenda came back out and walked over with a strange look on her face.

"Well?" asked Maggie. "Was it the right one?"

"The right foot?"

"Yes . . ."

"No, it was the left foot."

"What? It can't have two left feet."

"No . . . it was the right foot, but it was the left foot. Anyhow, I hate to tell you this, but a toe is missing."

"**What?** What toe?"

"The little toe. Didn't you count the toes before you put it in your purse?"

"Nooo, I didn't count the toes! Oh, Lord."

"Well, just calm down, and look in your purse; maybe it got caught on something . . ."

"Dear God in heaven." Here she was in broad daylight, searching for a dead stranger's little toe in the bottom of her purse. But after a minute, she found it and handed it to Brenda. She would never be able to use that purse again, and it was brand-new. But at least they had all the parts in one place.

The Man on the Wall

Monday, November 10, 2008

O n Monday morning, the cleaning crew Maggie had hired was crawling all over the house, so when Brenda came in after lunch with all the comparables in the area for them to go over, they went into the library to get away from the noise. Brenda sat down at the desk and opened her briefcase. "Did you know that eight out of ten of the houses that sold last year were Babs's listings?"

"I'm not surprised," said Maggie.

"How does she do it? She's like a shark: eat and swim, eat and swim."

As Brenda was busy getting all the papers in order, Maggie happened to glance over her shoulder at the oil portrait hanging above the fireplace. She had seen it several times before, but this was the first time she realized that the man in the portrait was dressed in the same formal Scottish kilt as the skeleton.

"Oh, my God! Brenda, look."

Brenda looked up. "What?"

"Just turn around; look. Is that what I think it is?"

Brenda looked.

Brenda said nothing, but she stood up and went over and peered more closely. "It's the same outfit, all right."

"Are you sure?"

"Oh, yes. Right down to the buckle on the sash." Brenda turned to Maggie with wide eyes. "Honey, we've got Mr. Edward Crocker himself over in storage."

"But it can't be him. Mrs. Dalton said he had been lost at sea; they never found him."

"Well, I can't help that; the gold plaque right here says 'Edward Crocker,' and I don't know about you, but I've got to get out of here. Bones is one thing, but looking at that man when he was alive is another!"

Maggie followed Brenda out of the room, still wondering how a man said to be lost at sea could wind up in a trunk. What next?

Later that afternoon, after Brenda left, Maggie went back into the library and looked at the portrait again. The man in the portrait, who appeared to be at least in his forties, had clear blue eyes, rosy cheeks, and sandy-colored hair and was standing by a tree, with a golf club, in a stiff formal pose. Although he was gazing off into the distance, as she looked closer at the face, she saw something about his expression that intrigued her, a slight softness around the eyes. All she knew about Edward Crocker was what Mrs. Dalton had told her and the things she had read about him in school: that he had been a rich and powerful iron, coal, and steel man and had done a lot for the city. Of course, she couldn't be a hundred percent sure the skeleton in the trunk **was** Edward Crocker, but still, there was something in his eyes that made her want to know more about him. "Who was he?" she wondered.

Edward Crocker Begins

1884

*F*rom the day of his birth, nurse Lettie Ross never left young Edward Crocker's side. Although she was still very young and pretty, she had no time for suitors. She was on call twenty-four hours a day, seven days a week and slept in his room at night. Angus Crocker was terrified of kidnappers. There were ruffians down in the valley that would do anything for money.

As a consequence of his father's mistrust of strangers, Edward played no games with other boys and mostly stayed indoors. Edward took after his mother's side and was delicate and prone to colds and fevers, but even so, Angus refused to let Nurse Lettie call in a doctor. He no longer trusted doctors. He had come through many childhood illnesses; so would Edward.

But Lettie, being a trained nurse, did believe in

doctors. Her own brother back home in Scotland was studying to become a physician. What Angus didn't know was that Lettie Ross, passing the child off as her daughter, had dressed little Edward as a girl, and they had visited many a doctor in Birmingham over the years. She would take no chances while typhoid and yellow fever ran so rampant. She had made a secret vow to God that nothing would ever harm this child in her care, and if the child needed medicine, Angus Crocker be damned, the child would have medicine. But other than those occasional visits to doctors and carefully supervised outings to visit the Crocker-Sperry mines and steel mills, Lettie and Edward seldom left the grounds of Crestview. It wasn't too uncommon. In the rarefied world of the wealthy, in the days of private tutors and private nannies, everything was brought up the mountain to Edward. Private barbers cut his hair; clothes were brought to the home and picked out for him by Nurse Ross. His schooling was conducted at home. He had everything a boy could want, except friends his own age and a loving father. The only real interest Angus seemed to have in Edward was to teach him the business so he would be prepared to take over one day. With no friends and a father who was absent most of the time, Edward's entire world revolved around Lettie Ross. And for Lettie, who was still young enough to miss her brothers and sisters, Edward was her only companion. They played together, made up games, and had fun together. But then one day, when Edward came of a certain age, they suddenly grew even closer. Edward and Lettie Ross had a sexual secret, a secret that must never be told.

A Hard Sale
Mid-November 2008

Maggie spent the next week studying the market and thinking about what the asking price for Crestview should be. It was tricky. You couldn't ask too little or it would be an insult to the house and the neighborhood, and asking too much might cause the house to linger on the market too long. Of course, to her, the house was priceless; nevertheless, she had to put a price on it, and so it officially went on the market at just under $3 million, at $2,800,000—much lower than it would have listed at in a good market, but it was still a fair price. And to Maggie, considering what the brand-new fake Tudor homes out in the new gated communities were going for, it was a bargain; more than a bargain. Crestview was the real thing, not some cheap imitation. To her, the house was a work of art.

But Maggie was afraid that as much as she loved Crestview, it would be a hard sell. These days, everybody wanted the exact same thing: a large family room and kitchen combined, with granite countertops and cherrywood cabinets; every house had to have a home office, walk-in closets, snap-off mullions on the windows for easy cleaning, a jetted tub, a sound system, an outdoor eating area with a built-in grill, a three- or four-car garage, and be near a good school and a shopping mall.

Crestview would have been perfect for Maggie. She didn't need to be close to a school, and she preferred a separate kitchen. As bad as she was at cooking, the last thing in the world she wanted was someone hanging around and talking to her while she tried to prepare a meal. And she didn't want to entertain at a breakfast bar; she wanted a real dining table that she could set beautifully with lovely folded napkins. She didn't want an outdoor grill. Eating outside on paper plates was not her idea of gracious living. But she was obviously in the minority.

Maggie knew that it was also extremely important to market the house correctly. Crestview was not a house where you could just stick up a For Sale sign in the yard. She thought she'd begin by quietly and discreetly making the right people aware that it was available. Maggie decided to forgo the usual realtors' open house. It would be a waste of time and money, considering that only a handful of agents dealt with high-end listings. But mostly, she didn't want to have to face Babs Bingington.

Late Tuesday afternoon, after Brenda and Ethel had gone home, Maggie sat down and typed out the brochure to be sent to her "over the mountain" client list. She would try that first.

FIRST TIME ON THE MARKET

One of the grand premier estates of the city is being offered for sale. Your exquisite taste will be reflected in this spacious and lovely landmark home. Elegant and understated; perfectly suited for the discriminating buyer, with vaulted ceilings, seven stone fireplaces, and beautiful original hardwood floors throughout. You are invited to attend an open house on Sunday, November 23, from 2:00 to 4:00.

She reread the brochure and hoped she was doing the right thing, but she couldn't be sure. Without Hazel to give her advice, she was concerned. She **had** to sell Crestview. She had sent all the money she had left in her bank account to the Humane Society and the Visiting Nurses Association, and she couldn't very well ask them to give it back. It hadn't occurred to her that she would still be here. She had been forced to take out a short-term loan from the bank to tide her over, and if the house didn't sell, she would be in big trouble. She just hoped she could do it. God, she missed Hazel. Hazel had made her and all the girls in the office feel so smart, so capable that they couldn't make a mistake, and strangely enough, they hadn't. But after she died, it seemed nothing ever went right. Maggie sat wondering what it was about Hazel that had kept her and the entire office going. It had been almost impossible to be in a bad mood around Hazel. But how did she do it? One day, Maggie had asked, "Hazel, don't you ever get depressed about anything?"

Hazel looked at her, surprised. "No. What do I have to be depressed about?"

"Well, I don't know . . . a lot of people might feel sorry for themselves if . . ."

"If they were a midget?" Hazel laughed, then said, "Oh, I guess I might have, but do you know what my parents did? When I was eight years old, they drove me all the way out to Long Beach, California, to see the Miss Long Beach Beauty Contest."

"Why?"

"Well, that's what I wondered, but after it was all over, the M.C. announced that now it was time for the Miss 'Pee Wee' Long Beach Division, and out came ten of the prettiest little midgets you ever saw. And the crowd just went wild. There was a pair of twins dressed up in evening gowns and one in a little red Chinese pajama outfit and a little blonde that looked just like a miniature Jean Harlow, and you should have heard the sailors stomp and cheer and whistle for her. The midgets got more applause than the big girls had. Anyhow, it was the first time

I had ever seen other people just like me, and I found out that people liked midgets. So I just made up my mind to be happy about it. My parents had read about the contest in a magazine and planned the whole thing. Wasn't I lucky? Not a high school diploma between them, but they were two of the smartest people I ever knew."

Maggie said, "Now I'm curious. Who won the contest?"

"Oh, honey, little Jean Harlow, hands down. And now that I think about it, I guess seeing all those cute outfits that day is what made me love costumes. See how life works? Everything happens for a reason. Just think: if I hadn't wanted an Easter bunny outfit, you and I might never have met." Hazel's eyes suddenly lit up. "You know what, Mags? This Easter, I'm going to wear that outfit and surprise the girls with it. Better yet, I think the office needs to sponsor a big Easter egg hunt every year over at Caldwell Park. And the Easter bunny can hand out a prize to whoever finds the golden egg. What do you think, Mags? Won't it be fun?"

Maggie hadn't bothered to answer. She knew no matter what she thought, once Hazel got an idea, there was no stopping her. And this idea meant that all the agents at Red Mountain Realty would have to spend all day Easter at the park, helping with the Easter egg hunt, and she would have to listen to the girls complain about it off and on for the next two weeks. It was a lot of work hiding all those eggs, but

Hazel was right. The Easter egg hunt did turn out to be a lot of fun, and the Easter bunny handing out the prizes was always the highlight. But now, with Hazel gone, Easter was just another day.

Hazel always used to say, "There's not enough darkness in the entire universe to snuff out the light of just one little candle." It was the first time that Maggie had ever known her to be wrong. Without Hazel, the world had suddenly gotten very dark. Maggie sighed and got up from her desk and went home to another TV dinner and another long night, waiting for her first open house on Sunday.

Officially on the Market

November 23, 2008

*F*ortunately the open house went well. the attendees were mostly neighbors and old friends of the Daltons who were curious to see it again. They all had fond memories of being at Crestview at one time or another when they were children. Maggie heard a lot of stories about Edward Crocker from the older ones who had met him. By all accounts, he'd been a shy man but well liked. One older woman shook her head and smiled. "My mother said every girl in Birmingham had high hopes of becoming Mrs. Edward Crocker, but the sly fox was never caught. He was one of those confirmed bachelors, not that he didn't like the ladies. Mother said he was very good friends with a lot of the married ladies in town. And, of course, he absolutely adored his sister, Edwina. They say that no matter how busy he was, every June, without fail, Edward sailed to Europe and spent three months visiting Edwina at her home in London."

Later, an older man in a wheelchair came through Crestview and said he had grown up in a house down the hill. He remembered Edward Crocker as being very fond of children. He said when he was boy, Mr. Crocker would let him and all his brothers and sisters ride their ponies all over the property and sent them wonderful presents every Christmas. The more Maggie heard about Edward that day, the more curious she became.

So after everybody left, she went back to the library and looked at the portrait again. This time, she realized what it was about his eyes that she hadn't noticed before. There was a strange sadness there, almost as if he was longing for something he couldn't have. Maggie related to that. "But what was it?" she wondered. Edward Crocker had everything in the world a man could want: money and power and Crestview. Even so, he looked lonely. He had not been an only child. He had a sister, so she wondered **who** it was he was lonely for. Had he been disappointed in love? Had someone broken his heart?

The longer she looked at his face, the more she wished she could have known him.

Crestview

Birmingham, 1935

$\mathcal{E}$very afternoon, after a hard day's work running the family business, Edward Crocker, like his father, Angus, before him, would sit out on the stone terrace until all the lights of downtown Birmingham started to come on one by one, sparkling like liquid jewels that twinkled and danced for as far as the eye could see. He sat and watched the cars as they snaked around the mountain like a chain of moving tiny glowing rubies, and it always pleased him. He had no art in the home, except the oil portrait over the mantel in the library, but unlike his father, Edward loved music and, when he entertained, would often hire a string quartet to play out on the terrace. On those summer nights, people said they could hear the faint sound of music playing all the way down the mountain and into the valley below.

Crestview was the only home Edward had ever

known, and as a young boy, he had played among the workers and stonemasons his father had hired to build it. He was happy on the mountain. There was, of course, that one great secret of his life, but as hard as it was to bear, he did have sister, Edwina, in London, and he had Crestview. And no matter how much noise and hustle and bustle in the city below, it was always quiet that high up on the mountain. All that could be heard was the far-off train whistle and the night birds in his vast gardens.

When his father, Angus Crocker, passed away at ninety-two, his last wishes were that he be taken back home and buried in Scotland. But having been raised in Alabama, Edward wanted to be buried at Crestview. He loved his home, and when he was out of town, he left standing instructions: "The home is to be lit with electric light from sundown to sunup, and the gardens are to be maintained per my instructions."

Twice a year, Edward opened up his home and gardens to all of his employees and always had presents for the children. A shy man, he observed the festivities from a chair in the attic. It had been very pleasant to watch all the children playing in the gardens below.

In 1928, little Ethel Louise Tatum, long before she became Ethel Clipp, had been taken up to Crestview for a Christmas party and, at one point, had looked up and waved at the man in the upstairs window, and he had waved back. But she didn't remember it. The only thing she remembered was the present she received. All the boys got toy trains, and the girls were given dolls. She would rather have had the train; only eight years old and already a malcontent.

Later as Maggie walked around Crestview turning off lights and closing all the drapes, Babs Bingington was across town (recuperating from yet another face-lift) sitting up in her bed, with her head wrapped in bandages, and squinting at her laptop computer, reading an email from the spy she had sent to Maggie's open house. And if she could have she would have smiled.

"No principals. Just lookie-loos and neighbors."

Just as Babs had thought. That old dog of a house would never sell; certainly not before Christmas. She didn't have to do a thing now. She'd wait and call the lawyer in New York after the first of the year with another proposal he'd be a fool to turn down.

The next morning, some eighty years after her first visit to Crestview, Ethel Clipp still had complaints. When Maggie came in the door, she started in: "I am so upset, I could just have a flying fit. You are not going to believe this."

"What?"

"Saturday, I went to the loveliest wedding over at

the Church of the Advent, and every one of the bridesmaids had tattoos and so did the bride. Can you believe it? Pretty young blond girls with tattoos. In my day, nice girls wouldn't even date a boy who had a tattoo. What are they thinking? And to make matters worse, the groom had a head full of dreadlocks, and he isn't even black. Can you imagine what the world is going to be like fifty years from now? A bunch of old ladies sitting around playing bridge with tattoos all over their big fat arms. I mean, Jesus Christ, who wants a grandmother with a tattoo? And I remember when boys used to be clean-cut."

"Me too," said Brenda.

"Now they all want to look scruffy. It was that TV show, **Miami Vice,** that did it. Since then, nobody shaves anymore. I swear to God, people are so stupid. Something becomes a fad, and everybody does it. What happened to the individual? I wouldn't be surprised if a show about nudists was a hit, and the next day, everybody in America stopped wearing clothes."

Brenda laughed. "Well, if that happened, I sure don't want to see it. I don't even like to look at myself naked, much less strangers."

Ethel made a face. "I'll tell you one damn thing. If that happens, and people start jogging in the nude with their altogethers dangling in the wind, I'm out of here."

Time on Her Hands
Friday, November 28, 2008

Thanksgiving came and went, and still no sale of Crestview. There were a few people that seemed interested, but nothing concrete. But every day that went by, sitting in the house, looking at his portrait, Maggie became more and more intrigued with Edward Crocker. Not having a plan for the future or watching the news, Maggie was finding out that between showings at Crestview, she had a lot of free time on her hands with nothing to do. Finally, one afternoon, she went down to the Birmingham Public Library and began doing a little research on Edward Crocker. She started looking up old newspaper articles on microfilm.

Most of the coverage was about business, but she found a few mentions of Edward in several articles. An interesting one came from the **Birmingham News,** in 1933.

Dapper and neat, with a razor-sharp wit, Edward Crocker is an avid golfer. As friends say, "He is not too long off the tee, but his short game has devastated many an opponent." While visiting Birmingham, legendary golf champion Bobby Jones was challenged by Edward at a hundred dollars a hole. Jones later declared, "We played a ding-dong of a game. I remember thinking how blamed stubborn he was. I was shooting pretty good, but this little fellow kept sticking and sticking, and every time I made the least slip, he won a hole from me." When a reporter asked Mr. Crocker if he intended to keep the money he'd won, he answered in the affirmative. "Indeed I do; after all, sir, I am a Scot."

Edward looked small and somewhat delicate in his photographs, but he was no weakling where business was concerned. Maggie read accounts of his stance in the thirties against the large influx of people who had been sent to Alabama to try to infiltrate and unionize his workers. In 1932, Edward had been photographed standing in front of one of his mines, holding a rifle, and underneath, he was quoted:

"I pay well, and I take care of my workers. Any Bolsheviks that come sneaking around bothering my men, I will personally chase them back to Russia. This is an American company. No slackers, no Bolsheviks. An honest day's pay for an honest day's work."

From what she read, he seemed to have been a tough but fair man.

Although some companies in Magic City have reported rumblings of unrest, the workers at the Crocker mines have been immune to outside influences. With a first-rate company hospital and top-notch schools for the children and adult education for those who want it and free home nurse care for new mothers, Mr. Crocker's workers have no complaints and have sent the trouble-makers packing.

Most of Edward's workers were poor sharecroppers who had come to town looking for work, or immigrant Greeks, Italians, or Poles who had ridden steerage to get there and had been assured a chance to move up in the company if they worked hard enough. All the workers seemed to like and respect him. As Maggie read on, she saw that many articles had been written about his business affairs, but almost nothing about Edward's social life. She started looking in some old society columns for any mention, and luckily, she was able to find a few. One, from the **Birmingham News** on June 19, 1932, was especially intriguing.

MAGIC CITY SOCIETY

BY CALEB KINSAUL

Birmingham's bachelor millionaire Edward Crocker's reluctance to be drawn to the altar is legendary; however, his appreciation for the fairer sex is also well known and reflected in this sentiment: "At the end of a long day, I prefer to see a pretty face across the table and leave business behind."

Mr. Crocker's friends and business associates speak of him warmly: "a grand little chap and a good and loyal pal in time of need." His numerous lady friends, by all accounts, find him attentive and delightful company. But so far, none have come away with a wedding ring. This has surely disappointed many a Birmingham belle gone on to marry another, but all have remained friends and received generous and lavish gifts on the occasion of their weddings. When queried about his famed bachelorhood, he has this to say: "I fear a lady would find me quite inadequate as husband material. I already have three wives: iron, coal, and steel. It would not be fair to ask a lady to play fourth fiddle."

And from the same newspaper in 1933:

Mr. Edward Crocker has left our fair city to embark on his yearly sail to England to visit his sister, Miss Edwina Crocker, who, I am told on the very best of accounts, is the toast of London society.

The more Maggie read, the more she gleaned that Edward had been unusually devoted to his sister and had left the business he seemed to love to spend three months in London with her every year. But what red-blooded man would devote so much time to his sister? People who visited Crestview had remarked that the only photographs he kept in his bedroom were of his sister. In an interview, he had once said, "My sister is my dearest friend and best companion." One article quoted his sister, Edwina, as having said to a London **Times** reporter, "My brother is as fine a man as any on this earth; there is none closer and dearer to me than my own beloved brother, Edward; our hearts and minds think as one."

Oh dear, Maggie thought. That was pretty close to saying something was going on between them. But then, considering the flowery language of the times, it was hard to know. Twins have a different relationship than just regular siblings. Still, something was strange. If they had been so devoted, then why had she never come to visit him in Alabama? Why did he always go there? Another mystery.

As she scrolled through the papers, Maggie found a few more photographs of him, but none taken with his sister, as she had hoped. He was usually standing in a group of other men. She could see he was a small man, but still very nice-looking, with a kind face. She could understand why the ladies had been so interested in him, and from everything she had heard, he had obviously liked women and had been very fond of children, and yet, he had never married. But why? It was a puzzle. There were only three good reasons she could think of:

1. He had been impotent.
2. He was a secret homosexual.

3. He was in love with his sister.
4. ?????????????????????????

Of course, from everything Maggie had read so far, the twin sister had never married either. Maybe she was making far too much of it. Still, it did seem odd.

Miss Edwina Crocker

London, England, 1920

Nurse Lettie Ross had gone ahead to England and opened the house in Mayfair for Edward and Edwina's visit. She had arranged Edwina's dresses in order and laid out the matching jewelry. Miss Edwina was particular about color, but never liked to waste her time having to mix and match her evening attire. Edwina was always happy to be in London, but one day, there was a particular excitement in the air.

At Buckingham Palace, Miss Edwina Crocker had just been presented to Queen Mary, also a lady of proud Scottish ancestry. A string quartet played as she descended the stairs, in a white dress, wearing three white feathers, having just received the title of Lady Edwina Crocker, due to her brother Edward's enormous contributions to England during the war.

Thanks to America, where one had the opportunity to rise above one's class, a member of a family who had once been thirled serfs now stood in line at a royal reception in her honor. As Edwina smiled and received guests, she wondered what all those poor men, women, and children of her family would have thought if they could see her standing there today. Could they even have dreamed it? Of course, there had been tremendous personal sacrifices for both Edward and Edwina, but still. "Oh, what a lovely day."

Although Edwina Crocker's home was on the north coast of Scotland and her brother, Edward Crocker, lived in Alabama, every year, they always spent three months together in London in a magnificent townhome Edward had purchased. Edwina loved to visit the city, and Edward loved to spoil his sister and cater to her every whim.

Whereas Edward was a shy and private man and, while in London, only came out for special occasions, usually having to do with business, his sister was quite the opposite. Edwina, famous for her beautiful clothes and quick wit, enjoyed a whirl of social activities. An invitation to her Sunday afternoon salon was the envy of all London. Noël Coward, Gertrude Lawrence, and Beatrice Lillie were among her many friends. Although not a great beauty, she had a bright mind, and men found her irresistible. Flirtatious by nature, she'd had numerous love affairs, some with quite powerful men, but like her elusive brother, she'd never married. When asked about it, she laughed it off, saying, "I'm waiting to meet a man as kind and as compassionate as my dear brother, Edward, and alas, I'm still waiting." This was not good news to the array of hopeful suitors who would have been more than happy to marry into the Crocker family. It was rumored that her brother's holdings were now up into the millions, and some disgruntled suitors began to wonder if Edwina had specific instructions from her brother not to marry. Some even suspected that Edward didn't trust her to be left alone in London without supervision, because when he departed London, Edwina departed as well.

They had heard that the father, Angus, had been ruthless, but it seemed that now the brother would go to any lengths to protect his fortune, even depriving his own sister of the joys of marriage and children. This was a sentiment felt on both sides of the Atlantic. When several of his eligible male friends from Birmingham had shown up in London on business and requested an introduction to Edwina, Edward had declined the request politely but firmly. However, as protected as Edwina's life was, it did not stop her from her fun with the men she fancied in London. She once said to a friend about her numerous affairs, "I know it's quite scandalous, but I have to make hay while the sun shines. All I have is my precious three months in London, and the rest of the year, I might as well be living in a nun's cell."

Although she clearly enjoyed the company of men, Edwina was quite a champion of women's rights. At a reception for the great Irish playwright George Bernard Shaw, she quipped, "In your delightful play **Pygmalion,** is it not true that you ask the question, Why can't a woman be more like a man?" "Yes," he said. "Quite true." "But my dear Mr. Shaw, my question to you is, Why can't a **man** be more like a woman?" The great man laughed and had to good-naturedly agree. Such public outspokenness from a woman of lesser means, or one not so closely connected to such a powerful man as her brother, might not have been so well tolerated.

While Edwina and Edward had always lived a protected life of privilege, their Scottish nurse, Lettie, had told them firsthand stories from her own childhood of how women of a poorer class were treated, and later, Edwina had observed it with her own eyes when she had visited the workhouses and tenements. Because of her enormous influence on her brother, Edward's eyes had been opened as well, and he had responded in kind.

Back home in America, Edward's Birmingham banker noticed that thousands of dollars were being donated to many female causes; one check alone for fifty thousand dollars was sent to Margaret Sanger in New York, a radical famous for promoting birth control. The banker later confided to an associate,

"I don't know who she is, but he has some woman in his ear, telling him what to do."

He did indeed. What the banker did not know was that both brother and sister had an immediate and personal interest in safe and effective birth control.

The Humdrum Motel

Friday, December 5, 2008

*I*f Brenda had a weakness, other than ice cream and doughnuts, it was wigs. She loved wigs—not just any wigs, but good, expensive wigs. She didn't shop at Miss Delilah's House of Wigs, like her older sister did, or at Wow Wigs out at the mall; she ordered her wigs online from ExclusivelyYoursWigs .com. She had the Tina Turner wig, the Diahann Carroll wig, and this morning, she came in to work wearing her new Beyoncé wig, which she was not happy with. "It looked better in the ad," she said.

At around ten A.M., Brenda came into Maggie's office and whispered, so that Ethel wouldn't hear her, "I need you to take me somewhere at lunchtime, okay?"

"All right, where?"

"I have an appointment with a psychic healer."

"Oh, no. Not another one."

"Yes, but this one's from the Philippines, and he's only going to be here for one day."

Maggie shook her head. "Oh Lord, where is this one going to be?"

"At the old Humdrum Motel, out on old Highway 8."

"Oh my God, honey, why do you want to waste your good money? You know those people are fakes."

Brenda said, "No, they're not! Tonya had a tumor removed last year."

"Brenda, that man had a chicken gizzard up his sleeve and just told her it was a tumor. You told me that yourself, remember?"

"Well, I could have been wrong . . . Whatever he did, it worked—she doesn't have a tumor anymore."

"How do you know she had one in the first place?"

"She might have; she said she felt a hundred percent better."

"Are you sure you want to go out there? I don't think it looks good for a reputable real estate agent to be seen going to some charlatan like that."

"Nobody is going to see us."

"All right. But why do you need me to take you?"

"Because I don't think I should drive after surgery. I want to see if he can help me with my kidney stones."

"I thought you were going to use the power of positive thinking on them."

"I am . . . this is part of it."

"Have you told Robbie where you're going?"

"No, she doesn't believe in alternative medicine."

"Brenda, I don't think this would be considered alternative. This is more on the hocus-pocus side."

"Oh, come on, Maggie, please. It will only take a little while."

"Well, of course, I'll take you, but promise me you won't tell Robbie I took you out there. I don't want her mad at me."

"I promise."

Later, Maggie sat in the parking lot of the Humdrum Motel, waiting on Brenda and flipping through the Multiple Listing Service book to pass the time. Forty-five minutes later, Brenda came out of Room 432 carrying a small brown paper sack and grinning from ear to ear. She opened the car door, announcing, "I'm cured! Here they are."

She opened the bag and pulled out a small glass jar, full of what looked to Maggie suspiciously like gravel from the driveway of the Humdrum Motel, but she didn't say anything.

"And it didn't hurt at all!" said Brenda.

"What are you going to do with them?"

"Keep them."

"Where?"

"Oh, I don't know; maybe in my medicine cabinet. Why?"

"Well, if it were me, I'd throw them out. What if Robbie finds them?"

Brenda thought about it and then took out her cell phone and called her older sister, Tonya. As soon as she answered Brenda said, "Listen, this may or may not happen, but if Robbie ever calls you about a jar of kidney stones, tell her they're yours. Okay?" And then she hung up. Five seconds later, Brenda's phone rang. After a moment, she said, "You don't need to know why, just tell her," and hung up again.

Maggie said, "I wish I had a sister I could boss around."

Brenda laughed. "Well, I would give you Robbie and Tonya, but nobody would believe it."

After she dropped Brenda and her "kidney stones" off, instead of going right home, Maggie changed her mind, and made another trip down to the library. When she got there, she sat down and started to look at microfilm again.

Maggie scrolled forward in time and found a January 16, 1939, headline:

EDWARD CROCKER FEARED
LOST AT SEA

Three days after the death of his beloved sister, Birmingham business tycoon Edward Crocker has been reported lost at sea in what appears to have been a sailing accident. The accident occurred off the northern coast of Scotland, where his sister was buried.

Then another, dated April 28, 1939:

EDWARD CROCKER OFFICIALLY DEAD

After two weeks of extensive search, officials say all hope of finding missing Edward Crocker has been abandoned. A family spokesperson in Scotland said that Edward was last seen on the morning of his sister's funeral, when he announced that he was taking his boat for a short spin to "clear his head." As he was known as a master sailor, some speculate that foul weather may have been a factor, in that neither boat nor lone passenger was retrieved. All Birmingham mourns the passing of this great industrialist and philanthropist.

Edward had died just three days after his sister. Maggie had been guessing about his being in love with his sister, but now she began to wonder if she had been right, and whether his death really had been an accident or if Edward had been so despondent over losing his sister that he had done exactly what Maggie was planning to do. Another clue that he had been in love with Edwina.

Maggie kept looking, but she did not have any luck finding anything more about the Crocker twins. Just as she was about to get up and leave the library, she saw Miss Pitcock walking over. Miss Pitcock had worked in the library archives forever, and Maggie had known her since she was in high school. Miss Pitcock asked her if she needed any help finding anything. Maggie told her that she was doing research on Crestview and on Edward Crocker and his sister, Edwina, in particular. Miss Pitcock's eyes lit up behind her thick glasses. She told Maggie she would be delighted to help, that anything about old Birmingham history was her specialty.

Miss Pitcock was one of the unsung heroines of the world; she had quietly devoted her entire life to helping thousands of struggling teenagers (like Maggie) find their way through the maze of the library archives, and now she was doing it again. God bless her, thought Maggie.

After that, true to her word, Miss Pitcock sent Maggie a little information each day. She had found several photos of Edwina Crocker in a few English newspapers. There was one of her standing alone and several of her in a crowd, but never a photo of Edward and Edwina together, as Maggie had hoped; body language could tell so much. Then

Maggie began to wonder why they had never been photographed together. They had spent so much time together in London. That seemed odd. What were they trying to hide? Had they just been un-usually close or had it been something else? And why had neither of them ever married? She couldn't tell Edwina's coloring from the black-and-white photos in the paper, but she certainly looked attractive. It was a mystery all right, and as the days went by, Maggie began to feel just like Nancy Drew in **The Secret of the Scottish Twins.**

A Bad Day
Tuesday, December 16, 2008

Maggie had really been hoping for a quick sale. but as the days dragged by, she was becoming more and more concerned. She'd had her hopes up a few weeks ago, when a nice woman who had come to an open house had loved Crestview, but today, when the husband came to see it, he had not liked the floor plan, so that was that. And to make a bad day even worse, when she got home that afternoon, Miss Pitcock had just faxed her some new information that had completely blown a hole through her entire theory about Edward Crocker and his sister, Edwina. Miss Pitcock had traced the Crocker-Sperry family's records all the way back to Scotland and had found a photocopy of Edward's birth certificate. There had only been one child born on that date.

To Maggie's surprise, there was no sister at all.

According to the records, Angus Crocker and his

wife had only had one child, a male named Edward. Then **who** was that woman in London, the one Edward claimed was his sister? Was it his mistress? Edward had supported her. But why hadn't he married her? It made no sense. She looked at the photos again. To her, they looked exactly like twins. They **had** to be related in some way. Maybe she had been a cousin. But that wouldn't make any sense either. If she was a cousin, why not say so? Maggie was completely stumped. Oh God, now she had a headache. She went to look for an aspirin and realized she had thrown them all out a few weeks ago. So she put a cold washcloth on her forehead and lay down on the couch.

While Maggie hadn't expected this news about Edwina, she guessed she really shouldn't be surprised. It was the story of her life. She had also expected that Hazel would live forever, but she hadn't.

Easter morning, about six years ago, the entire staff at Red Mountain Realty was already over in the park, hiding all the Easter eggs, and after church, Maggie had gone home with Hazel to help her get into her bunny outfit. Later, driving to the park, Hazel had been very excited. "Oh, Mags, don't you just love Easter? Christmas is great, too, but just think, every Easter, we get a chance to rise up and start all over again. And even when you're dead, you still keep going. Isn't that great? Isn't that wonderful?"

After another few minutes, she said, "You know,

Mags, I've been thinking, since this is my favorite
holiday, I've decided that I want to be buried in my
bunny outfit, okay? Will you see to that for me?"
Maggie was taken aback. It was the first time she
had ever heard Hazel mention anything pertaining
to sickness or death, but she said, "Well, of course,
Hazel, whatever you want, though you're a long
way off from being buried."

"Oh, I know that," Hazel said. "I'm planning on
becoming the oldest living midget in the world."

"You are?"

"Yes, and you know me, if I set my mind to do it,
I will."

Of course, three months later, when Hazel had
died so suddenly, it had been difficult when Maggie
and Ethel had shown up at Johns-Ridout's Funeral
Parlor with a bunny suit on a hanger, but last wishes
are last wishes.

The day of Hazel's funeral had been a real revelation. They had expected that all the real estate people in town and all of her friends would be there, but
a good hour before the service was to begin, the
church was packed to the rafters with people they
had never seen before. The governor and the mayor
were there, as well as all the local news media; repre-
sentatives from clubs, organizations, theater groups,
the fire department, the police department, and all
the charities she had been involved with; and girls
who had received scholarships from her. Plus, members from chapters of the Little People of America

from all over the country had shown up. They said everybody at the Birmingham airport had nearly had a fit as each plane landed and all these little people came piling off by the busloads, all going to Hazel's funeral. So many people came that hundreds had to stand outside the church and listen to the service on loudspeakers. As the preacher said, "It was a big turnout for such a little lady." Even Ethel, who had known her better than anyone, had been surprised at the number of people's lives Hazel had touched. That day, they heard stories about money she had lent and time she had devoted to people and causes she had never mentioned.

Poor Little Harry had been completely devastated by the loss. He had not even been able to come up with something for her tombstone. What could you possibly say about someone who had been your entire life? Ethel stepped in and took over and said as simply as possible:

HAZEL ELAINE WHISENKNOTT
1924–2003
GONE BUT NOT FORGOTTEN

Little Harry left for Milwaukee two days after the funeral and never came back to Birmingham again. The office kept in touch through his family, but they said all he did now was sit in his room. Maggie understood how he felt. They all missed that three-foot-four dynamo ball of energy, that silly little funhouse of a human being who had kept them amused and entertained, who had pumped them up, lifted their spirits, driven them crazy, but, most of all, had made them feel special. Hazel had been that one in a million who seemed to have come out of the womb and hit the ground running; one of those rare human beings who only comes along once in a blue moon.

Brenda Reflects
Friday, December 19, 2008

Driving back to the office from lunch, Brenda was in a rare reflective mood. She said, "You know, Maggie, when I was young, I used to want to be white, but not anymore. Ask me why."

"Why?"

"I'm not sure."

"Then why did you want me to ask you?"

"Well . . . because . . . I'm trying to figure it out. It didn't happen during the Black Is Beautiful thing or when Obama was elected; it's even more recent than that."

"Really."

"Yes, and I'm thinking that Oprah and Queen Latifah had a lot to do with it . . . I mean, if they don't mind being big and black . . . then I don't mind, you know?"

"I can understand that."

"And guess what else?"

"What?"

"I'm beginning to like being a little plump; what do you think about that?"

"I think it's great. You know all that's important is that you're healthy."

They drove a few more blocks.

"Maggie, I never told anybody this, but during the sixties, when all the marches and sit-ins were going on, with all the name-calling and the misery we had to go through, I sometimes used to wonder if it was even worth it. But not anymore."

"No?"

"No. I feel a lot better about everything now, because if you think about it, I'm really kind of in style these days. Lord, who would have ever thought it, but I guess that's what happens when you live long enough. Just think, not more than fifty years ago, most black women in Birmingham couldn't hope to be more than somebody's maid, and now one is getting ready to run for mayor."

"That's right," said Maggie. "The world has changed."

"Yeah, it's hard for me to believe but . . . I guess now with Obama being elected, black is the new white."

"It would seem so, honey."

Brenda then looked out the window and sighed, "I just wish I could get back all those years when I felt so bad about myself. I just wish . . ." She didn't finish her sentence, and tears rolled down her face. She said, "Life is so hard sometimes."

Maggie reached over and put her hand on Brenda's arm. "I'm sorry you had to go through that."

"Oh, Maggie, you just don't know how bad it feels to have people who don't even know you hate you, and for something you had nothing to do with."

Maggie started to tell Brenda something that she had never told anyone, but decided not to. But she did know how it felt. She knew exactly how it felt.

Brenda was right, of course; people of color were very much in style now, and as Ethel said, at the slow rate whites (particularly Presbyterians) were reproducing, she wouldn't be surprised if in fifty years, they would be the new minority. If that were to happen, Maggie wondered if there would be a White History Month on A&E to celebrate all the old customs and featuring native dishes like tomato aspic, chocolate mousse, and dinner rolls. She hoped they would get their own month, or at least a week.

Chicago

1975

෧

Brenda, like everyone else who had fought seg-
regation, still had bad memories of things that
had happened, not directly to her, but to other
members of her family and to friends. After college,
full of idealism, she had moved to Chicago to work
as a teacher in the inner city. But most of her students raised in the projects at Cabrini-Green had
seen too much too soon, and by the time she got
them, she looked out on a room full of dead eyes.
She tried so hard to reach them and thought she
had helped a few of the girls but then, a few years
later, she would drive by and see them working on a
street corner, strung out on drugs. It was a heart-
breaking experience. Having grown up in a nice
middle-class neighborhood, she had not been prepared to deal with the harsh realities of kids who
had been raised in the tough ghettos of the North.
And that last year, when one of her students had

pulled a gun on her after she had refused to let her go out in the hall to hang out with her boyfriend, she'd known it was time to quit. Like a lot of her friends who had moved north, she missed home, and when things eased up, they all started coming back to Birmingham. It wasn't perfect. Just like everywhere else, there were still stupid people around, black and white. Unfortunately for Brenda, three of the stupid people happened to be her nephews Curtis, DeWayne, and Anthony.

When she was growing up, her heroes had been people like Sojourner Truth, Thurgood Marshall, and Martin Luther King, but the nephews had their walls plastered with pictures of their favorite rap stars. Every one with a police record a mile long.

At present, all three nephews were strutting around town, sporting gold chains and diamond earrings, wearing baseball hats perched sideways on top of do-rags, with their underwear sticking out of baggy pants. Their grandparents and parents had been college graduates, but all three had dropped out of high school at fifteen and now, between them, they couldn't string a sentence together. If they said, "You know what I'm sayin'" one more time, she would scream. Instead of going forward, they had gone backward.

She was so disgusted with them that she wouldn't let them come over to the house anymore. Thank God for Arthur, her other nephew. He had a good job in Atlanta with CNN, and her niece Sandra, Robbie's daughter, was majoring in history at Birmingham-Southern College. Sandra had a head on her shoulders. But the nephews were driving Brenda crazy. She wished all three had one neck and she had her hands around it right now. They might be fooling other people, but she knew darn well what they were up to. When she got elected mayor, one of the first things she was going to do was round up every dope dealer and pimp in town, black or white, and sling every one of them in jail. And if she had to build new jails to hold them all, she'd do that, too.

Although Birmingham had had a black mayor since 1979, she would be the first woman mayor, and it was about time. She had no doubt she would win. Hazel had assured her she could do anything she wanted, and Hazel was **never** wrong. And after she became mayor, she just might go on to become the first black governor. Some of her friends were still a little apprehensive about her getting too hopeful. They said, "Obama or not, this is still Alabama." Maybe if she had been beaten or, like her sister Tonya, had been knocked down by the fire hoses or thrown in jail, she might think differently. Those who had gone through the marches said she had never really had the real "black experience," and they could be right. But, sadly, she couldn't change the past. She had to think about the present. She wanted people to do better right now.

Of course, she was angry about what had happened in the past, and she hated with a passion how her ancestors got here. But selfishly, she was glad she was here now. She loved her home, and besides that, Brenda believed with all her heart that God had a special plan for her and she was exactly where she was supposed to be at the exact right time. And who knew? The way things were changing so fast, anything could happen. A black woman from Birmingham had already been America's secretary of state, and Regina Benjamin, a black woman from southern Alabama, had just been named surgeon general of the United States. As Hazel had said, where else in the world could a three-foot-four woman become a millionaire? Or a black woman like Oprah become a billionaire? Brenda couldn't help but be a little hopeful. But as always, progress had not come without a price.

Another Side to the Story

⌒

*I*n history books, the civil rights movement will always be viewed as a great triumph, but for those who lived through it, black or white, it was not easy.

The year Maggie was Miss Alabama, she arrived in Atlantic City for the Miss America Pageant, excited and hopeful. And as the days went by, she had reason to be hopeful. In the preliminary judging, she won first place in the evening gown competition, and after seeing her for a few days, the press had already listed her as most likely to win.

Everybody had been so encouraging that when the time came to ride in the annual Miss America Parade down the boardwalk, Maggie was feeling on top of the world. It was a cool, crisp, September day, and hundreds of people had already lined up on both sides of the boardwalk, waiting for the parade to start. Every state had its own float, and alphabetically, the Miss Alabama float was always the first to appear, so naturally, they wanted it to make a big impression and be as beautiful as possible. The year Maggie was Miss Alabama, the float was particularly spectacular. A group of the top floral designers from all over the state had flown to Atlantic City the day before and had spent the last twenty-four hours decorating the Alabama float with bushels of Alabama cotton, magnolia, gardenia, dogwood, and azalea blossoms they'd had shipped in from all over the state. Then the entire float had been sprinkled with hundreds of silver stars, in keeping with their "Stars Fell on Alabama" theme song. That morning, they carefully placed her on the float and draped her white gown all around her throne and waved and cheered for her as the parade began. It was so exciting riding down the boardwalk, seeing all the people lined up on either side of the boardwalk and all the little souvenir and saltwater taffy shops. Her float had not traveled more than a block and a half when it happened. Maggie did not see who threw the first bucket, but she heard the gasps of the crowd, and when she turned to look, the contents of the second bucket of mud hit her on the side of her face. At first, it was simply such a shock, and she was not sure what had happened; it wasn't until a moment later that she looked down and saw her lovely white gown splattered with mud and garbage. But the float kept moving down the boardwalk, and she couldn't get off. She didn't know what to do, so she just sat there through the entire parade, trying not to cry, trying to keep smiling, hoping that maybe people wouldn't notice that her gown was filthy and that her hair was matted with mud.

Fortunately, the incident was kept out of the papers. Nobody, particularly Atlantic City or the Miss America Pageant, wanted bad publicity. "It was just a few crazy people trying to cause trouble," they said. It had only happened to her because Alabama's was the first float to go by. Everyone assured her it was just a fluke, a prank not personally aimed at her. But that was not the end of it. On the night of the pageant, when her name was called, it started slowly and quietly, and then as she walked around the runway, the boos and hisses became louder. Evidently, this had been a planned protest against the state. People had been strategically placed all around the auditorium, so no matter where she was on the runway, she would be sure to hear them. Each time she appeared onstage, she heard them, and later, during her talent number on the harp, the sounds of the booing rattled her so that her hands shook badly, and she missed a few notes and almost lost her place several times.

Later that night, after the pageant was over, Maggie could tell by the way her mother and her chaperones looked at her that they had also heard the boos and hissing and were anxious and worried that she might have heard them, but she pretended she hadn't. However, the judges must have heard them, because they had taken an unusually long time in reaching a decision that night. The next day, a lot of people in the press said she should have won. Some said she didn't win that year because she was from Birmingham. But nobody would ever know for sure. Everybody, including her mother, said that they had not even noticed that she had skipped a few notes in her talent number. Maggie knew, though, and she would never forgive herself for disappointing everyone.

However, a few days later, when she returned home from Atlantic City, hundreds of people met the train and cheered for her, just as if she had won. Alabama may have lacked a lot of things that other states had, but loyalty had never been one of them.

The mudslingers and the booers and hissers who had traveled to Atlantic City had been terribly disappointed that their actions had not made the papers, but no matter, they were still very pleased with themselves. They had made a statement.

'Twas the Day before Christmas

Wednesday, December 24, 2008

At ten A.M., Ethel was sitting in her living room in her lavender chenille robe, sipping eggnog and opening her last batch of Christmas cards, grumbling out loud to her two cats. When she read the card from one of her nieces, she said, "Damn it, I don't want anybody donating money in my name to some charity. I want a present, and look at this. Thirty-seven Christmas cards and not one says, 'Merry Christmas.' It's all 'Have a Joyous Season,' 'Happy Holidays,' or some such nonsense. It's **Christmas,** for God's sake! Well, you can thank the goddamn ACLU for that," she added as she continued throwing the cards away, one after another, in the trash can beside her, until she opened one from a friend in her handbell choir that actually had "Merry Christmas" on it. "Well, finally," she said, and she stood up and placed it on the mantel with the others. A couple of minutes later, she got up and put her new welcome mat out at the front door:

PEOPLE BRINGING TIDINGS OF JOY,
KINDLY STEP BEHIND THOSE
BEARING PRESENTS.

Across town, Maggie was getting ready to go to work. Although December was known as the "dead as a doornail" month for real estate, she had decided to hold the house open through the holidays. She had hired a crew to come and hang lights, and she'd had all the hedges trimmed neat and clean. And a week ago, she had hung a lovely evergreen Christmas wreath with a big red bow on the door. She'd placed little sprigs of holly on all the fireplace mantels and around the mirrors in the entrance hall and had Christmas music playing all through the house. Every day, after she lit a big roaring fire in the living room fireplace, she opened all the curtains upstairs and downstairs, and then she and the house stood ready, waiting in anticipation, just hoping for the right person to come in and see how wonderful it was. But day after day, almost no one came. Poor Crestview. It tried to be bright and cheery all day, and each night, Maggie could almost feel its disappointment as she closed the curtains and turned off the lights. It was the same today. She had suspected that the day before Christmas would not be very good for an open house, but she had hoped.

She had just finished closing the last curtain and was about to turn off the hall lights when her phone rang. It was Brenda.

"Are you sure you don't want to come over here and be with us tonight? Robbie said she'll come pick you up and take you home."

"Oh, honey, that's so sweet, but really, I just want to stay home by myself tonight."

It was her last Christmas Eve on earth, and for once, instead of making up excuses, she had actually told the truth. It was a start. Too late, of course. But as usual, that night, she started to worry that she had hurt Brenda and Robbie's feelings. Lord, it never ended. If you did tell the truth or if you didn't, there were always consequences. Human interaction was difficult at best.

Merry Christmas, Maggie

Thursday, December 25, 2008

At around ten on Christmas morning, Maggie had just finished eating two pop-up waffles off a flimsy paper plate and was now sitting in the kitchen going over figures. She hated to do it, but she had no choice. After the holidays, she was going to have to approach Mrs. Dalton about lowering the asking price. The phone rang.

"Hey, Maggie, it's David Lee. Merry Christmas!"

"Well, hello, David. How are you?"

"Listen . . . I hate to bug you at home on Christmas, but do you have any offers on Crestview yet?"

Maggie winced. She hoped she wasn't getting fired. She said as cheerfully as possible, "No, we had a few people interested, but nothing solid as yet."

"Well, Mitzi and I have been talking about it, and we think we're just going to go ahead and buy it ourselves, if that's okay with you. It would be an all-cash offer. Full price, of course. Both of us grew up right down the street, so it will be like coming home, moving back into the old neighborhood."

Then Mitzi jumped on the line: "Hey, Maggie . . . how are you, darling? Isn't this just wonderful? I'm thrilled to pieces! We've got to run, but I can't wait to see you."

David came back on the phone. "We won't keep you, but I'll call you at the office on Monday, and we can work out all the details."

This was the best Christmas present she could have received; Maggie couldn't think of two better people to buy Crestview. Now she could leave, knowing she had saved Crestview from the wreck-ing ball. She wanted to jump for joy; it was a perfect ending, except for one thing: she had been so ex-cited when they had called, she had totally forgot-ten about the little problem in the attic.

Oh, no. Should she tell them or not? If she did tell them, she might lose the sale, and if she didn't, could she live with herself? Selling it to a stranger without disclosing what had been found in the attic was bad enough, but David and Mitzi were friends; she would be just horrified if they were to somehow find out about it later and think she had been trying to deceive them.

Maggie spent the rest of the day going back and forth about what to do. She thought long and hard about how she would feel if the shoe were on the other foot.

She didn't think she would mind about the skeleton, but it was the deception that was the issue. She went to bed in turmoil and agonized all night.

The next morning, she sat down and made the dreaded phone call.

"David, it's Maggie."

"Hello!"

"Listen, David, before we go any further with Crestview, there's something you and Mitzi should know."

"Uh-oh. Is someone else bidding on it?"

"No. It's not that . . . It's, well, when we first got the listing, my partner, Brenda, and I were up in the attic, and we found a little something."

"Termites? Oh, I expected that."

"No. Not termites. We had a termite inspection, and it's really in good shape as far as termites go. It was uh . . . something else . . ."

"Mold?"

"No, no mold or structural problems. It's just that, when we went up to the attic, we found two big steamer trunks that hadn't been opened since 1946, and so we opened them. At first, we thought it was a bunch of old clothes, but . . . when we started looking through them, we . . . well, we unfortunately found a few old bones."

"Bones?"

"Yes. Well, more than a few really, uh . . . It was

a man's skeleton. Hanging on a hanger. Of course, we got it out of the house right away, and nobody else knows about it, but I felt that I had to disclose that information, and if you want to withdraw your offer, I will certainly understand." She closed her eyes and held her breath and waited to hear his response.

"A **real** skeleton?"

"Yes. Of an unknown man. Found upstairs in the attic. In a trunk." Maggie held her breath again.

After a long moment, David said, "Oh, hell, Maggie, it doesn't matter to me. I'm not superstitious about those things."

"Really?"

"No. I don't see it as a problem."

"Well, I think you better talk it over with Mitzi and call me back."

"All right. I'll call you back."

An agonizing hour later, the phone rang. "Maggie, it's Mitzi! Listen, I just walked in the door, and David told me about your finding a skeleton up in the attic, and I think it's the most exciting thing I ever heard, don't you? A real mystery. Just like Nancy Drew."

"That's exactly what I thought," said Maggie. "Then you don't mind?"

"Mind? Oh, honey, you're so cute to worry, but as I said to David, with so many skeletons in both our families' closets, what's one more or less? And it will make perfectly wonderful cocktail conversations, don't you think? I'm just dying to find out who it is . . . aren't you? Grandmother said Mr. Crocker was kind of eccentric; maybe he collected skeletons. It could be somebody famous for all we know."

"Well . . . I hadn't thought about that, but yes, I guess so."

"Oh, Maggie, I just can't wait to get back home to Birmingham. I'm so happy about Crestview; I always loved it, and it's perfect for us until we go on out to St. Martin's and a wonderful house for David Jr. and his family when they come back. I know you probably think I'm silly, but I've already started dreaming about all the parties I'm going to throw."

No, Maggie did not think she was silly at all. She had done the same thing for years.

After Maggie hung up with Mitzi, she immediately picked up the phone again and dialed Brenda.

"Brenda? We just sold Crestview. Merry Christmas, and Happy New Year!"

"What?"

"David and Mitzi Lee called, and they want to buy it. All cash. Full price."

"You're kidding?"

"No, and Brenda, guess what else?"

"What?"

"They **want** the skeleton!"

"They do?"

"Yes."

"Oh, hooray!"

"In fact, Mitzi was just delighted about it; she thought it would make great cocktail conversation."

"Oh, hooray!" Brenda said again.

There were some things about white people she would never understand, but the main thing was, they had a sale at last.

Three days later, after all the papers had been FedEx'd to and from New York, and the deposit check had arrived, Maggie could hardly believe it. She had sold Crestview to a member of a good old Birmingham family, one she could trust would keep it intact, and the office had a nice commission. They had a thirty-day escrow, and if all went well, it meant that she could leave the day after the house closed, knowing that Crestview had been snatched out of the jaws of the Beast and was safe forever. Maggie had forgotten how wonderful it felt to feel so good, and just when she was getting ready to leave, too.

A Woman Scorned
Monday, December 29, 2008

On Monday, Babs Bingington was back at her office on her computer scrolling through the Multiple Listings and saw that as of this morning, Crestview had a "sale pending" on it. Goddamn it to hell. The bimbo has-been beauty queen had somehow managed to get an offer. She knew they were probably sitting over in the office right now, gloating and laughing at her, but she consoled herself. They might be laughing now, but they wouldn't be laughing for long.

For the past few years, she had been secretly negotiating with Hazel's widower's lawyers in Milwaukee and was just waiting for the day when Harry the dwarf finally kicked off or was deemed incompetent, whatever came first. Then she was going to buy Red Mountain Realty right out from under them and throw Miss Alabama out on her ear, along with the other two. A lot of real estate business owners were hurting, but not Babs. She had been very smart about her investments. About ten years ago, Babs had heard from one of her wealthy buyers about a money manager who only handled a few ex-clusive clients and was doing very well for them. At first, he had politely declined to take her as a client. But Babs would not take no for an answer. As usual, she had pushed and shoved her way in and had even pressured his wife to intervene on her behalf and had almost blackmailed the poor man into taking her on. As a consequence, she had done **very** well in the market and was now ready to make her big move. Not as soon as she had hoped, but as Babs liked to say, "Revenge is a dish best served cold."

Babs was right. Ethel and Brenda **were** delighted that Maggie had sold Crestview out from under her. But despite all Maggie's efforts, she began to feel guilty about stealing the listing. Yes, Babs was not a nice person, but still, what she had done had not been exactly ethical. When her part of the commis-sion came in, after she paid off her loan and the rest of her bills, she would send what was left to Babs. It wouldn't be the full commission, but it was at least something, and then she could go with a clear con-science.

A Blast from the Past

Monday, January 19, 2009

Although Crestview was sold, Maggie still had to hold open houses until escrow officially closed, to try to get a backup offer. Today, as Maggie was about to lock up the house and go home, she heard a man's voice in the hall.

"Hello. Anybody here? Maggie?"

The minute he said her name, she knew who it was, and her heart began to pound. She walked into the hall, and there he stood. When he saw her, he smiled and said, "It's your old decrepit boyfriend, come to say hello. How are you, Maggie?"

"Charles . . . I can't believe it's you."

"Oh, yes, it's me. Only with gray hair."

They hugged, and Maggie said, "Well. I'm just stunned, but what are you doing here? Oh, not **here,** but in Birmingham?"

"We had to put Dad out at St. Martin's, and I had to sign some things."

"Oh, I see . . ."

"I'm sorry to drop in on you unannounced like this, but I ran into Mrs. Dalton, and she said you'd be here today, so I thought I'd take a chance."

Maggie was so thrown at seeing Charles that she was at a loss for words. "Well, I'm just stunned," she repeated.

"Me, too," he said. "What happened, Maggie? Seems like I just left home a couple of years ago . . . but it's been over forty years, and I have a grown granddaughter. Do you believe it? But I swear to God, Maggie, you don't look a day older than the last time I saw you."

"You're sweet to say so, Charles, even if it isn't true, and you look just the same yourself. Can you come in and sit down?"

"I can't, I'm on my way to catch a plane; I just wanted to say hello . . ."

"Will you be coming back?"

"Oh sure, we all do eventually; I just don't know when. Mrs. Dalton told me that David and Mitzi are buying the place. I'm glad."

"Me, too."

They stood and chatted a little about old friends and how much Birmingham had changed over the years, both avoiding the obvious two elephants in the living room: the subject of his wife and why Maggie had wound up unmarried and selling real estate.

As she stood there looking at him today, she was

struck by something. With his blue eyes and sandy hair, Charles looked exactly like an older version of Tab Hunter, one of her all-time favorite movie stars. Why hadn't she noticed it before?

After a few more minutes of small talk, there was an awkward silence. Then Charles suddenly looked at her and said, "Oh, Maggie . . . you broke my heart, you know."

Tears immediately came to her eyes. "I know I did. I broke my own heart, too. I'm so sorry."

"I've always loved you, you know."

"Yes, I do. I do know."

They stood for a moment, not knowing what else there was to say. Then Charles finally said, "Well, I guess I'd better go."

Just then, a beautiful blond woman cracked open the door and stuck her head in. "Hello? May I come in?"

Charles looked embarrassed. "Sure, darling, I'm sorry."

Maggie had heard that he had married a beautiful blonde, but this woman was much younger than she'd expected (they always are). But Maggie was gracious and said, "Oh, please, come in." Charles put his arm around the woman and said, "Honey, this is Margaret; Maggie, this is Christine." Christine put her arm around his waist and smiled at her. "Are you the famous Margaret I've been hearing about all my life?"

Maggie was a bit flustered. "Well, I don't know."

"Daddy always told us he had dated Miss Alabama, but we never believed him. But I guess it's true. I'm so happy to meet you."

Then Maggie said, "Oh. **Oh!** You too, Christine."

"Daddy was a nervous wreck all the way up here, and now I know why. You are just as beautiful as he said you were."

Charles looked very uneasy, then glanced at his watch and said, "Well, come on, sweetie, we have to leave or we'll miss our plane."

Christine shook Maggie's hand. "It was wonderful to meet you. If you're ever anywhere near Lake Lugano, Switzerland, come and see us," she said as Charles pulled her out the door. "Promise?" she added.

"Yes, I promise," said Maggie.

"Bye, Maggie," Charles said.

"Goodbye, Charles."

Of course, she should have known Christine was his daughter when she smiled. As she watched them drive away, a wave of sadness flooded over her. If she hadn't been such a complete fool, that beautiful girl might have been her daughter.

As they drove away, Christine said, "What a beautiful lady. Was she as pretty as you remembered?"

"Yes."

She looked over at her father. "Dad, why are you blushing?"

"I'm not blushing."

"Yes, you are. I think you still like her. Did you ask her?"

"No."

"Did she have a wedding ring on?"

"No."

"Then why didn't you just ask her? If she's not married, and you're not married, why didn't you?"

"It's much more complicated than that. I'm sure she's probably seeing someone."

"It wouldn't hurt to ask, would it?"

"Well, we'll see. Maybe the next time I come back, I'll give her a call."

"All right. But I just hope you don't wait too long."

Ready to Leave (Again)

Saturday, January 31, 2009

Escrow on Crestview closed right on time. and a few days later when Babs received the check from Maggie for her half of the commission, Babs looked at it and thought what a complete idiot Maggie was. But she kept the check anyway.

Friday Maggie had taken Ethel and Brenda out to dinner at the Highlands Grill for a big celebration dinner. Now she was free of all obligations and could get on with her plan.

This morning, she was headed back down to the river to hide her things (again) and be ready for her departure in the morning. She had saved Crestview, so even though there had been a slight delay, just like Hazel said, everything happens for a reason. She reached over and turned on the radio to the easy listening station. She was in the mood for something with violins, but then she was always in the mood for something with violins. It reminded her of old movies. Rosemary Clooney had just started singing "Tenderly," one of her favorites, when the mattress truck entered the highway. Maggie didn't see him, and he obviously didn't see her, because he plowed right into the side of her car.

It was such a shock; one second, Rosemary Clooney was singing, then a loud, sickening crash, and the next thing she knew, her car had flipped up in the air and had come down with another loud noise, then flipped up in the air again, and hit the side of the road and started rolling over and over down a steep embankment, until it finally landed on its roof with a thud.

She must have passed out along the way, because when she came to, she was hanging upside down in the front seat, with a strange terrible-smelling creature right beside her. It was staring at her with odd gold-and-green eyes and slanted pupils, but she couldn't tell what it was. She felt like she was spinning around inside a washing machine, and as hard as she tried, she couldn't focus on anything for more than a second. She didn't know if she was dead or alive. She could be in hell for all she knew, and the creature sitting beside her could be the devil himself. Then she heard voices yelling from a distance and the sound of people running toward her. A man approached the car, dropped down to his knees, and stuck his face in the window.

"Lady, are you all right?"

"I'm a little dizzy."

"Try not to move; you might have broken something." She heard another person run up, and a woman's voice said frantically, "Oh, my God. Is she all right?"

The man said, "I think so; she's talking." Then a woman's upside-down face appeared in the window and shouted at Maggie as if she were deaf, "Honey, I've called the paramedics, and they're on their way; the fire department is just a half mile down the road, so don't you worry; you just stay calm, okay? Does anything hurt?"

She was looking up at the woman's spinning nostrils and answered, "I don't think so; I'm just dizzy."

Then the woman clapped her hands loudly and shouted at the terrible-smelling black creature inside the car, "Leroy . . . get out of there!" But whatever or whoever Leroy was, he didn't move. The woman turned to the man. "Gary, go get Leroy out of the car." The man ran around to the other side and pulled Leroy out of the car and then said to his wife, "Stay here; I'm going to see if the guy in the truck needs anything."

The woman leaned back in and said to Maggie, "Dear, I'm Marian Conway, and that's my husband, Gary."

Maggie tried to nod, but it was almost impossible to nod hanging upside down, though she did manage a "How do you do?"

"They told us not to move you until they get here . . . Excuse me a minute," she said, and stood up and yelled at her husband again. "Gary. Get the goats! They're running out on the road!"

Maggie finally figured out that Leroy must be a goat. But Leroy was not out on the road. When he had been pulled out of one side of the car, he had promptly come around to the other side and stuck his face in next to Maggie's. The woman pushed him away with her leg. "Get out of here, Leroy, and leave her alone!"

Maggie asked, "I don't understand what happened. Why am I upside down?"

"That mattress truck pulled right out in front of you and sideswiped you, and you flipped over in our yard. I saw the whole thing. It's a wonder you're not dead. Is there anyone I should call? What's your name, honey?"

"Margaret Fortenberry."

There was a pause. The woman leaned in and looked at her more closely. "You're not Margaret Fortenberry—Miss Alabama, are you?"

"Yes."

"Oooh, for gosh sake, my mother was Jo Anna Horton! She was in the Miss Alabama pageant the same year you won; she played the marimba and tap-danced? Do you remember her? She always said you were just the nicest person."

This was not the conversation Maggie would have liked to be having at this moment, but still upside down, she answered, "Oh, yes. I do remember her. How is she?"

"She's just fine. Oh, my gosh, wait till she hears about this."

In the short time before the fire truck arrived, Maggie found out that Gary and Marian had bought the land she was now hanging upside down on about ten years ago and had started Sweet Home Alabama Goat Farm. Eleven years before, they'd found out that their second baby was allergic to cow's milk and realized how hard it was to find good fresh goat milk products and thought that starting a goat farm would be a great opportunity to leave corporate America, something Gary had always wanted to do anyway, and now he was having a chance to serve mankind as well . . .

Maggie was told in great detail all the many reasons why goat milk was far superior to cow's milk. When the fire truck with the paramedics arrived, they immediately cut her out of her seat belt and carefully pulled her through the window and laid her down on the ground. As the paramedics were busy checking her for broken bones, one remarked, "I'll tell you this, ma'am. If you hadn't been wearing your seat belt, you would be dead." As they continued to check out her arms and legs, she couldn't help but wonder. Why would a woman who was planning to jump in the river and drown herself be wearing a seat belt in the first place? How stupid.

After examining her, they found that other than a sore shoulder and a bruise on her forehead where her purse had hit her when the car was rolling, she was fine. But everything else around her was a mess. She had knocked down the Conways' huge sign and half of their fence, and her car had been completely totaled. Now she was going to have to fill out all those insurance forms, and God knows how long that would take. The truck driver, who was not hurt, was claiming the accident was her fault, and so there was probably going to be a lawsuit before it was over with.

Later, after the police had come and taken pictures of the accident site and filled out the report, she looked up and saw her car being towed away and realized, too late, that her raft, her glue, and her weights were still in the trunk.

A few minutes later, Brenda answered the phone at home.

"Brenda, it's Maggie . . . listen, are you busy?"

"No, why?"

"I need a ride. Could you possibly come and pick me up and take me home?"

"Sure, where are you?"

"I'm at the Sweet Home Alabama Goat Farm."

"A **goat** farm? What are you doing at a goat farm?"

"Well, I wasn't at a goat farm; I just wound up here."

"How?"

"A mattress truck hit me."

"A truck! You were hit by a truck? Oh, dear Jesus in heaven!" Brenda screamed down the hall, "Robbie, Maggie's been hit by a truck!"

Maggie heard Robbie's voice in the background. **"What?"**

"She's been hit by a truck." Suddenly, Robbie was on the phone. "Maggie, are you all right?"

"Yes. I just had a little car accident . . . but I'm all right."

"Have you been checked out?"

"Yes. The paramedics were here, and they said I was fine; no broken bones, but my car was wrecked. Could you and Brenda come get me and take me home?"

"Of course, where are you?"

"I'm out on the old highway, right past the old Silver Slipper Supper Club, at the Sweet Home Alabama Goat Farm on the right."

"Is there a sign or something?"

"Well . . . not anymore. But you'll see a lot of men out on the road, working on a fence."

"Okay, we'll be right there."

After she hung up, Robbie was out the door in less than twenty seconds, with Brenda running to catch up to her. Robbie wasn't an emergency room nurse for nothing.

Maggie sat on the front porch, waiting for them, with Marian and Maggie's new best friend, Leroy the goat. From the time she had landed in their yard, Leroy had followed her everywhere.

"I swear," Marian said, "Leroy has just fallen in love with you. He won't stop pestering you for one second; he's never done that before." It was really very sweet, and Maggie guessed she should be flattered, but she had never been this close to a goat in her life, and she had no earthly idea how to pet a goat. Still, she reached out and patted it on the head, trying to be nice.

Maggie and Marian sat and looked out across the pasture and watched as Gary, with a bunch of neighbors, tried to put up a makeshift fence so the goats wouldn't wander out on the road and get hit. "I'm so sorry about this," Maggie said. "Believe me, this is the last thing in the world I wanted to have happen today."

"Oh, don't you worry," Marian said. "It wasn't your fault; I'm just glad you're alive. Just thank your lucky stars. This could have been your last day on earth."

A few minutes later, Maggie had a long-distance conversation with Jo Anna, Marian's mother, which started out by Marian saying, "Momma, you will never guess who just wound up in our yard today." To Jo Anna's credit, she hadn't guessed. About forty-five minutes later, after Maggie and Marian had exchanged information and addresses, Robbie and Brenda arrived to pick Maggie up. As they drove home, Brenda, who was driving, looked at Maggie in the rearview mirror and said, "I'm not even going to ask you what you were doing driving around out in the sticks all by yourself."

After a moment of silence, Brenda said, "Well?"

"Well, what?"

"What were you doing?"

Robbie said, "Now, Brenda, that's none of your business."

"Well, I guess it is . . . she's my business partner, and I guess I have a right to know why she was way out here."

Maggie sighed. "Oh, Brenda. If I told you, you'd never believe it."

"Try me."

"I was just driving around in the country, that's all."

Brenda was horrified. "Why? There are snakes down here and everything!"

Snakes? My God, Brenda was right. Maggie hadn't thought about that. Oh, Lord. That's all she needed. To go to all this trouble to do it right and then get snakebitten by a big old water moccasin on her way down to the river. By the time they found her, she would probably be all swollen up and bloated, and they always photographed the body, and no telling where that photo would wind up.

On Monday, Brenda took Maggie over to the car leasing company to fill out all the papers about the accident. The owner had been very fond of Hazel and immediately gave Maggie a new car to drive. Then Maggie drove over to the auto body shop, where her old car was. They had to open the trunk with a crowbar so she could get all her things out and transfer them to the new car. What a perfect mess. This was going to mean yet another delay. She was not only the victim of an accident, she was also a key witness, and she had to be available to give a statement. Also, she had to make sure the leasing company was fully reimbursed for the car and that the poor Conways got their insurance company to pay for a new fence and a new sign. Having dealt with insurance companies in the past, she knew what a hard battle that could be. But as soon as that was cleared up, she would go on with her plans, as soon as possible. Every extra day she stayed was just adding up more debt. Being a woman in the business world was expensive. Just the sheer maintenance alone was costing her a lot of money. Hair, nails, makeup, cold cream, dry cleaning and laundry, not to mention food and gas for the car.

When Maggie finally arrived back home, she saw that Miss Pitcock the librarian had faxed her yet another document regarding the Crocker siblings. Oh dear. A few weeks ago Maggie had called and thanked her profusely for helping her with her research, saying that she had all the information she needed, so there was no reason to go forward. But evidently once Miss Pitcock got started, she could not be stopped. And today she had faxed Maggie something that had thoroughly confused her.

Miss Pitcock had somehow managed to obtain a photocopy of Edward Crocker's will, dated January 11, 1935, and after pages of instructions dealing with numerous foundations and charities, Edward had specified that in the event of his death, the business and Crestview were to be willed to the Dalton family. But he had left the entire bulk of his fortune (including Edwina's house in London) to Lettie Ross, his childhood nurse. There was not even a mention of an Edwina Crocker in the entire will! And who was Lettie Ross? If the woman in London who had passed herself off as Edwina Crocker had been his mistress or even a distant relative, then why had Edward not left her a dime in his will? It didn't make any sense. Oh, well, it was obvious that detective work was not as simple as Nancy Drew would have you think.

Brenda Gets a Surprise

February 2009

Brenda didn't know it, but her sister Robbie had been saving money to buy her a fifty-inch flat-screen television set for her birthday, in two weeks. This morning, Robbie had read that Costco was having a huge one-day sale on electronics, and the exact model Brenda wanted was marked down 35 percent. So that afternoon, with the help of two of her intern friends at the hospital, they borrowed an ambulance and ran out to Costco and bought one. Because she couldn't trust Brenda not to go through every square inch of the house and the garage looking for her presents, they took it over to storage to keep until her birthday, so it would be a surprise. But it was Robbie and the two interns who got a surprise when they moved the chest of drawers.

The next person to be surprised that day was Brenda. When she came bouncing in the door from her Youth at Risk meeting, she was feeling pretty good, until she saw Mr. Crocker sitting on the sofa with his legs crossed and Robbie sitting right beside him.

"I've been waiting for you," said Robbie.

"Uh-oh." Brenda understood that this was one of those times when changing the subject with enthusiasm was just not going to work. She was busted and she knew it, so she sat down and told Robbie the truth.

After she finished, Robbie shook her head and said, "Brenda, do you have any idea how insane you are?"

Brenda blinked her eyes and tried to look as innocent as possible. "Well, it sounded like a good idea at the time."

"And Maggie went along with this? That doesn't sound like her."

"I know, but you don't understand: we **needed** this sale. Our office depended on it. Please don't tell Maggie that you found him. Please."

Robbie thought about it for a minute, then said, "Well, okay, I guess it won't hurt anything. But why do you keep saying **he**?"

"Because we're almost positive we know who he is."

"Oh, really?"

"We think it's Edward Crocker, the man who used to live there. There's a painting of him in the house wearing this same exact outfit. Don't you think that's a pretty good clue?"

"I do. Except for one small detail."

"What?"

"Your little friend here is a female."

"WHAT? How do you know that?"

"Because I examined it."

"Are you sure?"

"Of course I'm sure; I know physiology. You can tell by the hips."

Brenda was not happy to hear this news. "What were you doing examining my skeleton's hips . . . and now that I think about it, **what** were you doing over at the storage unit in the first place?"

"That's for me to know and you to find out," said Robbie. "Other people have secrets, too."

Usually, as it was so close to her birthday, Brenda would have badgered Robbie until she found out what the secret was, but she had other things on her mind right now. She was wondering how she was going to tell Maggie that the skeleton was not Edward Crocker. After thinking it over, she decided that maybe she wouldn't tell her. What Maggie didn't know wouldn't hurt her.

Across town, after Ethel Clipp had poured herself a nice stiff drink, she was sitting in her living room in her purple velour pantsuit, looking out the window and watching the pigeons walking all over her yard. One big fat male pigeon was all puffed up, strutting around and pestering some poor female to death.

Typical. It could have been her ex-husband, Earl. If she thought there was any truth to the reincarnation thing, she would have gotten up and gone out in the yard and swatted it.

After the divorce, that son of a bitch Earl had just disappeared. He just took off and hadn't sent her a dime in alimony, not even a postcard. If it hadn't been for Hazel, she never could have gotten those two kids raised, much less been able to send them to college.

And after her working so hard to make sure they had an education and would be able to get a good job, they both wound up weird as hell, and neither one of them had a job. Now, just like crazy Dottie Figge, who had flipped out and gone all Hindu, they said they were on some so-called spiritual quest and needed to devote time to discovering the "path to happiness." Opal, her youngest, had just sent her a book. She said it was the most profound thing she had ever read. Ethel didn't want to burst her bubble, but it seemed like a bunch of gobbledegook. Back in her day, going to church every Sunday used to be enough. But now everybody and their brother had some new lamebrained theory or philosophy they were pushing. Years ago, you used to have to wait until someone asked you to write a book, but now with self-publishing, every wing nut in America was writing one. Ethel thought that maybe she should write one. She had a philosophy, too. She even had a title: **Fools and Idiots I Have Known or Have**

Been Married To. Her theory was very simple: there wasn't a thing the matter with the world, just the people in it. They never learned, and they just kept doing the same damned stupid things over and over again. Animals were fine, but all humans were fools. Herself included, or she wouldn't have married Earl in the first place.

The Kate Spade Affair

8:57 A.M.

March 15

On Saturday morning, Brenda and her sister Tonya were at the factory outlet mall for the annual Kate Spade March Madness handbag sale. They had arrived at five A.M. to make sure they got in the front of the line, and by seven, the line was already around the block, with women waiting to stampede through the store and grab as many bags as they could. When the doors finally opened at eight, Brenda shouted for Tonya to go to the left, and she would go to the right. Brenda had been rushing around the store for about ten minutes when she began to feel ill. She felt a burning pain in her chest; she was hot and sweaty and was suddenly having trouble breathing. She should have gone home, but this was a once-a-year sale, so instead, she ran in the ladies room and threw cold water on her face and headed back out again. When she did, she caught a glimpse of her sister across the room, and Tonya held up a bright red bag in triumph, and Brenda started over to that side of the store to try to find one just like it. She needed a red bag, too.

Meanwhile, across town at Avon Terrace, Maggie was busy with her last-minute details again. Finally, after weeks of waiting, her deposition and all the paperwork involving the wreck had been completed, and yesterday, the Conways had called and said that the insurance company had finally agreed to cover all the costs of the fence and a new sign. When Maggie had heard from them, she had gone back to the river, this time with her snakebite kit in hand, and left all her jumping-in-the-river items.

Yesterday, she had ordered a car to pick up a Mrs. Tab Hunter at eight-thirty in the middle of the block. Maggie had been up since seven, and now all that was left for her to do was put out the package with her Miss Alabama crown, sash, and trophy for Audrey and a box with her new clothes labeled for the theater out in plain sight, where they could be seen.

She had payed off her credit card, and yesterday she had put her last check for half of the commission on Crestview in the mail to Babs.

She made the bed and checked off the last items on her list. Clean towels in the bathroom, new soaps in all the soap dishes, ant traps under the sink. She then went back to the kitchen and put the "To Whom It May Concern" envelope and the envelope addressed to Lupe with the watch and, this time, one thousand dollars in cash on the kitchen counter, and did a last look around the room. She realized that after today, the two envelopes would be all that was left of her.

All she had now was just enough money to pay for the cab ride to the river. Oh, well. At least she hadn't left owing money, and that was something, she guessed. She then unplugged the toaster and the microwave oven and locked the kitchen door. She grabbed her purse and went down the hall to the front door. But when she tried to open the outer glass door, it wouldn't budge. Something heavy stood in the way. She looked down and saw a huge cardboard box with a card taped to the top, addressed to her from Sweet Home Alabama Goat Farm. Oh, Lord. How had they gotten in the gate? It was too early for mail, so the gardeners must have put it on her stoop, thinking they were doing her a favor. She reached down and opened the card; inside was a photo of Leroy the goat, along with a note.

Dear Maggie,

I am so glad you are alive and not hurt. Please come out and see me again soon. I miss you. The Conways send their love and said to tell you thank you for all you did to help them with the insurance claim.

Love,
Your friend, Leroy

Oh no, that really was very sweet of them, but why today, of all days? It was obviously some kind of food because the box had PERISHABLE, PLEASE REFRIGERATE written all over it. She couldn't leave it sitting out on the stoop in the sun—nothing smells worse than spoiled goat cheese—so she pulled the box inside the foyer and opened it and saw that they had sent twenty-four cartons of goat yogurt and at least ten pounds of a variety of goat cheeses. She had just spent over an hour cleaning out her refrigerator. She tried to think of someone she could give it to, but who would ever want this amount of goat products? She couldn't think of a single person, and she couldn't just leave it sitting in the foyer. There was nothing she could do. She was going to have to take it all out and put it in the refrigerator, and hopefully, Lupe would find it on Monday and take some of it home. As she was busy unloading the box, her phone rang, and she was so rattled, she completely forgot that she wasn't going to speak to anyone and picked it up. "Hello."

"Hey, it's me." Maggie winced when she realized what she had done. It was Brenda. Too late. Now she was caught.

"Can you hear me?"

"Just barely . . . where are you?"

"I'm at the Kate Spade sale. We got here early this morning, and I just got six bags for half price. I'm standing in line right now, waiting to pay for them."

"Oh, great, honey, that's wonderful." Maggie tried to sound interested and still concentrate on getting all the yogurt into the refrigerator.

"What are you doing?" asked Brenda.

"Oh, just putting a few things away. What's up?"

"Listen . . . I don't want you to get excited, but I may or may not be having a heart attack. But if I were, what would be the symptoms?"

Maggie was suddenly alarmed. "**What?** What makes you think you're having a heart attack?"

"I said, **may be.** I didn't say I was."

"Oh, my God. Have you called Robbie?"

"No."

"Why not?"

"Because. I don't want to hear her say 'I told you so' until I'm sure."

"Are you having chest pains?"

"Uh-huh, sort of. Off and on," Brenda said as she moved one step closer to the check-out counter.

"Are you short of breath?"

"A little."

"Brenda, don't fool around with this. You get out of that line right now and go get help."

"I can't. I haven't paid for my bags yet."

"Forget the damn bags! You find somebody right

now and tell them what's going on, and I'm not hanging up until you do!"

There was a pause; then Brenda said, "I'll call you back . . ." and hung up. She was sorry she had called now, but since she'd never heard Maggie cuss before, she figured she'd better do what Maggie said, so she tapped the lady in front of her on the shoulder and said, "Honey, would you do me a favor? Could you hold my bags and my place in line for me for just a minute? I have a little emergency." The woman said she would, and Brenda looked around the room and spotted a young security guard backed up against a wall, trying to stay out of the way of the crowd of stampeding women running through the store. The pain in her chest was getting worse as Brenda pushed herself through the crowd, and when she finally got to the guard, she looked at his name tag, then said, "Listen, Dwayne, I may or may not be having a heart attack, but if I was, what should I do?"

Dwayne looked at her wide-eyed and immediately pulled out a black walkie-talkie and yelled into it, "Heart attack in the basement! Heart attack in the basement!" He then asked her if she was there by herself, and she told him her sister was with her. Brenda started to go and find her, but he stopped her. "Don't move; wait right here," he said. "I'll find her; what does she look like?"

"She's a heavy-set woman in a black dress, wearing a red wig."

Dwayne quickly waded into the crowd and suddenly realized that the entire room was full of heavy-set women in red wigs, wearing black dresses.

Maggie stood in the kitchen, not knowing what to do. Should she wait for Brenda to call her back? Oh, Lord . . . what do you do when someone you know may or may not be having a heart attack? She tried to call Brenda back, but she didn't pick up. Brenda had been calling Tonya, who was standing in line on the other side of the store, and finally, Tonya answered.

"What?"

"Listen, Tonya, I may or may not be having a heart attack . . . and I—"

Tonya, who could hardly hear her above the crowd, interrupted: "Who's having a heart attack?"

"Me. Well, maybe. Anyhow, I have to go to the hospital, but I need you to go to the line at the cash register and pick up my bags from the lady who's holding them for me and pay for them, okay? She's wearing a black dress."

Tonya frantically looked around the room, searching for her sister, but she didn't see her, because at the moment, Brenda was being taken in a wheelchair to a waiting ambulance. At every big discount sale, there was always an ambulance waiting outside. They knew they would be called sooner or later.

As soon as she saw Brenda in the wheelchair, Tonya dropped all her purchases where she stood and began pushing her way across the store through the crowd, just in time to see Brenda being driven away in the ambulance with its sirens blaring full blast. Tonya was beside herself; she didn't know whether to do what she'd been told and go back in and try to find the woman with Brenda's bags or to just go on to the hospital. As she stood there trying to decide, a lady carrying two large shopping bags came out of the store and walked up to her and asked, "Do you know that lady they just took away?"

"Yes, she's my sister."

"Well, here are her bags. When she didn't come back, I just went ahead and paid for them. Tell her she can send me a check; I put my name and address inside."

"Oh, thank you so much."

"Well, that's all right. Tell her I hope she feels better. She got some great bags!"

A few seconds later, Maggie's phone rang again, and it was Brenda.

"Hey, it's me," she said.

"Brenda! Where are you? Are you all right?"

"Honey, I'm flopped up in the back of an ambulance, so they won't let me talk long."

"An ambulance! Oh, no. Where are they taking you?"

Brenda said, "Hold on," then asked somebody, "Hey, where are y'all taking me?"

Maggie heard a man in the background say, "University Hospital," and then heard Brenda say,

"University? Can't I go to Providence, out in West End? I'd much rather go there." Then a man came on the phone and said, "She can't talk now," and the phone went dead.

Maggie stood in her kitchen in shock. Oh, my God, her poor friend Brenda was in an ambulance on her way to the hospital. All she could think about now was getting over there as fast as possible. She was in her FISHERMEN DO IT WITH A BIG POLE shirt, but it couldn't be helped. She ran out the door and saw her taxi up the street. Thank heavens, she had a car waiting. She was so upset, she would have probably had another accident trying to get there and trying to park. Once she got in the backseat, she told the driver where to go. As they drove, she dialed Robbie's number at home, but no one answered. She just hoped and prayed Robbie was on duty at the hospital today. Although University Hospital was not far from Maggie's house, getting there turned out to be a long, slow process. Today was the annual Do Dah Parade, and they had to wait at every intersection. Life was so bizarre. While her best friend was possibly dying, she had to sit and watch people marching by with plastic trash cans on their heads.

As they slowly made their way across the south side to the hospital, she started to panic. God, what if Brenda died before she got there? In her preoccupation with making all **her** plans, she'd never dreamed Brenda could go first. What if it was too late? She hadn't even really said goodbye or told her that of all the people in the world, she would miss her the most. Now she might not be able to tell her anything ever again.

It's Good to Have a Sister

All of Brenda's efforts to have Robbie not find out that she might be having a heart attack had been in vain. She had forgotten that Robbie was the first person listed on all her ID cards to be called in case of emergency. But as the pain in her chest grew worse, and it dawned on her that she might really be having a heart attack, she got scared. When the ambulance finally arrived at the emergency room entrance, Robbie was the first person out the door. Brenda had never been so happy to see anyone in her life, even if she was going to get fussed at.

But Robbie was not mad. She just took Brenda's hand and smiled and walked alongside the stretcher, giving instructions to the attendants about where to take her. Then she said to Brenda, "Don't worry. Everything is going to be just fine."

An hour later, Maggie and Tonya were sitting in

the waiting room when Robbie came out and said, "They're still running tests, but it looks like she's fine. I'll let you know as soon as I know more."

"Is she awake?" asked Maggie.

"Oh, yes, she's in there babbling away about wanting to get back over to Kate Spade's before it closes. Tonya, do you know anything about some bags she hadn't paid for?"

"Yes, tell her I have them."

Maggie was so glad that Brenda was not dead, she finally began to relax a bit, until she suddenly remembered something. In her haste to get to Brenda, she realized that she had left the "To Whom It May Concern" envelope sitting on the kitchen counter, and now she had to get back home fast before anybody found it and read it. My God, what next?

Maggie told Tonya she would be back as soon as she could. She leapt up and ran out of the emergency room and down a block to the taxi stand on the corner and jumped in. It was now eleven-thirty, and she prayed the parade was over. It wasn't, and she spent the next forty-five minutes sitting in the back of the cab, a nervous wreck. What if some realtor came by? Finally, when they got closer, she jumped out of the cab and ran the last two blocks. She flew in her door and back to the kitchen and, to her everlasting relief, the letter was still there, exactly where she'd left it, unopened. She had never done so much jumping and running in one day in her life. It had paid off. She had been lucky. It was Saturday, but not one single real estate agent had come by to show the unit, and for the first time, she actually appreciated the terrible market. Unfortunately, in her haste to get to the hospital, she had left some of the goat cheese out, and the entire place smelled a lot like Leroy. She stuck the rest of it in the refrigerator, put the box outside on the patio, and opened all the windows.

She hated to do it, but Maggie had to take the gold watch and Lupe's cash back. She would need the money to tide her over, in case she had to stay for any length of time. She certainly couldn't leave while Brenda was still in the hospital. Maggie then took her To Whom It May Concern letter back to her desk drawer in the den.

She would have to wait a few days, until she knew for sure that Brenda was all right, and then reschedule.

A few minutes later, Robbie called with the latest report. Brenda had not had a heart attack, as they'd first suspected. It had been an esophageal spasm, which had similar symptoms.

"Oh, thank heavens."

"Don't bother to come back tonight; they just want her to rest."

"Is she going to be all right?"

"Oh, yes, you know Brenda; as soon as she found

out she wasn't dying and she got her bags, she was as happy as a clam, sitting up and asking for ice cream. Anyhow, she said to tell you to call her in the morning. We turned her phone off tonight."

After the call, Maggie pulled out another sheet of stationery and started another letter that she would leave in Brenda's desk before she left.

Dear Brenda,

I wanted you to know how much I have always appreciated your friendship and to tell you that afterward, you must never wonder if I knew that you appreciated mine. I did. You always made me smile. Thanks for all your help with the contracts. I couldn't have done it without you.

Sincerely,
Maggie

P.S. You will make a wonderful mayor.

It was short, but it said exactly what she wanted to say.

Gus's Famous Hot Dogs
Early April 2009

⌒

Maggie had to fill in at the office while Brenda was at home recuperating. She couldn't leave Ethel all alone. It was another delay, but at least she could depart knowing Brenda was going to be all right. Brenda had even promised to go back to Overeaters Anonymous, so the heart attack scare must have done some good.

A week later Brenda was back in the office bright and early and seemed to be happy and doing well. She was happy mostly because in the past week, she had lost seven pounds, and her Overeaters Anonymous sponsor had stopped by her house and given her a gold star. By Friday, with Brenda back to normal, Maggie was satisfied that the time was finally right. On Saturday, she drove back to the river with all her things, and this time around, she didn't even bother to hide them. No point. She was coming back early the next morning. She thought that since she was all ready to go, this afternoon she would go on her own private little Farewell to Birmingham tour. As she drove, a light misty rain began to fall.

This wasn't her first farewell ride. When she was five, just before midnight on the night of April 18, 1953, her father had bundled her up and they had ridden on the very last run of the Ensley Streetcar No. 27. It had been packed to the rafters with people and decorated from stem to stern with balloons and banners. There had been lots of cheering as it pulled into the streetcar barn and shut down for the last time. The wonderful old streetcar was headed to the scrap yard the next day. She supposed today, she was just like Streetcar No. 27, and was making her last run.

She had seen the end of so many things. The wonderful years with Hazel, the end of her one-year reign as Miss Alabama, and her last walk around the runway. There had been lots of tears and loud cheering that night, but today, as she rode through town, there were no tears or cheering; just the sound of her windshield wipers swishing back and forth.

She then drove out to East Lake, to where the old Dreamland Theatre used to be. When she got there, she saw that the entire side of the block was now a used-car lot, but as she passed by she could still remember the theater as it once was, and she wondered what ever happened to that nice man across the street at the Western Union office who used to wave to her?

As she drove up over the mountain and past the Mountain Brook Country Club and past English Village, the image of a young girl popped into her mind, a girl she must have seen in a movie once. But which one? Was it one of the girls in **The Sound of Music**? As the image kept fading in and fading out, she realized who the girl was—she wasn't from a movie; it was her. She was the one who used to feel this way, that same old melancholy feeling; a strange loneliness had haunted her, a deep yearning for something, but she never quite knew what it was she was yearning for.

Maggie felt a sudden pang of pity for that poor dumb dreamy girl with so many disappointments ahead, so many illusions to be shattered. Remembering her now was like remembering someone she had known in another lifetime.

Going back home, she drove through downtown, and just as a spur-of-the-moment thing, she did something she hadn't done in years. After a few times around the block, she found a parking space on the corner and went into a little hole-in-the-wall place called Gus's Famous Hot Dogs. She went in, sat at the counter, and ordered two chili dogs with mustard, onions, and sauerkraut and an orange drink. Gus's Famous Hot Dogs was one of the few places left where she and her parents used to go when she was little and then later, as a teenager, she and her girlfriends had always eaten there. The place had not changed a bit, and the chili dogs were as delicious as she remembered. Then she ordered two big pieces of lemon icebox pie. Why not? On her last day on earth, why not have a little fun? She knew she would probably have terrible indigestion tonight, but it was worth it. She remembered the days when she had been able to eat anything she wanted, French-fried onions and cheeseburgers, and not have to pay for it later. The last time she had eaten there was with four or five of her high school girlfriends, when they had been running from one place to the next, going to the movies or hanging out at the record store. She wished those days could have lasted longer. It was hard to believe that most of those giggling girls were grandmothers now.

Maggie looked down at her watch. It was still pretty early, and she wondered what she would do for the rest of the day. She started toying with the idea of maybe going on to the river this afternoon and not waiting until the morning. When she paid her bill, she was pleasantly surprised to see that you could still get a good meal and a cold drink for less than five dollars. She was in a good mood until she walked outside, just in time to see the traffic cop on a scooter driving away from her car. She had just gotten a parking ticket!

Oh, no! She had never gotten a ticket in her life. What had she done wrong? She had put money in the meter. Her time was not expired. She opened the ticket and read what the woman had written:

"Improper parking, too far away from curb." She stepped back and looked. Well, maybe her car was a little too far out in the street, so she guessed she was guilty as charged, but as she read further, she was greatly relieved to see that she could pay the fine by mail; it said DO NOT SEND CASH— PAY ONLY BY CHECK OR MONEY ORDER. She was in luck. As fate would have it, her next stop was the bank, to close out her account again. Had this happened later in the day, she would have been in a bind. After she had written the check to the Department of Motor Vehicles and closed her account, she mailed the ticket outside the bank.

After roaming all over town and driving down all her favorite streets and places, she went back down the mountain and parked her car across the street from Caldwell Park and watched the last afternoon light fade. She sat there until dusk, until the street lanterns in the park blinked on and reflected their yellow lights in the trees and on the shining sidewalks.

It was a fitting ending for her last day—just like life itself: incredibly beautiful, incredibly sad, bittersweet. She started the car, took one long last look, and then turned and headed back to Avon Terrace.

But before she went home, she slowly drove by Crestview one more time, and it made her happy to think about David and Mitzi living there. She had found Crestview good owners; not much in the scheme of things, but at least she had accomplished something. She could now leave without feeling like a complete failure. Maggie sat down and went over her "Things to Do" checklist again, and by the time she finished, it was almost six o'clock. She decided it was too late to go to the river today. She guessed she would just wait and go in the morning.

Is It Real or Is It Memorex?

April 12, 2009

Maggie woke up and looked over at the clock. six A.M. Good. She might as well get an early start, and there would be less traffic on the way down to the river at this hour. After she was dressed in her fishing shirt and jeans and men's boots, she emptied out the refrigerator, took out the garbage, placed the ant traps under the sink, and took out the "To Whom It May Concern" letter and laid it on the kitchen counter. When she left, she locked the front door behind her and put the key under the mat. The taxi was right on time, waiting, and to her surprise, the driver looked exactly like Omar Sharif from **Doctor Zhivago.** The bad news was, he could barely speak English, and she had a hard time explaining how to get to the river. But the good news: he was from Siberia, so he had no idea she was a former Miss Alabama or that she was not Mrs. Tab Hunter.

She tried to be pleasant and asked him how long he had been in America. When he told her eleven years, she asked, "Do you ever miss Siberia?"

He looked up at her in the mirror and said sadly, "Oh, yes, I can't wait to get back."

She couldn't imagine how anyone would long for Siberia, but she guessed everybody loved their home, no matter where it was. As they drove, Maggie sat and thought about how life was so full of surprises, even up to the very end. She was sure a lot of other people must have considered ending it all at one time or another but had chickened out at the last minute. She'd bet that a lot of people would be surprised that **she**, of all people, had actually gone through with it. But then, they say it's always the quiet ones you never suspect. She was even surprised at herself and was amazed at how calm and serene she felt. She knew intellectually that this should be a big dramatic moment, but she didn't feel it. She had been more nervous just going to the dentist than she was now. But real life was never the same as they showed it in the movies. And then, too, she had made this same trip so many times that now it all seemed anticlimactic.

When they reached the river road, she had the driver let her out a few minutes from the old Raiford Fishing Camp. She gave him a nice tip, and when he was out of sight, she walked the rest of the way to the spot where her things were waiting. When she reached the clearing, she went down the path, snakebite kit in hand, but luckily she didn't see one snake. Near the water, she was glad to see that everything was still there, exactly as she'd left it. Maggie inflated the raft with the pump that came with it and placed all four weights in the boat. She then climbed in and pushed herself off with the paddle and started rowing out to the middle of the river.

It took her about fifteen minutes to get there and, just as she expected, there was not a single person or a boat in sight. She picked up the two ten-pound ankle weights and applied a generous amount of the sticky, white, As Seen on TV "miracle glue" onto the Velcro and wrapped them around her ankles; she did the same thing with the two wrist weights. Now all she had to do was wait the twenty minutes for the glue to dry and she'd be good to go. She set the egg timer on the seat and realized that she had worn her expensive watch. She should have left it in the envelope at home for Lupe. That was so stupid. Oh well, one small detail missed. Everything else had been taken care of. As she sat there waiting for the glue to dry, she found out that twenty minutes is a long time, especially if you have nothing to read. She should have brought a magazine.

As she sat there, an old song ran through her head, and she began to sing, "Oh, Mr. Sandman . . . bring me a dream, make him the cutest that I've ever seen . . ."

After singing the entire song all the way through,

twice, she looked down at the rooster egg timer again . . . Good Lord, eleven more minutes to kill. So she started another song that had always been one of her mother's favorites: "Blue champagne, purple shadows and blue champagne."

It was a strange sight, a woman alone, sitting in the middle of the river, singing all the "oldies but goodies" she could remember. Finally, after another ten long minutes, the timer's bell went off. She put one leg over the side of the boat, then the other, and slowly lowered herself into the cold water. She held on to the side of the boat with one arm for just a moment, then let go.

The second she let go, she immediately began sinking straight down to the bottom at a surprisingly rapid speed, and her last thought was "Well, I did it." As the cold water rushed past her ears with a loud roar, she sank deeper and deeper, and the water became darker and darker. But just at the very moment she was expecting to black out, a brand-new thought suddenly hit her.

"Wait a minute, this is a **mistake!**"

In that one second, she had completely changed her mind and now wanted to go back up to the surface. Maggie began to flail around in a panic, kicking and struggling with the weights around her wrists, desperately trying to pull them apart, and as she continued to sink, she jerked and pulled at them with all her might, but to her horror, she could not get free. As advertised, the "guaranteed-

or-your-money-back magic glue" was holding tight. Sinking deeper, she could hear herself screaming and yelling underwater, "Wait! Stop!" And then came the terrible moment, the horrible realization that she could not save herself. It was too late.

As she gasped for what she knew was her last breath and felt the heavy ice-cold water rushing down her throat and into her lungs, just as she was on the very verge of losing consciousness forever, she suddenly shot straight up in bed with her heart pounding in her chest, covered in sweat, still screaming at the top of her lungs, "Wait! Stop!" She sat in the pitch dark struggling for breath, still in a blind panic, not knowing if she was dead or alive. Had the river been a dream or was this a dream? She could still hear the sound of the water rushing past her ears. Was she dead? She reached over to the nightstand and grabbed the remote and, with shaking hands, clicked on the television set, and when the gray light came into focus, there sat Rick and Janice on the set of the **Good Morning Alabama** show, and Maggie had never been so happy to see any two people in her life.

Still, her heart continued to race out of control. It was pounding so hard that she wondered if she was having a heart attack and if she should get up and take an aspirin. Ironic that someone who was planning to drown herself was now terrified about having a heart attack and dying, but she was. She jumped up out of bed and ran into the bathroom and opened the medicine cabinet, but it was empty. She had thrown everything away last night. So she just stood at the sink and did some deep breathing until, finally, her heart slowed down a little. She was still slightly disoriented, but now that she thought more about it, she realized that of course it had all been just a terrible nightmare, a bad dream. She should have realized it sooner. What had she been thinking? Omar Sharif was from Egypt, not Siberia!

She made her way into the kitchen and fixed a cup of herbal tea. Still sweaty and shaky, she then went outside and sat on her patio in the fresh air, just as the sun was starting to come up over the mountain. She sat there, still in a state of shock. She had had nightmares before, but never one that vivid or real and certainly never that terrifying. Up until a few minutes ago, she'd had no idea she wanted to live, but clearly, she did. She had fought with all of her might. Even though it had just been a dream, she still felt exhausted from the struggle. What a total surprise! She had assumed she was perfectly ready to go, but she had been wrong. Just yesterday, she couldn't think of a thing to live for, but right now, a hundred reasons flooded her mind. For one, it felt so good just to be able to breathe; why hadn't she noticed that before?

Maggie looked up at the sky and watched as it turned from early morning pink to a pretty robin's-egg blue. The colors were so amazing; she hadn't sat out on her patio in months, and almost never at dawn. How beautiful it was!

As she sat there looking up at the sky, she realized something else. This happened every morning. No matter what was going on in her silly little life, the sun always came up. Why hadn't she remembered that? Then something Hazel used to say popped into her mind: "Remember, girls, it's always the darkest right before the glorious dawn." Hazel had been referring to real estate at the time, but it could apply to her this morning. Hadn't she just gone through her darkest hour? And hadn't there just been the most glorious dawn? Certainly the most glorious one she had ever seen. And now, in the early morning sunshine, everything looked so fresh and beautiful, like something out of a movie. The world had suddenly turned from dark gray to bright Technicolor. She fully expected Gene Kelly to come dancing around the corner and swing on the lamppost at any moment. She felt absolutely **joyful**. But then she thought, Wait a minute. **Why** was she feeling so happy all of a sudden? Could she have just had a break with reality? Had she finally just snapped and flipped out and gone completely crazy? Or had she been crazy before? Surely, planning to jump in the river was a pretty good indication that **something** had been off. Could the dream have scared her so badly that it had shot an overload of adrenaline into her system and flipped her back into her right mind? Or maybe this euphoria she was feeling was just some sort of temporary chemical imbalance from all the lemon pie and hot dogs she had eaten yesterday. Of course, her heart had been pounding pretty hard, so there was the possibility that she could have just suffered a minor stroke, but whatever it was, she was feeling absolutely—what was the perfect word? Hopeful, that was it.

And thank God she had had that dream last night; tomorrow night would have been too late. But what had caused the dream? Could it have been a simple case of indigestion that had saved her life? Or had it been something more? Could it have been someone from another dimension? Her parents or Hazel or a guardian angel of some kind trying to reach her, to stop her, before it was too late? She didn't know who to thank, the hot dogs or an angel, but she was grateful to whatever it was, because she was so glad to be here to enjoy this perfect beautiful morning. She looked up again at the blue sky, just in time to see three little puffy white clouds float over Red Mountain. She smiled and waved at them as they passed by. "Hello, you pretty little things. I've missed you."

Everything was so quiet this morning that she could hear the bells of the big Highlands Methodist Church start to ring way off in the distance. Church bells, what a happy sound. But wait a minute. Why was everything so quiet? The dull roar of Highway

280 traffic usually started around six A.M., but this morning, she couldn't hear a thing, except for a few birds chirping. Had there been some big accident, had something happened? Then she remembered what day it was. No wonder it was so quiet. She had completely forgotten. It was Sunday; not only Sunday, but Easter Sunday. Imagine. She **must** have been out of her mind. How could anybody forget that?

Now Maggie began to wonder if having that dream on Easter had been some kind of miracle— or was it just a coincidence? She would like to believe it was a miracle, but of course, she had no idea if it was or not. But then, a few seconds later, she glanced over to her left and saw something she had not noticed before. She couldn't believe her eyes. Standing right in the middle of her rock garden was one large white Easter lily! After all these years, it had somehow managed to survive and push its way up through the rocks. And it was now just blooming away, happy as a lark and enjoying the sunshine.

Oh, my God, she thought, **it must be Hazel.** Hazel had sent her those Easter lily bulbs, and she had planted them years ago, and not one had ever bloomed. It couldn't be just an accident that this one had waited all these years to bloom, could it? Of course, they'd had a lot of rain this year, so was it just a coincidence? A fluke of nature? She wanted to believe with all her heart that it was Hazel, but she couldn't be a hundred percent sure. Now she didn't know what to think. Then, as if on cue from some stage manager in the sky, a large white dove flapped its wings and flew directly across the patio and landed on the edge of her bird feeder and looked her right in the eye, blinking at her twice. Oh, my God. Not **one** sign from Hazel, but **two**! After she got over the initial shock of seeing the bird and looked at it more carefully, Maggie saw that it was a light gray pigeon and not a white Easter dove, as she had first thought. But she didn't care. As far as she was concerned . . . it was close enough.

Maggie wanted to jump up and run inside and call everyone she knew and tell them she was back. But since nobody knew she had been away, they might think she was insane. And they could be right. A moment ago, she **had** been talking to clouds, but if this was insanity, she would take it. And most of all, she thought, God bless Hazel Whisenknott. Hazel obviously didn't want her to jump into the river; she just knew it!

HAPPY EASTER. HOORAY AND HALLE-LUJAH!

Later that morning, after Brenda got up and listened to the message Maggie had left on their machine at 6:47 A.M., she remarked to Robbie, "If I didn't know her better, I'd think Maggie might be drunk or stoned or something."

"Why?"

"She sounded funny."

"What do you mean, funny?"

"Sort of silly . . . or something."

"Oh, she's probably just happy; it's Easter."

Just the same, Brenda called her back, but Maggie did not answer.

As Maggie drove across town in the clear, bright sunshine, she looked around and was amazed to see that spring had already arrived in Birmingham and she hadn't even noticed. The dogwood trees and the azaleas were all in bloom, and every yard was full of yellow and white jonquils. She had her windows down, and the smell of the clean, fresh air was wonderful. Just being able to breathe was wonderful. Everything was wonderful! She turned on the radio and heard the swelling of the organ music being broadcast from the big Baptist church on the south side and sang along with the choir as she drove. She thought this was exactly what Scrooge must have felt like on Christmas morning, only it was Easter.

Maggie realized that it was she who had changed, not the world. The birds still chirped, the sky was just as blue, the dogwoods still bloomed in spring, and the stars still twinkled at night. And the good news was that she was still here to see it.

She stopped at a roadside flower stand and bought a dozen white roses. When she arrived at the cemetery, she walked over to where her parents were buried and was surprised to see that there was already a huge beautiful bouquet of flowers on their grave. She bent down and opened the card. It read,

"Happy Easter. Love, Margaret." They were from her. She had completely forgotten, but the woman at the Bon-Ton florist had delivered them, right on time as promised. As she stood there looking across the cemetery, Maggie realized just how lucky she was to be here. She wouldn't have been if Crestview had not come up for sale and if the mattress truck hadn't hit her and if Brenda hadn't thought she was having a heart attack and if she hadn't eaten those chili dogs and had that nightmare. Contrary to what she had always thought, she was one of the luckiest people in the world.

As she stood there, Maggie wondered how many people in those graves would have loved to have lived for one more year, one more day, or even just one more hour. How could she ever have been so ungrateful, to just throw away whatever time she had left? How could she have ever even thought about it? All right, so life wasn't great and wonderful all the time. So what if she couldn't work a BlackBerry or program her oven or parallel park? What difference did it make if the napkins weren't folded properly or the silverware was not set correctly? Who cared?

Suddenly, being her age seemed great. She didn't have to look perfect. Hooray! And think of all the senior discounts she had to look forward to, not to mention Social Security, Medicare, and Medicaid. So what if she was afraid of getting old? Big whoop-de-doo—who wasn't? She wasn't alone;

everybody her age was in the same boat. She was going to relax and just let herself get older. Who cared if she wore two-inch heels instead of three-and-a-half-inch heels? Her feet hurt, and not only that, she was going to have a piece of cake once in a while, and she wasn't going to go anywhere she didn't feel like going anymore, either. Bring on the Depends! And the bunion pads and the Metamucil. And if she liked pretty music and old movies, so what? She wasn't hurting anyone.

Hazel had always said, "If you're still breathing, you're ahead of the game." And she'd been right. Life itself was something to look forward to, and so for whatever time she had left, she was going to enjoy every minute, wrinkles and all. What a concept! What a relief. She looked down at the flowers again and noticed something. She then bent over and picked a four-leaf clover growing right beside the headstone, and she had to laugh. It was Hazel all right.

Across town Babs Bingington had just picked up Mr. and Mrs. Troupe, her Texas clients, the ones she had stolen from Dottie Figge, to drive them to the airport, and they asked if they could stop by the model unit at Avon Terrace for a few minutes and measure the rooms once again before they left. Babs tried calling both Maggie's home phone and her cell phone to let her know they were coming by, but she couldn't reach her, so she guessed she was not home and drove the clients on over to Avon Terrace. She knocked on the door several times, but when no one answered, she used the key in the lockbox, and they went in. As her clients walked around, measuring for their furniture, Babs sat on the stool in the kitchen and waited. Then she noticed a blue envelope addressed to "To Whom It May Concern" lying on top of a stack of papers on the counter. She figured she'd better read it. It might have some instructions about showing the unit that she needed to see.

Back at the cemetery, as was usual on Easter morning, carloads of families started arriving with flowers. Maggie had completely forgotten how pretty children looked on Easter. When she went back to her car, she could hear her cell phone ringing away in her purse, to the tune of "I'm Looking Over a Four-Leaf Clover," and she had to laugh, since she was holding a four-leaf clover in her hand at that exact moment.

She figured it was Brenda calling. "Hello . . . Happy Easter!"

"Maggie?"

"Yes?"

"Where the hell are you?"

"At the cemetery—"

"Jesus Christ!"

"Who's this?"

"Babs Bingington. You haven't done anything stupid yet, have you?"

"What?"

"You haven't taken anything, have you?"

"What are you talking about?"

"What do you mean what am I talking about . . . I read your note."

"What note?"

"The note you left in the kitchen . . ."

"What kitchen?"

"Your kitchen, you idiot!"

"My kitchen? What are you doing in my kitchen? What note? I didn't leave you a note . . ."

"It says, 'To Whom It May Concern.' "

Maggie felt all the blood drain from her body. Oh, no. And just when she'd thought there was going to be a happy ending.

Babs continued her tirade: "What the hell's wrong with you, leaving a note like that? You must be nutty as a fruitcake. I've got a good mind to call the police."

Maggie panicked. "Wait, please, don't do anything. Just stay there, and let me come home and explain."

"I don't have time to wait around on you; I have to take my clients to the airport. But you need some serious help, sister." And she hung up.

Just then, Mrs. Troupe heard Babs yelling in the kitchen and came in and asked, "Is there anything wrong?"

Babs cocked her head to one side, smiled, and said in her phony southern accent, "Why no, darlin', not a thing."

Maggie sat with the phone in her hand, wondering what to do. She tried speed-dialing Babs back, but Babs wouldn't pick up. Of all the people in the world to find her letter, why did it have to be Babs? She had to somehow try to stop her from spreading it all over town, and knowing Babs, it would be just like her to post her letter on the Internet. Oh, God! She had to stop her before it was too late. She started the car and headed out to the airport as fast as she could. When she got there, she parked in front of the Southwest Airlines terminal and waited. This being Easter morning, the airport was almost deserted, and thank heavens, the airport police did not make her move her car the way they usually did. Fifteen minutes later, she saw Babs drive up in her big silver Lexus and let her clients out. Maggie pulled up behind her and got out and walked over just as Babs was smiling and waving goodbye. But as soon as Babs's clients went inside the glass door, she turned and glared at Maggie. "What the hell are you doing here?"

Maggie leaned in the window on the passenger side and said, "Please, I really need to explain. Can I get in and talk to you for just a minute?"

Babs quickly pushed the locks on all the doors, and they snapped shut with a loud click. "No! I'm not letting you in my car. You're as crazy as a loon; you might have a knife or a gun."

Maggie stepped back. "All right, okay, but please, just meet me somewhere and let me talk to you. I need to explain to you about the letter. Please . . . just for a little bit . . . let me buy you a drink or coffee or something. It won't take more than five minutes, I promise; just hear me out, and then you do whatever you want. But please just meet me somewhere."

Babs looked at her for a moment, then looked at her watch and let out an exasperated sigh. "Well, all right, but I'm still going to the Board of Realtors first thing in the morning to get your license suspended. Where do you want to go?"

"Anywhere. You pick it."

"Wait a minute. It's Easter, there's nothing open. Oh, forget it . . ."

Maggie desperately racked her brain and then said, "Meet me at Ruth's Chris over at the Embassy Suites Hotel. I know they'll be open; I'll meet you there."

Maggie ran and jumped back into her car and sped across town and arrived at the restaurant first. They were open and serving a lovely Easter brunch, but Maggie wasn't interested in food. As she sat in the booth waiting for Babs, she was scared to death that she wouldn't show up and that any second now, men in white coats would be coming through the door to cart her off. But to her relief, a few minutes later, Babs walked in and plopped down across from her. Maggie was a nervous wreck and when the waiter came over, she said, "I'll have a Pink Squirrel, and make it a double."

Babs looked at her and made a face. "A Pink Squirrel? Is that a joke? What's a Pink Squirrel?"

"I don't know, but it's good."

The waiter said, "It's like a Grasshopper, only it's pink."

"All right, whatever," said Babs. "Bring me one, too."

After the waiter left, Maggie thought about telling Babs Hazel's joke about a grasshopper named Harold to try to lighten the mood a bit, but she decided against it and started with "First of all, Babs, thank you so much for coming. I know it's a big imposition, but before I say anything else, I want you to know that the letter you found doesn't mean a thing. I wrote it at a time when . . . well, anyhow, I just didn't expect anyone to find it."

"What was it doing there, if you didn't expect anybody to find it?"

"I had planned to go to the office this afternoon and shred it. It never occurred to me anyone would be coming to the house on Easter. Anyhow, I know it was very upsetting for you, and I'm sorry."

Their drinks arrived, and Maggie slugged hers down in two gulps, then motioned to the waiter for another one and continued.

"When I wrote that letter, I wasn't thinking very clearly. I may have been having some sort of a little mini-breakdown or something. I've had an awful lot of disappointments lately."

"Oh, boo hoo, who hasn't?" said Babs. "Are you sure you're not just some nut job? That letter sounds wacko to me."

Maggie had no good quick comeback to that.

"I think you need to go and have your head examined."

"Well, you may be perfectly right about that, but in the meantime, I can assure you I'm not going to do anything stupid."

Babs took a long sip of her drink and made a face. "God, this is **sweet**!" She looked at Maggie and said, "Not that I care, but I am curious. Just how were you planning to dispose of your own body?"

"Oh . . . well, if you promise not to tell anyone, I'll tell you."

When Maggie had finished telling her the entire plan from start to finish, Babs nodded and said, "Pretty good, but you forgot one thing."

"What?"

"The raft. They have serial numbers. Somebody could have found it and traced it right back to you."

Oh, dear . . . Babs was right. She hadn't thought about that, but she didn't want Babs to know it, so she leaned back and smiled. "Very true . . . however . . . there was absolutely no way that anybody would ever find that raft," she said, while trying to quickly come up with a reason why not.

Thankfully, just then the waiter walked over with two more drinks and announced that they were from the nice man in the brown gabardine suit at the bar. Maggie smiled at him, pleasantly but not too friendly; she didn't want to encourage him.

Babs said, "Well? How were you going to get rid of the raft?"

"Oh . . ." Maggie said, making it up as she went along. "Well . . . okay . . . so after I got out to the middle of the river, I was going to tie myself to the raft with a piece of clothesline."

Babs frowned. "A clothesline?"

"That's right. Then I would puncture a hole in the raft, and when all the air was out, instead of me going down with the ship, the ship would go down with me." Maggie couldn't help but feel a little pleased with herself for coming up with something so fast.

Despite herself, Babs looked impressed. "Well, you're either crazier than I thought you were or smarter. I don't know which."

"Well, thank you, Babs. Anyhow, I'm sorry that you of all people had to be the one to find the letter; I know you don't particularly like me."

Babs agreed. "No, I don't," she said. "Even if you had done yourself in, it wouldn't have mattered to me one way or another."

"Then why were you so upset?"

"I didn't want you to mess up my sale of the unit in your complex before we closed escrow. After that, you can go jump in the river for all I care."

Maggie looked at her. "Oh, Babs . . . surely you don't mean that."

"Yes, I do. Look, I feel the same way about you as you feel about me."

"What do you mean? I don't dislike you."

"Oh, come on, who's kidding who here? I know you and every other realtor in town hates my guts."

Maggie tried to protest. "Oh no, we don't hate you, Babs . . . My heavens." But then the three double Pink Squirrels on an empty stomach started taking effect, and she said, "Well, yes . . . I guess we all kinda do."

"Of course you do, but the difference between me and all of you is that I couldn't care less what you think about me."

"But Babs, how can you not care what people think of you?"

"Easy. I just don't care."

"You really don't?"

"No, I really don't."

Maggie sat back in the booth and mulled it over, then leaned in and said, "Well, Babs, and I don't mean this in an ugly way, but considering that you obviously don't have a conscience or any ethics whatsoever or even one ounce of human decency . . . I think it's much easier for you not to care."

Babs thought about it a second, then nodded. "I guess that's true."

Maggie continued on with a pleasant smile. "In fact, you're probably the meanest, most despicable and evil person I've ever met."

Babs looked at her. "Is that so?"

"Yes. You are without a doubt the most perfectly horrible person I've ever encountered in my entire life." Maggie put her finger up in the air to make a point. "And, I might add, a thoroughly rotten human being, rotten to the core. Frankly, I wouldn't be surprised if somebody didn't wind up running you over with a car someday."

Babs, now on her third Pink Squirrel as well, started to laugh. She suddenly thought everything Maggie said was hilarious.

"Really, Babs. I don't see how you can live with yourself. You are a vicious fiend, a two-faced vampire-bat snake-in-the-grass bully. And by the way, those shoes you have on went out of style in the seventies and, Babs, garnet earrings? Nobody wears garnets anymore, much less in the daytime. You have absolutely no morals. You're rude, hateful, and thoroughly unpleasant, a liar and a cheat and a criminal."

By this time, Babs was almost doubled over, she was laughing so hard.

"In fact, you probably should be in jail right now." Maggie stopped and looked at her. "Come to think of it, I wouldn't be surprised if you weren't a complete sociopath!"

Babs screamed with laughter at the word "sociopath," and so did Maggie!

A woman sitting in the corner of the dining room, wearing a pretty pastel green dress with a lace collar, scowled at them, then punched her husband on the arm. "Look, Curtis, both of them drunk as lords, and on Easter, too!"

After they finally were able to control themselves, Babs reached into her purse and handed Maggie a Kleenex and sighed. Then she said, "But what do you really think about me?" And they both started laughing all over again.

When they had recovered and could talk, Babs looked over at Maggie and said, "You may have cotton balls for brains, but you're funny."

Wiping her eyes, Maggie said, "Thanks. I hope I didn't hurt your feelings calling you a sociopath."

"Me? No, I've been called worse than that."

Maggie gave out a big sigh and looked at Babs somewhat wistfully. "Oh, Babsy, what's it like not to care about what people think?"

"It's great."

"It must be. I wish I didn't care so much, but really, tell me the truth . . . deep, deep down, don't you care just a tiny bit?"

Babs thought, then said with some certainty, "No, I really don't."

"Truly?"

Babs shrugged. "No, like I said, what people think about me is no skin off my nose."

"Aaah," said Maggie, "but I think it is. I think it probably affects you in ways you don't even know about and will probably never even find out."

"How? I'm the top seller in the Southeast. How bad could it be?"

"Yes, but even so, I still think it's important to have people's good will."

"Why?"

"Why? When something bad happens to you, don't you want people to say, 'Oh, that's too bad,' instead of 'Oh, goody, she had it coming'?"

Babs shrugged again. "Don't care."

"Don't you want people to wish you well?"

"Don't care."

"Oh . . . Babsy," said Maggie, reaching for her drink and missing it, "you must have had a terrible childhood. That must be the reason you're so unethical."

"My childhood was fine. But while we're on the subject, let me ask you something. How did you manage to steal Crestview away from me?"

"Oh, that."

"Yes, that."

Maggie was caught red-handed and had to admit the truth. "I know the man who handles the Dalton estate, and I called him."

Babs was surprised. "Oh, really."

"Yes. Of course I'm not proud of what I did."

"Why not? I would have done the same thing."

Maggie looked at her in amazement. "You're not just saying that to be nice, are you?"

"Me? No." Babs looked around the room. "I think I'm getting hungry. Should we eat?"

"Of course, order anything you want . . . the sky's the limit."

Babs ordered her steak rare, and Maggie was not surprised.

After they finished eating, Babs said, "I don't have any plans. Do you?"

"No, I'm free as a bird."

Twenty-four hours ago, if someone had told Maggie that she would wind up at the Alabama Theatre, still half drunk on Pink Squirrels, seeing **The Sound of Music** with Babs Bingington, she wouldn't have believed it. After the movie, when they were walking back to their cars, Maggie said, "Do me a favor, Babs: if you ever do buy our company, you can fire me, but keep Ethel and Brenda, okay?"

Babs smiled and said, "Not on your life," and got into her car and drove away. Like her or not, there was one thing you could say about Babs: she was consistent.

Home for Good

⌒

After Maggie had left Babs in the parking lot, she realized again just how lucky she was that she had not jumped in the river. After all her long and careful planning, the serial number on that raft could very well have given her away. No matter what they said, there really was no such thing as a perfect plan.

When she got home and walked into the house, her phone was ringing. She picked it up, and it was Brenda on the other end. "What happened to you? Are you all right? I've been worried sick. Where have you been all day?"

"Oh, honey, I'm sorry, but I'm fine, better than fine . . . in fact, I'm just perfectly . . . wonderful!"

"Well, I'm glad you're so wonderful, but you almost worried me to death. I tried calling you all afternoon. I almost came out looking for you. Why did you have your cell phone turned off?"

"Oh, well, after we had lunch, Babs and I went to the movies, and I had to turn it off."

There was a long silence on the other end. And then Brenda said, "Have you been drinking?"

Maggie laughed. "Why, yes . . . as a matter of fact . . . I have."

"Well . . . I think you'd better take some aspirin and go to bed."

Maggie said, "Yes, Mother, I will. Good night . . . Sleep tight . . . Don't let the bedbugs bite."

Brenda hung up the phone and said to Robbie, "I told you she sounded drunk. She's loaded to the gills. She thinks she went to the movies with Babs Bingington."

After the phone call, Maggie decided that ever telling Brenda what she had **really** been planning to do today would be far too upsetting for her. There was no need for her to ever know. She'd get to work early Monday morning and take the note out of Brenda's desk. But for now, she was suddenly very thirsty. It must have been all that Easter ham she had eaten for lunch and the salty popcorn at the movie. Maggie had just poured herself a glass of water when she heard the sound of a fax coming in on her machine in the den. She wondered who could be faxing her this late, and on Easter, too. Oh God, she hoped it wasn't her cousin Hector Smoote. She walked back to the den. Just another fax from Miss Pitcock. The woman was like a dog with a bone. She was still at it, and on a holiday, too. Miss Pitcock had now gone online and was searching all the English and Scottish newspapers and the Hall of Records for any information. But after all her digging, she had never been able to locate a birth or a death certificate for Edwina Crocker. She had just faxed over a picture of Edwina Crocker at some reception in a white dress and wearing three big white feathers in her hair. Well, whoever the woman was, she looked like she was happy. Good. Tonight, Maggie wanted everyone in the world, dead or alive, to be as happy as she was.

As Maggie kicked off her shoes and looked around the empty den, she now wished she hadn't shredded all her photos and all her old press releases, but maybe it was for the best. She had spent far too much time dwelling on the past, and maybe it was a sign that she should concentrate on the future. What an odd thing. Just a few weeks ago, she'd had no future. And now, she had nothing but a future, with so many things to do. She sat down at her desk and started a new list.

Old Age, Pros and Cons

Pros	Cons
1. You are still alive!	1.
2. Senior discounts up the kazoo	2.
3. No more high heels	3.
4. You don't have to be nice	4.

5. You can say what   5.
   you think
6. You still don't have   6.
   to watch the news
7. You can watch Turner   7.
   Classic Movies all night
8. You don't have to do   8.
   anything you don't
   want to
9. You are still alive!!!   9.

When Maggie saw it all written down in black and white . . . no question about it, no matter what might be coming up in the future right now, there were no cons she could think of. She turned off the light and went to bed and realized for the first time in years, she was actually looking forward to another day.

The first thing the next morning, Maggie jumped up out of bed and fixed her tea and went outside to greet another beautiful spring day. It was so wonderful to look up and see Crestview. As she sat there, she reviewed her list; No. 4, "You don't have to be nice," stuck in her mind.

After she went back inside, she picked up the phone and did something she should have done years ago. When he answered, she said, "Hector? It's your cousin, Maggie, from Birmingham, calling . . ." But before he could begin his usual greeting, she said, "I think you should know that it is extremely rude to make fun of someone's home and their accent."

"What?"

"Goodbye, Hector," she said and then hung up and felt quite good about it. She had actually said what she had been thinking for years, and she didn't seem to regret it one whit or even care what he thought. What a wonderful feeling that was. As she ate her waffles, she had another thought. While she was at it, she might just call that late-night television host and tell him she didn't appreciate his ugly little remarks about beauty queens either.

But on second thought, she decided against it. She had the rest of her life to say exactly what she thought. There would be plenty of time for everything. How thrilling was that?

Several days later, the most amazing thing happened. Maggie had run out to the cleaners to drop off a few things and was headed back to her car when she heard someone call her name. When she turned around to look, she saw that it was Jennifer Rudolph, who she had not seen since the fifth grade. After they hugged and chatted a moment, Jennifer said, "Oh, Maggie, I was always so proud of you. You are the most famous person I ever knew. I always brag and tell my kids I went to school with Miss America, and are they impressed."

Maggie felt her old shame rising up and said, "Well, you know, honey, I wasn't Miss America."

Jennifer looked surprised. "You weren't?"

"No, I wish I had been, but I was only the second runner-up."

"Really? Oh well, who cares—you'll always be Miss America as far as I'm concerned." Then she laughed. "Honey, it's like the Oscars; after so many years, nobody ever remembers who won, just who was nominated."

After they said goodbye, Maggie was still amazed by what Jennifer had said. Jennifer clearly hadn't cared, one way or the other, if she had won or not. Good Lord, had her not winning really been that unimportant? Wouldn't that be wonderful? Wouldn't it be a relief not to dread running into old friends again? She suddenly began toying with the idea of calling a few people just to say hello. A few years ago, the Miss Alabama people had asked her to be one of the judges in the state pageant, and she had declined; but maybe if they asked her again, she would reconsider. She might even go to the next ex–Miss Alabama reunion. Life was so odd; only two days ago, she had felt just like the last fox-trot on the **Titanic** . . . but today, it was full speed ahead!

More Revelations

Friday, April 24, 2009

*T*he days flew by, and spring became prettier and prettier. Ever since that Easter morning, something had shifted a little for Maggie; a small shift, but still a big one for her. It had happened so gradually that at first she hadn't noticed, but then one day, it suddenly dawned on her. That old gray dread that she used to feel when she woke up was not there anymore, and as strange as it seemed (for her, at least), she hardly ever worried about things anymore. And what a relief that was. Of course, nothing was perfect; she still had all the same old shortcomings that she had been struggling with for years. But in the past few weeks, Maggie had realized something that had never occurred to her before. She didn't have to be perfect. Yes, she had made a lot of mistakes in the past and she would probably make many more in the future, but it wasn't the end of the world. And okay, so she was still just a little bit stuck in the fifties. She enjoyed seeing reruns of **I Love Lucy** and hearing a pretty song every now and then. She still cried when they played the national anthem. Maybe she was too old-fashioned, but she still loved celebrating the Fourth of July and seeing the Thanksgiving parade and watching the same old Christmas movies on television each year . . . but so what? As she had found out the hard way, life was too short to be unhappy about anything. Hazel had been right all along. She'd said, "I don't have time to be unhappy; I'm having too much fun being alive." And Maggie agreed. She wasn't thrilled about having to go back to the gym two days a week, but she had signed up for a cooking class that she was enjoying very much. She had taken up her harp lessons again and was learning the song "Blue Skies" in honor of Hazel. With so many new things going on, Maggie had mostly forgotten about her quest to solve the mystery of the Scottish twins. Even the unstoppable Miss Pitcock had finally been stopped. She had just faxed Maggie and informed her that she had reached the end of all available information in the British archives, or anywhere else in the world for that matter. Maggie immediately faxed her back and thanked her profusely for all the good work she had done.

Maggie was sure that if Miss Pitcock couldn't find any more information, there wasn't any, but when Maggie got into bed that night, she found herself thinking about Edward and Edwina Crocker once again. Of course, now she would never know for sure who Edwina really was, but having seen her photograph taken at Buckingham Palace, and considering the uncanny family resemblance, she was convinced, birth certificate or not, that Edwina really was Edward's sister and **not** his mistress as she had once suspected. Besides, now that she thought about it, Edwina never would have been given the title of Lady Edwina Crocker if she hadn't **really** been a Crocker. The British wouldn't have made a mistake like that in a million years. But still . . . it was odd that there was no record of birth for a person as important as Edwina. Oh well, it would just have to remain unsolved. Maggie rolled over and turned off the light.

At around two A.M., Maggie suddenly sat straight up in bed and said, "Oh, my God." Why hadn't she seen it before? It was as obvious as the nose on her face. No wonder Edward and Edwina had never been photographed together and Miss Pitcock had never been able to find a birth certificate for Edwina. There was no Edwina Crocker. There never had been. Edward and Edwina were the same person! Of course. The two sets of clothes in the trunks had both belonged to Edward.

At last, it all made perfect sense. Edward Crocker had been a cross-dresser. He had lived as a woman in London and as a man in Birmingham. No wonder he had never introduced Edwina to any of his friends. He couldn't. Oh, that poor man. How Edward must have suffered all those years, trying to keep it a secret. Well, bless his heart, he needn't worry about anyone finding out. His secret was safe with her. She didn't need to tell anyone. But she did feel relieved to know that she was obviously not as dumb as she'd thought. She had solved the mystery of the Scottish twins. She had finally figured out the real story.

Maggie had no way of knowing it, but she was dead wrong. That was not the real story at all. There had been only four people in the entire world who knew the real story: Angus, the father; a doctor; Nurse Lettie Ross; and, of course, Edwina. The only other living creature who knew the **real** story was the fly on the wall that day in 1884, when it all began.

What the Fly on the Wall Saw
Edinburgh, Scotland, May 22, 1884

The day Edward Crocker was born, the doctor in attendance was jubilant. His patient had just given birth to twins, a boy and a girl. Nurse Lettie Ross ran to the top landing upstairs and announced to Angus, waiting below, the good news: his wife had given him the son he wanted and a daughter.

But an agonizing hour later, the weary doctor came down the stairs and slowly walked down the long hall to the study, dreading the task at hand. Angus Crocker was a man he had wanted to please. He needed a benefactor, and if all went well, Angus had promised that he would build him a hospital. But all had not gone well. Due to unforeseen complications, he had lost the mother, and the weaker twin had died soon after.

Sometime later in the evening, after all the servants had been sent home, the young nurse was called down to the study, and the door was closed behind her. No one knows how much money was exchanged or what was said, but in the middle of the night, a baby was wrapped in blankets and taken away, and by morning, the baby that lay in the cradle upstairs was named Edward, and the word "male" written on his birth certificate. The doctor got his hospital, and the young nurse had a position for life. With the death of Angus's wife, there would never be another child with both Crocker and Sperry blood. Half-mad with grief and half-mad with power, Angus had made a deal with the devil that night.

There would be a Crocker son. Not the one he had hoped for, but this child would carry on as best it could. What if there were sacrifices? Hadn't he sacrificed to create an empire? Hadn't its mother died bringing it into the world? This child would be made to understand that this was the only choice. A female child was not a blessing to a wealthy man; a female was a liability. Who knows, down the line, what fortune hunter could come along, marriage laws being what they were; and after Angus's death, this stranger could gain total control of the Crocker-Sperry holdings. Hadn't he done the same thing? Angus was not about to give away his life's work to some unknown thief or scoundrel looking to steal another man's fortune. It could happen. And by God, this child would understand that it was for her own good that it was done. The child would thank him one day.

After the funeral of his wife, Angus wanted to get as far away as possible from the place that held such painful memories. He sold all the company's holdings in Scotland, and as soon as the child could travel, father, nurse, and baby sailed for America and, upon arriving in New York, boarded a private train headed to Birmingham. Acting on a tip from his friend and fellow Scot Andrew Carnegie, in Pittsburgh, Angus had purchased thousands of acres of land he intended to develop into the largest coal, iron, and steel company in the South.

Lettie Ross, the young nurse, knew that the bargain she had made was ungodly, but she had eight younger brothers and sisters and a sick mother who would be saved from the grinding poverty of the poor working class. With her salary, there would be money for doctors, food, warmth, and education for her brothers and sisters. Maybe she would go to hell for what she had agreed to, but it was a small price to pay for an entire family's salvation. And the child in her care would want for nothing, other than being deprived of its natural gender; but as far as Lettie was concerned, that was also a small price to pay. Given a choice, what female wouldn't want to live as a male? Males were free to move about the world as they chose; males could vote; they could not be beaten by their drunken husbands like her poor mother. But most of all, this child would never be forced to submit to a man for anything, the way she had been. When the child came of a certain age, she would make her understand that what had been done was for her own good. The child would thank her someday.

As the years passed, she began to see what a lonely, unhappy life the little girl was leading. When she was sixteen, it was Lettie Ross who first came up with the idea of Edwina. And what fun it turned out to be: all the trips to London, shopping for clothes. A few years later, a townhome in May-fair was purchased, and the grand deception began. In June of 1912, Miss Edwina Crocker, twin sister of Edward, was launched into London society, and Lettie Ross was happy. For once, the girl could be who she really was, and although it would only be for a few months once a year, it would provide some relief from the tremendous burden of having to be Edward the rest of the year. When her father, Angus, had died, she had taken over the family in-terests and was now in charge of all the Crocker companies. It was quite a responsibility, with little time for fun. Edwina cherished the months she spent in London: her friends, the parties. There was even a time when Edwina fell in love and enter-tained the idea of giving up the charade forever. But by then, it was too late. The revelation would have caused too much of an uproar, and the scandal might have destroyed the company. She had hun-dreds of employees' welfare to think about, so al-though she loved him, she said goodbye to the young man. But there was another reason she did not give up her life as Edward and marry. Unlike most women, Edwina had felt what it was like to have power, to be a male in society. And once having tasted that power, she was not willing to give it up, even for love.

She was, after all, her father's daughter, and she liked the business of making money. She was smart, capable, and, having lived as a man and a woman, even more intuitive about people than old Angus Crocker had been. Since taking over, she had more than tripled the company's assets. In 1932, she foresaw the decline of coal as a fuel source and, unlike the other stubborn coal men, she followed her gut intuition and sold most of her coal interests and invested the money with oil prospectors in Texas.

Years later, looking back at what her life would have been as Edwina, with all the restrictions and limitations of being female, she came to believe that although it had been a terribly reckless and selfish thing that had been done, in the long run, Lettie was right; it had turned out to be for her own good.

As Edward, the son, she'd had total control of her own life. As Edwina, the daughter, she would have had money, but never control of it; she would have borne the Crocker name, but never the power that went with it. And there had been other advantages. When Edward had spoken, people had listened. When he had championed women's causes, he had not been dismissed as just another emotional female. When Edward had ordered men about, they had not balked at receiving orders from a woman.

And her life had not been without fun. She and Lettie had laughed over the years, picturing the faces of men: if they had only known a female was running one of the largest companies in the world and had bested most of them at golf, if they had known a female was the president of three all-male clubs, it would have boggled their minds. She knew men's real opinion of women. She'd heard it first-hand. At the time, even in a deeply racist society, the mostly uneducated black man had been given the right to vote before college-educated women, black or white. If she could do more as Edward to help the cause, then as Lettie said, it was a small price to pay.

But as the years passed, the strain of living a double life began to take its toll. And in 1939, while in London, Edwina suddenly became more tired than usual. Insisting that she needed a complete rest, Lettie took her to her family home in northern Scotland to be attended to by Lettie's physician brother.

But after an examination, the news was not good. Edwina had an advanced case of leukemia and was dying. Devastated, Lettie never left her side for a moment. A few weeks later, Edwina Crocker died in Lettie's arms, the same arms that had been the first to hold her at her birth.

With her beloved Edwina gone, Lettie now had

to solve the problem of informing the world about what had happened to Edward. People in Birmingham would soon begin to wonder where he was.

The next morning, she sent a wire. Soon after it arrived, the **Birmingham News** carried this headline in bold letters across the front page:

EDWARD CROCKER FEARED LOST AT SEA

Three days after the death of his beloved sister, Birmingham business tycoon Edward Crocker has been reported lost at sea in what appears to have been a sailing accident. The accident occurred off the northern coast of Scotland, where his sister was buried.

Everyone in Birmingham sat waiting for news; when it came over the Teletype, it was rushed into print and broadcast on the radio.

EDWARD CROCKER OFFICIALLY DEAD

A week later, over a thousand people came to a memorial service for a man who had never existed. Edward Crocker, the person they had known as the rich, powerful industrialist, had died quietly in an obscure little village in northern Scotland as Edwina.

But before Edwina had died, she had made one last request. She wanted to be taken home and buried at Crestview. Lettie had promised her that it would be done, but in 1939, war was brewing in Europe and travel was difficult, so the trip home would have to wait. In the interim, Edwina's body was buried in a small country cemetery outside the village in an unmarked grave until it was safe to sail again.

Returning Home to Crestview
Scotland, 1946

Seven long years later, with the war in Europe finally over, Lettie began her plans to bring her beloved Edwina home to Crestview, but under the circumstances, it would be hard to do. They couldn't send the body out of the country through official channels; too many questions would be asked. Edwina Crocker had no record of birth. Although Edward Crocker had a birth certificate, they couldn't risk having the body examined by the trained eye of a government official or a coroner. How could they explain the remains of a woman traveling with a male birth certificate? But Lettie was determined to get the body home and to keep the secret of Edward and Edwina. She had made a vow to Edwina to take her home to Crestview, and she was honor-bound to keep it.

With the help of her brother, the body was exhumed and taken to a family friend who was an undertaker, and the remains were prepared for the long journey home. The skeleton was cleaned, then dressed in the formal Sperry family kilt and hung in one of two steamer trunks containing the twins' clothes. Lettie had wanted to sail with the trunks, but her brother, although he was indebted to Lettie for his education, was too frightened to travel on the same ship, in case there was trouble. And so, on his advice, the trunks were shipped ahead. When word came that the two trunks had arrived safely, he and Lettie would follow on the next ship and arrange a private burial at Crestview.

Edward had left Crestview to his business partner, George Dalton. Lettie knew Mrs. Dalton very well. She was a delightful lady who had served as Edward's hostess on many occasions and was one of Edward's favorite lady friends, and she had adored him as well. They had spent many cheerful hours together planning parties. Lettie knew Mrs. Dalton could be trusted to do anything Edward wanted done, and a wire was sent to her at Crestview.

Mrs. Dalton,

Following Mr. Crocker's last instructions, am sending two trunks containing personal items. Upon receipt, please hold for my arrival. Would appreciate notification of safe delivery.

Lettie Ross

When the trunks arrived, Mrs. Dalton immediately had them taken upstairs and locked in the attic. Her children were incurably curious, and she didn't want them to break open the locks and rummage through Edward's things.

Miss Ross,

Trunks arrived safely. Awaiting your arrival and further instructions.

Mrs. George Dalton

It was a simple plan. After she and her brother arrived in Birmingham, she would explain to Mrs. Dalton that Edward wanted certain personal items to be buried at Crestview. She knew Mrs. Dalton would understand and would respect his final wishes. Then they would make arrangements to have both unopened trunks buried in the shady gardens below the house, and afterward, she could go back to Scotland and die happy, her life's work done.

Once Lettie received word that the trunks had arrived safely and intact, she and her brother booked passage to America. A week later, Lettie, now almost eighty, was preparing for the upcoming trip when she had a stroke. She was never able to make it to Birmingham and died a couple of years later, in 1949.

Until November 5, 2008, when Brenda banged the door open, the body had been locked up in the attic and forgotten.

Beauty Secrets

Friday, May 1, 2009

Sometime after Maggie realized she wanted to live, she began to reexamine her life and try to figure out why she had become so unhappy. Then one day, it occurred to her that although she had never purposely lied to anyone, she had been living a lie for years. Brenda thought Maggie was so good and virtuous, but she deserved to know the truth. She hoped it wouldn't affect their friendship, but it was a chance she had to take.

She picked up the phone and called Brenda and invited her to lunch out at the old Irondale Cafe. She wanted Brenda full of good food before she told her. Brenda did not let her down. She had the chicken livers and the macaroni and cheese and lemon icebox pie. As Maggie was driving them back home, she gathered her courage, took a deep breath, and said, "Brenda, there's something I think you should know about me . . . something I've never told you before. Something you might find quite shocking."

Brenda said, "I doubt it."

"Well . . . you might."

"Oh, right. What are you going to tell me? That you're really the midnight bandit who's been robbing all the 7-Eleven stores?"

"Oh, no. Nothing like that, but it's something I'm not very proud of."

"What?"

Maggie took another deep breath. "Well, the man I was involved with in Dallas that I told you about . . . Richard?"

"Yes? What about him?"

"He was married."

"And?"

"That's it. He was a married man. I had an affair with a married man."

"Oh."

"The reason I didn't tell you before is that I didn't want you to be disappointed in me."

"I see."

"Oh, Brenda, I'm sorry." Maggie looked at her with concern. "Are you just terribly shocked?"

"Well, yes. I am shocked, but not disappointed."

"Really? You're not?"

"No. We all make mistakes; we wouldn't be human if we didn't."

"You wouldn't lie to me just to make me feel better?"

"Of course not."

Brenda was unusually quiet as they drove along, and Maggie began to wonder if she had made the wrong decision by telling her. They drove along for quite some time, Maggie getting more anxious by the minute, until Brenda said, "Maggie, do you remember the college professor I told you I had the affair with?"

"The one who broke your heart when you were a senior?"

"Yes . . . well, there's a little something I never told you about, either. Or anybody else for that matter . . . not even Robbie or Tonya."

"What?"

There was a long pause. Brenda said, "She was married, too."

"Ahhh . . . no wonder it was so—" Maggie suddenly stopped when she realized what she had just heard and looked at Brenda. **"She?"**

"Uh-huh."

"Oh, Brenda . . . really?"

"Oh, yes, honey; married, white, and Jewish. What can I say? So you see, you're not alone. Everybody has their little secrets." She looked over at Maggie. "Are you surprised?"

"Well, yes . . . I guess I am."

"Are you disappointed? You look funny."

"Oh, no . . . I'm not disappointed. How could I be? I just feel . . . oh, I don't know, flattered that you trust me enough to tell me."

Now Brenda was relieved. "Whew, I'm glad that's over. I'm a nervous wreck. I'm all sweaty," she said as she grabbed an emergency Hershey bar out of her purse and took a bite. When she finished, she looked over at Maggie and said, "Well, then . . . now that both our cats are out of the bag, like the song says, ''Tain't nobody's business but our own,' right?"

"Right."

"Life is hard enough. I say everybody deserves at least one little secret, don't you think?"

"I do." A few minutes later, Maggie said, "Brenda, let me ask you something. Do you think I'm too old to learn to parallel park?"

"No, I do not. I think you can do anything you set your mind to."

"Really?"

"Absolutely."

"Oh, Brenda . . . you don't know how happy I feel—like a hundred-pound weight has been lifted off my chest."

"Me, too."

"I feel so much closer to you now . . . do you?"

"Oh, yes."

They both smiled all the way home. It was so good to have a best friend.

A Message from Mitzi

Friday, May 22, 2009

⤬

*F*or Maggie, life was just getting better and better. in addition to her cooking classes, she was now taking driving lessons. Just as she was walking out the door this morning, headed for the office, the kitchen phone rang.

"Maggie? It's Mitzi. Listen, honey, I'm just heart-broken to have to make this call, but poor David's company has been so whipped around by this awful economy thing. He's not going to get to retire when we thought."

"Oh, no."

"Yes, can you believe it? He's going to have to stay in New York at least another three years and help them get it straightened out and try to make sure his clients don't lose everything."

"Oh, Mitzi, I am so sorry."

"Well, me too, but the worst part is, honey . . . we can't keep Crestview and our place here, and as much as we hate to, we're going to have to just turn right around and sell it."

Maggie's heart dropped, and she sat down. "I see."

"I can't tell you how disappointed I am. I know you think I'm silly, but I practically had the place furnished and was already planning the parties I was going to give and everything."

After she hung up, she felt badly for poor Mitzi and also for Crestview. She was afraid she would never be able to find more perfect people than Mitzi and David.

Later, when Maggie walked into the office, Ethel looked up and greeted her with even worse news.

"Little Harry died," Ethel said.

"Oh, no. When?"

"Sometime yesterday."

"What happened? What was it?"

"They didn't say; just old age, I guess. But we need to send flowers or something, don't we?"

"Oh, absolutely. Oh, poor Little Harry. I'm surprised he lived as long as he did. You know he must have been so lonely without Hazel."

"I'm sure he was."

"Little Harry must have been what? Eighty? Eighty-five?"

Ethel shook her head. "No, Little Harry was not that old; he was at least ten years younger than Hazel. I don't know if he knew or not, but he was. Anyhow, you know what this means, don't you? I hate to be the bearer of bad news, but it's curtains for

Red Mountain Realty. I always said, 'The minute Harry goes, his family will sell the company.' "

Maggie nodded. "I'm sure you're right."

"I know I am. The lawyer just called ten minutes ago, asking to see the books."

"Oh really, did he say why?"

"He said he wanted to look them over before he sent them to an interested party, and I'll give you three guesses who the interested party is. Hint: she's been circling over our heads like a buzzard for years."

"Does Brenda know yet?"

"Oh yes, she was here when the lawyer called."

"Was she upset?"

"Does a cat have a tail?"

"Where is she?"

"Back in her office, I guess."

Maggie walked down the hall and called out, "Brenda. Where are you, honey?"

But at that moment, Brenda was already walking in the front door of the Krispy Kreme doughnut shop six blocks away. The idea of Babs Bingington taking over Hazel's company made her sick. She needed a doughnut, and she needed it right now. Brenda sat down at the counter, looked the waitress in the eye, and said, "I want a dozen glazed, a dozen assorted, and four cinnamon buns to go, and bring me a coffee and two jelly doughnuts for here." Her cell phone started ringing, but she ignored it. It might be her Overeaters Anonymous sponsor; she had not called this morning, but Brenda was in no mood to be saved from herself.

Ten minutes later, just as she was about to bite into another jelly doughnut, she heard a familiar voice behind her saying, "Okay, Brenda, step away from the counter!"

Brenda froze in her seat. It was Ja'ronda Jones, her Overeaters Anonymous sponsor!

"You heard me. Step away from the doughnuts; put the doughnut down now!"

Brenda knew you didn't fool with Ja'ronda; she was a six-foot-one retired policewoman and could do you some real harm if she wanted to. Brenda slowly placed what was left of her doughnut back on the plate, and before she knew it, Ja'ronda had snatched up her purse and had her by the arm, walking her out the front door. The girl called out, "Don't you want your to-go order?"

"No, she doesn't," said Ja'ronda.

Not only was Brenda losing her job, she had just been ratted out by a fellow member of Overeaters Anonymous, who'd happened to be driving by and had seen Brenda's car, with the Red Mountain Realty sign on the door, parked in front of the doughnut shop. It was that **damn** car's fault! Some days, it just doesn't pay to get out of bed.

Maggie sat at her desk and continued to dial Brenda's cell phone number, feeling pretty low herself. After all of her hard work, Babs Bingington would wind up with the listing on Crestview after

all. What had ever made her think things were looking up?

The very next day, their worst fears had come true.
The sale happened so fast, one couldn't help but
wonder if the lawyer and Babs hadn't had everything in place before Little Harry died. Four days
later, the lawyer came to the office to explain the
transition to the staff of Red Mountain Realty. The
terms were simple. They were to be out of the office
in two weeks, and at that time, all their existing
properties under contract were to be absorbed into
the parent company, and they were to turn in their
leased cars on the last day.

Ethel said, "I don't suppose we can expect any
sort of severance pay."

The lawyer shook his head. "No, I'm sorry, the
new owner feels that two weeks' notice is suffi-
cient."

Ethel said, "So after fifty-six years with the company, it's 'Here's your hat, what's your hurry'? If I
were a drinking woman, I'd buy a bottle of champagne—and hit her over the head with it."

The lawyer smiled. "I understand how you feel,
Ms. Clipp," he said while pulling out yet another
set of papers. "However, I wouldn't let it bother me
too much if I were you. The previous owner, Hazel
Whisenknott, made certain arrangements that I
think will more than make up for it."

Certain Arrangements

In the 1980s, when the world had gone litigation-crazy, and so many frivolous lawsuits had been filed against businesses, Hazel had quietly transferred her other company, L.P. Investments, into Harry's name. They all knew that Harry owned another company that handled a few commercial real estate holdings. But what they hadn't known was that in the late 1950s, when land was cheap, L.P. Investments had quietly bought block after block of property on the south side, the same property where the huge University of Alabama Medical Center sat today. Although Hazel had lived modestly, she had died a very wealthy woman. Naturally, being a smart businesswoman, she had wanted to protect herself, so if either company was hit with a lawsuit, the lawyers would not be able to tie up everything she owned. At that time, Hazel had verbally specified to Little Harry that if anything happened to her and he sold the companies, he was to make sure that all the current members of Team Hazel were well taken care of. And so, according to her wishes, they were to share 50 percent of the profits from Red Mountain Realty and L.P. Investments. Since there were only three members of Team Hazel left, the lawyer handed each a check for $8,278,000! He went on to explain to them that they would each have to pay income tax on the original amount, but even after taxes, Team Hazel would still be sitting pretty. All three were astonished.

Brenda was the first one able to speak. "But I've never heard of L.P. Investments. Who is L.P.?"

The lawyer checked the original and informed her that L.P. wasn't a person at all. "L.P." stood for "Lucky Penny."

Later, after they got over the initial shock and could think straight, they all started talking about what they were going to do with their money.

Ethel said she was going to take a trip around the world, get a new hip and a face-lift and cataract surgery.

"I'm putting mine in the bank," Brenda said, "and keeping my mouth shut. If those nephews of mine find out I've got money, I'll never hear the end of it."

"What are you going to do, Maggie?" Ethel asked. "Have you decided yet?"

Maggie knew exactly what she was going to do. She smiled. "I'm going to buy Crestview."

That night, David and Mitzi were thrilled when she called and told them. Mitzi said, "Oh, Maggie, as much as I hate to give it up, I can't help but wonder if you weren't supposed to have it all along. Isn't it strange how things work out?"

After she hung up, Maggie had to smile. It wasn't so strange how things had worked out. Hazel had been right about people all along; they never do really die, they just go on and on. Just when they had thought that all was lost, little Hazel had come riding in on her white horse and saved them once again. Now everything made sense. No wonder Hazel had stopped her from jumping in the river. After all, Hazel had always said "Don't give up before the miracle happens." And if this wasn't a miracle, Maggie didn't know what was.

A few days afterward, Audrey got home from the Brookwood Mall and stopped at her mailbox and was surprised to see a personal letter addressed to her. She rarely ever received a real letter anymore. It was always bills or ads or a fake letter that was really an ad. But inside this envelope was a cashier's check made out to her for a hundred thousand dollars; no note, just the check. She didn't know who had sent it or if it was a real check or a fake, so she didn't want to get too excited until she could go down to the bank and find out, on the off chance that it was real. Oh, the things she would do. The first thing she would do would be to get all dressed up and take herself out to a fine restaurant and enjoy herself for a change. Why, she could think of a hundred little things she needed and some she didn't.

The same day, the Visiting Nurses Association and the Humane Society received nice checks, and a fund for the annual Hazel Whisenknott Easter Egg Hunt was established. Maggie thought her friend would have liked that.

Maggie could hardly believe it. Her life was going to have a happy ending after all. Crestview would be hers. She could hang Thanksgiving corn on the door, Christmas lights, Halloween witches, flags on the Fourth of July; place eggs and baskets of white lilies on the front lawn at Easter. It would be hers to decorate forever. To Maggie, it wasn't just the house, the bricks and stone. It was the idea behind it; it was a constant reminder of beauty, grace, and symmetry. To her, Crestview was a dream that one man had imagined, a dream that had come true and still stood all these many years later. And then, too, something Hazel used to say about the one little candle came to mind. Maybe that was it. Maybe she was supposed to keep that one little candle burning as best she could. If nothing else, who knew, maybe someday a little girl might look up on the mountain and be inspired the way she had been. There had to be something left for people to look up to and dream about, didn't there?

Of course, Ethel said that with all our problems these days, it was just the beginning of the end for Western civilization. Maybe so, but Maggie, for one, was going to hang on to it for as long as she could because no matter what ugly things people said about it, she **liked** Western civilization. It was just so civilized. And, okay, maybe we weren't perfect, but my heavens, hadn't we given the world movie stars, musical comedies, electricity, baseball, hot dogs and hamburgers, not to mention Disneyland? And if anyone thought women would give up their equal rights now that they had them, they needed to talk to Brenda. She, for one, could tell them that that just wasn't going to happen. Just like the old iron statue of Vulcan, Maggie would stand up on the hill overlooking the city she loved. And just the other day, she had seen a bumper sticker on a car being driven by a young man that read, LIFE DOESN'T SUCK! Crudely put, perhaps, but the message was certainly hopeful . . . She hadn't liked the way she'd started out in life, but she sure loved the way she was ending up. Maggie began to think that maybe she didn't have to change. Maybe it was all right to be who she was. Just a little bit out of step with the rest of the world, but very happy.

Then all of a sudden, an idea hit her. Hazel had always said, "Look around and see what the public needs, then supply it." That was it. She certainly could see the need, and she could supply it. She went to her desk and started to turn on her computer, but then stopped. No, something as important as this should be written by hand; at least the first draft. She pulled out a sheet of paper and started outlining the chapters for her new book entitled:

Real Estate Etiquette
by
Margaret Anne Fortenberry

Outline

Chapter One
  For Sellers
  Showing Your Home
    a) Do not remain at home during a
       showing
    b) Do take your animals and children
       with you
    c) No dirty dishes left in sink, please

Chapter Two
  For Buyers
  Looking for a Home
    a) As a courtesy, leave your animals and
       children at home
    b) No rude comments while attending an
       open house

   c) If you do not care for the home, try not
     to insult the real estate agent

Chapter Three
  For Agents
    a) Leave your animals and children at home
    b) Try not to speak ill of other agents
    c) Do not steal other agents' listings

First she would finish the book; then hopefully, she'd enjoy many more years at Crestview; then over to St. Martin's in the Pines for bridge, lovely bus trips, and maybe golf lessons; and then, too, in the meantime, there was Charles.

As it turned out, he had been a widower for over six years and had called her and told her he was moving back home for good in a month and would love to take her to dinner. And if that wasn't a good enough reason to be glad she hadn't jumped in the river, she didn't know what was.

Of course, as the new owner of Crestview, she was now also the new owner of the Crocker skeleton and was left with the responsibility of deciding what to do with it. Maggie thought about that. She knew that if people found out the truth about Edward Crocker, there would naturally be a lot of talk; anything involving someone's sexual life (dead or alive) was fodder for the worst kind of titillation and gossip, and his life would wind up being just another amusement for people to speculate about; all the good he'd done forgotten, and just the one fact remembered. Maggie decided that he deserved more dignity than that. So in the end, the Edward Crocker legacy would remain exactly as it was: Edward Crocker, a kind and generous human being who had been lost at sea. She would have the remains buried in the gardens below, and they would remain at Crestview with her.

It was the least she could do.

Life continued to be full of unexpected surprises. Not more than a month after Babs Bingington bought Red Mountain Realty, her hotshot money manager in New York (the one she had pushed and shoved to get to) was hauled off to jail, and she was completely wiped out in one day. She had to sell everything. It was a terrible blow and quite a comedown, after owning her own agency, to now have to apply for a job as just another agent. She submitted a job application to the brand-new owner of Babs Bingington Realty, Ethel Clipp. No surprise, she was turned down flat.

As for Maggie, she had heard people say, "Be careful what you wish for, and make sure it's what you really want." All her life, Maggie had imagined she would be happy if only she could live in a big beautiful home atop Red Mountain. And whether it was luck or not, she had been right. She loved living in the house as much as she'd dreamed she would, even more so.

A year later, although Maggie was in her living room arranging flowers and couldn't see her, a skinny ten-year-old girl was visiting the statue of Vulcan with her fifth-grade class. When she looked up and saw Crestview standing up on the mountain for the first time, she thought:

A. That's the most beautiful house I have ever seen!
B. I wonder if it's haunted?
C. That's where I want to live someday.

The End

or

Maybe just the beginning.

Epilogue

A few years later

*B*irmingham had elected its first lady mayor, who had won by a landslide. Her campaign slogan: "Compassion . . . to a point."

With Brenda, there was no "three times and you're out." With her, it was one time. Two days after she was elected, when she appointed her no-nonsense OA sponsor, Ja'ronda Jones, as the new police commissioner, all three of Brenda's dead-beat wannabe-rap-star nephews suddenly joined the army.

The other big news in Birmingham was that at age ninety-three, Ethel Clipp had just been listed in the **Guinness Book of World Records** as the oldest living working real estate agent in the world. Of course, Ethel was furious. She hadn't wanted anyone to know how old she was.

Charles and Maggie had married and were very

happy. How kind nature is. Just when she was beginning to wrinkle, Charles's eyesight was beginning to fade. But for Charles, Maggie would never
grow old. He would always look at her and see a
beautiful young girl in a white evening gown.

ABOUT THE AUTHOR

FANNIE FLAGG is a bestselling author as well as an actress, TV producer, speaker, and performer. Her book **Fried Green Tomatoes at the Whistle Stop Cafe** became a bestseller, as well as a heart-winning major motion picture. Flagg's script for the film was nominated for an Academy Award and a Writers Guild of America Award, and won the highly regarded Scripter Award. Her other bestselling novels include **Daisy Fay and the Miracle Man; Welcome to the World, Baby Girl!; Standing in the Rainbow; A Redbird Christmas;** and **Can't Wait to Get to Heaven.** She lives happily in California and Alabama.